AN UNCOMMON WOMAN

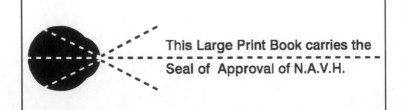

This Large Print Book carries the
Seal of Approval of N.A.V.H.

An Uncommon Woman

Laura Frantz

THORNDIKE PRESS
A part of Gale, a Cengage Company

LIBRARY OF CONGRESS CIP DATA ON FILE.
CATALOGUING IN PUBLICATION FOR THIS BOOK
IS AVAILABLE FROM THE LIBRARY OF CONGRESS

ISBN-13:978-1-4328-7598-5 (hardcover alk. paper)

Published in 2020 by arrangement with Revell Books, a division of Baker Publishing Group

Printed in Mexico
Print Number: 01   Print Year: 2020

Heart of my own heart, whate'er befall,
Still be my vision, O Ruler of all.
                              Dallán Forgaill,
                        "Be Thou My Vision"

1

Buckhannon River, Western Virginia
Spring 1770

Why could she not quit pondering that flounced petticoat?

The rule of the river was vigilance, Pa had always said. Embraced by blooming redbud and dogwood on both banks, the Buckhannon gushed snow-cold in the spring thaw, its muddy depths a maelstrom of danger. Yet even the high water could not keep Tessa's thoughts from wandering over-mountain. Nor silence her eldest brother's promise to return from there with a gift fit for a town-bred lass.

Despite the sweat that slicked her brow and the fierce tug of the queasy current, despite the swarm of insects like a white blizzard over the water's surface or the immense catfish that was visible mid-river, her woolgathering loomed larger than the ferrying at hand. Starved for frippery, she was.

Might Jasper bring her a pined-for petticoat that fell with a flounce to the top of her ankle bone?

"Tessa!"

Her uttered name was half hiss. Rarely did Ross speak so. If he'd jabbed her with his iron-tipped setting pole she'd have been less startled. While his gaze swung wide, taking in the opposite shore, hers narrowed to her youngest brother. His wary stance bespoke danger as much as the nervy, blindfolded horse they'd taken aboard their ferry. Ears back, nostrils flaring, tied to both railings by the bridle, the nag looked near to bolting. 'Twas always the creatures that sensed danger first. The ferry rocked from the horse's skittish dance, slapping the muddy water and sending up frothy spray.

Squinting, Tessa scanned the west shore. Beyond the muted birdsong and wildflower-fringed bank they were hurtling toward were three . . . six . . . eleven Shawnee streaked with war paint, their bald heads befeathered, all wending single file among the leafing trees. Their blackened eyes so like a coon's, their split earlobes adorned with flashing pendants and hoops, and their near-naked, hard-muscled forms sent a tremor through her. Even without war clubs, knives, and muskets likely gotten in

Pontiac's Rebellion, these were the deadliest of forest warriors, dark eyes trained on the ferry.

"Lord Almighty," Ross breathed.

'Twas something their mother oft said, the start of many a silent prayer. Here and now, in their predicament, it seemed more epithet.

"Pole backwards!" Tessa choked out.

"Backwards ain't no better!" Ross shot back.

Jerking her head around, she saw more Indians along the riverbank they'd just left. But not Shawnee. Cherokee.

Bitter enemies.

At mid-river now, the blindfolded horse's owner began a slow raising of his rifle. But at whom? Which side?

"Drop anchor!" Tessa spat out the hasty words like rancid cider.

Ross was already at work, abandoning his setting pole for the heavy, forged-iron weight roped to the deck. Trapped between the Buckhannon's banks, they were at the mercy of the current's ruthless tug. Any second the anchor might give way and sweep them sideways downriver.

Breaking from the line of warriors to the west, the lead Indian moved to the riverbank, every muscle tensed, bow drawn.

His target?

Stomach fisted and nerves raw, without so much as a barrel to cower behind, Tessa braced for the whoosh of his arrow. All life seemed suspended in that instant, her pining for a petticoat a vain, trifling thing.

A shrill Cherokee war whoop split the tense air at her back. Defiance pulsed in every syllable. The answer was a rapid release of two Shawnee arrows. Tessa whirled as an outcry erupted on the opposite bank, one taunting Cherokee doing a macabre dance. Stoic, the Shawnee reached into his fringed quiver, then drew his bow again.

The whooping Cherokee fell, and his agile companions dragged him into the brush even as the triumphant Shawnee faded into the forest. With a swollen river between them, little fighting would be done.

Knees soft as candle wax, Tessa sank to the gritty deck. Slowly, their foot passenger lowered his rifle. Ross studied the anchor chain as if in no mood to lift it and reach the Shawnee side.

"Best tarry a spell," the frontiersman said beneath his breath.

Ross gave a nod even as the ferry strained to be free. Raising her knees, Tessa folded her arms and rested her head on them, stricken thoughts spinning to those in the settlement. Trapped on this river, how could they sound an alarm?

Quickly she ticked off the whereabouts of those in gravest danger. Cyrus, her third-eldest brother, was farther up the valley helping raise the newest fort in a string of such defenses. But the rest of her clan? Sadly, she'd missed the usual breakfast jabber as she'd gone searching for a milch cow in the woods.

She raised her head. "Where's Zadock and Lemuel?"

"Clearing the new cornfield." Ross wiped his damp brow on his sleeve. "Ma's still at the cabin, likely, though she talked of going to help feed the crew at Fort Tygart."

"Tygart?" The frontiersman's gaze left the Shawnee shore and settled on the bank where the Cherokee had fallen.

"Aye, the newest garrison a league or so north of here," Ross answered. "Named after some officer in the Seven Years' War."

"I served with a Tygart at Fort William on the Hudson River under General Webb." He grimaced. "A bloody business."

"Never heard of Tygart myself, but he's on his way south to take command of the militia." Ross's chest seemed to swell before

Tessa's eyes. "I can muster now that I'm of age."

"Sixteen, aye? We've need of stalwart souls if we're to keep this land." He continued to talk quietly as his gaze swept both banks. "Last time I was this way an older man with the look of you kept this ferry."

"Pa was killed some time back by Indians."

Tessa felt an inward flinch. That dismal wound was still sore as the day it was made and rarely mentioned. The frontiersman fell silent. No telling his losses too. Everyone on the frontier had a chair that sat empty, a place unoccupied. Who would be next?

They floated in silence a good quarter hour, and then the sky darkened with cinder-colored clouds, turning the woods more shadowed.

"Let's put to shore," their passenger finally said. "I'll cover you if needs be on the west bank."

Tessa stood as Ross lifted the anchor. With dogged determination, they soon landed the horse and rider, then pushed off again with such haste that Ross nearly fell overboard.

"Reckon we'll make it back before the heavens open?" Tessa asked. Already the wind carried the scent of rain and was ruffling the hem of her homespun skirt.

Ross's smile was feeble. "If my scalp's still attached I'll not complain about a little damp."

Never had they landed and tied up the ferry so fast. They abandoned the setting poles, taking care not to turn their backs to the trees. Tessa knew what was next but could barely stomach it.

"You see to Ma," Ross said in a rush, "and I'll run to the fields then the fort and raise a warning."

If the fort still stood. *If* Ma —

Tessa forced the thought away as Ross vanished, the soles of his bare feet a dingy white against the greening ground. At least no smoke smudged the sky. The Indians were forever burning things. Crops. Cabins. Captives. That was the shining thread in the Swans' dark tapestry. Dear Pa, Lazarus Swan, had died outright, felled by a tomahawk. Swiftly if not painlessly.

Heading the other direction, Tessa ran along a deer trail till her lungs cried for air and she nearly couldn't stammer out a sensible greeting. Ma stood in the fenced garden patch, hoe in hand, planting squash and beans. How Tessa hated to end her tranquil task.

"Ma, get to the cabin fast as you can."

Without comment, Rosemary leaned her

13

hoe against the split-rail fence and made for the log structure just a stone's throw away, taking her prize hen with her. Inside the cabin, she and Tessa shut the massive black walnut door, heaved the crossbar into place, then barred the sole shuttered window. Embers glowed in the blackened hearth that overtook the west wall, built inside lest the stones be torn down and entry gained through the outside opening. Through an adjoining door was the two-story blockhouse that earned the name Swan Station, with no openings save loopholes to jam a rifle barrel through.

All smelled damp. Rank. The hen strutted about, making discontented noises, deprived of its bug eating and dirt baths. Ravenous when she'd left this morn, Tessa now eyed the barely visible stack of corncakes atop the table with woozy disinterest.

"Tell me everything from start to finish," Ma said in her easy way, as if they'd been bedeviled by no more than a swarm of yellow jackets.

Tessa told the tale with far more detail and elaboration than her taciturn brothers would. Save Ross, all were men of action, not words. She recalled with special force the whoosh of Shawnee arrows and the precise moment the Cherokee brave had pitched headfirst onto the riverbank before being pulled away by his fellows. How the lone frontiersman spoke of the war hero Tygart. The telltale pewter hue of the river warning of the coming rain, which even now drummed with such force on the roof she lifted her voice to finish the telling.

Ma's gnarled, liver-spotted hands opened the Bible resting on the mantel, and she began reading. "The Lord is my rock, and my fortress . . ."

But Tessa was too focused on the sounds outside the walls to pay the holy words much mind. Their cur, Snuff, began howling from the edge of the clearing, a low, mournful lament. Their livestock were belled, all but the pigs, and roamed the near woods. Prickles shivered her skin.

Passing to the wall, Tessa looked out a loophole to the pasture. Her brothers had taken two of their fastest horses to Fort Tygart. Another was missing. Likely Ross had taken a third bareback, making a precarious dash to warn their brothers in the far fields and their nearest neighbors on his way to the fort.

Mimicking her mother's calm, Tessa built up the fire, then took her father's worn rifle from its perch on a pair of antlers to check powder and bullet lead.

15

Lord, let the wait be not long.

They had been lulled into a lethargy after a long, quiet winter when the Indians kept to their villages and ceased raiding. Spring meant yet another season of watching their backs had begun. Her muscles tensed at the thought. Not till hallowtide or chestnutting season could they rest easy.

All her life had been spent looking over her shoulder. Such unceasing, ingrained guardedness wore a body down. Day was never begun without a long, measured look out a cabin loophole. Ever clever, her second-eldest brother, Zadock, had designed a straw man to thrust in the doorway when it first opened of a morn. How they'd laughed at the foolish sight bedecked in their homespun rags and a tattered hat! Yet here the straw man remained just inside the door to do its duty, a burnt hole through the worn felt brim proof of its purpose. She couldn't imagine a day not dogged by danger, when one's own shadow wasn't suspect.

Folks overmountain didn't live on the razor's edge of peril. Soon Jasper would return from there with far more than salt or the needed stores. He reappeared just as heavily laden with word of society's ease, of bread and sweetmeats to be had in confec-

16

tioneries, shiny cloth in shop windows, books and ink and reams of spotless paper brought in by tall-masted ships from England. Was it wrong that her girlish heart longed for an unfrayed ribbon or sturdy cobbled shoe? A book to call her own? She'd never known such, born in this wilderness place, and doubted she ever would.

But oh, what she'd give for a pretty petticoat.

2

Philadelphia, Pennsylvania
1770

The overly crowded parlor reminded Clay of why he preferred the far-flung frontier. Chambers like this, no matter how genteel, were a cauldron of barely civilized scents that left him longing for clean air and expansive views. Heavy perfumes barely masked perspiring, unbathed bodies layered in lush fabrics amid the city's heat. He pulled discreetly at his own freshly laundered stock, casting a baleful eye at the tall, closed windows with their British crown glass.

Two more days. No longer would he be confined to brick buildings and slop-strewn streets. True, he could turn a corner here without being met with a hatchet, and a pint of ale was as easily gotten as the plague. But in the bowels of teeming Philadelphia he felt tethered. Suffocated. Even dimwitted. Lulled into a civilized lethargy that the wilderness never allowed him.

Close to a hundred Philadelphians had come to hear him talk, crowding into his kin's glittering parlor on Front Street atop the Delaware River's western embankment. He was far from an orator, yet they sat spellbound, starved for news about the latest unrest from a region most had never seen nor wanted to. Or mayhap drawn by him most of all, the white Indian, a so-called redeemed savage brought back from the brink of heathenism in the nick of time.

The aftermath of the last war weighed heavy. He read the questions on their faces, the fears there would be another. Mayhap his coming was a blessed reprieve from the angry outpourings about the Stamp Act being forced on the colonists by Parliament. Mayhap it gave them reason for thankfulness that somewhere else in the world there was more danger, turmoil, and uncertainty.

"Colonel Tygart." His host — and uncle — was before him, a blushing belle on each arm. "More of your admirers wish to meet you."

Clay inclined his head. Gave a small bow. If she'd lived to see it, his aunt would be pleased her training had taken hold. The young women looked at him coyly, each

fluttering their fans hard as a humming-
bird's wings.

"I was captivated by your speech," said
one. "We only glean the scantest bits from
newspapers and broadsheets of exploits in
the West. Never have I heard a firsthand account such as yours."

"No doubt your call for men and arms
along the border will be heeded after so
rousing a message," said the other, touching
his coat sleeve with the tip of her fan. "From
a true hero of the Seven Years' War — and a
former captive. How horrifying!"

"I didn't mean to paint so grim a picture,"
he returned, "given I lived to tell the tale."

"I'm sure you've spared us the most
distressing details as any gentleman would.
My only wish is that you looked more the
part."

Bemused now, he smiled. "Greasy buckskins, feathers, and the like?"

They giggled like schoolgirls, though his
uncle remained unsmiling. His Quaker kin
still found it hard to make peace with his
straddling both worlds. And his forsaking
their faith had widened the rift. Though
he'd been back among the whites for as long
as he'd been with the Indians, he retained
an Indian taint.

"I regret hearing that the abundance of

20

game grows less and less the farther colonists push west, the prized elk and buffalo foremost." His uncle's thoughtful comments surprised him. "Though I'm glad the predatory wolves are not the threat they once were."

"Wherever you hear the ring of an axe you'll find it so." Could they hear the lament in his voice? "But there are still deer and bear aplenty. And panthers are just as much a danger as the wolves."

The dining room doors were being opened, a long table a-glitter with candlelight. Offering each lady an arm, Clay started a slow walk across the carpeted floor, aware of too many appraising glances. His senses, honed sharp by his past, provided ongoing entertainment. He took note of the beauty patch, big as a tick, on the chin of the mayor's wife. The missing gilt button on one gentleman's waistcoat. A servant's bruised eye and tarnished buckle. The failed soufflé at supper.

While tolerating some aspects of civilization, others he embraced. An overburdened table was one of them, laden with Philadelphia's beef and pork pies and hearty northern fare. Many a winter he'd scraped by on wild game and roots. The ravenous frontier was as much a force to be reckoned with as the treacherous frontier.

Soon he'd be three hundred miles to westernmost Virginia and Pennsylvania's borders, with a tattered, winter-weakened militia in dire need of powder, mustering, and more, and the back settlers, as they were called, in need of defense.

As he took his place around the elegant table, he pondered all he hadn't said in his honest speech about British America's embattled borders. Best save that for a more hardened audience.

Packhorses and provisions. Indian trade goods. Powder. Bullet lead. Rifle pouch. Flint and steel. Salt. Clay surveyed the growing heap and the pawing horseflesh before him. The journey out was always more comfortable than the journey back. For now, he familiarized himself with his stores, gotten from a list he'd made that would be paid and supplied by the colonial treasury.

He had no need of a guide as so many did — those who were unfamiliar with the backwoods and the deer or buffalo paths connecting stations and settlements. Seasoned bordermen knew to avoid the treacherous Indian trails that ran the depth and breadth of the frontier, spiderwebbing in every direction.

"We're going to ride to Pitt in fine style." The jovial voice cut into Clay's musings as his longtime partner descended the mercantile steps. A man who, if pressed, could likely outwit him and every other borderman Clay knew.

Jude Early looked at the line of horses and provisions that needed loading, then cast a baleful glance at the spring sky as the Quaker merchant appeared behind him, list in hand. "Think we'll clear Philadelphia by the forenoon?"

"If we cut to the chase," Clay replied, settling a packsaddle into place.

He'd thanked his host, bade farewell to his city kin, and prepared himself mentally for what lay ahead. Barring mishaps, he reckoned on seeing Fort Tygart by May. The backcountry, that region of particular concern to the king and colonial government, would be aflame with Indian raids after a long, white winter.

Lord willing, he and Jude and Maddie would reach Fort Pitt first, then drop down some hundred miles to the war-torn Monongahela country. There his unseen, picketed namesake stood on an overlook above the Buckhannon River, smack in the middle of what he himself considered the ring of fire that was western Pennsylvania, northwestern Virginia, and the Ohio.

"Colonel Tygart . . ."

He stilled, catching Jude's bemused expression before the genteel voice turned him around. All thoughts of the journey ahead vanished.

"Miss Penrose." Of all the women who'd graced his host's parlor, she was, like the Monongahela, most memorable. Not that he'd tarried on that fact.

"Pardon the surprise, but you left the other night before I could bid you goodbye." Her smile was coy beneath her wide-brimmed, beribboned hat. In her mitted hands she held a folded paper. When his gaze landed on it, she held it out to him.

Full of the wilderness as he was, he easily caught the fragrance of some cultivated scent he couldn't name. Lavender?

"I'm hoping we can keep a correspondence. You are a man of letters, and I . . ." She paused, the intensity of her green gaze not lost on him. "I am not impartial to the post."

"Obliged." He stifled a rueful smile, the fragrant letter betwixt his callused, dirt-brown fingers. "But lest you wait too long for a reply, a reliable post is yet to be had where I'm headed."

24

"How many months will you be away?"

His shoulders lifted in a slow shrug. He rarely talked details and dates. The wilderness wouldn't let him. "As the good book says, 'If the Lord wills, we shall live, and do this, or that.' "

"Are you a Scripture-abiding man, Colonel Tygart?"

"I purpose to be." The half-truth stung, but she gave him a smile nonetheless.

"I shall pray for you then, in the hope that we shall meet again."

He gave a noncommittal nod, loosening the subtle cord she'd attempted to tie him with.

"Godspeed, Colonel Tygart." She turned away with her maid and swept down the cobbled street, skirts trailing.

The shop merchant stood on the top step and guffawed, having surveyed the exchange with no small amusement. "Are the flowers of the frontier so much fairer than our city sirens, gentlemen?"

"Best ask Colonel Tygart, sir." Jude's grin widened, a flash of brilliant white in his dark face. "Seems like he attracts attention where'er he goes, even in buckskins."

"Oh?" Kneeling, Clay resumed checking and tying and buckling. "I've been too preoccupied with staying alive to notice."

"Truth." Jude ran a hand down a pack-horse's withers. "Besides, there's precious few frontier flowers beyond the mountains, and too many menfolk."

"Glad I am of the comforts of the city then." With another cackle, the merchant stepped aside as Jude's wife stepped out the mercantile door, arms overflowing.

Jude gave a good-natured groan as Maddie approached, pleasant determination on her face. But Clay felt a warmth and appreciation for any feminine graces she brought to the grit of the trail. Maddie was, in her own way, as necessary as Jude. Owned by an English officer who'd fallen during Braddock's defeat, they'd aligned themselves with Clay soon after. Maddie had been a laundress, Jude a hostler. When Clay had almost died from a case of fever, Maddie had nursed him back to health. In turn, he'd saved her and Jude from a deadly ambush. Together they'd returned to eastern Pennsylvania with the tattered army, having formed a lasting if unusual friendship.

"Looks like you raided the shop, all right. Anything left?" Jude took an accounting as she began tucking things into saddlebags. "Thread. Scissors. Hairbrush and dressing glasses. Tea leaves. Loaf sugar." He lowered his voice discreetly. "Ribbon garters. Pet-

26

ticoat. Hooper's Female Pills." He opened a small sack. "Candied . . . ginger?"

Maddie smiled patiently. "Husband, don't you want something else to chew on besides that foul tobacco?"

With a chuckle, Jude returned to his own packing.

"Saved this one just for you." Clay gestured to a well-fed mount, a young mare that nickered softly as Maddie approached.

Maddie thanked him, her pleasure plain. Despite her frontier garb and manly felt hat, she was decidedly feminine. Childless, she and Jude preferred the wilds just as Clay did but for far different reasons. Clay didn't have the worry of slave catchers on the prowl for freed blacks to seize and then sell into captivity. At least on the frontier, dodgy as it was, they owned their personal freedom.

By the forenoon, they'd left Philadelphia far behind. Farms and fences spread on both sides, but only occasionally did they have to maneuver around a fence line. 'Twas like a long march, a drill he knew by heart. The Forbes Road, cut into the lush Pennsylvania landscape by General Braddock, led west to Fort Pitt. But first countless waters to cross, mountain ranges that tested stamina and sanity, signs of life diminishing as the wilderness opened up, crowned by the magnificent Alleghenies.

His stallion, Bolt, settled into a steady rhythm once they were free of the city. Clay couldn't deny the stirring in his own blood the closer they came to the borderlands, the farthest reaches. No matter the wood gnats or the spiking heat or the prospect of eating pemmican for endless days and nights, the wilderness was in his marrow, pure and simple. Bone deep.

Maddie yawned an hour past dusk, drawing Clay's notice. "Look to make camp," he said.

Men had little care for where they bedded down, at least in warm weather and free of danger. Maddie had a gift for choosing a winsome spot. They spent a good quarter hour unpacking what was needed for the night, the hiss of a kettle and sizzle of a frying pan accompanied by the spring chorus of tree frogs.

Feet to the fire as spring's chill crept in, Clay cleaned his rifle, thoughts adrift till Jude said, "Been a while since we saw Fort Pitt. Wonder if it's as wild and raw as ever, what with the Indian traders and the like."

"No doubt," Clay said.

"We best lodge at Semple's." Maddie stirred the meat and potatoes with a long wooden spoon. "Respectable and tidy."

Nodding, Jude reached into the skillet for a pinch of supper and earned a rap on the hand. After a wink at his wife, he glanced at Clay. "Who's the commandant at Pitt here lately?"

"Captain Edmonstone of the 18th Royal Regiment."

"Reckon the fort that bears your name along the Buckhannon River is big as Pitt?"

"Reckon not." Clay cracked a smile and put away his rifle. "More the size of a privy." At their amusement, he added, "No reason to name a fort Tygart. Better to call it after some fallen hero."

"I'd rather honor the living than the dead," Maddie said matter-of-factly.

Jude nodded his agreement as they commenced eating. "So, Colonel Tygart, what sense do you make of the colonial government opening a land office at Pitt? Ain't that in violation of the Indians' treaty rights and the king's proclamation that forbids all settlers west of the Appalachian Mountains?"

"Forbids? Rather, 'at least for the present, and until our further pleasure be known.'" Clay echoed the oft-repeated phrase of the king's men. "The boundary lines are pushed further and further west treaty by treaty.

'Tis a twisted business."

Jude rolled his eyes. "Your red blood is plenty affronted, I reckon. I seen how your hackles rose at the sight of that newly plowed field which used to be the grandest forest we ever saw. The land grabbers keep moving west. Ain't hard to understand why those settlers tomahawked along the New River not long ago got their mouths shoved full of dirt."

Clay said nothing to this. 'Twas a sore subject he didn't tarry on long.

Maddie's voice raised a notch. "Let bygones be bygones, aye, gentlemen?"

The steady chirrup of crickets replaced conversation. Rolling up in a saddle blanket to keep off the damp, Clay listened for Jude's sawlike snoring and Maddie's soft snuffling before an uneasy sleep claimed him.

3

By dusk Tessa and nearly everyone she knew had forted up within the walls of an unfinished defense that crowned the Buckhannon River bluff like a rude castle awaiting its lord and master. Settlement spies were sent out to determine the whereabouts of the warriors, settlers within Fort Tygart praying any hostiles had left the country. But where one settlement was spared, another was assaulted. Soon they'd hear of other raids, captives, stock stolen, if not their own. Such was the weft and warp of everyday life.

"Could be worse," Ruth Schoolcraft said as they kept to a stockade corner. Her gaze rose to the high pickets before falling to the wood shavings at their feet. " 'Tis so new a structure 'tis not yet rank. And I've not seen you since Christmastide."

Had it been so long? Tessa marked time by chores and seasons. Being penned up in this place kept her from sowing the needed seed, accomplishing the next pressing task. The Indians, ever clever, understood that too. Masterful observers and raiders, they knew a bountiful corn crop carried settlers and their livestock through another winter. Flax kept them clothed, firewood warm. Nuts and berries were an added boon at table. The Indians did everything they could to disrupt that circle of survival.

Ruth touched the faded ribbon of her cap. "Times like these make me remember things I'd rather forget. We're nearing June . . ."

"June, aye. You're pondering Keturah," Tessa murmured. "As am I."

Was it guilt that shadowed them? The fact that she and Ruth had been spared that long-ago spring day?

Ruth shivered. "Seems like Keturah's kinfolk should have stayed on here, not gone back overmountain. Their leaving seemed to say they'd lost hope she'd ever come back."

"I suspect their cabin was too empty without her." Was it not the same with Pa gone, every glance about their homeplace bringing a barbed memory? His clothes. His tools. His pipe and tobacco pouch. How they'd grieved then and grieved still. Nothing felt safe. All seemed haunted. Keturah seemed but a haint too.

"We were but twelve." Tessa took her place at a loophole, tamping down the memory much as she tamped down the powder in her gun. "And now four and twenty."

So many years had passed. Would they always wrestle with the day's details? If they'd stayed close to home, might Keturah still be with them? Once they'd seen the full strawberry moon, off they went berry picking, chasing after the first succulent fruit in the thaw of a lean winter. Giddy, mouths stained scarlet, they'd lost track of time and then one another, determined to fill their baskets the fullest. A foolish, hapless task.

How quiet it had been that day. How innocent. Till the warm air was slashed open by a high-pitched, panther-like scream. Standing on a little knoll, Tessa saw Keturah's basket tumble, berries spilling like red hearts every which way. If she'd but toted her gun that day, Keturah might be here now.

"Sister, need any bullet lead?" Lemuel's voice yanked her back to the present.

She stared at him absently. "Nay."

Reaching out, he yanked Ruth's dangling braid in passing. Ruth's answering giggle grated. It seemed wrong somehow to make merry with such a dark memory hovering. Betimes her patience wore out with Ruth, moonstruck by anyone in britches. She dallied with all the unmarried men but never settled on one, earning her the reputation of fort flirt.

As if sensing Tessa's tetchy mood, Ruth moved on to help with the children now making a commotion in a near cabin, as eager to be penned up as their parents were opposed. With their lighthearted laughter in her ears, Tessa tried to make peace with her surroundings.

By day's end there'd be noise, stink, gossip aplenty. Nary a speck of lonesomeness or a quiet corner to be had.

She drew a deep, steadying breath, squinting out the loophole to the stump-littered clearing. A lone redbud tree clung to the cliff's edge, its purplish blossoms showy as a Sabbath skirt.

At least the fort was fresh hewn, the privies newly dug. Whoever this hero named Tygart was, she hoped he'd be pleased with the place that bore his name. Though they'd never met, she already knew the gist of him, of every enduring borderman. All were crafted with the same uncanny courage, that hard-bitten fearlessness. Not all men had it. Those who didn't were soon run off or cut down. Cowards were not to be borne.

Somebody within these walls said Tygart had eyes like a rattler, so intense was his gaze. A shiver coursed through her. If he had such eyes, she'd not look into them. Snakes were an abomination ever since Eden's garden. Copper snakes and rattlers wound themselves amid her flax patch, an everlasting dread. A vicious snakebite had carried off her favorite cur, Absalom. She still visited his grave.

"Come away, Daughter." Ma was at her side, all but prying the flintlock from her hands. "We're to sup with Hester."

With a nod, Tessa looked up at the rifle platform where men stood watch, all armed to the teeth. Yet not one contrary shot had been fired. For that they could be thankful. She might eat her supper in peace. No need for a feminine hand just yet till time came to spell one of the men when the fray turned exhausting. With Jasper overmountain, were her other brothers safely here? Amid all the homespun and felt-hatted men at dusk, 'twas hard to tell.

Eyes down, she followed Ma through the melee. Folks were still coming in, the gates manned by no less than a dozen guns. The whine of new iron hinges nearly made her wince. Last time they'd forted up downriver the Indians had stormed the gates and nearly gained entry till a quick-thinking settler had poured molten tar on them. Their anguished howls stalked her for days.

Once inside Great-Aunt Hester's cabin, Tessa leaned her rifle in a corner. Cornbread baked a deep buttery gold sat at the hearth, and a pie, likely made of last season's dried apples, cooled on a table. Pewter plates and tankards were placed just so, the eldest Swan exacting even in old age.

"Tessa, you're a sight for sore eyes," Hester said as she bent to poke a pot of beans.

Tessa gave her a peck on the cheek. "Need a hand, Auntie?"

"Set out this round of cheese and the last of the quince preserves."

Despite Hester's spinsterhood, the cabin had a comfortable feel full of homespun touches, unlike the temporary quarters of those who dashed in when an alarm was raised, then scurried out again when the country was calm.

Ross appeared for supper, though her other brothers remained at the wall. A few others joined them, in need of feeding. The Swans were a generous lot, with ties to Williamsburg and Philadelphia. Talk even now turned to overmountain. Tessa reckoned she was one of the have-nots, born and bred on the frontier, hearing about such faraway places secondhand.

After all but Ross returned to their posts, Hester served sassafras tea. "Two Swan spinsters are too many." She began her familiar rant, darting a stern look Tessa's way. "Thankfully, with so few women here, there's a blessed glut of men to choose from."

Tessa breathed in the beloved scent of sassafras as her own cup was filled, shutting out Hester's timeworn words. Spring tonic, sassafras. When sweetened with maple sugar, no finer remedy could be had.

"I'd rather talk about Jasper," Ma said after a sip from her own cracked treenware cup. "He promised to bring flower seed from overmountain. I've a mind to plant a tea garden. Liberty tea, it's called."

"Oh? And what is this so-called *liberty* tea?" Ross teased as he reached for the last piece of cornbread. "We are anything but at liberty."

"Likely the Indians will cut down that sort of nonsense too." Hester's words were punctuated by a gunshot. "Save your seed for more peaceful times."

Tessa said no more as another shot rang out. So, the fracas had begun. Talk was pointless amid so much noise.

Ross left the cabin, cornbread in hand, shutting the door after him. The women sat listening. A baby cried and the corralled animals near the fort's front gates began making frightful noises of discontent. Already the biting smoke of black powder snuck between the cabin's chinking, snuffing the fragrance of sassafras.

Steeling herself, Tessa bowed her head briefly.

Lord, let it end soon, please. Spare Tygart, whoever he is, the sorry spectacle of his fort under siege.

4

Clay took in the distant, dark silhouette of Fort Pitt. Of all the frontier outposts, Pitt had the most presence. Bordered by three rivers that were nothing short of jaw-dropping no matter the season, Pitt was a behemoth of brick and earth and stone, a formidable stronghold, the celebrated gateway to the west. Now, overfull from the spring thaw, the entangled waters held a special sheen, unspooling to faraway places.

The Monongahela River he knew best. It flowed north and was a mere hundred or so miles in length, shallow enough to walk across in places, leading south toward Virginia and the fort that bore his name. He preferred the seldom-seen waters farther west, the Indian-sacred Muskingum and Tuscarawas and White Woman of his former life.

For now, they'd reprovision at Pitt after a week's travel. Digest any news before journeying on.

Clay reported to Captain Edmonstone while Jude and Maddie found lodging at Semple's beyond fort walls. Bypassing swaggering soldiers and sotted traders, steely-eyed Indian guides and half bloods, Clay gained the garrison's inner sanctum only to be steered beyond its walls to the newest commandant's house, a fine brick building with cut stone steps.

"After a brief time of peace following the last treaty, there's fresh trouble," Edmonstone told him straightaway, gesturing to a large map spread across a table. He jabbed an ink-stained finger toward the westernmost Virginia border. "Numerous raids, large and small. A great many scalpings and captives taken. Most of the unrest seems to originate with the Shawnee. You'll muster a much-needed militia at Fort Tygart, where settlement is the heaviest and danger is the thickest. Pick your spies and send them out to scout with care. There are many able bordermen who should serve you and the government well, the Swans, Clendennins, and Schoolcrafts foremost."

Noting the settlers' names, Clay studied the map. Though Pitt was virtually immune to Indian attack, word was that the British no longer wanted the encumbrance of so costly an outpost, no matter how well forti-fied and strategically placed. Ransoming captives, making treaties with the tribes, and supervising the oft-brawling Indian traders was what Pitt did best. Though subject to the king's and Parliament's whims and dictates, Pitt turned a blind eye on the tide of settlers flooding west despite the king's waffling displeasure. The lure of the land was too great.

That night Clay, Jude, and Maddie sat down in the crowded dining room.

"Semple's is becoming quite proper," Maddie said, eyeing their linen-clad table and fellow diners. "I spy John Connelly, agent of Virginia's royal governor, over in the corner."

"Mistress Semple's famed kin, aye," Clay answered.

Jude picked up a serviette suspiciously, accustomed to his shirtsleeve. "You fancy yourself back in Philly?"

Maddie offered a wide smile. "After time on the trail, I'm just glad for a fork and a chair."

Semple's did not disappoint. Venison col-lops and fried catfish aplenty, even mince-meat pie. Dishes were passed even after Clay pushed his plate away.

Jude took an eager bite of pie. Stopped chewing. Tried to swallow. "That crust wouldn't break beneath a wagon wheel."

Bypassing the pie, Clay tasted the bracing coffee. Black as hades but nothing to complain about.

"I heard tell Colonel Washington likes to lodge at Semple's when he's here," Maddie said, stirring cream into her cup. "And that the best rooms are reserved for him, some secret bower the rest of us plain folk never see."

"He's one officer I wouldn't mind crossing paths with again. I ain't seen Wash since Braddock's defeat in '55." Jude took another stab at the pie. "He's got some powerful medicine taking four bullets through his coat and two horses shot from under him and living to tell the tale."

Clay pondered Washington's miraculous escape till the commotion in the tavern foyer stole his attention. Unruly dogs barked outside while a burly man in an Indian blanket stood at the dining room's entrance, gaze settling on Clay.

Alexander McKee, Fort Pitt's Indian agent.

With a slight limp, McKee made his way to their table, shook hands, and took a seat. A harried serving girl brought him coffee, then refilled Clay's own cup.

"I've been looking for you, Tygart." McKee drank half the brew in two swallows, hot as it was. "You're headed for the Buckhannon settlement, Edmonstone tells me. Still aim to leave out soon as you're provisioned?"

"Day after tomorrow, likely."

McKee said nothing for a full minute. In the time he'd been an Indian agent, he'd absorbed some of their reflective, taciturn ways. "A fortnight ago, a prisoner exchange took place. The Lenape surrendered a young woman thought to be from the Buckhannon River country."

Clay remained as stoic as McKee. "Her name?"

"We don't know for certain. She won't speak. One of the men who served in the Buckhannon militia remembers her. Said she's daughter to a Dutch family by the name of Braam who was raided a few years back."

"And you want me to return her to her kin."

"If there's any left, aye."

Clay mulled this latest development, making no promises. Former captives were fraught with complications. Some were glad to return to their white families. Others

43

balked. Which would Miss Braam be? And if she didn't talk . . .

"Might be a good time to travel with another woman along." Maddie's voice was quiet. Thoughtful.

Clay rubbed his whiskered jaw. "Best make her acquaintance first."

"She's no trouble," McKee said gruffly. "Keeps to herself mostly. Partial to sewing and beadwork. But quite frankly, I'm concerned for her safety."

Clay eyed him with intensity till he explained himself.

"She draws too much notice. Some of the men even ask for extra guard duty just so they can be near her. I've never seen a woman so . . ." He paused, searching for the right word, clearly flummoxed. "Womanly."

Maddie smiled. Jude chuckled. Clay tried to gauge just what that meant. McKee was not given to praise or overstatement. Simply put, the returned captive was pretty enough she put herself at risk. Fort Pitt was overrun with soldiers, traders, drunkards, even criminals. Given time, someone would break into the blockhouse or accost her on the street. McKee wanted her gone.

"I've seen a lot of women, Indian and white, French and British and half bloods.

She's an uncommon one," McKee concluded.

Jude rubbed his furrowed brow. "Why you reckon she don't speak? Been gone so long she forgot her mother tongue?"

McKee finished his coffee and stood. "Mayhap she doesn't want to remember."

The next forenoon, Clay and Maddie trudged through a steady spring rain with its accompanying ankle-deep mud to Fort Pitt's westernmost blockhouse. An armed sentry stood guard at the blockhouse's massive door.

"We're here to see the returned captive," Clay said.

With a nod, the sentry thrust the door open. Clay and Maddie stepped into a shadowed interior lit by lantern light. His gaze fell on a figure sitting on an Indian blanket along one far wall. Shoulders slightly bent, the young woman did not look up, engrossed in the beadwork trailing across her lap and in her hands. Her world seemed to extend no farther than her trade blanket.

Maddie hung back as Clay moved forward. Taking a cue from the former captive, he lowered himself to the floor just beyond one woolen edge. Only then did she look up. And in that fleeting, lantern-lit instant, Clay understood the Indian agent's concern.

Flawless.

Mesmerizing azure eyes. Braids of woven white-gold. Bone structure a bewitching blend of lofty lines and pleasing angles, lips full and unsmiling. Even seated, he could tell she was tall and lithe. Yet bosomy and narrow-waisted. And dressed as a Lenape down to the thunderbird and tortoise design on her moccasins. On each high cheekbone was a dot of red paint gotten from the bloodroot plant. Her parted hairline bore a telltale red streak.

He swallowed past his astonishment and gave the customary Lenape greeting. *"Hè, kulamàlsi hàch?"*

She looked away from him, and he sensed her surprise though she did not show it. And then her attention returned to her handwork. Nary a word did she speak.

Reaching out, he took a cluster of wampum beads in hand. He'd always been partial to purple. Small baskets were scattered around her, each holding the decorative items the Indians were so fond of. Dyed quills. Glass beads. Small, metal tinkling cones. Bright ribbon. Trade silver. Feathers. Even a small pot of vermillion, the prized color of every tribe. How long had she been with the Lenape? The artistry of her hand-work bespoke years.

He continued quietly in Lenape. "Tomorrow when the sun is two fingers high we will follow the Monongahela south to the back settlements. Just you, me, the woman you see behind me, and a man named Jude. You'll ride a mare with your belongings. My intent is to return you to your white kin."

Her slender hands stilled.

"The Indian agent here believes you are called Miss Braam. Your people settled along the Buckhannon River in western Virginia prior to the raid that took you away from them years ago. If you know different, you need to tell me, else we'll begin a fruit-less chase."

Her lips parted. Would she speak? A voice seemed the very soul of a person. Much could be had by its pitch and tone, its peculiar resonance. Like a moccasin print, no two alike, a voice was one's own unique possession. And if it was as fetching as all the rest of her . . .

He released the wampum he held, the beads making a faint tinkling sound. His last look at her before he pulled himself to his feet left him gut-wrenched.

A single tear slid down her pale cheek,

trailing to her jawline, then falling to a dark splotch on the coarse weave of her blue duffel skirt.

All at once, Maddie was beside him, holding out a brightly dyed Philadelphia handkerchief. But would the woman take it? Lashes lowered, she reached out gracefully, even gratefully, and accepted the offering.

A good beginning.

Clay paused. Repeated the hour of their leave-taking, this time in English. Best get used to the white man's talk if she was to live among them.

Miss Braam, if that was who she was, did not look his way again.

5

Two days the siege wore on and then the shooting sputtered to a slow stop on both sides. Sleepless, Tessa grew winded in running hot bullets in her apron to waiting guns, finally replacing a man at the wall whose elbow had been shattered by a musket ball. Sighting and firing, she ignored the thudding of a headache determined to crack her skull. A smoky haze lay about Fort Tygart, not all of it from the discharge of black powder. The Indians had set ablaze a few outlying buildings, namely the corncribs, which held the little sustenance left to them at winter's end. Till the gardens came in, the settlers would live on game and more game till their whole being cried out for bread.

Parched, she took a long swallow from a gourd dipper and piggin that Ruth brought round.

"It's finally dying down." Ruth looked as

beleaguered as Tessa felt. "Maybe by morning we'll shed this place."

If so, Fort Tygart had done its namesake proud. Not one man had fallen and only a few injured. Spirits stayed high, and a good deal of talk during the lull was about the coming of the war hero. Scraps of it returned to her now as she resumed her place at the loophole, her gaze on the still, smoky clearing.

Tall, Tygart is . . . From fine Philadelphia stock . . . English Quakers . . . Acquitted himself well in the Battle of the Wilderness by using Indian tactics, even war paint, during ambushes . . . Rescued valuable papers and a military chest containing thirty thousand pounds from the French . . . Known to shoot a man at 250 yards, the enemy fleeing like chickens before a fox . . . A devilish brave fella.

All thought of a pretty petticoat was pushed aside.

Then came the hour that wreaked the most havoc in Tessa's spirit, the pall after the siege, that chancy hour when the newly hewn gates of the fort were cautiously opened. First a crack as they waited for a flicker of opposition, then flung treacherously wide to allow the unshaven, ex-

50

hausted, bleary-eyed settlers out. The hair on the back of Tessa's neck rose at such times, though her brothers surrounded her, some afoot and some on horseback.

She missed Jasper, the eldest, with a soul-clenching fierceness. Was he on his way back to them, laden with salt and needful things from parts east? Circling her and Ma were Ross, Lemuel, Zadock, and Cyrus, each reminding her of Pa in different ways. Jasper, possibly the most fearsome of the Swans, was sorely needed.

She tensed for a sudden commotion — outright ambush — during the league home, as wary fellow settlers sought their own outlying farms. Once at Swan Station there'd be animals to tend, the ferry to check, supper to fix. All within easy reach of a rifle. For now, the woods were downright boastful, bedecked in blossoming dogwood and redbud at every turn.

"Tessa," Ma remarked when they broke the silence within view of their cabin, "Hester asked about you coming to the fort for a spell."

"What for?" she asked, dismounting.

"I expect she has courting in mind. Way out here . . ." Ma left off.

The age-old concern weighed on Tessa's spirit.

Way out here, busy from daylight to dark with nary a man in sight, what prospects have you for a husband, a family?

"I'll scout the ferry." Ross spoke in measured tones. "See if any more mischief's been made along the river."

"I'm in," Lemuel replied, the two melting into the newly leafed brush.

"May's a-wasting," Zadock muttered. He was always the last for meals and worked far into the dusk, hating labor lost from Indian unrest. "Glad we weren't gone at corn planting." He and Cyrus moved carefully into the clearing, taking quiet account of their cabin and outbuildings, the outlying gardens and fields and fences.

Tessa betook herself to her favorite place, the springhouse. 'Twas Pa's legacy as a stonemason, a two-story stone marvel built over a limestone spring that bubbled up in a cellar, passed out an opening in the wall through a long, deep trough, and then meandered away through the western meadow. Always cool, unmoved by arrows or buckshot or fire, the springhouse seemed a promise of peace, of better days to come despite the loopholes in its walls.

Shutting her eyes, Tessa breathed in the smell of cold water and crockery, a reminder of her need to gather splint wood for baskets, particularly yellow birch when the new sap was running. Tarry too long and the wood wouldn't budge. She had in mind to plant a tea garden like Ma said, if Jasper remembered to bring the coveted seed. Little solaced her like harvesting and hanging bunches of herbs to sweeten the place.

Returning to the cabin, Tessa drew an easier breath. All was as they'd left it, save some critter had gotten to the abandoned corncakes on the table, a scattering of crumbs left to sweep up. These she fed to the birds outside their door, her favorites being the mourning doves beneath their west eave, cooing again in late morn.

All the while she held her breath as the steady routine of life took hold. No more rifle fire and choking smoke. No Indian cries that curdled the blood. No vexed, harried settlers obsessed with powder and bullet lead. No squalling babies and restive animals. Just quiet. Calm. Birdsong. The sigh of the wind around the cabin's corners.

Her mind resumed its usual rhythms too, the groove worn by Keturah especially deep. She daren't speak of it. Ma got that stricken look when she did. As if she feared the same fate would befall Tessa in time. Keturah had been dear to Ma, something of a second daughter. Her wrenching absence struck a lasting lick. Ma had even dreamed of a match between the comely Keturah and one of her sons. There'd been a bit of tomfoolery about it back then. Every one of her brothers was smitten save Ross, too young to go moon-eyed over her. But Keturah was not only lovely. She was good-hearted. Hardworking. Kind.

And then she was gone.

Tessa gathered eggs as Ma ground fresh meal in a giant mortar just beyond the front stoop. A glance outside told her Zadock and Cyrus were repairing a plow by the barn. She'd pray Lemuel and Ross home from the river.

Supper found them all at table, save Jasper, the door barred. Bedtime came early after a sleepless siege. A few unstifled yawns went around.

Zadock set down his fork. "I'll finish plowing the flax on the morrow."

"I'll be on the Buckhannon," Ross told them, always drawn to the river more than the field. "With the spring thaw, more settlers need ferrying."

"Pass along a warning." Zadock lit Pa's pipe, the fragrant smoke spiraling toward the rafters in aromatic wisps. "And take care to watch your back."

Ross simply nodded. Being the youngest,

he was the most unguarded. Foolhardy, Jasper called him. Yet he was the handiest with a rifle, fixing anything from a broken stock to a blocked touchhole, his talk full of flints and jaw screws and frizzen springs. He was also a dead aim, much to the chagrin of his brothers. Pa had planned to apprentice Ross to a gunsmith, but all that went awry at his passing.

"Tessa best keep to home and away from the river lest you truly need another setting pole." This from Cyrus, ever cautious. "That flaxseed begs to be in the ground, and I sense more rain coming."

Though she'd rather be with Ross at the ferry, the flax wouldn't wait. Tessa sipped her sassafras tea as remarks flew between her brothers, some barbed, some in jest.

"I hope you put all that foolishness about Tessa forting up to rest." Zadock aimed his low words their mother's way.

Betimes Zadock grew too big for his britches in Jasper's absence. Tessa gave him a wry smile as Ma pondered her reply.

"Before your father was cut down, one of the last things he said to me was that he wished to see his only daughter marry well. I've not forgotten, and neither has your great-aunt Hester."

Her thoughtful words led to a chastised

silence. Tessa stared at her mother. 'Twas news to her, Pa's wish.

" 'Tis hard enough having no daughters-in-law or grandchildren," Ma finished, eyes a-glitter, as her sons shifted uneasily in their seats.

This Tessa understood. Other than their shared faith, what joys did they have beyond family? Though the natural world was a wonder, betimes it seemed more foe than friend. Truth be told, Tessa longed for female company near at hand, a bosom friend like Keturah had been. Surely Ma's need for other daughters, especially grand-children, went bone deep.

"There's not a man hereabouts worthy of Sister's hand." 'Twas a rare burst of words from the reserved Lemuel. "If you want bet-ter for her, best look elsewhere. Or send her east to our city kin."

"Seems like I should have some say in the matter," Tessa stated, every eye on her.

"Well, have at it then," Zadock told her.

She winked. "What need have I of a husband when I can't keep track of five brothers?"

They laughed, easing the tense moment. She stood and began clearing plates, refill-ing their applejack as needed, occasionally going to a loophole to peer out. In time her brothers finished their evening chores and betook themselves to their blockhouse bunks. Their combined snores were her usual signal to seek her cozy corner behind a quilt strung from a beam near the glow of the hearth.

Ma slept on the far side of the cabin, her bed open to the room. It had been that way for as long as Tessa could remember. The trundle bed beneath it had been hers in childhood before Ma moved her here.

Pulling at her petticoat strings, she untied the knot at her waist and shed her garments to her stays, then her shift. Neatly hung on pegs about her bed, the clothing helped block wintry drafts. Since no one came behind the quilt, she had adorned the small corner with the shelf Lemuel had made her, home to a river stone polished smooth, a dried flower and wad of soft moss, and a fetching feather.

Pressing her knees to the hard floor, she folded her hands and bent her head. So many needs, including Jasper's safe return any day now. But first, thanks.

Clay led out, the former captive just behind, followed by Maddie then Jude. The journey from Philadelphia to the Forks of the Ohio had been mostly carefree. Now it turned treacherous. Never again could he let his guard down with Fort Pitt at his back.

He reckoned on seeing Fort Tygart by week's end, barring foul weather, illness, or ambush. If they kept to the creeks and streams that first day, they'd avoid leaving too noticeable a trail.

Miss Braam sat in the saddle like an Indian princess. If it was indeed Miss Braam. What was her Lenape name? Aside from her Dutch paleness, there was little that was white about her. Maddie asked him if she shouldn't shed her Lenape garments, but Clay urged otherwise. He had an inkling Miss Braam wouldn't be so obliging about changing clothes.

"It'll confuse a war party," he said, to Maddie's amusement.

Glad he was that the Lenape's former captive was behind him. If she was in his line of sight, he'd be plenty distracted. As they'd readied to head out, he'd discreetly searched for some flaw in her comeliness, aside from the faint pox scars barely visible. Hair too white-gold. Complexion a tad freckled. Eyes too blindingly blue. Waist too willowy. Nay. He'd schooled his surprise at how tall she was. Taller than many men, yet it somehow only lent to her loveliness and set her further apart. An uncommon woman, aye.

But nary a word did she speak. Not even to refute him when he continued calling her Miss Braam. The Indian agent had shown him an old, weathered notice in the *Virginia Gazette* that wrenched him in its anguish and seemed to confirm her identity. McKee had thrust it at him at the last as if Clay might balk and leave her at Pitt.

Taken by the Indians from Augusta County, Keturah Braam, then in her twelfth year, fair-haired, and much freckled. Her father and mother beg that she may, by all good people, be helped on her way to them as they are very desirous of seeing her.

He blew out an aggravated breath. The Braam woman's sudden appearance, the plaintive plea of her parents, began chipping away at his shuttered memories with deft, axe-like strokes. The call for his own return years before had seen print in the eastern papers, but he'd had to relearn his letters before he could read the words.

That night they made a cold camp, Maddie and Miss Braam on their bedding beneath a rock overhang while he and Jude minded the provisions and horses.

"You're awful quiet," Jude said in low tones.

Clay looked up from his task. Was he? If anyone noticed, Jude would. Sliding his hand down the mare's fetlock, Clay paused while she picked up her foot. He worked the hoof pick by rote, Jude's words lodging like a stone in his own moccasin.

"Many an idle word's gotten a man ambushed," Clay answered.

"A man can ambush his own self." Jude ran the curry comb over Maddie's mount in rhythmic strokes. "You seem plumb eat up pondering. Reckon it has to do with Miss Braam unearthing some things best forgot."

"Mayhap."

"Still sore over that Bouquet business back in '64, I reckon, when you called the colonel out on account o' those smallpox blankets."

Six years had done little to blunt the worst of the memories. Serving under Bouquet's command in the Ohio country and at Fort Pitt, Clay had witnessed the forced return of two hundred white captives, the Indians given infected goods from Fort Pitt's hospital in exchange.

"Heard tell thousands of Indians perished, more from the pox than all the powder and lead in the colonies. That true?"

Clay gave an aggrieved nod. Had Miss

Braam sickened as a result?

He doubted she was a *miss* at all. Likely she'd married within the tribe, had children. For all he knew they could have succumbed to the pox or flux or some other pestilence. Like his own Indian kin had.

Jude straightened. "Then the colonel got cut down himself."

A small flicker of triumph overrode Clay's angst. Shortly after Bouquet's promotion to commander of British forces in the southern colonies, he'd been struck down by yellow fever.

Vengeance is mine; I will repay, saith the Lord.

How he wanted to believe that wholeheartedly. But his beliefs were dusty. Rusty as an old iron nail. Doubt called Bouquet's demise pure happenstance. His own tired faith made a poor defense.

Finished with hobbling the horses and securing the provisions, they sought the rock overhang. Jude's snoring soon commenced, then Maddie's soft, even breathing told him she too slept. But he was unsure of Keturah Braam.

He finally dozed lightly like he usually did on the trail, not too soundly, one ear cocked, rifle at hand. A wolf's howling roused him once, then the comely captive herself. Fully awake now, he lay perfectly still. She was an arm's length from him, her head pillowed on her outflung arm.

"Kètatamihtit mahtakenk nëwitèch."

Though the words were mumbled, they were spoken fervently.

If they want to have war I will go. Because I do not think about my life.

She rolled over as if agitated, nearly brushing his arm. Such telling words. *War. Life.* The Lenape sentences, strung together like beads on a leather string, told a piece of Keturah Braam's life story.

He'd not spoken a word to her since they'd first met at the blockhouse. Needs be he would try to converse with her in Lenape. She might have completely forgotten the white talk. Just how many years had she been away? He tensed as she mumbled again, this time indistinctly. If he had his druthers, she'd be gone by first light, fleeing west into the forest, before she reunited with her white kin.

Betimes the return was as terrifying as the capture.

6

Clean tow apron. Piggin in hand. The creak of the cabin door opened onto a dewy, sunlit clearing. Tessa stepped outside in the sleepy haze of first awakening, ears tuned to unbroken birdsong, spirit tuned to the day's prospects. The cow awaited milking. The butter churning. After that she'd help Ross at the ferry.

Ma was near, humming softly as she watered the vegetable garden. Together they'd sown the flax yesterday. Lemuel was chopping wood while Zadock and Cyrus took to the fields. No sign of Jasper. With the recent Indian unrest, they all but held their breath till they saw him again.

A week had passed since they'd forted up. Tessa rued returning to the river and the unsettling memories there, but at noon she took her rifle and a dinner pail to Ross. With the last killing frost far behind them, 'twould soon be strawberry season. Long daylight.

Riotous growth. On the heels of that came another unwelcome, stubborn thought.

'Twas in June Keturah had been taken. Three Indians had encircled her. Or were there four?

Keep quiet, Keturah.

Tessa had only mouthed the words that day, panic choking her. Though she'd screamed at first, Keturah then turned to stone. One painted brave reached out a hand, lifting a strand of her corn-silk hair. Pure Dutch she was, terror in her delft-blue eyes.

Tessa was struck by a peculiar thought. If the Indians were bestirred by beauty, might it save her lovely friend?

Ruth had run like a jackrabbit. But Tessa, torn between fleeing or making a stand, hunkered down behind a screen of mountain laurel. Keturah was bound, her wrists knotted with rawhide, and shoved to a start. She'd not walk far before she'd trip in those petticoats. One was singed from the hearth's fire. Tessa had teased her about it that very morn.

In moments, Keturah stepped into a thick stand of chestnut and vanished. 'Twas the last memory Tessa had of her beloved friend.

Ever since, regret had been her bosom companion. What if she'd tried to save her?

Would she not have been taken too? What could one have done with only a basketful of berries?

Sidestepping a mudhole, Tessa tried to banish all dark thoughts. Impossible. A sudden snap of a twig just behind caused her to swirl around so fast her skirts caught on a bramble bush. A timid doe took a step through the leafy undergrowth, a bespeckled fawn not far behind. Jerking her skirts free, Tessa pressed on, gaze swinging wide. The rifle grew cumbersome, the dinner pail a nuisance.

Ahead of her the trail forked. The path to the ferry was well trammeled while the other was scraggly and overgrown, leading to the Braams' abandoned homestead. No one had walked that way for years to her knowledge save some animal or passing Indian. Haunted, some said, all much as it had been the day the Braams had left. Mayhap *haunted* was the reason no one else had claimed it. In a time of land grabbing, 'twas a wonderment it was left alone.

She veered left toward the river, startled to find a wistful longing pulling her right. Long ago she'd felt that same beguiling pull, a young girl on her way to visit friends. How bright the Braam cabin. How welcoming. Was it because they'd had only daughters?

Mistress Braam oft made sugar bread, *sûk-erbôle,* its welcoming aroma reaching to the edges of the clearing, warm as an embrace. Mister Braam was always in the fields. Deprived of sons, he did the heavy work. In her mind's eye he stood tall as his corn, his silhouette against the horizon scarecrowish, he was so lean. Come harvest time, Tessa's brothers were sent for. With Keturah, the eldest daughter, nearby, getting the Swans to lend a hand had not been hard.

At last Tessa emerged on the riverbank. Squinting, she adjusted to the water's glare, glad to the heart to see Ross returning from a ferrying.

"I was starting to fret," he called out when he spied her.

Across the Buckhannon was a large family, the two youngest secured in hampers straddling a packhorse. One was wailing. The older boys herded the few sheep and cows from behind. A chicken squawked in their midst. The clan looked vulnerable. Weary. Her heart squeezed as they struggled up the rocky bank. On the opposite shore, Ross made a smooth landing, leaping from the ferry's rough edge.

"Current's sluggish today." He poked around in the pail. "Better partake right quick. Look over yonder."

Over yonder meant east. Tessa's eyes widened at the sight of a large party in the distance, two buckskinned men leading. Rarely did such a pack of armed men come to harm. Mayhap the struggling family could travel with these backwoodsmen, who usually swam their horses across if unencumbered by pelts and trapping gear. Not all relied on the ferry.

"Virginians, likely," Ross said, biting into his cornbread. "Surveyors. Land stealers."

She regarded them with a mix of disdain and fascination. The parceling of western land meant peace, Pa had once said, yet she'd not known a speck of peace in all her hard-won years. Soon these bold men sprawled along the riverbank like they already owned it, burdened with their chains and markers and axes, looking her up and down as if set on surveying her too. Paying them no mind, she took hold of a setting pole, having shut her rifle in the ferry house.

Ross set his fixings aside. One particular nervy horse needed to be blindfolded, the party ferried in batches. Such a mess of men and baggage! Reeking of spirits and unwashed parts, they were, and she aimed to stay downwind of them if she could, listening as Ross warned of the latest spate of trouble and the coming of the war hero.

"Wait till Tygart gets here," one man said, no hint of jesting about him. "A good many redmen stay clear of him. And not only because he fights like the devil."

Her ears nearly burned to hear the rest. Other than Boone and Washington, both revered up and down the frontier, few men were worth mentioning. The rest of their blustering was lost to her as the man nearest her began to cough and spit tobacco into the muddy water. Such coarseness left her craving the cabin and Ma's hymn singing.

By and by, all were ferried to the far shore. They paid in coin. It made a merry jingle when Ross dropped it into a leather pouch. Stepping around a mound of horse leavings, Tessa eyed the trail to the ferry that would soon be a rutted wagon road by midsummer.

"Take your leave," Ross urged, likely remembering Cyrus's caution to keep her home. First he fetched her rifle. His own was near at hand.

She hesitated, never liking him to be alone, before kissing his sun-browned cheek. It bore a faint, red-tinted stubble. Though the smallest Swan both in stature and by birth, he was fast becoming a man. And he had little need of her with the current so peaceable and the day nearly done.

Grudgingly, she left him, her bare feet returning her to the forked trail she knew so well. Only this time, borne along by some contrary whim, she took the overgrown path, the one she usually shunned. Maybe she should face the past and thereby shake loose the memories that still dogged her.

Her steps slowed. She nearly turned back. Her childish heart had long clung to the Braams' homeplace, but now she hardly knew it. The tumbled-down fences and caved-in well met her first. How often they'd played near the well on hot days, arranging their dolls for tea parties with acorn cups and other forest furniture.

The log house was much as she recalled with its rare split-shingled roof. How big it had been in childhood. How full of life. Now the woman in her saw it for what it was. Smaller. Faded. A hard beginning. A bitter end. The corncrib and outbuildings all burned and blackened. Weathered farm implements held fast to the ground by a stranglehold of thorny vines and tangled weeds.

Did the wilderness, all this wildness, only take? Did it give nothing back?

Her throat clenched and her eyes smarted as she surveyed what was once hard won and well kept. She came closer, mindful of the tall grass and snakes. The smooth door stone, untrod all these years, was green with moss, the thick slab of door leaning open on rusted hinges. A spasm shuddered through her, half sorrow, half fear. But her hankering for this old place, or the way it used to be, pulsed on.

One foot on the porch and she paused. Dare she go in? Replace her treasured memories with tarnished ones? Swiping at a spiderweb, she stood in the yawning doorway, breathing in dust and disuse.

Little remained inside but a bat in a high eave. Slowly, Tessa walked the edges of the dwelling, at last kneeling in one shadowed corner. Marysee's rag doll? Or Annika's? Her fingers closed around it, and she struggled to stay stoic. Leaning her rifle against a log wall, she caressed the worn fabric and faded embroidered face.

Lord, help Keturah. Bring her back to her family.

'Twas a prayer she had prayed for so long it seemed rote as arithmetic. Keturah's family was not here but somewhere overmountain. Inexplicably they'd left the settlement not long after their daughter's disappearance. To protect their other children, Ma always said.

Without thought, she reached for one of the few remaining things in the cabin. A cobwebbed broom. The floor was littered with last autumn's leaves swept in by the wind. She swept them out again, though some crumbled to dust, and then she closed the door behind her, her gun in hand, the doll in her pocket.

Three days into the journey, Clay traded the river valley for a ridge, glad for the shade and invisibility. Moccasin tracks — a party of six all told — along a rushing creek the day before had led to a cold camp last night and today's wary heights.

Jude had gone ahead on foot, his horse tethered at the end of the column. Few could outfox Jude. With Miss Braam behind him, Maddie came last. She preferred walking to riding and did so now, acting as rear guard. Tireless, keen-sighted, she seemed twin to Jude.

Clay took advantage of the near privacy to speak to Keturah Braam. In English. On foot beside her mare, he never let his gaze settle as he kept watch, pitching his voice purposefully low.

"We're halfway to the Buckhannon River, where I believe you once lived." He spoke slowly, giving her time to adjust to the fact he would not resort to Lenape. "Might behoove you to talk the white talk. *Father . . . Mother.*"

Though he didn't look at her, he sensed she understood some of what he said, her lovely face at first clouded with confusion and then clearing.

"Kahèsëna Hàki?" Her voice was pleasing, even delicate, with that whistling lilt peculiar to the Lenape.

"Mata." Nay. He continued slowly. "Not our mother earth."

"Kahèsëna Xàskwim?"

A smile pulled at him. Was she . . . teasing? *"Mata,"* he said again. "Not our mother corn."

Her gaze held his unflinchingly when he said, *"Anati." Dear mother.* There was no mistaking it, the tender word still sweet, though he'd not tasted it for years.

She gave a cursory nod, erasing any playfulness of before. And then, as if wanting to please him, she said slowly and unmistakably in English, *"Mo-ther."*

He repeated it if only to reinforce it. Would she even recognize her birth mother with so many years and experiences between them?

His thoughts veered to Colonel Bouquet's wrenching release of Indian captives years before. One circumstance rode roughshod over all the rest. Taken as a little child, one young woman looked forlornly at the strange white faces waiting to claim lost kin. No hint of recognition stirred on either side. Someone finally suggested the mother sing a hymn. The poignant words were easily recalled.

Alone, yet not alone, am I,
Though in this solitude so drear;
I feel my Savior always nigh,
He comes the weary hours to cheer.
I am with Him, and He with me,
Even here alone I cannot be.

Before the song had ended, the tearful captive had flung herself into her aging mother's arms. The words and image had clung to him ever since.

Let it be the same for Keturah Braam.

7

Tessa set the tattered rag doll on the cabin mantel, then thrust it back into her pocket. 'Twas only a matter of time till her keen-eyed brothers spied its presence. Jasper, likely. Though he wouldn't place the doll, he'd want to know the story behind it. Ma would get misty-eyed as she always did on the rare occasions the Braams were mentioned. Mayhap she'd best secret the doll away in her curtained corner. Yet as she took a step in that direction, a voice she'd not heard for more than two months cut across the clearing. Jasper's bottomless laugh filled Tessa to the brim. Home from overmountain?

Tessa nearly tripped in her haste to the cabin's open door. She drank her oldest brother in as he stood there. Mercy, how lean. And bewhiskered. The string of packhorses behind him bespoke weariness and distance, saddlebags stuffed with necessities in exchange for ginseng and furs.

Ma was just ahead of her, already running to meet him with the gait of a girl. Spry she was at midcentury, her silvered braid spilling down her back. Skirts in hand, Tessa dashed after her, the dust of the yard soft beneath her feet.

Jasper caught them both up in a bearish, trail-worn embrace. It squeezed the breath right out of Tessa.

"A few weeks overmountain and I find you taller and even prettier," he teased, winking.

"I quit growing a long time ago, you furry rascal," she shot back.

He spat a stream of tobacco juice into a clump of weeds, making her wrinkle her nose in distaste. Trail tobacco was a reward for so arduous a journey. She'd tried it once, but it made her fluttery-stomached.

"Nary a speck of trouble," he replied to Ma's question. "Though the price of a pretty petticoat now trumps a brass kettle."

Tessa smiled. He'd remembered? But first the unpacking and inspecting and storing. Anticipation made her steps light.

By suppertime, all was in order, the seven of them lining the trestle table. Jasper always brought something for them all.

For Ma, a Holland handkerchief and a

hard cone of loaf sugar wrapped in purple paper. For her brothers, some hand tool or implement sufficed. Enjoying her expectation, Jasper made her wait till everything else had been distributed. Her parcel was store wrapped and tied with twine. She sat it upon her aproned lap as every eye settled on her.

Zadock cut the string with a swipe of his new knife. Her eager fingers did the rest. Even Ma sighed with pleasure when Tessa held up a tiny vial. Toilette water? She'd heard of such among fancy folk. Uncorking it, she shut her eyes and breathed in a distillation of rose and lavender and something she couldn't name amid her brothers' chuckling. Though impractical, it made her heart sing and the rough-hewn log walls fade away.

She smiled her thanks, setting the tiny bottle on the table for all to see or pass around. But her brothers merely regarded it dismissively as if too manly to touch such. Next came something silvery. Shaped like an acorn, it fit in the palm of her hand, the initials of *TS* engraved on the shiny top. She looked at Jasper in question.

"Pocket grater," he said. "Open it."

She twisted it apart, finding a curious brown nut within.

"Nutmeg," he told her, swiping Lemuel's refilled tankard of cider.

To her astonishment, he grated a dusting of the russet brown atop the drink and bade her taste it. She did, brows arching. The fine spice elevated simple cider to the sublime.

"Brother spoils you," Ross teased. "You won't be worth a hoot and a holler 'fore long."

The cider was passed round. A small bag of nutmegs was next, enough that she would not hoard the one. Dropping the grater into her pocket alongside the rag doll, she turned her attention to the final gift. Candlelight gave the creamy linen a special sheen. Finely sewn and flounced, the petticoat was a snowy marvel, more art than garment.

"Nary a cinder speck to be found," Jasper remarked, reminding her of her hole-ridden garments from where the hearth fire threw sparks.

Leaning nearer, she kissed his bristled cheek. "All this took a passel of furs, I reckon."

He shrugged broad shoulders, his mind clearly on another matter. "Heavily laden as I was, I took care to come the untrammeled way." He lit his pipe, the fragrant smoke hinting of Tidewater tobacco from eastern Virginia. "Came upon a party of two men and two women near the north fork of Drowning Creek. They knew what they were about, leaving little trail. Though I tried, I could never catch up to them. The white woman in particular drew my notice. The white man I believe to be Colonel Tygart. I heard the black man in their party call him by name."

"Tygart's wed then?" Zadock looked surprised. "Bringing his bride to the wilderness?"

Tessa digested this, dismay hollowing out her middle. But why? Because she'd heard he was handsome. In his prime. Many a settlement maiden would be sorely disappointed. Ruth, foremost.

"If you're here, then they're there," Cyrus surmised. The Swan homestead was south of Fort Tygart just a league.

"Reckon they're causing a stir at the garrison then." Lemuel lit his own pipe from his new tobacco pouch. "Makes me wish I was forting up for once."

"Not me," Ma said, pushing away from the table to clear the last of the supper dishes. "Good enough to see you safely home again, the door barred."

Tessa set her disappointment over Tygart aside. In this circle of candlelight and kinship, Jasper's return was gift enough.

The men continued talking in low tones as she took her new belongings to her corner. The flounced petticoat soon hung from a peg, the toilette water on the shelf. Already she wished for something more to dust with nutmeg. Gingerbread or warm milk or applesauce.

With all the fuss, sleep was long in coming. What had Jasper said about happening upon that party of four?

The white woman in particular drew my notice.

It wasn't like him to say such a thing about a woman who might be another man's wife. Yet no one questioned him about it. Something else begged considering. Jasper was unsettled by the woman, enough to mention her.

Why?

Leave it to Maddie to convince Keturah Braam to change garments before they entered Fort Tygart's gates. Clay admired the way Maddie managed it. Slow and gentle-like, making much of the beadwork and fringe before wrapping the Lenape doeskin and trade cloth into a tidy little bundle hidden away in a saddlebag.

Thankfully, Maddie was skilled with a needle, fingers flying nimbly to remake her best dress into a garment the white woman would wear, without any sign of haste or second-handedness.

Clay rued that the indigo cloth made Keturah's eyes even bluer, the cut of the dress far more form-fitting than her looser Lenape garments. Biting his tongue till it nearly bled, he kept himself from reversing Maddie's choice to cushion Keturah's return to the white world.

No doubt shedding the Lenape clothing had cost Keturah something, yet she had consented. Still, her sunny braid hung unaltered to her hips, the center part of her hair painted Lenape red.

Once Fort Tygart's gates swung open wide in welcome, a barrage of questions was sure to pepper them like buckshot. He, Maddie, and Jude would be all but invisible when the women-hungry men spied their comely captive.

His gaze swept across the heavily forested valley that led to the rocky bluff forming the foundation of the distant garrison. Compared to the sprawling Fort Pitt, Fort Tygart was in miniature. Yet four sturdy blockhouses stood at its far-flung corners, a few hats showing above the white oak pickets impaling the sky.

A welcoming volley of shots ushered them

in. They'd been seen and now recognized by some who'd served under him prior. Those few men were firmly behind him. Others — strangers — would need proof of his authority. Mustering a militia and assigning spies to scout the woods would be the least of his challenges.

Though their horses went at a slow walk, they raised the dust. Aggravated by a south wind, it partially obscured the gates as they groaned open. Several men lifted two fingers to the battered brims of their hats as he rode past. Others gawked openly at Keturah Braam. She kept her eyes down, dismounting after he did but from the right side of her horse, Indian fashion. This surely did not go unnoticed either.

To Maddie he said quietly, "Take Miss Braam to the nearest empty cabin."

Maddie nodded, gaze already roving the enclosure where twenty-odd cabins hugged the fort's inner walls.

"Colonel Tygart, sir." A burly, balding man extended a firm hand. "Glad you've arrived unimpeded." His homespun clothes belied his cultured voice and vocabulary. "I'm Joseph Cutright, storekeeper."

After shaking a good many hands, Clay made a short speech about the impressive appearance of the garrison and his priority of mustering the militia in hopes to spread the word that more hands were needed. Answering questions about the latest news from the east and Fort Pitt took time. Able to sum up a man quickly, Clay made quiet note of those who looked to be leaders before he took possession of the blockhouse.

After the sparseness of the trail, the edifice assumed a rosy glow. Smelling of green wood and chinking, its cavernous hearth bore a small cook fire, a kettle over the coals. An assortment of empty pots dressed the fieldstones. At the room's center a trestle table and six rare Windsor chairs garnered his attention, but it was the hefty desk with its smooth walnut top and the nooks and crannies along the wide back wall that bespoke the commandant's domain most of all. Upstairs were his sleeping quarters, gained by a wide set of roughly hewn steps.

"There's a granny woman in the next cabin who'll cook for you," said Cutright. "Unless you brought your wife along . . ."

"Nay." Clay ended any speculation. "The white woman is a returned captive. The black woman is free and wife of the free man who rode in with me."

"Captive?" Cutright ran a hand over his bearded jaw.

"Aye. From along the Buckhannon River south of here. What little we know, that is. Goes by the name of Keturah Braam, mayhap."

No recognition kindled. "I've been here but six years. Truth is, there's so much raiding and killing and stealing up and down the border that all the victims ball into a nameless jumble."

"Anybody hereabouts with a history?"

A decisive nod. "That would be the old crone, Hester Swan, who'll keep you fed. Say the word and I'll summon her."

"Once I'm settled, aye." Clay hung his shot pouch and powder horn from a wall peg. Releasing his rifle felt strange after a sennight's grip. His stomach rumbled so loudly that Cutright laughed.

"Once you've eaten, you mean." He moved to the open door. "I'll try to stem any business with you till tomorrow. Today's spent."

With an appreciative nod, Clay examined a map of sorts laid out on the desktop.

"I took the liberty of drawing the fort for you and naming all the occupants cabin by cabin down to the privy pit and such," Cutright said. "If the cabins aren't marked they're empty, though they fill quick enough when folks fort up."

"Well done." The inked map was precise and detailed. "Surveyor as well as store-keeper?"

Cutright chuckled. "Years ago, I ran the line with Colonel Washington."

"Your skills are appreciated." Clay aimed to memorize the map by morning.

"I'll fetch the cook." Cutright shut the door, ushering in a blessed, spacious calm.

Slivers of light shone through half a dozen loopholes. Clay climbed the steps to the loft slowly as if testing their strength. Upstairs was a window open to the fort's common. A dragonfly winged in iridescent flight around the wide, curtainless frame. Taking a stool, he sat down and surveyed his new realm like a lord might his kingdom. The lofty, albeit foolish, thought made him smile.

Frontier forts were, by necessity, meant for little but survival. But as the sun pulled west and dappled the dusty common with flattering gold light, the blockhouse door below opened and closed repeatedly and soon sent him downstairs again.

At the hearth a tiny, tidy woman poked at a sizzling skillet. On the table was a pewter plate piled high with corncakes. He cleared his throat to announce his presence and she straightened, turning around to face him. He worked to hide a smile as she cocked her head this way and that, sparrow-like, piercing gaze boring into him.

"So, you're Tygart, I suppose." Around her wrinkled neck was a monocle strung on a badly frayed ribbon. She placed it over one faded blue eye, squinting to hold it in place, and peered up at him in obvious disapproval. "Well . . . not handsome exactly. More striking looking." An onerous sigh. "The unmarried women are bound to be sorely disappointed. But there's no denying you're an excellent woodsman from the look of you, built like a young bull. No savage'll lay a hand to your scalp."

The honest appraisal both amused and stung. Ever since he was knee high, he'd been a tad thin-skinned about his appearance. *Salt Boy,* the Lenape had oft taunted him on account of his white skin. A deep-seated Scripture jumped to mind as it always did, sown by his ma long ago.

For the Lord seeth not as man seeth; for man looketh on the outward appearance, but the Lord looketh on the heart.

"I hope I'm as kind about your cooking," he said with a wink. "Mistress . . ."

"Swan." She cackled, and the monocle fell to dangle upon her bodice as she turned back to the fire. "Hester Swan."

He pulled out a chair and sat down, the

lure of a meal too much. Silently he watched as she produced a pewter plate and piled on thick slabs of ham, with crisply fried potatoes and onions atop it. The butter in the small crock made his mouth water even before she'd smeared it generously on the corncakes.

He took out his knife, for he saw no other utensil, but she withdrew a two-tined fork from her pocket and passed it to him. Fully armed, he commenced eating the most mouthwatering meal he'd had since leaving Fort Pitt.

"You're not a praying man then," she queried, her wrinkled face pensive.

Did she mind? He deflected the stab of guilt her words wrought. At his continued silence, she took the Windsor chair across from him, the curved back arching above her head, she was so tiny. A Swan trait?

To his surprise, she uncorked a jug and poured them both a drink. "You're liable to need this if you're to last."

Liquid fire. Once down, the whiskey spread in a languorous stream to all the saddle-sore parts of him. But it did not quell his noisy stomach. He forked a bite of ham, swallowed, and said, "How long you been here?"

"In this very valley since '55." Her pointed

chin rose proudly. "Carolina before that. Came overmountain with my nephew, who was killed by savages a while back at the Buckhannon ferry."

One good man gone then. "My condolences. Mention was made of the Swans at Fort Pitt, along with the Schoolcrafts and Clendennins."

"None finer." She downed the corn whiskey in two swallows without a sputter.

"What do you know of the Braams?" he queried between bites.

She studied the wall behind him without focus. "Good Dutch stock. Comeliest daughters I ever saw. The oldest was took by Indians long ago. I recollect the Braams mostly because the daughter they lost was with my niece that sorry day."

"Your niece wasn't taken?"

A slow shake of her head and again that faraway look. "Out picking strawberries, the both of them. Bosom friends. Seems to me there was a third girl. I forget her name. The Braams' daughter got ahead of them, and then like lightning she was gone."

"And her kin?"

"Took it awful hard. Some folks would rather their kin be killed than took. Soon after, the Braams abandoned their homeplace. Don't know what became of them."

The food now seemed a tad tasteless. He'd wanted more for Keturah Braam than an abandoned homestead. This new hitch brought disappointing complications.

"I suppose the missing Braam girl is now the flax-haired woman you rode in with." It was a statement, not a question. "My eyes may be dim but my ears aren't. Word got round right quick that she looked familiar."

Before he could reply, Jude darkened the doorway, Maddie in his wake. "Just got your supper summons from Cutright. Got enough to share?"

Clay looked to the frying pan, still half full, and motioned them in. Jude gave a low whistle of appreciation while Maddie perused the unfamiliar blockhouse. Clay made introductions, the name Swan easily remembered.

"Miss Braam's sleepin'," Maddie told him quietly.

He took an extra plate and saved a portion for Keturah along with two corncakes. The tall stack hardly dwindled. Hester Swan left with a brisk farewell. Was she being compensated for her cooking? Another question to settle. But Keturah Braam was foremost on his mind.

"Appears Miss Braam's kin left these parts after she was taken," he said, "and I've yet to discover where to."

Maddie's face fell, but a famished Jude only looked up from his plate to reach for the salt cellar.

"Where does that leave her till you figure out what to do next?" Maddie asked.

Clay pondered his answer.

"She won't tolerate the fort long, living free like she's been," Jude said as he chewed. "A fort is naught but a cage to an Indian."

"And all those white eyes." Maddie knew firsthand what it was like to be an outsider. Though free, she wasn't always treated so and often chafed against a fort's narrow confines herself.

"Once I put out the call to muster the militia tomorrow, I'll take Miss Braam out to her old homeplace and start there." Why he'd start there Clay couldn't explain. It was bound to be emotional for her if any of her childhood memories remained or resurfaced, not to mention the absence of her white kin. "Care to come along?"

"I'll join you," Maddie answered without pause.

"Till the forenoon then."

8

They rode out under a ten o'clock sun that promised to melt them by noon. Keturah Braam was abreast of him, Maddie behind. Clay sensed the Dutch captive's relief to be beyond fort walls. It matched his own. Out here they escaped the rising stench of the fort's privy pits and the manure-laden livestock pens, a potent combination in the May heat, and breathed deeply of the forest-cleansed air.

Now, in late spring, the lush woods were at full frolic before starting a slow slide toward autumn. It didn't take long for Keturah to slip from her unsaddled mare and gather a palmful of early strawberries. She extended a hand, offering the first pickings to Clay, a smile on her berry-stained lips.

How could he refuse? He thanked her in both English and Lenape, popping the offering in his mouth. Next to marrow bones slow roasted around a campfire on a cold winter's day, strawberries — summer's best fruit — were his favorite food.

Maddie soon dismounted and joined Keturah while he stayed atop his horse, rifle resting in the crook of one arm, gradually getting his bearings in new territory.

Joseph Cutright had told him the whereabouts of the Braam cabin, but they were in no hurry to get there. He'd kept quiet about their destination, and now Keturah had turned it into a strawberry-picking expedition.

"Do you know the legend?" he asked her in Lenape.

She looked over at him, her hands busy with the berries. "How the Great Spirit made the first man and woman, and they quarreled? The woman ran away and the man could not catch her."

Surprised by her wealth of words, Clay tamped down his desire to hurry. "To help him, the Great Spirit created a patch of strawberries, hoping to delay her. She stopped and ate this new fruit, and finally the man caught up to her and said he was sorry."

Keturah nodded. "They called the fruit *heart berry* because it is shaped like a heart and reunited them forever."

"Tehim," he said, resurrecting the old word. "Strawberry."

He studied her as she remounted her mare. Had she no angst about the day she was taken, picking berries as she'd been? Mayhap she'd forgotten that or refused it entry.

She looked at him, a curious light in her eye. "Someday you must tell me your own story. And why you speak the Lenape tongue so well."

He said nothing to this, kneeing Bolt forward.

It took an hour of dense woods, two creeks, a thorny tangle of grapevine, and a bear sighting before they reached what looked to be the border of the Braams' deserted homestead.

Out of the corner of his eye, Clay watched Keturah's expression. Placid as a doe's. At least till they got in sight of the cabin. In the noon glare, all the abandonment lay exposed. Every overturned cart, barrel, and rusted hinge. The sagging springhouse roof. A lightning-split hickory crushing a corn-crib. All told that the Braams had been gone a long time.

Once again Keturah slid off her mare and began a slow walk to the well. She knelt there by the tumbled stones, eyes on the grass as if searching for something.

Maddie came abreast of Clay, her words more whisper. "Reckon we should follow?"

"Best let her go first." He looked to the pommel of his saddle, the downward slant of his felt hat cutting the sun's glare but turning his hairline itchy.

Something about the scene was too tender to witness. Half of him was glad she'd returned to ghosts. Betimes an actual reunion was too much to bear.

"What did McKee say happened to her Indian family?" Maddie asked him. "Before she was brought in to Pitt?"

"Something about disease cutting half the tribe down." He watched a ring snake slither away beneath a rotted stump. "Notice the old scars on her throat and arms? My guess is she survived the disease as a child before living with the Lenape, then lost her Indian family to it not so long ago."

"I wondered why she's not put up a fight to rejoin the Indians. She seems surrendered to coming back here."

"So far, aye."

After a few minutes Maddie dismounted, intent on the cabin. Keturah had set foot on the porch but made no move to open the cabin door. What would she find? Moreover, what would doing so unleash?

Clay's gaze dissected the surrounding woods for any untoward movement. He blinked, eyes stinging from lack of sleep in an ill-fitting bed. Since his captivity he'd preferred the ground, a cushion of moss or leaves beneath him.

At first light he'd met with the fort's four spies, needing to add to their number. Scouting was an unenviable job. He'd gotten his start spying at Fort Henry under General Amherst years ago.

Veering away from that sore mental trail, he pondered telling Keturah his story as she'd asked. Rarely did he unearth it, letting his past gather dust and fall into disuse like the Braams' homestead. Most folks didn't understand the path he'd trod. Or didn't want to.

The women went into the cabin, Maddie leading. Keturah hovered on the threshold for a few indecisive seconds. Maddie was a godsend even if she didn't speak Lenape. In her quiet way, she'd begun teaching — rather, reminding — Keturah of simple English words. Soap. Bowl. Milk. Corn.

A flicker of movement by a laurel to his left snagged his eye. A sun-dappled fox was all it amounted to. His shoulders relaxed though his mind stayed wary. The last spate of trouble, Cutright told him, started near the Buckhannon ferry last month. Two clashing tribes. One brave killed. The fort was briefly besieged after that by a small party of Wyandot, leaving one settler with a shattered elbow but no fatal wounds. Since then, nary a whiff of unrest, though Indian sign continued to be plentiful.

Keturah and Maddie emerged into the sunlight. The cabin door closed. Keturah lingered at the well again, picking up the water pail severed from its rope as if wondering how it happened to be so. Finally, they were on their way again, Keturah looking lost in thought.

"Where to now?" Maddie asked Clay.

"Closest neighbor — Swans. Their land borders the river."

Mightn't Keturah remember her former neighbors?

Their horses went at a walk, Clay intent on giving her ample time to adjust to her former surroundings. Once the Swan homestead spread before them, Keturah's expression seemed unchanged. Or did he note a faint flicker of recognition?

Unlike the Braams', all was order and industry here. Corn thriving ankle high in the surrounding fields. A cabin clearing free of stumps, with half a dozen sturdy outbuildings at first glance, including a new stable. A large fenced garden patch in colorful array to the south. Not just any house but a fortified blockhouse on the west end of a handsome cabin. Most surprising of all was the stone springhouse, the equal of any he'd seen in the east. Swan Station, Cutright had called it. The place looked to have been along the Buckhannon for some time.

They rode in slowly but had already been seen. A great many noises set up at once. A hog grunted noisily and a chicken squawked. The aproned woman coming out of the cabin made a beeline toward them while a bewhiskered young man emerged from a smithy, leather apron tied about his lean waist, red-faced from a small forge fire. His hammering had been heard a ways off.

Clay slid his rifle into its pouch and dismounted to the woman's greeting. "Colonel Tygart?"

"Aye, Tygart," Clay replied. "And company."

"Welcome then. You're the talk of the border here lately. I'm the widow Swan." Her gracious manner warmed him. He didn't miss the start of surprise in her eyes when her gaze fixed on the former captive. He held his peace, waiting for recognition to kindle and confirm one of the Braams was truly among them.

"Keturah?" Uncertainty framed her words. "Heaven be praised! Can it be?" Mistress Swan took a tentative step toward her, a wealth of emotion in her tanned face. "So long it's been, yet you look the same, only taller. Like your ma."

Her poignant words narrowed Clay's attention, yet he didn't miss the gawking men now in their midst, all in varying degrees of befuddlement. The Swan brothers he'd heard about?

Mistress Swan enfolded Keturah in a plump, homespun embrace once she'd dismounted. And the single, inexplicable tear Clay had witnessed at Fort Pitt faded to the far reaches as Keturah cracked open like a broken water pitcher.

"Watch your hide," Ross cautioned as Tessa left the river, trading her setting pole for a small willow basket.

Up at first light, she'd accompanied Ross, glad few folks needed ferrying since her mind was set on berrying. Strawberries were abundant this year, bits of scarlet amid the sun-stroked, loamy places. Telltale white blooms promised a good gathering. Never mind if winter-starved deer got there first or the ruby gems had been bird-pecked in places. Such creatures helped scatter the seed.

Her gait was light as she neared home. Her gun she'd left behind at the ferry house. The heavy rifle was an encumbrance, but she'd catch what for from her brothers for her carelessness. Yet sooner or later she must set it aside much like they did when plowing and sowing and doing their many chores.

A peaceable hour passed. Sweat-spackled, her belly and basket full, she came into the cabin clearing. Odd how a body was ill prepared for the most heart-wrenching surprises. No warning hullabaloo. No shadowy feeling. Just a rare lull about the cabin. What had made her brothers abandon their pressing tasks at midday? Had it something to do with the three strange horses grazing around the springhouse?

Voices floated to her across the empty clearing. Most she knew. One was distinct in cadence and tone, a manly volley of English and . . . Indian?

Basket dangling from one arm, she pushed open the cabin door. All her brothers but Ross were gathered around the table. The man at the head, occupying Pa's place, was one she'd never laid eyes on, as was the black woman to his left. Ma sat with her back to the door in her usual place, unnervingly close to a woman whose pale braid snaked down her slender back.

The woodsy giant was the first to acknowledge her, his gaze swiveling to Tessa as she hovered in the doorway. As it wasn't his house, he didn't motion her in.

"Tessa . . ." Jasper spoke in the sudden lull as she entered.

Mindlessly, Tessa set the berries aside.

"Best sit down," Cyrus said, voice full of portent. "Your long-lost friend has come back to us."

The braided woman turned, delft-blue eyes searching. Disbelief struck Tessa like a blow.

Keturah?

Her old friend sat before her, once a mere bud of a girl, now blossomed into a full-blown flower of a woman. Keturah . . . who once taught her to write her name . . . who made a game out of chasing deer from the fields . . . who sang like a bird . . . who always called her *lieverd* . . . who stuffed tow linen in her ears at the firing of the fort guns . . . who kept all Tessa's secrets and laughed with her like no one since.

Emotion tightened her throat. No greeting could she give that fit the mighty chasm that time and distance had wrought. Yet every eye was upon her, willing her to do something.

Coming from behind, Tessa opened her arms and embraced her old friend. Smoke and earthiness suffused her senses instead of the milky, sugar-laced scent of before.

The conversation resumed around her, none of it answering her needling questions. She sought the open seat between Zadock and Lemuel while Keturah turned around again as easily as if she'd never left. The lively talk was hard to track till her surprise simmered down. Scraps about the militia. Fort spies. Enemy sign. Provisions. Gun powder and bullet lead.

They seemed to skirt the heart of the matter, that Keturah Braam was here, had come back to them, was at their very table. Another discreet glance told her that Keturah was worn. Spent. The slight sag of her features might be called resigned. And her cheeks bore the faintest imprint of dried tears, the dust of the trail marking their downward course.

Was this strapping tree of a man Keturah's husband? Though seated, he was a full head taller than her brothers. And not nearly as loose-lipped.

"Why, without any kin close at hand, she'll stay right here," Ma was saying. "Just us women in the cabin. The men keep mostly to the blockhouse when they're not in the fields or at the ferry."

Murmurs of affirmation went round. Finally, Tessa snapped to. The tense tickle in her middle nearly erupted into a laugh at the sight of her brothers' barely restrained glee. She swallowed all mirth while the man at the head of the table looked straight at Keturah and spoke Indian again.

So, they weren't wed? Was he asking Keturah where she wanted to be? Penned up at the fort or with the Swans along the spacious Buckhannon? The cabin stilled again. Keturah answered in the dulcet voice Tessa remembered, though the words were gibberish. Somehow it hurt her that she couldn't understand her former friend yet this tall stranger could. And how was it that a white man could speak Indian so well?

"Seems our company manners have fled, what with all the excitement," Ma said, looking from the stranger to Tessa. "Colonel Tygart, this is my only daughter, Tessa Swan."

"Pleased to meet you," he replied as Tessa inclined her head to acknowledge the introduction.

All her expectations and presumptions collapsed in a disheartening heap. Was this truly Colonel Clayton Tygart or some buck-skinned imposter? He was not at all like she'd expected. Nothing like she'd hoped.

She studied him beneath lowered lashes, but the shadows in the cabin were too deep even in daylight to grasp hold of him. All she knew was that he was tall and as soot-haired as Keturah was fair.

They were locked out of the conversation for several more moments as he spoke to Keturah. And then he said in plain King's English, "She will stay."

9

Clay moved toward Bolt, who'd mowed down the tallest grass around the Swans' springhouse and was now eyeing the sweet timothy by the smokehouse. Maddie lingered with Keturah and Mistress Swan in the cabin while the brothers returned to their work.

Belly full of mincemeat pie and coffee, he'd formed a pleasant association at first meeting, given all the Swan brothers would muster with the militia. The youngest, Ross, was absent but just as eager, they said. All in all, a satisfying day's work, mayhap the most important matter being Keturah's settling till her kin could be found.

Though the half-dozen horses in a near pasture bespoke plenty, he'd leave Keturah's mare here. One less animal to tend at Fort Tygart. One less to steal. Indians had a terrible penchant for horseflesh.

"Colonel Tygart, sir."

He swung round to face the one Swan whose voice he hadn't heard till now, though her uncommon name had stuck to him like pitch. Tessa. In a world of Marthas and Janes and Annes, it rang refreshing. And now she stood in front of him, catching him by surprise again.

"Mightn't you send round Keturah's belongings?" she asked.

He regarded her in thoughtful silence. In the cabin's dimness, he'd not grasped her features. Here in broad daylight he saw she was a deep tobacco brown, her eyes a startling indigo — nay, more violet — and the dominating feature in her oval face. Had she no hat to shield her from the sun?

"Redeemed captives have precious few belongings," he replied.

She looked toward the cabin. "I missed most of the talk. I never figured on seeing my friend again."

He checked his rifle. "Miss Braam's been gone a long while. She'll not be as you remember."

"Has she forgotten her mother tongue?"

He stared down the rifle's barrel before snapping it shut. "Seems so."

"Maybe she can teach me Indian."

"Lenape?" That nearly made him chuckle. "I've never heard the like."

"Oh? Else you can teach me a few words before you go."

She was all earnestness and entreaty. Any notion that she was being coy shattered. This was no coquettish Philadelphia miss. For a moment he stood stupefied.

"Well, Colonel, are you going to give me some words, or aren't you?"

The gentle jibe hit its mark and wiped the amusement from his face. He eyed the cabin. What in thunderation was taking Maddie so long?

"Words." He ran his fingers along the stubbled edge of his jaw. All the Lenape he knew left his head in exasperating fashion. "Mayhap you'd best teach her the white talk. She's more in need of that than your learning Indian."

The hopeful light left her face.

He wasn't being ornery, just honest. "Speaking of words, how is it you have such a" — he stopped short of *comely* — "uncommon name?"

She picked a burr off her berry-stained apron. " 'Twas my granny's name. She hailed from Scotland."

She'd turned a tad bashful, no longer looking at him. Beyond the gentle slope of her shoulder, he saw Maddie emerge from the cabin, Keturah and Mistress Swan in the doorway.

He swung himself into the saddle, reining around to face the deer path that had led them here. *"Winkalit."*

Tessa echoed him. "What does it mean?"

"Ask Miss Braam," he said as Maddie joined them.

Tessa nodded, a bit of the light he'd snuffed returning to her face. Bidding Maddie farewell, she began a slow walk toward the cabin, as bare of foot as she was bare of head.

Maddie waited till they'd entered the woods to tease him. "You in a courtin' frame of mind, Colonel?"

"Miss Swan, you mean?"

"She's awful pert."

He ruminated on that till they'd crossed the first creek. Crooked Creek, Cutright's map said. "She merely asked for Miss Braam's belongings."

"Mighty kind of her." Maddie studied him knowingly. "Those town-bred gals seem to bore you. Maybe a frontier flower'll do."

He chuckled and pulled the brim of his hat lower. "You have some foolish notions."

"Do I? Even Scripture says it's not good for man to be alone. Take me, for instance. I get to ride into Fort Tygart to Jude, my lawfully wedded husband, while you face a cold bed and an old crone of a cook. What comfort's to be had in that?"

"My being here is all business, remember," he countered. "I aim to do my part to secure the frontier so the Swans can farm and ferry in peace and no one is taken captive like Keturah Braam. And I'm just as set on seeing no peaceful Indians abused or retaliated against for their more warring brothers."

"Well, seems like you could enjoy yourself while you're doin' it," she chided good-naturedly. "What's more, I overheard you say you'd send Keturah's belongings by a fort spy. Why not honor Miss Swan's request yourself instead of rounding up somebody else?" Her gaze held his. "Or maybe Miss Braam's more to your liking."

He stayed silent, used to Maddie's ribbing.

"I do believe it's better for Miss Braam to be with the Swans than at the fort." Her expression brightened. "Maybe we should pray one of them handsome brothers wins her."

"Recollect their names?" He asked himself mostly. What he most remembered were faces. Names told little.

"Jasper. Lemuel. Zadock." Maddie pursed her lips in contemplation. "I disremember the rest. The youngest was at the ferry."

"That would be Ross. The other's Cyrus."

"And Miss Swan?" A low, throaty chuckle. "Remember her given name, Colonel?"

Tessa.

"Nay," he lied. He purposed to forget it.

Tessa sought the privacy of the barn to gather her scattered thoughts before returning to the cabin. She kept close the Indian word the colonel had given her, still battling disbelief that Keturah had come back to them. But like the colonel said, 'twas not the Keturah of before.

Leaning against the ridgepole, she listened to the cooing of a dove in the rafters. The plaintive sound only aggravated her already tumbled feelings, which had little to do with Keturah's sudden return. What had happened out there betwixt herself and Colonel Tygart? Not the words but all the rest. The long looks. The weighty pauses. Like heat lightning, something had passed between them, something immediate and intense.

Succumbing to a childish habit, she fell back into a pile of old hay, hardly feeling the scratch and prickle. Maybe it was on account of his eyes that she was so a-snarl. Never had she seen such a sight. One fiercely blue, the other a deep, earthy brown and mossy green. It startled and mesmerized her and turned him half feral.

Colonel Tygart couldn't pass as handsome. Not with a nose too narrow and a jaw too wide. Few could fault his frame. She doubted all five of her brothers could take him. He oozed an immense vigor like a sugar maple oozed sap. When his odd gaze met hers, she felt all ablaze, flushed and tongue-tied and weak-kneed all at once.

Was she moonstruck?

"Tessa?" From the cabin doorway came Ma's voice. Its strident tone yanked her back to the present and had her picking bits of straw from her skirt and hair as she collected herself and left the barn.

Laden with firewood, she returned to the cabin to find Keturah cross-legged on the floor, playing with a kitten. Ma was busy shelling peas, the first from the garden. Bacon crowded a skillet, overriding the stale tobacco smoke of the night before. Overpowering everything was the last wintered-over cabbage from the straw-filled trench near the springhouse. Seasoned with onion, it could be smelled clear to the barn. All familiar, welcome sights and scents now made strange by the presence of the woman more Indian than white and the rattling presence of the man who'd brought her here.

In the lull of lost years, she'd forgotten how lovely her friend was. Once again Keturah's beauty struck her hard. Beautiful in ways that she herself could never be. Fair. Flawless. The colonel intruded again. Surely a man like Tygart would find her plain as a sparrow in comparison. Maybe Tygart was as smitten with Keturah as her brothers were or had once been.

Ma looked up from her task. "Set Keturah a place between us, aye?"

With a nod, Tessa put utensils on the table, pausing at Pa's place. A thin sliver of mincemeat pie remained, which she ate if only to clean and put away the dish. Colonel Tygart had even pushed in his chair, a courtesy rarely practiced by her brothers.

Tessa kept busy till supper, skirting Keturah as she played with the kitten and then walked about the cabin as if familiarizing herself with a place she'd once known well. If only Keturah would speak. Should she try to remind her old friend of English things? Say simple words? Maybe Keturah knew them, had not forgotten, but was holding back. Being around so many Swans might loosen her tongue in time.

When her brothers came into the cabin before supper even graced the table, Tessa bit back a smile. As if being first would garner a seat beside their unexpected guest.

Keturah settled between her and Ma, eyes down demurely as they all found their usual places, joined hands, and prayed. 'Twas Ross, most like Pa, who said grace.

"Lord, we would ask Thy blessing on this food. Bless it to the good of our bodies that we may be better prepared for the battles of life. For Christ's sake we ask it. Amen."

After so lean a winter, everyone wanted a fair helping of the first peas of the season. Their very greenness was odd at table after winter's barren sameness of hog and hominy. Keturah ate sparingly, her continued quiet hardly noticed as the Swan men revisited the eventful afternoon.

"The colonel seems a right capable character," Jasper said, murmurs of affirmation following.

"I never saw a gun-toting Quaker before," Cyrus said. "No *thees* or *thous* to speak of neither."

Jasper shook his head. "He's no Quaker other than his roots and raising. Rifle-bred to the bone, sure to rile his Quaker kin. Word is he's not on the best terms with them."

"Militia musters when?" Ross asked, clearly dejected at all he'd missed. "Week's end?"

"Saturday noon. Nominations will be made for office of captain and lieutenant." Lemuel balanced his peas on his knife. "Frolic to follow."

Tessa perked up. Frolic? A rare occasion to dress in their humble best and step a reel or a jig. With women so few, she never lacked for partners. It would be a fine time to don her new petticoat.

"Going to barbecue that white ox of Westfall's," Cyrus added.

Ma took note of this, setting her fork down. Westfall was their nearest neighbor to the north, a widower of some merit.

As bowls and plates emptied, Tessa listened to the usual manly banter — of the white bear with dark nose pads and white claws seen near Dog Run, of the proper way to roast a brace of turkeys, if the Ohio River was mightier than the Monongahela, why Fort Pitt had become little more than a spirit-sated gaol, of the spreading conviction that western Virginia belonged more to Pennsylvania, and how Ross had nearly sunk the ferry by overloading oxen the day before.

Discreetly, Tessa watched Keturah. She'd seemed reluctant to eat, waiting till the men began, and had shunned her fork, preferring to partake with her fingers. How was she handling all this male talk? Any jabber about Indians and Indian sign was altogether missing, thankfully.

To Tessa's surprise, at meal's end Keturah began clearing the dishes from the table amid the men's pipe smoke and sated belching. Tessa stayed still, though Ma rose to do the washing.

"So, Sister, going to set your bonnet for Colonel Tygart?" Cyrus teased with a wink.

"What bonnet?" Ross joked of her perpetually bare head.

"Shush," she chided, pushing away from the table.

"Spied you two talking before he left. A mite bold to sashay up to him that way." This from Zadock, who missed little. "Hope you remembered to call him Colonel."

"Aye, that I did." She felt pinned by their stares. "I merely asked him to send round Keturah's things."

"Is that right?" Lemuel drawled. "You seemed to be taking your sweet time doing it."

They hooted when she crossed her eyes, stuck out her tongue, and ended the matter.

Across the cabin, Keturah's yawn had Ma making plans for bedtime. Would their guest sleep in the trundle bed? With a wave of her hand, Ma shooed the men to their blockhouse quarters, the door betwixt them and the main cabin soundly shutting. They took it without complaint, for Ma was above any teasing, though Tessa sensed they wanted to linger.

Her private corner was hers no longer. Yet she didn't rue the loss except to feel a slight qualm when she got on her knees to pray before she snuffed the bedside light. Keturah's searching look sent her thoughts spinning every which way but heavenward. Had Keturah forgotten to pray, at least the white way? Indians kept their own religion, their practices deemed heathenish by most.

After a hasty amen, Tessa rose reluctantly to crawl between cool linen sheets while Keturah regarded with suspicion the trundle bed that had been moved to Tessa's corner. Pulling the bedding free, Keturah wrapped it round her and lay down upon the wooden floor, her back to the shunned frame.

Tessa felt a qualm. Needs be she should stay on her knees all night. A great many matters needed praying for.

Father, bring the Braams back or Keturah to them. Let it be a gladsome reunion. Help me befriend her again till then. And if it pleases Thee, let her look kindly on one of my older brothers who so need a wife.

10

The strong, greasy aroma of roasting beef invaded every corner of Fort Tygart. After so much venison, Clay welcomed the change. He'd been at the fort a week, the days a blur of inspections and meetings and forays in and out of its walls. Not one whiff of trouble that he knew of along the border other than a few warriors bent on personal glory stealing horses. But instinct told him their every move was being watched. His coming here had not gone unnoticed. Little happened at military outposts that bypassed the tribes. Every inch of ground the settlers gained thrust the Indians back. That he felt caught in the crosshairs of the conflict mattered little.

"Colonel Tygart, sir." At the blockhouse door stood an express rider. "Dispatch from Fort Pitt."

Clay motioned him in even as he sealed his notice about Keturah Braam for the eastern newspapers. Jude had returned Keturah's meager belongings to the Swan homestead a few days prior, saving him the trouble. He himself expected the Swan brothers for today's muster and the frolic to follow.

"Best stay on for the festivities," he told the weary courier. "Nothing urgent that needs sending to keep you from it."

"Obliged." Appreciation eased the man's bedraggled features. "I smelt that beef long before I caught sight of them pickets."

They left the dispatches atop his desk and emerged into a morning marred by distant thunderheads. "There's to be horse racing and a turkey shoot just beyond the gates," Clay told him. "And guards posted within and without."

The courier removed his cocked hat and slapped it against his thigh to dispel the dust. "I'm wearied to the bone of watching my back."

"Someday you won't have to."

Thunder boomed along with a drum, the signal to muster. While the courier took his rifle and joined the turkey shoot, Clay stood at the gate as a party of eight came through the line of trees to the south, the Swans and Keturah Braam on some of the finest mounts seen in these parts.

116

Maddie went out to meet them, Jude not far behind. Maddie seemed especially fond of Miss Swan. Pondering it, Clay moved on to the muster, pleased that nearly every eligible man in the settlement had turned out. There were the usual no-goods among them, the hotheads who resisted authority, even a few shirkers and sots. The Swans were among the better men. It was no surprise that a vote decided Jasper Swan as captain and a Schoolcraft as lieutenant. A roster for guard duty was begun and the most dauntless assigned as spies.

Their first drill played out and the regulations were read aloud, a great deal of commotion, questions, and dust clouding the day. Clay spent much time moving among the crowd as time unwound, committing each settler's name and face in his thoughts, assessing their weapons and woodcraft and deciding who'd best serve where. Glad he was the summer twilight lasted late into the evening.

A fiddle twanged, followed by a shout signaling the dancing was about to begin. A bonfire glowed at the fort's center, its snap and crackle building till light was cast into the farthest corners. Children flitted about like fireflies, the rare merriment like a contagion. He kept an eye on the guarded open gate, the other on the cavorting. 'Twould be a long, mosquito-laden night.

"Let me look at you." Great-Aunt Hester turned Tessa this way and that behind the closed door of her cabin, just as she'd done since Tessa was no bigger than a minnow. With a forceful snap, Hester beheaded a stray string from Tessa's new petticoat, then moved on to smooth the modesty piece about her bodice, anchoring it with an heirloom, a coral cameo from Scotland.

Beside her, Ruth sighed with delight, mayhap with a beat of envy. In her plain homespun, though she did wear a finely made cambric apron, she wore no jewelry, even borrowed. Tessa had lent her a dab of the toilette water from overmountain, which Ruth declared ornament enough.

"Now, go and choose well," Hester admonished, shooing them out the door to the common just beyond. "A wedding would be a fine thing after so many buryings."

Out onto the common they went, Tessa's eye drawn to Ma sitting with Keturah on a bench beneath a cabin eave.

"Think she does those wild Indian dances we hear about with drums and rattles and such?" Ruth whispered.

Tessa simply shrugged. Who knew what Keturah had learned or unlearned in those lost years? With only a few nights together under the Swan roof, their days filled with unending tasks, Tessa was left wishing Keturah had returned in winter when the pace slowed to a trot and more talk could be had as they huddled near the hearth.

A great many couples were swirling over the trammeled ground to a sprightly reel. Ruth's focus shifted. "How does Colonel Tygart strike you?"

Like lightning, Tessa didn't say, her gaze traveling through the crowd in search of him. "Seems respectable enough."

Across from them, silhouetted by the bonfire's orange glow, the colonel seemed to have fixed his attention more on the gates than the rumpus around him, the light calling out his irregular features and the furrow between his eyes, the way his hair was tied with leather string so that it tailed down his back. He did not dress for the occasion or set himself apart, his fringed shirt with its belted waist, worn leggings, and moccasins no different than any other borderman they knew.

Ruth's disappointment was plain. "Seems he could have at least donned a fine frock."

She understood Ruth's complaint. Surely

in that newly hewn blockhouse of his was a handsome linen shirt and breeches, stock and waistcoat, maybe even buckled shoes.

"Reckon he'll dance?" Ruth nearly shouted above the music.

"I doubt it."

But something told her he could not only dance but dance well. 'Twas in the way he moved and held himself, that odd glimmer of refinement despite the roughness. It was even in the way he spoke, never stumbling in speech like some folks, but able to set forth a matter simply without a blizzard of words. He had a knack for listening intently to any who spoke to him, his manner one of quiet courtesy and control. She couldn't abide rudeness or arrogance or cowardice. There was none of that about Clay Tygart. Though she'd only just met him, he seemed to embody the verse "Let every man be swift to hear, slow to speak, slow to wrath."

She fingered Hester's cameo absently till whisked away for a jig. Whom she danced with hardly mattered. Her attention was fixed on Clay Tygart. Not one dance did he step as the night wore on, instead keeping to the shadows even beyond the firelight's reach. She couldn't dismiss a niggling worry that his holding back might lead some to label him contrary, even big-headed. She could see it already clouding some countenances, those settlers who took offense easily. Having grown up with them, she knew. And it was in her nature to counter it if she could.

She worked her way through the boisterous crowd till she stood behind him. Keen observer as he was, he'd likely been aware of her movements from the first.

"Miss Swan," he said over his shoulder, confirming it.

She would not play coy. "Why are you not dancing, sir?"

The firelight revealed his amusement. "And who would you have me partner with?"

"Granted, there are few petticoats here, but surely you can delight one of them."

Her ready answer turned him round. For a second he seemed to consider it. "Name her."

Her own rueful smile surfaced. "If you dance with me we'll set every tongue wagging. Best partner with Great-Aunt Hester or some widow woman. There are those who'll hold it against you if you don't."

"Such folks are seldom appeased either way."

"True." She pondered this as the fiddler

finished a frenzied jig and struck a spritely reel.

At the first beat, Colonel Tygart reached for her with a swift decisiveness that left no room for a nay. A self-conscious warmth drenched her that had nothing to do with the humid summer's heat. The dusty dance floor seemed to clear. They were the head couple for the set, without a doubt. She was partial to the English country dances, especially Sir Roger de Coverley, which she'd learned when she was small. She'd partnered with all manner of boys and men since then, but none like the odd-eyed giant before her.

What drawing rooms had he seen over-mountain? He swung her around with a gentle power, unlike most clumsy men who all but sent her flying. With him she was at her nimble best. Not once did he misstep, while she felt stretched to the seams keeping up. Swirling past Maddie and Jude, she realized Maddie's look of pleasure.

Winded, Tessa came to a stop as the dance ended. She curtsied as prettily as she could, color still high, and was drawn to the punch bowl, a rude piggin of mostly rum. Hester oversaw the beloved concoction, pouring the brew repeatedly between pitchers till well blended. Tessa tasted molasses, cream, egg. She only allowed herself half a cup. No sense entertaining the likes of Colonel Tygart by weaving about the common like a drunkard.

Ruth pushed toward her, barely heard over the squeal of the fiddle. "How'd you get the colonel to dance with you?"

"I all but asked him," Tessa confessed. No need to reveal her deeper motives to Ruth.

"You always was one for getting things done." Ruth made a face. "If only your brothers were as bold as you."

Before the words left Ruth's mouth, they were both spirited away by men who'd tired of squiring each other. Tessa tried to shut the thought of the colonel away, to not compare, as one gollumpus yanked her about the common now dampened by a warm drizzle. But there was simply no dodging Colonel Tygart in her mind.

Clay, Maddie called him, while she herself hadn't moved beyond the ramrod-stiff *sir* or *Colonel Tygart.* Maddie's term bespoke a familiarity Tessa craved.

Free of the clutches of yet another fawning man, she fled again to the punch bowl, taking a rare second helping before standing in Jasper's shadow by the gunpowder magazine. Rain made a frizz of her hair, the damp wisps pushed back by a hasty hand.

"Enjoying the frolic, Sister?" Jasper asked.

She followed his gaze to Keturah beneath a far cabin eave, Maddie keeping her company. She nodded. Once Jasper had been sweet on Keturah. Since then the long, hard years had lined him, even scarred him with the pox. He'd assumed his place as head of the family at Pa's passing without complaint, tamping down his grief. Betimes he seemed a powder keg ready to explode. And since he'd returned from overmountain there'd been a new edge to him that unnerved her. Had something happened in the East? Or was it Keturah's coming?

"You might ask her to dance," she dared him.

Jasper shot her a dark look. "Ask an Indian?"

"She's no more Indian than Pa was at their hands."

Her simple logic brought a smirk. "Keturah talks like an Indian. Moves like an Indian. There's little white left about her."

"But she's come back. And it's up to us to help her find her way."

"Nay." He spat into the dirt. "Keturah's not our concern. I expect she'll run. That's the only reason I didn't naysay it when Ma wanted her to stay."

"She's not gone yet."

"Give her time."

She'd struck a nerve without wanting to, the jut of his jaw fueling her own ire. Still sore over Pa, would he somehow besmirch Keturah simply because she'd associated with the murderous savages, as he called them, through no fault of her own?

Her voice held the iron of Hester's. "A warm heart is a fine thing to have in a cold world, Jasper Swan."

He shrugged, clearly unmoved. Turning his back on her, he helped himself to the punch Hester was replenishing.

Stung, Tessa started toward the southwest corner of the fort, where a limestone spring cascaded over mossy rocks. A few children, bored with the dancing, played in the water that ran cold and pure. After a heavy rain, the spring rushed up from the underground with such force it seemed to seethe. Fort folk called it The Boils. But now, in the gray shades of twilight, the water flowed serenely, its surface dimpled by the rain.

"Miss Tessa." A bare-chested boy smiled up at her, holding out a small, speckled stone. "For you."

She knelt, unmindful of the mud and her new petticoat, and took the offering. "Mighty handsome, Matthias. My thanks.

See any frogs or lizards?"

"Nary a one," he said in a grown-up voice so like his pa's.

She pocketed the stone, fingertips brushing the rag doll taken from the Braams' abandoned cabin. Kept away from Jasper's disapproving gaze, maybe meant for Keturah in time. How her brother's words wounded. Any rosy notions she'd had about him and Keturah as sweethearts took wing.

Tessa moved on, making her way along the south wall past cabins and knots of folks savoring the evening. A silvered spear of lightning lit the horizon far beyond the fort's pickets, yet the dancing showed no signs of ending despite the chancy weather.

Smiling at Keturah and Maddie, Tessa passed to Hester's cabin, suddenly aware she would lodge by Clayton Tygart himself, the sturdy blockhouse casting a large shadow. Thankfully, Hester's dwelling was empty. They'd stay the night here, her brothers bedding down on the fort common.

Alone in the cabin, she took a turn. On the hearth's mantel was a small collection of books. *Gulliver's Travels* had been Pa's favorite. Beside it was Hester's worn Bible. A collection of Matthew Henry's sermons. Old copies of the *Virginia Gazette* papered the log wall in a corner, the ink so faded it escaped perusing. No new reading material beckoned.

Still tetchy over Jasper, she stood in the cabin doorway, knowing she'd catch what for if she holed up alone for long. Dutifully she took herself outside again, occupying Maddie's place by Keturah when Maddie danced with Jude. And then the lively fiddling ground to a halt mid-reel at the upward thrust of Colonel Tygart's staying hand. All high spirits halted with it.

She stood abruptly as the gates were closed and barred, any dawdlers outside coming in. Beside her, Keturah stayed seated and eyed everything with solemn stoicism, hands in her lap. Something was amiss, enough to stop the merriment of the fort's first occasion. Next came not the thought of firsts but of lasts.

Last dance with the colonel. Last taste of Hester's punch. Last argument with Jasper. Last jaunt to the spring . . .

The colonel was deep in conversation with the newly appointed militia officers nearby, their grave expressions telling. Tessa knew that look. One of the fort's spies had just ridden in from a scout, based on the disheveled, rain-smeared look of him, his gestures and winded answers to the colonel's questions gnawing at her.

Orders were given, and men who'd been at the punch bowl or dancing assumed their places along the rifle platform. The mood grew more and more grim. But at least the colonel was here. Somehow that fact comforted Tessa in her oft-comfortless world. Here on the savage border, things changed in a heartbeat, a breath.

Life was lived in the shadow of lasts.

11

Hester's waspish gaze settled on Tessa as she descended the loft ladder at first light. Not one gunshot nor war whoop had troubled her sleep. With Ma gone to milk and Keturah still abed, Tessa braced herself for whatever Great-Aunt Hester would say.

"My rheumatism's raging this morn."

"You look hale and hearty to me," Tessa returned.

"Nonsense. You know nothing about my old bones. Now tie on your apron and finish what I started."

Tessa looked to the hearth's fire, where a lone kettle simmered. Nary a whiff of breakfast to be had. Resigned, she did as her bossy aunt bade and reached for her apron, eyes going wide at Hester's next brow-raising order.

"Colonel Tygart likes his coffee hot and his hoecakes brown." At that, she pulled a rocking chair nearer the window and sat

129

down hard, adding an exclamation point to her words.

Tessa set her jaw. Did Hester truly expect her to fix the commander's breakfast? She'd rather face a multitude of redmen than obey this blatant attempt at matchmaking. Her great-aunt had many fine qualities, but tact wasn't one of them. Nor was patience.

"Quit your dawdling!" Hester scolded as Tessa took a quick look in a cracked looking glass hauled overmountain long ago. "The man can't manage a garrison on an empty stomach."

Tessa shot a glance at the half-open cabin door. Doggone the milking! Where was Ma when she needed her to put a stop to such foolishness?

"Oh, and he's overfond of sweetening, just so you know," Hester said with a wave of her hand. "Prefers loaf sugar but he'll take molasses in a pinch."

Biting back a retort, Tessa stepped outside into a morning of warm mist, the sky a pleasing pink, the common littered with last night's revelry. A stone's throw away was the blockhouse, door open wide, the hearty smell of bear bacon beckoning. Her own stomach rumbled.

Shutting her eyes, she uttered a hasty, heartfelt prayer and then, still addled as a bee in a butter churn, bridged the short distance to the blockhouse. There at the hearth were the fixings of a commander's breakfast. She noted both coffee and tea. Plenty of sweetening.

No colonel.

From the loft above came a few decisive sounds. The thud of a boot. The opening of a shutter. *Singing.*

Though low, the voice was distinct and melodious, even rich. "The Nightingale"? 'Twas a tune she knew well. She bit her lip to keep from joining in and focused on the task before her. First, a daub of grease in a hot iron skillet, then hoecake batter fried a deep brown. She herself liked them golden with butter, no sweetening.

"Good morning, one morning, one
 morning in May,
I spied a young couple all on the highway,
And one was a lady so bright and so fair,
And the other was a soldier, a brave
 volunteer . . ."

She half chuckled at her old aunt's prank on Colonel Tygart. What would he think of that?

"Good morning, good morning, good
    morning to thee,
Now where are you going, my pretty
    lady?"

Clay paused singing long enough to shave,
maneuvering the razor with long, even
swipes over his bristled skin. He toweled off
on a soft piece of tow linen, taking a last
look at the common below through his open
window.

A few discarded wooden cups, even a
pewter one, glinting in the dirt and grass. A
muddy shoe and colorful handkerchief. A
few crude toys. All evidence of a merry
time, even if one of the fort's spies had
brought a grim report. Few who'd come for
the frolic would likely leave the fort till better news was brought.

He resumed his low song, something he'd
missed on the trail, though he heard Boone
oft sang at the top of his lungs in devil-may-
care defiance. But he couldn't risk the
women in his party, so he'd stayed silent all
the way from Fort Pitt to Fort Tygart.

As his boot struck the first step, a warm,
womanly voice joined in from below. Not
Hester. The old woman hadn't a song in
her wilderness-hardened soul. His steps

quickened till his boots sounded like a small storm.

"Good morning, good morning, good
    morning to thee.
Now where are you going, my pretty
    lady?
I'm going to travel to the banks of the
    sea,
To see the waters gliding, hear the
    nightingales sing."

There at the hearth was a becoming if surprising sight. Miss Swan? Her back to him, she deftly flipped his favored hoecakes, using a free hand to grasp hold of a kettle's handle with her apron.

Taking a seat at the table, he hated to end her singing. She had a lovely voice, sweet and full-bodied. When she swung around armed with his breakfast, her blatant consternation made him chuckle.

"And your great-aunt is . . . ?"

"Fit as a fiddle," she answered. A telltale pink stained her features, confirming his suspicions.

Best say it outright. "And bent on a little matchmaking."

Tessa gave an aggrieved nod. It wasn't hard to figure. Hester Swan had left a trail

133

of bread crumbs to her niece since she'd cooked his very first meal.

"Tessa is a hand with her garden. Her quince preserves are second to none. She can knit a pair of stockings nearly as fast as I fry an egg. Ever since she was small, my niece has been a wonder digging ginseng. Fleet of foot too. She may not be fancy as a town-bred girl, but she steps a fine reel . . ."

Tessa turned her back on him, retrieving a rasher of bacon. Molasses and butter were already before him, including his usual pewter plate and cup. Eyes down, she set the meat on the table. In the ensuing quiet came a noisy growling. Her stomach?

"Let's give Hester some satisfaction, aye?" Forking two hoecakes off the stack onto his plate, he added meat and the neatly turned eggs she'd almost forgotten, then reached across the crude table and plunked down the plate.

Their eyes met, hers befuddled. Already she'd begun backing out the door.

"Nay, Miss Swan. Stay."

A slightly sheepish smile and a blush graced her face. "Is that an order, sir?"

He nodded and started to rise to fetch a second plate, but she'd already whisked it from a shelf. "Overmountain tea or coffee?" he asked.

134

She sat, eyeing both. "Tea." Slowly, she reached for the jug of cream yet bypassed the sweetening. "No trouble during the night, I reckon."

"False alarm, mayhap," he said, taking coffee with plenty of cream, the fragrant steam rising. "Or a close call."

Fork mid-mouth, he stayed his hand when she said without a flinch, "I'd be obliged if you'd bless breakfast."

Tarnation. Suddenly at sea in his own fort, Clay simply stared at her like the heathen he was. Her earnest gaze was violet-gray in the morning shadows, reminding him of polished silver in a shop window.

"We always hold hands doing it," she said, reaching across the bountiful plates between them.

Humbled and caught off guard, he took her warm, callused fingers in his as she bowed her head reverently and waited. The words that lodged in his throat were so dusty, so tarnished, he had to reach to the uttermost to grasp but a few.

"We thank Thee, Lord, for this our food for life and health and every good . . . . By Thine own hand may we be fed." He swallowed, still groping. "Give us each day our daily bread. Amen."

Somehow she looked satisfied. He felt

he'd successfully run the gauntlet. They released hands, returning to their blessed breakfast, the finest the frontier had to offer. Closing her eyes, she took a sip of fine English tea from Morris and Willing of Philadelphia. Her childish delight tickled him. She was used to making do with nettles and sassafras, likely. City tea was a luxury.

This morn she'd exchanged her pretty party dress for plain homespun. The linen fichu about her shoulders was spotless and smooth, tucked into a striped bodice of common frontier weave, her skirt indigo blue. Covering her dark hair was a linen cap, the barest ruffle at the edge, its strings untied and dangling.

Bare of foot, she accidentally brushed his boot beneath the table. Mercy, but she made it hard for a man to mind his meal. Despite the heavy aroma of fried meat and the more delicate fragrance of hyson tea, he detected clean linen. Herbs. Something else he couldn't name. Thankfully, he didn't reek of the trail and was clean-shaven to boot.

She ate slowly, pinching off a bite of hoecake, then taking another sip of tea. A caution for him to slow down, rein in his plans to clean up the common and meet with the settlement men before the sun was three fingers high.

136

She chewed on a piece of bacon. "Maddie and Jude don't eat with you?"

"Sometimes."

"How'd you make their acquaintance?"

He swallowed a last bite, washing it down with more coffee. "In the last war. Jude was a hostler and Maddie a laundress with the army under Braddock."

"And you?"

"Spy. Scout. Sharpshooter."

"How'd you come to talk Indian?" Unlike some, she asked carefully, her voice respectful. Free of distaste.

"I was taken as a boy by the Lenape."

She stopped eating and refilled her tea. "Like Keturah."

"Aye." He steeled himself for more questions, but none came. Yet he sensed they simmered beneath the surface and would be asked and answered in time. He had a few for her, but they too would wait.

For now, it was enough to enjoy the novelty of her homespun company. In this room there were no airs, no pretense, no rules, no noose-tight stock pinching his sunburnt neck. Just a simple man and woman thrust together by a fearsome wrinkle of a woman who might well be hovering outside the blockhouse door.

He couldn't resist a final, amused parry.

"There are so many men here and so few women that your aunt has little reason to ply her matchmaking skills."

"Aye, but Great-Aunt Hester is besotted with you."

"And you're not?"

"Nay." A downward sweep of her lashes. "I've had my fill of five brothers. No need to add a husband."

"A husband is an altogether different matter than a brother."

"A man's a man," she said quietly. "You're all a hand at snoring and scratching yourselves, belching, and making a mighty mess of laundry."

This was uttered with such spirit that he nearly spat out his coffee as he laughed. "Mind if I start calling you the Spinster Swan?"

"Doesn't pain me."

"Neither does it cure Hester's matchmaking."

"I'd be pleased to tell her you're promised to somebody overmountain," she offered.

"That would be a lie." The perfumed, pampered Miss Penrose flashed to mind and was quickly set aside. He refilled his coffee. "If it eases you any, I'm here to defend the settlement, not marry into it."

"A shame, Colonel." A finger of light from

the open door turned her eyes purple as a blooming thistle. "If you change your mind, there's a few unwed women and two young widows within Fort Tygart's walls."

He sat back, looking to his desk across the room and the stack of correspondence and ledgers that needed tending. "I'm more in need of spies."

"Spies are hard to keep alive." Her face clouded. "You might have better luck with a wife. Then you'd no longer have Hester to do for you and we'd both be free of her badgering."

She spoke simply. Logically. Like one of her brothers might. Despite her noncommittal words, he was taking too much stock in her company. "How goes it with Keturah?"

Something flickered in her eyes. "She's quiet. Keeps close to Ma." A slight smile. "She recollects how to milk."

A rooster crowed outside, nearly snuffing his words. "I've sent a post east to print in city papers about her return."

"So her kin might happen upon it?" She looked downcast now, staring at her empty plate. "I'd hoped she'd settle here in time. Once I wished she'd make a match with Jasper. He's nigh on thirty now."

The eldest Swan. He tripped over her

brothers' names and faces at times, as they looked and spoke alike. "Before the Indians took her, was there some tie?"

"She was awful young back then, but aye, seems like. She always took to Jasper and he was always teasing her. But here lately . . ."

"But?"

"Jasper wants her gone." Her voice dropped as if she was afraid of being overheard. She fixed her gaze over his shoulder, staring at the buffalo robe pegged to the wall behind him. "Says she's now more red than white and will likely return to the Indians."

He mulled this a moment. "What happened to your pa?" Whatever had become of Mister Swan bled through to Jasper's regard of Keturah, likely.

Swallowing, firming her chin, she answered, "Tomahawked at the ferry three years back. Jasper found him first."

"I'm sorry." He meant it. He'd seen his own parents slain as a boy. The horrific memory was like a brand, embedded deep. Nobody could blame Jasper for shunning Keturah, yet Tessa and Mistress Swan made a bold bid to keep her at their cabin. To them she was clearly innocent, a helpless survivor of her circumstances.

Tessa met his eyes again. "Do you think

she'll return to the Indians?"

Would she? "Time will answer."

A sudden shadow turned their attention to the door. Keturah stood there in Maddie's borrowed garments, sunlight illuminating her white-gold hair. She'd wrapped her long braid about her head in a sort of crown. Maddie's doing?

"Come in," he told her with a welcoming motion.

Keturah hesitated, gaze rising to the wood rafters. In a touching gesture, Tessa rose from her seat, went to the door, and took her hand, leading her to the table. Sitting down at Tessa's bidding, Keturah watched as Tessa served what was left of their breakfast.

Keturah tasted the tea with some curiosity, then eyed the bread. "Indian mush cakes?" she asked him in Lenape.

"Hoecakes," he replied in English, watching as she spread them with butter and poured a generous amount of sweetening on top.

He eyed his desk again, still impatient to begin but feeling pleasantly full of far more than breakfast.

He owed Hester.

12

Tessa began removing dirty dishes, humming beneath her breath the song she and Clay had sung. After setting things in order here she'd best find her brothers, who seemed in no hurry to leave the garrison. With Jasper now captain of the militia, he'd no doubt be at the fort more than their homeplace. Whereas once this would have pained her, now it brought an odd relief. She'd count on Lemuel to light a fire under the others and get them back to the Buckhannon. For now, she must make peace with the sight and sound of Keturah and Clay at the table, speaking mostly Lenape.

"Achsuntuimunschi," Keturah said, reaching for the molasses.

"The stone tree, aye," he replied. "The white word is sugar tree. Maple."

Keturah repeated it in halting tones before taking a bite.

"The stone tree?" Tessa ran a cloth over

the table to catch crumbs. "Why is it called such?"

"On account of maple being hardwood," Clay explained. "Keturah's sorry to have missed sugar season, being at Fort Pitt."

Sugar making with the Indians — or the settlers? Returning to the hearth, Tessa banked the hot coals and adjusted the crane, refilling the kettle in case Clay wanted more coffee or tea.

He and Keturah made a striking sight. Did he sense Keturah's fondness for him? Note the way her eyes followed him? Even now as he pushed back from the table and moved to his desk, she watched him from beneath her lashes.

The significance of it made Tessa's stomach clench. Was Keturah sweet on the colonel? Well, why wouldn't she be? He was striking as the day was long with his mismatched eyes. He spoke the Indian tongue, had even rescued her from Fort Pitt. All the makings of a hero, a fairy tale. Though he'd spoken against marrying, Keturah seemed to suit somehow.

"There you are." Ma hovered in the doorway, smiling approvingly at Keturah's breakfasting and Tessa's tidying up. "Both my girls."

"Morning, Mistress Swan," Clay said as

he inked a quill.

"Fine day to you, sir," she returned. Behind her appeared Ross, who squeezed past his mother and approached the colonel's onerous desk.

"You wanted to see me, sir?" Hat in hand, Ross eyed the commander with a dash of awe.

Clay signed a document and set aside his quill before turning toward the youngest Swan. "I hear you're quite a hand with a rifle."

"Fixing and firing them, aye, sir," Ross replied with a marked flush.

"Can we count on you for the militia muster?"

"Aye, sir." Ross turned banty rooster before Tessa's scrutiny. "And more besides."

Hiding a chuckle, Tessa moved her mother's way. "Ready, Ma?"

"If the colonel gives us leave to go," she replied.

"The latest scouting party should return by dusk." Clay stood, an ink stain on his sleeve. "I'd advise delaying your leaving till we've heard their report."

"Might behoove us," Ma answered. "I'm sure Hester won't mind."

Tessa went outside, breathing deeply of the fresh air. Passing from blockhouse to

144

common, she squinted at the brightness. The damp of the night before had given way to the bloom of day. Heat shimmers would soon skew her view as the day soared to summery heights. Her gaze trailed to Hester puffing on her clay pipe on the cabin's stone stoop. The pungent smoke held still in the windless air.

"And how," Hester queried between smokes, "did the colonel like his breakfast?"

"He made no complaint."

"A mite crowded in there with Keturah."

"Nay, Auntie. The blockhouse is room enough for the entire militia." Sensing what would come next, Tessa added, "I'll not make his noon meal, mind you."

A sharp cackle. Oddly, Hester seemed satisfied. "No matter. Plenty of meat left from last night. You might fetch some fresh water. This heat turned yesterday's brackish."

Taking two pails near the woodpile, Tessa headed toward the far end of the fort, glad for the welcoming shade of the lone elm by the spring. A few women made small talk as they drew water, children wending between their skirts. A peaceful morn after a frolicsome, abruptly ended night.

For a moment she stood, eyes closed, and savored the morning. Maybe in time, when no more bullet lead or arrows flew, these forbidding pickets would be taken down and used to build a dwelling fit for a family.

"Well, if it ain't Miss Swan."

The warm voice turned her around. "Morning, Maddie. Just call me Tessa, aye?"

Maddie smiled, brows raised. "Where'd you disappear to last night? All that dancin' wear you out?"

"I went to hunt for a book." Tessa set the water pails down. "Betimes I'd rather read."

"Who learned you?"

"Keturah's ma." In the blur of years she'd almost forgotten.

"Next time you go nosin' around, try the west blockhouse. Clay has a whole saddle-bag of books."

"Army manuals and such?"

"History books mostly. Poems and novels. From Philly-delphia."

"Is he jealous of them?"

"Jealous? Meanin' he won't share 'em?" Maddie gave a decisive shake of her head. "Clay's many things, but tightfisted he ain't."

High praise. Maddie, she was coming to realize, never said a sorry word about anyone. A rare trait in the fort's close confines. But might she be in league with Hester, wanting to do a little matchmaking through book borrowing? The fanciful thought was quickly cast aside. Maddie knew better than to foist a woman on Clayton Tygart.

"You two seem on friendly terms. Maybe you could borrow a book for me." Could Maddie read? Most could only mark an *X* for their name, her brothers included. "I'm the only Swan who can read and write save Hester."

"You, Hester, and Clay are the only learned folk I know hereabouts. Oh, and that storekeeper, Mister Cutright."

Maddie's admiration gave Tessa a quiet pride. "Where'd Colonel Tygart get his learning?"

"At the Friends School in Philly-delphia."

Plain folk. She'd almost forgotten. "Quakers?"

A solemn nod. "Clay don't talk much about it. Was took by Indians before that. Once his kin got him back, he was wild as an unbroke horse, and only the Friends could tame him."

Another missing piece of the colonel's history fell into place. All that learning made a fine gloss, yet she still sensed an unbowed beat of wildness beneath his cool courtesy.

"I suppose the Friends did themselves proud." Tessa bit her lip to stem further

147

praise and began drawing water. Balancing the full-to-the-brim buckets, she bade Maddie good day. "Best hasten back. Come by Hester's and have some flip with us tonight. We shan't leave out till morning."

"All right." Maddie unwound the yellow handkerchief from about her neck, wet it in the spring, and wrung out the cloth before donning it again.

Tessa set down her buckets and lifted her apron to dab at the sweat beading her own upper lip. Near the front gates, Lemuel sat atop his favored white-stockinged bay horse. Was he going home? She watched him depart with a check in her spirit, yet Lem's heart for the land was always greater than his fear of Indians. Two days away from the fields meant twice the work on his return.

"Hotter than Hades," he called to them at the last, lifting his hat in farewell as the gates swung open. "I misdoubt even the Indians are about in this heat."

Ma's mouth formed a solemn, wordless line as she watched her beloved son ride away. And Tessa wondered, did Ma quietly frame him in her head and heart in case it might be her last sight of him alive?

They returned to their simple tasks within fort walls, the same stroke of uncertainty beneath all they did. Hester read aloud from an old *Virginia Gazette* as if to distract them from their cares.

"Well, wonders never cease." She raised her monocle and peered at the paper. "Just listen to this. 'A newly invented instrument for knitted, knotted, double-looped work, to make stockings, breeches pieces, or silk gloves, cotton or worsted.' "

"A knitting-machine frame?" Ma shook her head. "I'll take my two hands, thank you."

Tessa's own knitting needles flew, her face turned to the window to catch a cooling breeze. To rest her eyes, she sometimes paused and looked out the window. The fort's activity was never dull, its commander never idle.

Even now Clay walked with a purpose as he left the blockhouse, stooping to the humble chore of redding up the common as he walked. He spent a fair amount of time with Ruth's blacksmith father at the smithy, where the ring of the hammer and the hiss of the quenching bucket never ceased, though he seemed most preoccupied with the magazine, the garrison's precious store of gunpowder. Her brothers accompanied him at times as they examined this or that. All watched the gates as if anticipating the return of the spies.

An afternoon at the window had gained more gawking than knitting. An unfinished pair of stockings was proof. Tessa hid them in the basket she'd brought from home. She rubbed her neck, stiff from looking sideways so long.

As the sun sank behind the westernmost trees, Hester prepared stew for supper, the kettle a-simmer with wild onions, potatoes, and leftover meat from the frolic.

"Set out nine bowls and spoons," Hester told her. "Then make extra cornbread."

Glad for another task, Tessa emptied the cupboard of dishes, then went about making batter from the corn Keturah had ground.

"Serve those persimmon preserves I've been saving for company. The pickles and head cheese too."

Company meant more than Keturah, likely. With Lemuel gone, she counted eight at supper. Was the extra place, the head of the table, reserved for the colonel?

Time soon told. Changing out of her grease-spackled apron for a clean, cambric one of Hester's, Tessa noticed her great-aunt didn't squawk at her borrowing as she sometimes did. The mirror's cracked reflection had her repinning her flyaway hair and cap, the ruffled edge as ragged as she herself felt. Closing her eyes, she found her thoughts full of a fragmented verse.

Strength and honor are her clothing . . . she shall rejoice in time to come.

'Twas one of Ma's beloved Scriptures, oft spoken at wit's end when heartache and uncertainty pressed in. To remember it now seemed to renew her courage, straighten her shoulders. She wasn't fancy, but she had the Bible to bolster her. She would be a woman of strength and honor, however humble.

When Clay appeared in the cabin's open door, holding something behind his back and looking cleaned up, her insides did a little dance. He greeted her mother and Hester, saying something in both Lenape and English to Keturah, who responded in kind.

"Miss Swan." His voice turned her away from the looking glass.

Had he seen her preening? How like her mother she sounded with her formal words, "Colonel Tygart, do come in."

The women around them stayed busy while Tessa crossed the distance, hating the fire he'd raised on her face. She wished her brothers would come tumbling in.

"What have you behind your back?" she asked him.

His gaze lit with mischief. "Guess."

She drew back a bit. "I'm used to men — boys — hiding things. Snakes and toads and the like."

He chuckled, stepping aside as Zadock entered. "A small gift for the Spinster Swan."

The teasing in his tone tickled her. "Give me a hint, aye?"

He paused, a small scar she hadn't noticed before stealing her attention. It ran like a whipstitch beneath his blue eye. This close she saw that he had especially long, dark lashes, maybe even longer than her own.

He held out a small, brown-skinned book. Maddie had told him of her hankering to read, then. Could he tell she was glad to the heart?

"Does poetry suit you?" He regarded her intently as if ready to return to Philadelphia or at least the blockhouse for something else instead.

"Aye, though I've had little of it." Taking the offering, she clutched the book to her chest. "I've yet to meet a borderman with poetry in his soul."

"A few words, aye. 'Beside some water's rushy brink with me the Muse shall sit, and think.' " His voice, agreeable enough in song, was doubly so in verse. "The poet

152

Thomas Gray."

She pinked again despite herself. His sudden intensity was not the antidote she needed to root out this sudden and silly enchantment. Nor did it help when Hester placed them side by side at supper. As if sensing Keturah's fondness for the colonel, Hester seated her by Ma at the table's opposite end.

Mince tarts concluded the meal, served with strong coffee. Maddie and Jude joined them in time, filling the cabin to bursting. Talk and laughter ebbed and flowed, and as the night ripened Hester made her praiseworthy flip, beating up a froth of eggs, ale, and rum. Tessa took the new grater from her pocket and ground a dusting of nutmeg atop each cup, giving Clay an especially generous dash.

Come morning, would the rest of the Swan clan leave? Or would a spy's dire report forbid them? For once their slow return didn't chafe, though she longed to know if Lemuel was well. If she had her druthers she'd take her book of poetry and retreat from so many eyes and ears, feel her soul take flight at a pretty turn of phrase. How she wished for a little of that refinement interwoven with the roughness that was Colonel Tygart. She was all homespun when what she craved was a bit of lace.

In time, the men began a dice game. Tessa looked on as Clay explained the rules of play to her eager brothers. Inexplicably, Keturah became visibly excited at the rattle of the dice in the wooden cup, hovering over the men's shoulders and watching their every move. The dice were cleverly painted peach pits, the scoring depending on which number landed atop the table. Here Clay had the upper hand, his every move confirming he'd played it long and well.

"Mamantuhwin," Keturah said to Tessa with a touch of pride, as if pleased to be teaching her for once.

Tessa repeated the lengthy word as Jasper scored and the tension mounted. Would Clay win?

Candles sank into their holders as the game reached fever pitch. Though Hester was yawning, she didn't dare bring the rare merriment to an end.

Quietly, Tessa slipped out into the May twilight to clear her head of the smoke and noise and cure her craving to watch Clay's every move. Finding a crude bench at the heart of the common garden, she caressed the book's smooth cover, breathing in the vanilla perfume of sweet rocket and phlox interwoven with the pungent spice of thyme and sage. Night insects winged about in swarms amid the lazy wink of fireflies. Bedtime at the fort was far later than at home. Yet neither Hester's flip nor the late hour tired her. Lights were snuffed in the surrounding cabins one by one. A dog barked, and a baby gave a plaintive cry.

'Twas the first time she'd be sorry to face first light. No longer could she deny the reason why. The fort's gates no longer spelled freedom but absence. Tonight her whole being stood on tiptoe because a man who'd left her addled by asking her to breakfast had addled her further with some poetry.

Lightning struck, she was. To the bone.

13

Clay left Hester's cabin not long after Tessa, his gaze circling the fort's two enclosed acres. Rosemary passed him on her return from the necessary, likely. He doffed his hat. He'd not refer to her as *widow* as some did. The way Westfall eyed her, she'd not be widowed long.

Above him, assigned men stood along the rifle platform, one of them yawning. He'd soon mount those steps come midnight watch. Hester's flip had done its mellowing work for a time, but now his every sense was needlelike in its sharpness.

Somehow he managed to lose sleep and still function when others fell into a stupor. Seasons of hunger and being on the move with the Lenape had toughened his frame and his temper, another reason this precariously situated fort bore his name.

He paused at a loophole, scanning the stump-littered clearing that led to the river.

The spies still hadn't returned, a worrisome matter, though any minute they might ride in with good news or ill. If the country continued calm, they might overnight at some agreed-upon rendezvous place till first light. Thankfully there were no shirkers among them anxious to return to the fort for their own comfort. They served the settlement well.

He walked on through the dark, finding all in order but for the incessant barking of a dog near the spring, the only flaw in the moonlit scene. Most of the fort folk were abed, the cabins shuttered, dark boxes.

His moccasined feet trod the slight slope to the east corner, where the cur stood at bristle-backed attention as if desirous of charging that lofty picketed wall. Panther, likely. Jasper had spoken of seeing tracks.

Kneeling, he spoke in Lenape, an old habit he'd never been able to shake around animals. Indians were notoriously fond of their dogs, and he'd come of age with Half-moon, a lame pup given him at his adoption into the Wolf clan. Of all the things torn from him at his reentry into the white world, he'd missed Halfmoon most.

He ran a callused hand down the dog's rough back, then gave him a bone he'd picked up on the common. Returning the way he came, he listened, ears taut for the slightest sound. Indians weren't often night raiders. They mostly struck at dawn after studying their intended target, be it farm or fort.

He checked the locked magazine, the corralled horses, both gates. Bypassing the blackened hulk of the smithy, he skirted the garden, breathing in the scent of sun-warmed soil.

A seated silhouette stopped him. Tessa? She'd left the cabin during their dice game, but he hadn't thought much about it. The moon slipped free of a cloud, casting her in a gentle pool of light. Tonight her pale cap was the only ruffled thing about her. She looked serene, the poetry book he'd lent her in her aproned lap. Other times it seemed she'd rather spit than speak, like this morning when Hester had sent her to make his breakfast. Now she regarded him coolly, shoulders straight, showing no signs of the wear and tear of the day.

"I thought you'd be abed," he said in that candid, cut-to-the-chase way he'd never speak to a town-bred girl.

"Hard to sleep of a night when it feels like summer." There was no complaint in her tone, just honest appraisal of a stifling May eve.

"You can tell your great-aunt I won't be needing breakfast."

Her mouth twisted wryly. "Am I that sorry a cook, Colonel?"

"Hardly. I'll be out on a scout." He wouldn't add that her leaving in the morning was the reason that sent him beyond fort walls. Since sign had been noted near about the Swan homeplace, he wouldn't rest with a secondhand report.

She was studying him now — rather, his rifle, as if recognizing it for the work of art it was. Moonlight glinted off the brass inlays and mountings as the gun dangled from his hand.

"Pennsylvania made, I'd wager," she said. "Lancaster lines. Stocked in black walnut. Smoothbore. Twenty-nine balls to the pound is my guess."

He schooled his surprise. "Aye."

"Pa had a cumbersome Jäger."

"Have your own rifle?" It was a foregone conclusion, which another nod of her head confirmed. "Something tells me you're a fine hand in a siege."

"I'm at the wall with the men most of the time. You won't oft find me in the cabin."

Raised at the wall, no doubt. Buckhannon born and bred. Somehow it pained him that she had to make do with such. "Have you never left this valley?"

"Nay."

"Ever want to?"

"Aye." No hesitation slowed her answer. "In the worst way."

Her delight over a small, saddle-bruised volume of poetry bespoke much. She hungered for things she hadn't had, not all of them material. Namely the freedom to move about, to not dodge shadows. Though she was fresh as spring, she owned that same steadfast wariness that wore down both body and soul before its time. He knew because it owned him too.

He rested his rifle on the ground. "If you could leave here, where would you go?"

"Williamsburg or Philadelphia. I've a hankering to visit the ocean too, which I've only heard tell of. Something tells me you'd make a fine guide."

"If I was to squire you, I'd take you to Philadelphia. Bradford's booksellers and the thriving Blue Anchor tavern might suit. Or the more refined London coffeehouse." He paused, struck by the pleasure it brought him. "You could lodge at the Indian King, the finest ordinary I know, though I prefer the Conestoga or Black Bear Inn with their wagon yards. If it was fair we'd walk along the waterfront . . ."

"You paint a pretty picture but for one thing." She looked down at her lap. "Overmountain I'd be naught but a fish out of water, as Chaucer says."

He grimaced and recalled his schooling, his disdain of Chaucer enduring. "If you can manage the frontier, you'd find town quite tame. Especially in a new bonnet to match that pretty petticoat." His wink was likely lost on her in the darkness.

"Who told you about my petticoat?" Rather than acting affronted, she gave him a delighted smile. "That rascal Jasper, likely."

Tipping his hat to her he excused himself with the deference he used in parlors. She bade him good night with a little laugh that lit up the darkness. What was it about her that made him want to tarry and tease her?

'Twas his turn at watch. If not, he might still be here come morning.

Tessa's lingering memories of the fort and frolic, particularly Clay's banter about her petticoat and all the talk about town, were soon swallowed up by the return home and something else far more unsettling. Their first night back, she was kept awake by more than the itch of poison ivy she'd gotten while tending the flax.

She tried to stay still, mindful of Keturah's soft snoring on the floor beside her. Toward dawn, she woke, the pink haze of morning on the horizon, the trundle bed empty. She blinked, adjusting to the cabin's dim lines. Had Jasper's prediction come true? Had Keturah run off?

By the time she reached the door, her dismay was bone deep. With Indian sign along the Buckhannon of late, why had Keturah risked the door being open? Because she was now more red than white and even her thinking had altered?

As Tessa pondered it, her brothers began to stir on the other side of the log wall. If Jasper had been the one to find the door ajar, Keturah would no longer be welcome.

Raising her rifle, she pushed open the door farther with her foot, body tucked to one side of the door frame. The cabin clearing was still heavily shadowed, but nothing seemed out of place. No queer bird call or movement marred the sultry morning.

Already her shift stuck to her in places, though it fell just below her knee and would allow her to run if needs be. She waited. Watched. Stepped outside. Snuff came out from behind the woodpile, tail wagging.

Safe, then.

She lowered her gun and went in search

162

of Keturah. A footprint in the moist dirt by the smokehouse pointed north. Through the brush she trod, unsurprised when she came into the tangled overgrowth of the abandoned Braam homestead.

Keturah was near the well, head bent like a broken flower stem. Crying — more a keening — turned the dawn eerie, the sound unlike any Tessa had ever heard as it bespoke anguish.

Setting her rifle aside, Tessa walked toward her, wishing Ma was near. Tears were so contrary to her nature she felt bewildered in the face of them. Her brothers' unwavering stoicism was far easier to take.

Kneeling on the ground beside Keturah, she felt the heavy dew wet her shift. Might it be time to use the one word she knew in Lenape, thanks to Clay? She'd practiced saying it in private till the word became natural on her tongue.

"Winkalit." Unsure of what it meant, she awaited some response.

Keturah raised her head and studied her, her welling eyes a spectacle of pain.

Tessa repeated the word, praying it held some meaning, some solace.

"Winkalit." Keturah nodded, chin quivering. "Friend . . . you are my friend."

Bereft of other Lenape words, Tessa pulled

163

the discarded doll from her pocket. A flicker of recognition? Keturah's fingers wrapped round the offering in unmistakable wonder. She brought the doll to her chest, her watery gaze returning to the empty cabin. Unable to look at her friend for the ache in her chest, Tessa stared unseeing at the ground. In the forlorn light of early morn came a shared, crushing sorrow. For girlhood. For what was gone, never to be regained. Tessa bit her lip till it nearly bled.

"Ma will worry," she finally said softly. "Best be home."

In time they got to their feet. Tessa retrieved her rifle, then took Keturah by the hand much as they'd done when they were small. Together they wended through the woods to the Swans' clearing, where they were met with the whack of an axe and two belled cows ready for milking. Ma stood in the doorway, her watchful expression fading to relief when she saw them. The taint of burnt toast sent her back inside.

Breakfast was a somber affair as if all sensed Keturah's turmoil. Though dressed, hair braided, the old doll tucked in her pocket, Keturah kept her eyes down and ate but a few bites of porridge.

Jasper shot Tessa a questioning look. Aggravated by his stance regarding Keturah —

mightn't he be the reason for Keturah's sudden sorrow? — Tessa regarded him coldly. Of all her brothers, Zadock seemed the most moved by Keturah's plight. He sat across from her, regarding her kindly as if wishing he could help in some way. Betimes he tried to talk to her.

"Colonel Tygart mentioned a large party needed ferrying," Cyrus spoke into the silence. "Seems they've all got Kentucke fever."

"Best leave out then." Ross looked at Tessa as she finished her crust of blackened bread. "Care to lend a hand, Sister?"

No one naysayed her going. They abandoned the table, taking the well-worn path to the river. Ross, usually chattering like a squirrel, seemed sunk in tongue-tied reflection.

"Something the matter with Keturah?" he asked in time, clearly uneasy about such matters.

"Nothing but returning to the place that bore her and finding it empty," she replied a bit testily, as angry with the circumstance as with Jasper. "And having to reside with a hostile instead."

"Something's about to boil over, aye." Ross blew out a breath. "You think Jasper might —"

"Hatred clouds a man's mind. Makes him do things he'll soon regret."

"Maybe you should talk to Colonel Tygart. I've seen the way he regards you. It's clear he respects what you have to say."

"If Tygart is half the man I think he is, he doesn't need telling." Though Ross's words warmed her, she had no desire to dwell on the colonel. "Saw you dancing with that Parker girl at the frolic."

"Her pa won't let her out of his sight."

"Stands to reason. She's his only daughter." Head down, she watched where she stepped. Just yesterday Lemuel had killed a copper snake, the largest they'd ever seen.

Ross shouldered his gun. "Tired of old Hester trying to foist you on Colonel Tygart?"

"He needs none of Hester's help, able as he is in any matter."

"He sure beat all our britches at the dice game." Ross grinned. "I ain't seen Cyrus so het up since Schoolcraft bested him shooting."

They emerged onto the riverbank, where the ferry house, always a mournful sight as it marked Pa's passing, stood stalwart. The ferry rested partly on the bank, the green water lapping at one end edged with a lacy ruffle from the west wind. Tessa exchanged her rifle for a setting pole, as did Ross, both looking east to the buffalo trail becoming wide enough for wagons.

Already overwarm, Tessa dipped a sun-browned foot in the cold water. "Hear any more about those Kentucke-bound folks?"

"Nary a word. Cyrus is a bit sparse with details."

Kneeling, she set down her pole and splashed cold water on her blistered hands. Already the rash was creeping across her arms and reddening her neck.

"Best allow Ma a look," Ross said, slapping at a mosquito. "Reckon they're plagued with poison vine and insects in the city?"

She made no reply, ears tuned to the expected pack train, the clamor of harness and horses. But 'twas a lone rider, one who made her completely forget her enflamed skin. For such a powerfully built man, his horse was smallish, more Indian pony about fifteen hands high, but nonetheless a sturdy, dun-colored stallion with black points.

Ross called out a greeting. Tessa stayed silent, pleasure edging out surprise. This was the colonel's first visit to the ferry that she knew of. He dismounted, never at a loss for words, she was learning, though he often spoke only a pointed few.

"Morning," he greeted them, removing

his felt hat. Sweat had run riot with his hair, amassing it into inky wisps and waves beneath the brim. He raked it back with a quick hand.

She took care not to stare. 'Twas unmaidenly, Hester oft scolded. But what a sight he made, standing in a shaft of sunlight that called out every single angle of him.

"First passenger of the day?" Clay queried.

"First, aye, sir," Ross replied with a grin. "And no ferrying fee either."

"Obliged. You lend a hand often?" Clay pinned Tessa with a gaze that left no question as to how he felt about the matter.

"I'm no town-bred miss, mind you."

Ross's grin faded to mortification. "Best take care not to sass the colonel, Sister."

Clay merely chuckled, and she began loosening the mooring lines. He helped Ross position the horse atop the boat's cleated bottom, then reached for her setting pole like he was born to it. She startled slightly at the touch of his hands on hers.

"Allow me," he said. At her amusement, he added, "Rather, give me the pole. Betimes my parlor manners follow me onto the frontier."

She curtsied in reply, earning his appreciative wink. When he turned his back to her, she blew out a silent sigh. Just when she had him boxed up in her thoughts, contained to a quiet corner, out he'd spring again and surprise her, leaving her topsy-turvy.

They shoved off just as effortlessly as they'd done since Pa was alive. Clay threw the heft of his muscled frame into the crossing, and they reached the west shore in record time, a feat that left Ross wide-eyed.

"Ever lost a passenger or animal?" Clay asked.

"In a sudden squall, aye," Ross replied. "A sow and a goat but no two-legged folk."

Clay was studying the far shore from which they'd embarked, eye on what Pa had called the River King. It was a towering, fully leafed hardwood, lightning struck at the center but still standing strong.

"Ever consider building a rifle platform in that silver maple?"

Ross and Tessa stared at him.

"Ponder it," he added, handing back her pole. "Might make a fine lookout with so much sign reported."

He led his horse up the sandy bank, then swung himself in the saddle. With a fare-thee-well, they poled back across the Buckhannon, the west wind hastening them.

"Pa never saw a need for such," Ross said

in wonderment as they bumped up to the shore.

"And Pa got himself killed," she replied.

The remainder of the afternoon was spent awaiting the expected party that never materialized, fishing, and pondering the treed platform. Ross even shimmied up the giant maple to determine a suitable height. Soon she was peering up the soaring trunk to see the worn soles of his shoes dangling.

"You all right?" she called.

"Speechless is what I am. Up here you can see clear to Fort Tygart."

"I'm not much concerned about that," she answered, setting her jaw against the poison itch now at her back. "The colonel keeps harping about sign. Any of that to be had from up there?"

Silence. And then, as if the wind had knocked him from his perch, there was a soul-shaking rustle as Ross came crashing down through the branches in a flurry of torn leaves and twigs. Breathless, he landed with ankle-bruising force, nearly toppling her.

"The colonel ain't wrong." Winded, face stricken, he began backing up the riverbank toward the trail to home. "There's half a dozen redmen or better at the falls."

Perilously close. Breath snatched, heart in

her throat, Tessa followed him. They were no longer walking but running, she herself hardly slowed by her ten-pound rifle. The fat crappie they'd caught for supper stayed on the bank.

14

They burst into the Swan clearing, alerting Zadock stacking wood and Jasper corralled with the horses. In one agile leap, Ross jumped atop the nearest mount and dashed north to sound an alarm.

Tessa looked about wildly. "Where's Cyrus?"

"Gone hunting," Jasper replied as coolly as if she'd merely warned of wasps.

Soon all were barred inside the cabin save Ross and Cyrus. Cyrus's fondness for turkey, the deafening shot that brought one down, might spell the end of him.

And Clay? Tessa paced by the hearth, the sound of guns being readied and positions taken in the adjoining blockhouse raking her nerves. Clay was out there somewhere. *Lord, hedge him in.*

Just as she'd heeded Ma's advice and settled on a chair, a terrific roar tore through the cabin. She started, staunching the urge to throw her apron over her head like she'd done in childhood. The very cabin seemed to shake.

Who had shot — and why?

In its aftermath came a dreadful silence before a resonant halloo in the clearing.

Clay?

Her very bones seemed to melt, an odd comingling of joy and stark relief. She rose from her seat and went to peer out a loophole. Clay was at the edge of the north woods, bare chested, his linen hunting shirt suspended like a flag of truce from his upraised rifle. Fury — and fear — soared.

"Hold your fire, you *blatherskate*!" She hurled the words at whichever brother had misfired behind the blockhouse wall. 'Twas one of Pa's Scots terms, reserved for the most heated moments.

She rushed to the door and unbarred it, the seconds till Clay reached the cabin stretching taut. He brushed past her, the earthy scent of pennyroyal riding the air. Ma and Keturah regarded him with deep concern as they stood by the hearth.

Tessa took in the whole of him in one grateful glance, beginning with his sodden buckskins now as black as the hair plastered to his blessedly intact skull. Never mind the indecency of wearing no shirt. Ma took the dripping garment from his rifle tip and hung it from a peg to dry while he looked out the loophole Tessa had forsaken, rifle ready.

It grew eerily still. Too still. The closed-up cabin felt like a bake oven. Only the Lord knew how long they'd be cooped up together. No doubt Clay had come across the same Indians Ross had seen from his lofty seat. Had he abandoned his horse? Likely he and the stallion had swum the river, as the ferry hadn't been waiting. Maybe the Indians would pass them by.

Supper waited on the table, a savory kettle of stew and a stack of corncakes a foot high. The fare grew cold, all appetites lost.

Clay reached for his still soggy shirt. Pulling it on, his arms overhead and head hidden, he was a riveting sight. Tessa tried not to gape. Hester would be scandalized. 'Twas a moment meant for a wife maybe, intimate and unguarded. But her close scrutiny gained her something else besides.

In the shuttered, barred cabin, where the day's dying light crept through an occasional crack, she saw blood pooling beneath his moccasin. Confounded, she went to him and knelt, reaching out a hand to examine his leg in a way that made Ma gasp.

"You got hit," Tessa said, calling for rags

in the next breath.

But how badly? And by whom?

"Hope it wasn't you," he teased beneath his breath.

"Not I. One of my blatherskate brothers."

"Blatherskate? From the Scots song 'Maggie Lauder.' " He chuckled. "His aim's off, so it's nothing to fret about. I've had worse."

The flesh below the knee was torn, warm, and bleeding in a way that made her stomach sink. His buckskin breeches were ruined, but better them than his leg.

When Ma brought warm water, Tessa cleaned the wound, grateful for the shadows even though they made her task tricky. She prayed for a clean mending and no infection. Ma hovered, neither of them paying much mind to Keturah's exchange in Lenape with Clay.

Keturah crossed the cabin to the corner she shared with Tessa and returned with a highly ornamented buckskin pouch. They watched as she mixed water and a white powder from her stores to form a poultice.

"Buck brush and yarrow," Clay told them, answering their unspoken questions. "A cure-all for many ailments, especially wounds."

Expertly Keturah applied the paste before finishing what Tessa had started and binding his leg with clean cloth.

"She's a *kikehwèt,*" he said, eyes on Tessa. "A healer."

Tessa repeated the odd word, noting Keturah's face light up when she echoed it without stumbling.

"You ought to let her treat you too," he finished with a lingering look at her reddened forearms. "The Lenape are known for their curative powers no matter how savage some think them."

Preoccupied with him, she'd forgotten herself, yet at the mention her inflamed skin began itching anew.

"An oatmeal poultice usually cures poison vine," Ma said.

"Mayhap it's not poison vine," Clay replied, switching to Lenape and looking at Keturah again.

Their unintelligible exchange made Tessa feel fenced out. Apart. And left her wishing herself away from the cabin, even in the chancy woods.

Keturah said a few words and Clay translated, "Jewelweed." He looked at Tessa. "Want me to get some? You look right miserable."

"You'd go out that door again? With your leg like it is?"

"My leg is less worrisome."

176

She flushed, the heat of it tying her tongue. "Maybe when the danger passes."

As if sensing her befuddlement, Ma motioned toward the table. "Might as well eat." She began ladling stew into a bowl while Tessa brought butter and filled a mug with buttermilk. "When you're done I'll take the kettle to my sons."

To Tessa's surprise, Clay bowed his head briefly before eating. At table's end, Keturah sat and sorted through her medicine pouch while they adjusted to the novelty of having the commander of Fort Tygart at their table again. Other than an occasional noise from the blockhouse, all was still but far from peaceful. Any minute the firing might begin in earnest. Her ongoing fear was that Indians would fire the cabin, burning them all to ashes. 'Twas a dread she'd carried since childhood.

As if privy to her thoughts, Clay began speaking in low tones. "Once it's full dark I'll return to the fort."

Another twinge of regret. "We sighted the Indians at the falls — rather, Ross did — near the top of that silver maple."

"So, you took my counsel to heart after all." He glanced at her as he ate. "I tracked four Shawnee on my return to the ferry. God be thanked you weren't there."

Another tremor shot through her. So close. If they'd dallied . . . If they'd not heeded his words to make use of that high perch . . . Woe to anyone in the Indians' path.

"I owe you," she said quietly.

Their eyes met, held. Even in the darkness she felt a sudden charge as if he'd reached out and brushed her flushed cheek with callused fingers. She wanted him to with a deep-seated need stronger than her hunger or her fear. With effort she looked away.

"You're exposed on the river," he continued softly. "I'd rather you keep to home."

Like any sensible woman would.

His warning was one she'd best heed. She ran a frightful risk, as did Ross. After Pa's passing Ma had talked of forsaking their ferry license, but Jasper had stood his ground. "One day, when that ferry's lined our pockets with velvet and that ferry house becomes a tavern with nary a bed to spare, you'll thank me."

If he'd voiced such to Clay, there'd have been a verbal tussle, she knew. Though the ferry was a chancy endeavor, some adventurous soul had to do it.

"Hester tells me you make a fine pair of stockings." He pushed his empty bowl aside.

"I've need of some."

What all was Hester telling him? "Stockings seem meager thanks for saving our hides."

He got up and returned to the loophole, favoring his hurt leg only slightly, his rifle waiting. She picked up his empty bowl and spoon and cup, struck by the odd delight it gave her while Ma took the kettle and remaining corncakes to her brothers.

In time, a shame-faced Zadock appeared, having mastered his humiliation and dredged up an apology. "Might have been worse had Jasper not grabbed hold of the barrel once he saw it was you."

"No harm done," Clay returned easily with a shake of his hand. "Nothing that won't mend."

Visibly relieved, Zadock returned to his loophole. Dusk came calmly, the time Clay would depart. Till then, Tessa and Ma began knitting in the dark while Keturah curled up like a cat on the trundle bed behind the quilt wall. Here lately she'd forsaken sleeping on the floor.

"Where's your horse?" Tessa asked Clay, sensing his restlessness.

"Likely returned to the fort by now," he answered with a glance at his bandaged leg as if pondering his next move.

She abandoned her knitting, both of them moving to the barred door. He was so near she breathed in the earthy scent of his river-soaked shirt. "Take one of ours. They're fleet and know the way same as your stallion."

"Obliged," he said in that low, easy manner that flipped her stomach. "I'll be back for my stockings."

She knelt to make certain the bandage would hold. "Don't tarry long or you're liable to have more stockings than savages to fret about."

Reaching up, he brushed back the wisp of hair that strayed free of her cap. Again, that woozy spark charged through her. Did she imagine it or was he a bit beguiled, same as she? Glad for the darkness, glad he couldn't see how hard his leaving was for her, she unbarred the door and he passed outside. Overcome, almost light-headed, she let the bar drop back into place with a thud.

She took his place at the loophole, her prayers making a way for him in the darkness. The heartache was not knowing if he would reach the fort. If she would ever see him again. But at least her worries about Cyrus faded when he returned, humming, with a brace of turkeys. He was surprised to find them cooped up inside, his day unspoiled by trouble.

With plans to feast on turkey and dumplings on the morrow, the women went to bed, or tried to, while the men continued an all-night vigil in the blockhouse.

By week's end, Tessa had made Clay enough stockings for every day of the week. Four of blue and gray worsted wool, three of white linen, even embroidering clocked patterns at the ankles on the Sabbath pair. No word came that he'd failed to reach Fort Tygart, though she doubted he'd ever die at the hands of Indians. He'd been one of them, spoke their language, knew their ways. If anything, the recapture of Colonel Tygart would be a coup of the highest honor. Keeping him captive was another matter.

Her skin had nearly healed, the jewelweed Keturah applied surprisingly effective. Ever since Clay had told them Keturah was a healer, she spent as much time in the woods as she could, adding to her medicine pouch.

Sometimes Zadock would follow her. 'Twas he who took pains to teach her — reacquaint her with — the white talk. Through his gentle, persistent efforts, Keturah began stringing words into simple sentences, her halting speech becoming surer. As days passed, she seemed more at ease around

181

them, if not the simple, openhearted girl of before.

Jasper regarded this in sullen silence, taking the edge off Tessa's pleasure. He was often away at the fort in his new duties as captain of the militia, his absences relieving the festering tension she now felt in his presence.

"What's the matter with my oldest son?" Ma wondered aloud as she and Tessa watched him ride off once more.

Tessa looked away from the field of blooming flax flowers, so rich a blue it seemed the sky had turned upside down. "Once Jasper was sweet on Keturah, so long ago you might not remember. Now Zadock is sweet on her and Jasper is aggravated by them both."

"Jasper's discontent with her being here is plain enough." Ma's eyes narrowed. "He's keen for word from her overmountain kin. To muddle matters, I sense Keturah is fond of Colonel Tygart."

Overly fond? Tessa toyed with the strings of her cap and tried to view things dispassionately, yet something green and irritating uncoiled in her belly. Or did Keturah simply look to Clay as a kindred Lenape spirit and former captive?

"Reckon Colonel Tygart's wound's still

ailing him?" Ma asked her. "A man might lose a leg if poisoning set in."

"I pray not." Still sore with disgust over the incident, Tessa pointed out the obvious. "Jasper sees the colonel right regular and hasn't made mention of such."

On this hung her hopes. A lesser man would begrudge her brother, stay clear of them all. She'd seen feuds erupt over pigs and property lines. Taking a bullet was ample grounds for some too.

"And you, Daughter? What of your heart?" Ma took a step forward, plucking a frail flax flower whose lifespan was but a day. "Dare I hope Hester's matchmaking is bearing fruit?"

"Fruit, nay," Tessa replied wryly. "Stockings, aye."

But he'd not returned to claim his stockings despite her admonition not to tarry. Had he forgotten? Granted, he had far weightier matters to ponder than leg coverings, but it was the one fragile tie between them, however foolish. She'd knitted the stockings with greater care than she'd knit anything before, fashioning spatterdashes from stout woolen cloth to better protect his legs on forays, at least from brush if not bullet lead.

"I saw the colonel take leave of you that

night" — a knowing smile softened Ma's deeply lined features — "with a reluctance that had little to do with Indians and a lame leg."

Though the bottom dropped out of her stomach at the mere mention, Tessa said nothing, unwilling to read more into their parting banter at the cabin door than she should. Reaching out, she plucked her own flax flower, the blue not unlike the hue of Clay's contrary eye.

"A man like that could take you away from here," Ma mused. "To civilized parts."

"Nay. Clayton Tygart's a borderman to the marrow, come to the fort that bears his name. I've heard no talk of his returning east."

"Well, word is the Tygarts are of sound Quaker stock, some of his kin wealthy Philadelphians."

"Which means he wouldn't settle for a rough-shod woman who goes about barefoot with her bonnet strings untied."

"You can mend your loose ways," Ma said.

"Make a silk purse from a sow's ear?" Tessa opened her hand and let the wind whip the flax blossom away. "Not likely."

"My worry is that the colonel will dally with you here in the wilds yet disown you in town."

"As common soldiers do?" They'd seen it often when eastern regiments came through long enough for some flip and a romp. More than one settlement baby lacked a father when all was said and done. "I'm not the dallying kind, Ma. And Colonel Tygart is no common soldier."

"Love makes fools of us all," Ma said.

"Aye, at any age, 'twould seem." Tessa couldn't resist a jibe of her own. "What's this I hear about you and the widower West-fall?"

"Fort gossip, is all." Still, Ma flushed so deeply she had the look of a girl. "I'm speaking of Colonel Tygart, not Eb Westfall. I'd not want to see you ill used."

Their talk dwindled when Keturah rejoined them, the sun making a dreamy halo of her hair. A white honeysuckle basket of her own making hung from her slender shoulder, the straps fashioned of sturdy bittersweet. The basket overflowed with dwarf ginseng, starflower, and the tender leaves of the stinging nettle.

Tessa greeted her, dispelling the tetchiness of a moment before. "I'm partial to nettles with ramps and bacon."

"He-he," Keturah replied with a smile of her own, falling into step beside them. "Tea?"

Zadock had taught her this. Each night after supper he lingered at table while they had tea fashioned from some wild root or berry of Keturah's making. Jasper, refusing to partake, swore Keturah would poison them all, but Ma hushed such talk.

Tea, indeed. A dusty memory resurfaced, of Dutch cups from a tidy corner cupboard and Mistress Braam's blue-veined, work-worn hands. For Candlemas and May Day she would serve her girls, Tessa included, a fine brew that tasted of flowers. What had become of that finery? Had it somehow given Tessa a taste of life beyond these mountains, as Ma claimed?

She opened her mouth to mention it, but the memory of Keturah weeping by the well reined her in. Best leave the past in the past. Some memories needed to lie undisturbed.

15

"Maddie looks a mite green." Though said beneath his breath at a distance from the fort's worst wags, Clay sensed it didn't matter. That Maddie was poorly was plain to see. "What's ailing her?"

"A misery in her stomach." Jude's frown made him years older as he watched his wife lean over the washtub, scrubbing half-heartedly. "Been plaguing her ever since Fort Pitt. And no doctor to be had."

"Take her to Keturah." Though he pondered the healing herbs to be had, Clay's mind leapt toward Tessa instead. Here lately she colored his every thought, making him balk at Jude's inevitable request.

"Sounds wise. But we'll need you to go along to Swan Station. Interpret."

Turning away from the sun-soaked common, Clay entered the cooler shade of the blockhouse. He hated to see Maddie suffer. All manner of maladies paraded through his head. Though he didn't pry for decency's sake, he suspected dysentery, given her frequent trips to the privy.

"I could have Keturah brought here," Clay told him, pouring them both cider. "Spare Maddie the distance to Swan Station." But even as he said it, difficulties arose. Jasper would likely be her escort, but with his frame of mind, Keturah deserved better company. "Let Maddie decide."

Clay drained his cider and sat down while Jude went out. He surveyed the growing papers atop his desk with stoic dismay. He was a fighter and borderman, not a scrivener, but as commander of a military garrison he was to document anything and everything that happened during his tenure, including supervising the fort's overall affairs — living conditions, disputes, the preservation and use of equipment and supplies, and the enforcement of military and frontier law, loose as it was in the backcountry. An onerous amount of scribbling that made his hand cramp more than his wounded leg.

In minutes Jude was back, no less grim than before. "Maddie's partial to riding to Swan Station to seek a remedy once she's done with the laundry."

"Aye." Clay's quill dangled precariously

over the paper, a drop of ink threatening to fall and mar the document as he dredged up details unrelated to the Spinster Swan.

The report prior to his arrival here was grim. Along the westernmost border of Virginia and Pennsylvania was an uncurbed trail of destruction that necessitated Fort Tygart and other, smaller stations being built. More than two hundred settlers dead. Fifty-some homesteads burned. Countless captives taken. Entire back settlements deserted, easing the way for enemy encroachment. And now, other than Indians combing the country, an inexplicable lull in any outrages.

"Musta heard you were coming," Cutright had quipped that morn, his belly with its gaping weskit shaking in mirth. He reached into a jar on a shelf and handed Clay a twist of celebratory tobacco.

Clay dismissed the jest. "My sense is that they're amassing. Strategizing. Preparing to strike collectively."

The big belly ceased shaking. "We've enough powder and bullet lead to withstand a prolonged siege, aye?"

"There's no such thing as enough," Clay answered, leaving the storekeeper to tend his depleted wares. Few pack trains ventured over the mountains in these uncertain times.

Pressing the ink to paper, Clay wrote today's date — *6th June, 1770.* More men were needed. Cannons, not just bullet lead and gunpowder. Wilderness warfare was fought by a different, ever-changing, endlessly taxing absence of rules. Such demanded all his focus, all his faculties. And yet an uncommon woman with a promise of new stockings danced at the corners of his conscience.

If Maddie weren't so miserable, if Jude didn't have a glint of desperation in his eye, if the woods weren't so mysteriously still . . . Combined, they forced his hand to revisit the Swans on a mission for Maddie. Hard on the heels of his desire swelled stiff resistance. He had no time to indulge any heart-related whims. With any luck, Miss Swan would be at the ferry and he'd miss her altogether.

"Ready, Clay?" Maddie stood in the blockhouse doorway, her dress hanging with alarming slackness around her already spare frame.

"Aye." He took up his rifle, shot pouch, tomahawk, and other accoutrements.

"Mighty big of you to act as escort, busy as you be." Maddie looked askance at his injured leg, unbandaged now and hidden beneath buckskin breeches. "Reckon you'll get shot at again?"

His grin was half grimace. She hadn't lost her humor at least.

They walked toward the front gate, where Jude had readied their horses. Clay tried to quell his rising anticipation. Though few knew, he'd patrolled the perimeter of Swan land so often he could find his way blindfolded.

The first mile passed in silence, his senses tuned to the slightest infringement on the peaceful summer's day. How he longed to enable the back settlements to farm and hunt and live in freedom, as unconcerned about danger as any city dweller.

A noisy splash through a creek and a slight climb over a rise brought them to the border of Swan land. Their cur, Snuff, began to bark the closer they came. Smoke hung in the humid air about the cabin, as did the reek of boiled turnips. The slant of the sun bespoke two o'clock. Clay pushed back his hat to cool his brow as Rosemary Swan stood up amid the kitchen garden. Keturah was nearby at the creek, rinsing out piggins.

Nary a trace of Miss Swan.

Disappointment pummeled him, and then relief reined him in. He dismounted as Jude helped Maddie down then led the horses to a water trough.

"Well, Colonel Tygart, honored by your coming," Rosemary said, walking over to meet them and glancing quickly at his wounded leg.

"A fine day, aye?" Clay removed his hat. "We need to speak to Keturah in private. Maddie's ailing."

Concern crumpled the older woman's features. "Of course." She gestured to a wide stump beneath the shade of a rustling elm. "It's a mite close in the cabin, but out here's a breeze. Care for something cold to drink from the springhouse?"

At their combined ayes, Maddie sat down with relief. Jude left the horses to forage while he talked to Zadock and Cyrus near the barn. 'Twas just Clay, Keturah, and Maddie now.

Keturah took a seat by Maddie, her long, pale braid coiling in her aproned lap. *"Keko windji?"*

Both of them looked to Clay, who was determined to master his unease if the conversation turned delicate.

"Maddie's in need of your medicine," he began, interpreting as carefully as he could in both Lenape and English.

At last Keturah's thorough questions and Maddie's honest answers came to an end. Mysteriously, the women disappeared inside the cabin. He sipped the cider Rosemary brought before she returned to the garden, keeping his eyes on the dense woods that blocked his view of the Buckhannon. If they were cut down, the river would be in plain sight. For now, the willow-skirted trail to the ferry was bereft of a rifle-toting slip of a woman, heaven be thanked.

In time Maddie emerged, her face slack with surprise, while Keturah's features bore a telling amusement. She studied him beneath finely arched brows before her gaze shot to Jude across the way. "Summon the father to hear the good news."

Hear — what? Clay stared hard at her, unsure if *he'd* heard correctly.

Keturah nodded. *"Mimëntëta."* Baby.

Maddie regarded them both in bewilderment. Had she not added up this puzzling equation? Suddenly her expression cleared as joy took hold.

"You'll be free of your misery in a few months," Clay told her, thanking Keturah with a hasty, *"Wanìshi."*

Jude nearly toppled as Maddie threw her arms around her stunned husband. "Did you hear that, Jude? I feel a bit like the women of old in the Bible, about to have a child despite my years."

Jude stood stupefied. "You sure?"

Keturah smiled. Clay laughed. And Tessa stepped into the middle of the merriment with a look of wonder on her face, two dots of color pinking her cheeks. Darting a look at him, she rested her rifle on the ground, her smile for Maddie. The two women embraced, the hullaballoo halting all work. Rosemary brought more to drink, Zadock and Cyrus joining them in a toast. Ross appeared next, toting a broken oar. Had they hit a snag crossing the river? Throwing it aside, the youngest Swan joined in, drinking thirstily from the jug Cyrus uncorked and drawing laughter.

Clay was far too aware of the woman nearest him. He held himself apart, a bit stilted despite the good news. Having steeled himself in the fortnight since he'd seen her, he'd not let slip a too friendly word or a long look. His new resolve was to treat her no different than he did Maddie or Keturah.

But Miss Swan was not bound by any rule of restraint, let alone overmountain etiquette. Nor did she play parlor games. It was part of her charm, that folksy groundedness. He recalled all too easily her playful curtsy at the ferry, as pretty as Miss Penrose's might have been. He never doubted where he stood with this border belle, or where anyone else stood with her for that matter. Dragging a hand over his stubbled jaw, he braced himself.

"Colonel Tygart, sir." That clear, lilting voice was like no other. "For a man about to glean a great many stockings, you're scarecrow stiff. Are you well?"

He thawed a bit but avoided her eyes. Aye, those eyes made her the belle of the border. He wouldn't think about the rest of her enticements.

"I see no stockings," he said, draining his drink.

At that she took up her rifle and headed to the cabin, leaving him feeling a mite guilty. Maddie was looking at him as the conversation swirled around them, a rare reproof in her gaze. He winked to ease her, unwilling to dim her enjoyment of the moment as he tried to adjust to the news himself. No longer would she and Jude be his trail companions. A baby changed everything.

Ross had begun telling the story of how the oar broke mid-river on a snag when Tessa returned with a small bundle bound in linen and tied with twine.

"Obliged," he said, taking the offering and tucking it beneath his arm.

"How is your wound?" she queried, obviously determined to draw him out.

"Nearly healed."

A prickly silence fell between them till Jude motioned to him, wanting to return Maddie to the fort.

"Won't you stay for supper?" Rosemary asked. "We've ham and hominy aplenty. And my daughter's made a fine custard tart."

"Nay," Clay replied, despite every fiber of his being pulled toward the cabin table. "Best hasten back, as I've a scouting report to hear." His stomach rumbled, mocking his refusal. Hester's victuals would serve tonight, and he'd invite Maddie and Jude to join him. But even that was no match for the Swans' culinary skills and robust company.

While Maddie said her farewells, he and Jude rounded up the horses. Clay didn't look back, squashing the ongoing urge to do so. The return trip was made in an altogether different mood, not the uncertain wretchedness of before but jubilant, slack-jawed wonder.

"If that don't beat all," Jude exclaimed, regarding Maddie with awe. "I never figured me for a father. Maybe we better get ourselves some corn-patch-and-cabin rights. Don't want our child to grow up behind fort walls."

■ ■ ■ ■

Benumbed, Tessa gathered eggs, soaked a deer ham in buttermilk for supper, and swept the yard with a sturdy brush broom Cyrus had made to ward off weeds and snakes. Despite her many chores, the hurt of yesterday followed her about, nearly swallowing her whole each time Clay cut across her conscience. And he cut across without mercy.

Somehow, in the short span of time since she'd first seen him sitting at their humble table, having delivered a redeemed captive to their door, she'd become captivated by this unlikely hero. And her every waking thought had threads of him woven into them, not unlike the weave of the woolens with a bright blue stripe that Ma preferred.

The book of poetry. A dance. Their moonlit rendezvous by the garrison's garden. The low talk at the cabin door that seemed about more than stockings. And then all shattered by his cool regard of her yesterday when Maddie had gotten her glad news. The book of poems now hung heavy in Tessa's pocket. She had no heart to ponder any now, nor even knit.

Sakes, Tessa, let no man cause you such

misery, even as fine a one as Clay Tygart.

She hated the lingering humiliation of it. Hated her wholehearted response to him. To try to right herself, she buried the book of poems beneath a pile of hay in the barn. Forced herself to begin fashioning a baby garment for Maddie till she felt less burnt. Yet even then her heart tugged her traitorously toward him, and she looked at the tiny, unfinished garment and pondered Maddie's happiness instead.

"What's turned you mute as a mackerel?" Ross asked her after supper as their brothers, all but Jasper, sat playing the dice game with Keturah.

Tessa stilled her needles long enough to say, "I'm recovering from being made a fool of."

"With Tygart, you mean."

An inner wince. "So 'twas plain even to you?"

"Only because you're my sister and I've studied you." He scooted his stool closer lest their voices carry. "As for the colonel, I reckon he's partial to you being out here right regular. Only he's trying to hide it."

"Hush."

"It's plain as daylight."

"Colonel Tygart's likely beholden to a sweetheart overmountain somewhere." This was what she'd settled on. Some former tie, despite his denial.

"Well, she ain't here."

Her needles clacked with a vengeance. "Sometimes I sense Keturah's sweet on him, which muddles matters further."

"What? I don't see that at all. But sure enough, Zadock is sweet on Keturah. Seems like we could turn all that around somehow, especially you and the colonel."

"I'll not help you," Tessa vowed.

Ross leaned back with a grunt of disgust. "Here we all sit, not a one of us married, and no sign that'll ever change."

"What about you and the Parker girl?"

"Mary Rose?" Ross scowled. "It's like courting her pa."

Tessa chuckled despite herself. "We're a hopeless lot, us Swans. Colonel Tygart even refers to me as the Spinster Swan."

"Fighting words."

"No need to act roosterish." Weary, eyes smarting, she put her handwork away. " 'Tis true."

Stepping away from the game, Keturah took the steaming kettle off the grate and served tea. Blackberry root tonight. Ma dozed in her rocker near the hearth, waiting for her sons to tire of the game. A gentle rain was slurrying down, a welcome sound.

The fields needed a good drenching.

'Twas almost haying time. Soon the scythes hanging from the barn rafters would be readied for the harvest. Her thoughts canted to the waiting dye shed. Thanks mostly to Keturah's foraging, they now had elderberries for blue dye, white birch bark for buff, and scaly moss for brown. And a fine field of flax to turn to linen in time. For now, the pulled stalks lay rotting by the creek to ensure a fine sheen for cloth, creating so fearsome a stink it might even drive the Indians away.

"So, Sister, I reckon you won't be making any more garments for the colonel, though it was big-hearted of you. He won't find any finer even east of the mountains."

She sipped her tea, aiming for a dispassionate view. "Stands to reason he shuns a back-settlement woman who's rough as butter spread over stale bread."

Ross's amused snort roused Ma, who got up and began checking the fastened window shutters and barred door. He scratched the beginnings of a beard. "A prim overmountain miss don't seem right for the colonel somehow."

"I'm done thinking about it." Getting up, Tessa set her cup on the table and went behind the quilt to her corner.

With any luck, Clay Tygart wouldn't invade her dreams.

16

For a woman of rustic domestic endeavors, Tessa's knitting needles were a wonder. Even Maddie exclaimed over Clay's gift, though a rebuff remained in her eyes.

"Will you look at that. Fancy clocking to boot," she said as she clucked over the detailed embroidery. "Part of me hopes these stockings don't stay up your long legs. Not till you ask forgiveness."

"Maddie . . ." Clay began, a note of caution in his tone.

"I won't stand by without speaking my mind. You've got to get out from under that burden of believing a lie."

"A lie?" Temper frayed, he swallowed the epithet between his teeth. "You can't deny that when I fix my affections on someone, something dire follows."

Her prolonged pause seemed confirmation. "It's just chance, Clay. Seems otherwise, but it's perilous times we live in. Folks you care about get cut down, so you stop caring, stop letting folks in. Time after time I watch it happen. Don't you know Miss Swan is partial to you? What's more, you're partial to her."

"All that aside, it's a matter best left alone. I wasn't sent here to conduct a love affair but manage a militia and guard the border. All else is a stumbling block."

"Since when is love a stumbling block?" she countered. "My worry is that you're going to keep passing it by till your only companions in old age are aches and pains and a great many what-ifs."

"Not everyone is meant to marry, Maddie."

"Well, seems like a man of your years should give it some thought."

He made no reply. Trouble was, he didn't know how old he was. Two and thirty, mayhap. His Quaker kin reckoned he'd been seven or so at the time of his capture. But who knew?

Maddie aside, he'd not had a moment's peace since leaving Swan Station. But why? He usually kept his distance from anything in petticoats. His reserved stance had even been in place when the beguiling Miss Penrose cornered him on a Philadelphia street. That caution served him well in every overdone parlor and ballroom, frustrating more than a few women he'd not thought twice about since. So why had all this misfired and left him feeling gut shot instead?

Because he'd let his guard down and Tessa Swan had ambushed his affections.

To make matters worse, the spatterdashes Tessa fashioned were equally well made, thoughtful even, and wore a deeper hole inside him.

Alone now in the blockhouse, Clay did another unthinkably foolish thing. Lifting a stocking Tessa had fashioned, he breathed in its scent and felt the wool softened by sheep's lanolin. It held the very essence of her, of all things earthy and honest and good.

Gathering up the work of her hands, he climbed the stairs to his sleeping quarters. A trunk was open, home to his finer garments, and he put the stockings inside, closing the lid with a resounding thud.

Out of sight if not out of mind.

What did Maddie mean by believing a lie? How could it be a lie when nearly every person he'd cared for deeply was lost to him, severed from his life with hatchet-like ferocity? His parents by an Indian raid. His adopted Indian family by disease. A tutor to a duel. And the one woman who in hindsight he might have married had she survived a riding accident.

He was no prize. Raised among Indians, more at home in the wilds than a cabin, always on the move and exposed to every danger. What sensible woman would stake a claim on a man who'd likely leave her a widow? With children who'd be apprenticed, bound out, because he had no inheritance?

Aye, he had wealthy Pennsylvania kin, Plain folk who looked askance at him because his years with the Lenape had eroded any white kinship or familial feeling. That and his gun-toting. Though his aunts, uncles, and cousins still welcomed him into their homes, they seemed to regard him as half-feral still. No doubt due to the fight he'd given them as he became Clay Tygart again after being seized from the "red brethren" and Christianized.

How ingrained was the memory of his first day at Hallowells Friends School. He'd been dragged toward civilization scratching and kicking and been tied fast in a chair, the cold scrape of the razor against his sunbrowned neck shearing the hair that had grown out on his recapture. He'd nearly lost his spirit those years in Philadelphia, before he'd run away to rejoin the "sons of the forest," as the Quakers called them, only to become a scout interpreter for the British army instead.

Averting his gaze from the burgeoning trunk, he went below and resumed studying his maps, preparing for the fort's spies who would soon ride in and give the latest report.

"Like this, *lieverd,*" Keturah said, taking a leather thong and stringing a shiny tubular bead the likes of which Tessa had never seen. "Wampum." In her lap was a hill of purple and white shells that had been hidden in her medicine pouch, along with two fetching feathers.

"Wam-pum." The echoed word felt flat, even foolish, on Tessa's tongue. Surely such pretty beads deserved a prettier name. But Keturah had again called her by the Old Dutch endearment. Such was cause for joy.

"From the big water," Keturah told her, clearly fulfilled by her task.

"The sea?"

Their eyes met, each of them grappling with new words. They sat on a quilt near the creek that shot through Swan land like a blue arrow, spared the sun by a sycamore's shade. 'Twas the Sabbath, the quiet hours between their morning Bible reading and hymn singing and supper. Axe and anvil were idle. Jasper and Zadock had gone to the fort. Ma napped in the cabin, worn down by a summer fever. Lemuel sat beneath the barn's eave, whittling. Ross was repairing a rifle near the well. No telling where Cyrus was. Her own rifle was primed and within reach.

"Who taught you to do such fine beadwork?" Tessa asked. "Your Indian mother or sister?"

"Chitkwësi." Keturah's fingers stilled. "No talk of the dead."

Was this Lenape custom? Tessa mumbled an apology, sorry for the flash of pain in Keturah's face. Forehead furrowed, Keturah returned to her beading.

Tessa's fingers worked the wampum a bit hesitantly, even clumsily, slowly creating a passable design. The undertaking was more troublesome than she expected, maybe because her thoughts of late scattered like dandelion seed. How did fort folk spend the Sabbath?

With no preacher to be had, there would be no preaching, just a quiet observance of the day while overmountain folks gathered to worship in a church, a structure she'd never seen. More miraculous still, some of these civilized places had bells and pointed spires called steeples. The mere thought lanced her with a peculiar longing. On the other hand, the wilderness surrounding her, the glory of creation, called for worship without walls every day of the week.

No doubt Clay had seen a man-made church, even worshiped in one. Was he a God-fearing soul? He'd once commenced eating breakfast at the fort without saying grace, then bowed his head at their supper table. Troublesome to her at the time, it raised other questions that would possibly never have answers in light of his callous treatment of her.

She sighed, spying an error in her second row of beads. Despite her keen concentration, her thoughts could not be corralled. How long had Clay lived among the Lenni Lenape, the True People, as Keturah called them? Forced west by the tide of settlers, scattered bands were now in the Ohio country, a place few whites had ever seen. Keturah had come from there, somewhere along the Muskingum River. Deep in the heart of Indian territory.

Betimes Keturah still seemed to be there. Even now, though an arm's length away, Tessa sensed she was still on the Muskingum in spirit, her beadwork returning her to places and people she could not talk about. Maybe she was even pondering Clay, the one person in the white world who understood her red ways. Despite his sudden coldness to Tessa, at least he was kind to Keturah. Had they crossed paths at some point prior to this?

Tessa pondered their predicament, Jasper's scowl ever before her. Just yesterday he'd come from the fort having served as spy, churlish and ravenous. "The militia's set to muster again at week's end. I plan on asking about the Braams, see if there's any word from Keturah's kin. The colonel's posting in the eastern newspapers should relieve us of the burden of her care."

Keturah had continued setting the table while Tessa stabbed a skillet of venison collops at the hearth with a long-handled fork, wishing it was her brother instead. Jasper set her blood to boiling like never before.

Ma regarded him with fevered eyes from her rocking chair in that way that bespoke she was still the head of the household no matter what her eldest son had to say. "And what makes you think she's a burden?"

"Feeding and lodging her. Letting Zadock get witless over her. She's better off under Colonel Tygart's charge at the fort."

"It's not all give, understand," Ma countered firmly if quietly. "She does her share of the work without complaint, and her wildcrafting serves us well. But all that aside, 'tis simple Christian charity to do as we've done, and I'll abide no Indian haters in this house."

Tessa froze, fork suspended over the sputtering skillet. A quick glance over her shoulder told her Keturah had finished setting the table and seemed unaware of the testy exchange. Jasper strode out the door, heading to the woods, anger stiffening his stride.

Later that day Zadock came in as she was drawing water at the well. He'd gone with Jasper to the fort hours earlier, whistling as he went. Now he faced her darkly, one eye blackened, a gash on his jaw, nose and cheek swelling. She went hot, then cold. Clearly, Zadock had gotten the brunt of the beating. Over Keturah, no doubt.

"Jasper's orneriness just backfired," Tessa said, linking arms with him as they turned toward the cabin. "Keturah will see to what ails you."

Keturah waited on the cabin stoop, eyes on Zadock, a certain softness in her face Tessa hadn't seen before. And so Keturah tended him, applying from her medicine pouch whatever remedies would mend his battered face.

Jasper had not returned for supper, his

empty place at table glaring but making Tessa glad. Nor had he returned this morn for the Sabbath. How could he stand before them and read from the Bible with hatred in his heart?

Tessa pondered it now, praying for some spark, some sweet feeling to kindle on Keturah's part. Zadock would make a good husband, his indifference to Keturah's Indianness remarkable.

Her pleasure in any pairings, her prayerful petition that they might soon celebrate a wedding, was blunted when Keturah said, "Soon go to fort."

"Soon, aye, when the militia musters." Tessa slid another bead onto the string. Her girlish delight over muster days had turned to gall.

Out of the corner of her eye she saw Ma approaching. Her mother surveyed the woods surrounding the clearing as she walked, ever more wary since Pa's passing. Never did they dodge the shadow that this day might also be their last.

Ma settled on the old quilt beside them, admiring their beadwork, her lined face finally free of the flush of fever. A breeze stirred the loose strands of her silvered hair, once the inky gloss of Tessa's own. "Come Friday we'll be at the fort. Zadock says

211

Hester's after us to stay the night."

Tessa strung another bead. She couldn't confess she feared folk's reactions to Keturah. Ruth had already shown her disdain, as had other fort dwellers, Ross had whispered in warning. This she would spare Keturah if she could. "I say let's keep to home and let the men muster."

Ma's surprise was palpable in the beat of silence that followed. "You've not said such before, Daughter. Ruth and Hester will be sorely disappointed."

"We've a busy week ahead with salting that buffalo and making ticks for beds."

"Which is why a little merriment is in order. Besides, there's to be a contest amongst the women this time, not just the usual wrestling and shooting matches of the men."

At this, both Tessa and Keturah looked up from their handwork.

"A baking contest, of muster-day cakes," Ma said.

Partial to cake, Tessa felt a bit of her dander melt. "I've never heard of such."

"They muster so overmountain, Maddie told me. Muster cake sounds to me like gingerbread. Each woman bakes one and a judge decides which is best."

"Who's to judge?" Tessa suspicioned it

was none other than Clay Tygart himself. That prospect alone made her want to forsake her apron.

"Maddie didn't say, except that she's craving cake. You even have nutmegs, a boon for baking. I misdoubt another settlement woman can say the same."

"What's mine is yours. You use the nutmegs." Extending an open hand, Tessa accepted more wampum from Keturah. "I'd rather bead than bake."

Ma chuckled. "But baking, not beadwork, is what's called for."

"And the prize?" Tessa asked despite herself.

"We'll soon find out." With that, Ma stood and returned to the cabin, closing the door on Tessa's resistance.

17

Hands stained purple from the dying shed, nutmeg grater in her pocket, and an unwavering dread in her spirit, Tessa rode her mare, Blossom, into Fort Tygart at week's end. She'd gladly give a day of her life to move Hester's cabin as far away from the commander's blockhouse as she could, even down by the nose-curling privy pits. As it was, she had to sashay past that open blockhouse door, concoct a muster-day cake, and try to stay atop her fractured feelings as the summer slid into July.

If the man said but a few words to her at their last meeting, spared her nary a glance, and went on his way, what cause had she to care? Why did it feel like he'd horsewhipped her instead? Because of it she'd taken no pains with her person. No flounced petticoat. No fine cap and apron. Her careless braid hung to her hips.

Out of sorts, she dismounted, taking care

to stay near her brothers, who always made a great deal of commotion mostly because of their number. Hester's door yawned open, but before she'd walked but a few feet in its direction, Ruth stopped her. Tessa regarded her friend without a smile, in no more of a mind to chat than she was to cross paths with the colonel.

"You're a sight for sore eyes, Tessa." Ruth gave Keturah nary a greeting as she and Ma walked past.

The slight turned Tessa tetchier. "Seems like you could call upon your Christian self to bestow a kind word to a former friend."

"*Former,* aye," Ruth spat.

A hasty retort sprang to mind, but Tessa set her jaw. She didn't care to decipher the depths of Ruth's dislike. The morning sun poked heated rays into her back as it scaled the east palisades, adding to her present angst. She longed to be free of Ruth as well as her linen stockings and heavy shoes, but being barefoot would unleash the full measure of Hester's ire.

Ruth looked at her askance, riveted to Tessa's braid tied with a string of purple wampum. "You think it's wise, the both of you wearing them beads?"

"I don't know why not." Tessa itched to be on her way as well, not stand amid the bustling common like a block of wood. But Ruth's grip on her arm stayed steadfast.

"You entering the cake contest? Every woman within these walls aims to win."

"What's the prize?" Tessa said as Ruth fell into step beside her.

"It's secret, part of the reason it's all the buzzle. As for who's judge, that's hush-hush too."

They passed the magazine with its dwindling ammunition, then the garden nearing its riotous peak. Tessa glanced at the west blockhouse, her brothers just entering to mark their mustering.

That terrible tightening coiled inside her, a low-spiritedness born of high hopes shot down. She listened to Ruth's recitation of the latest settlement happenings, of birthings and grievances and maladies, of Indian sign along Cougar Creek, and of who had gone overmountain.

"Well?" Hands on her hips, Ruth awaited Tessa's own accounting.

"I'm plumb out of words," she replied, to Ruth's disgust.

Ever since they were small they'd chattered like magpies, mimicking their mothers. But today, nay. Absently fingering the nutmeg grater in her pocket, Tessa gave the sky a last look, wishing it would rain in the slim hope the festivities would be dashed. Yet why rob another's sport with her sour mood?

Without another word, Ruth strode away, spite stiffening her spine. Tessa entered Hester's cabin, joining Ma and Keturah, the humid air already fragrant with gingerbread. Hester's cake sat proudly on a tarnished pewter platter at the table's center.

"We can't all of us be at the hearth at once," Hester exclaimed, looking pleased with herself, her usually tidy apron bearing a spackle of grease.

"Keturah's brought some strawberry cakes," Ma announced with a smile.

Hester's focus narrowed to the linen-wrapped offering in Keturah's hands. "A dish as Indian as your beads, I reckon."

"Glad I am Keturah won't be in the contest," Tessa said, "as her baking might well trump ours."

They'd grown as fond of Keturah's corn-cakes mixed with strawberries as her medicinal teas. Hester pinched off a bite and chewed thoughtfully. Tessa did the same, and soon only the berry-stained linen remained, leaving Keturah looking satisfied.

"Best begin," Ma announced, giving them ample time to remake a cake if a first one fell or succumbed to some other mishap.

But even a failed cake would be devoured. Little was ever wasted.

Summoning her nerve, Tessa set to work, glad Hester had already laid out supplies. Butter. Eggs. Sweetening. Flour. Mace. Cloves. Candied lemon and orange peel. There was a sweet sameness to baking that restored Tessa's sagging spirits.

By noon the entire fort common was overcome with spices as cabin after cabin turned out an abundance of muster-day cakes. Maddie was soon at their door, looking less wan than before. Had the herbs Keturah given her helped?

"Feel almost sorry for the judges with so many sweets to sample," Maddie jested as the women rounded the table to look at the three cooling cakes from every angle.

Tessa had dusted hers with a sprinkle of hammered sugar and nutmeg, giving it a special polish. Ma had refused Tessa's offer of nutmeg and Hester was not fond of the spice, so Tessa's cake alone bore that touch. Next the women began the communal task of making the noon meal. With so many hands at the hearth, Tessa took a seat and snapped green beans by the window.

Near the flagpole stood all the able-bodied men from sixteen to sixty. Though Tessa tried not to dwell on him, Clay couldn't be missed. His unusual height made a fine target. 'Twas a wonder he'd survived the wilderness and numerous forays for a decade or better. She'd heard tell he'd served with George Washington, who was widely known for his military bearing and physical prowess. That and their wits kept such men alive, surely.

The men stood in neat rows, equal distance apart, as the colonel inspected their weapons in a blinding haze of sunlight. Free to study him unawares, she did so, another tendril of affection wrapping itself round her hungry heart.

Clay vowed to pray for rain, or at least clouds, on future muster days. A coastal Philadelphia wind would be welcome this windless morn. No breeze stirred the earth they stood upon or dispelled the aroma of unwashed bodies and garments begging lye. As he passed in front of the Buckhannon militia, all in need of spring water and already craving their fair share of muster-day rum, he took solace in the heavily spiced air.

One of his earliest — and rare — memories of his boyhood was of his mother at her hearth. She'd been tall and graceful and capable to a small, clumsy boy. He'd been her firstborn, his vision of her unclouded by other images and voices. Oddly, his fragile grasp of her was scented with what he thought was gingerbread, the lingering aroma so familiar, so fragrant, his eyes smarted from more than the sweat stinging his vision.

He stepped sideways as he finished his inspection, to the very end of the last column, and came face-to-face with Zadock Swan. The sun's glare highlighted every bruise and bump, rescuing Clay from his bittersweet memory.

"Tussle with a panther in the woods?" he asked Zadock quietly.

"Nay, sir. Kin."

"Your sister, mayhap?"

A broad smile strained Zadock's split lip. "Jasper."

Unsurprised, Clay examined Zadock's rusted musket, a sad affair from the last war, woefully inaccurate and making a frightful amount of noise. It underscored his concern that there were more farmers than frontiersmen here, forced to carry weapons because of the ongoing hostilities. He far preferred the arrows of his youth. Unlike guns, arrows fired repeatedly and with deadly accuracy, the bows easily maintained and repaired. The tomahawk served well in a hand-to-hand tussle, yet few had them along the Buckhannon, most relying on skinning knives instead.

He swallowed his aggravation. How was he to improve the tattered reputation of the colonial militia, who were not only ill equipped but undisciplined? He'd penned a bold letter to Virginia's governor, placing an order for gunsmiths to make as many flint-locks as possible to be transported by wagons under guard. Highwaymen east of the mountains were as much a threat as Indians west of them, the governor fired back, and gave no promise of weapons.

The remainder of the morning was spent drilling, the activity curbing the staunchest appetites as the aroma of the coming meal overrode the spicy gingerbread. Clay called a halt just after noon, his voice carrying over the common like a gunshot.

Once the muster-day cakes were cut, they'd roll out the Caribbean rum from Fort Pitt. Keeping a tight rein on the unruliest men was an ongoing challenge. He'd not have them awash in kill-devil by nightfall. Hester had already lectured him unneces-sarily about that.

For now, spits of roasting meat puffed enough smoke to keep the insects at bay as women served bread and vegetables from the fort's garden on makeshift tables. He held off eating till the men had their fill, knowing Hester would save him a trencher full.

Heading to the blockhouse, he removed his sweat-stained hat and came face-to-face with Tessa as she stepped out of Hester's cabin, a crock in each hand. Their eyes met and then a mutual mortification set in. Just as quickly they went their separate ways with nary a word betwixt them.

On his desk sat his noon meal, flies hovering in an unappetizing mass yet failing to dint his appetite like his near collision with Tessa had. Once upstairs, he shed his shirt with short, jerky movements, wishing he could rewind time and give her a nod, at least. He leaned over the washbasin and poured the entire pitcher of water over his sweltering head and shoulders. Sweet relief. After toweling dry, he pulled on a clean shirt, gaze drawn to the open window.

From here he could take in the entire garrison in a glance. Inevitably his gaze hung on one petticoat. Tessa paused at the end of one makeshift table near the lamb pen, garnering the attention of one too many men. Why, with the odds so in her favor, had she not wed?

He sat down on the closed trunk, wishing

for closure on his conflicted feelings, this warring desire to be near her yet push her away. Even the distant sight of her made his pulse gallop. Despite his best intentions, he was no longer commander of a garrison in hostile territory but a hopelessly smitten, double-minded, would-be suitor. Didn't Scripture even warn about such a thing?

Yet he gave in to the guilty pleasure of watching her from a distance. She was, by any measure, the most striking woman he'd seen this side of the mountains. Even Keturah's blonde, blue-eyed beauty failed to move him in light of Tessa's fiery warmth.

He forced his gaze away. Hester was now leading the charge, the women parading a great many cakes from cabins and setting them on the judges' table at the edge of the common garden. A few huzzahs sounded as Cutright and Jude rolled out casks of rum to wash the cakes down.

Jasper was supervising as the men drew straws to act as judges. Once the selection was narrowed, Clay would cast the deciding vote.

Had Tessa done any baking?

The thought sent him downstairs again to shoo the flies from his meal and take a few half-hearted bites. Best save his appetite for rum and cake.

He rejoined the melee on the common, counting nineteen cakes on various plates from pewter to wood. Six judges gathered, none of them Swans. Clay stood in the smithy's shade by Jude as the cake cutting began. Even unliquored, the men were full of tomfoolery, the chosen six making such a show Clay was cast back to the theater in Williamsburg. Plenty of chewing, belching, and patting of stomachs ensued to earn these ruffians their backwoods standing. In a half hour, amid a fair amount of seriousness and ceremony, three cakes were singled out, the rest sliced and served to any comers.

"Colonel Tygart, sir." Maddie smiled at him, gesturing to the waiting cakes. She sliced the first with a sure hand, balancing his sample on a broad knife. Every eye was upon him and nearly made him squirm.

He tasted, swallowed. A bit dry. Crumbly.

The second sample was overwhelmingly spicy and a tad overbrown. How in the name of all that was holy had it cleared six judges?

But the third . . . Even before it met his tongue he breathed in the essence of nutmeg, cast back the thousandth time to his mother's table. Moist. Well seasoned. Redolent with molasses, with just a bite of lemon and orange peel. And perfectly browned. One bite wasn't near enough.

He picked up the pewter plate it rested on and looked to the knot of aproned women. "Who's responsible for this creation?"

He expected Hester to step forward. Mayhap Mistress Schoolcraft or Rosemary Swan. In the throng he'd lost track of Tessa. The women looked about in question. Maddie eyed him apprehensively as a hush fell over the gathering. He set the prize cake down just as the winner appeared.

Men hooted and hollered, the women all abuzz. Tessa stood before him, hands twined behind her back, bewilderment on her flushed face. All thought of the prize left his head.

"Kiss her, kiss her, kiss her!"

What? The heat of the moment swathed his own face. This was no cornhusking where a red ear earned a kiss. Even Tessa seemed to take a step back at the suggestion, which soon became a deafening chorus surrounding them.

"Kiss her, Colonel!"

He looked to the ground. Willed the crowd's tempting chant away. Jude thumped him on the back. He looked up and caught that telling spark in Maddie's eye. Tossing his hat to Ross across the circle, Clay mastered his waffling and slid an arm around Tessa's slim waist, lowered his head, and kissed her full on the mouth. His senses spun. She tasted of nutmeg and molasses and had the feel of warm clay beneath his hands. And if there'd been no crowd he'd have kept on kissing her till she told him to stop.

They drew apart to huzzahs of approval. Tessa brought her fingers to her lips, studying him with a sort of stern surprise. If he read her right, she wasn't altogether indignant.

She recovered enough to say, "Is that my prize, Colonel Tygart?"

"Nay, that's theirs." He angled his head toward the crowd. "Your reward for such foolishness is the pick of anything you please from Cutright's shelves."

Her eyes widened at the prospect. "Anything?"

With a nod, he wondered what she'd choose. "A pack train made it in day before yesterday, so the shelves aren't so bare." He gestured for his hat, which Ross handed over with a grin.

The crowd began to disperse in search of a new diversion. The remainder of the long July afternoon there'd be contests among the men while the women cleaned up. But for now, Tessa.

"So what sets that cake of yours apart from the pack?" he asked, returning his hat to his head.

"Nutmeg." A shy smile. "You favor it, whereas Hester can't abide it."

"Hester's loss." He paused. What had just happened between them was hard to put into words. "I suppose I should apologize —"

"Nay." She met his gaze.

Those violet eyes, so clear and earnest. They did things to a man . . .

"Can't make too much of a called-for kiss," she said without rancor.

"Meaning they would've wanted to thrash my hide if I didn't oblige." At her nod, he said, "So you don't begrudge it."

"Maybe a town-bred girl would take offense. But I'm hardly that. And I know there was no heart behind it."

A called-for kiss with no heart. The honest appraisal, though said without heat, was razor sharp. He rubbed his jaw, more at a loss for words here than in any stilted, formal eastern parlor. "I wasn't making sport of you. There was more heart behind it than you realize. If it'd been Hester, nay."

She chuckled, and some of the tension between them gave way. "Hester will be mighty pleased Colonel Tygart kissed the Spinster Swan."

"*That* I meant in jest."

" 'Tis true."

"The only reason you're not wed is because you don't want to be. It's easy to see you could have every unmarried man along the Buckhannon at your beck and call."

"Nay," she said shortly.

"Why nay?" 'Twas the one question that clawed at him.

"My mind is set on other things." She looked past him with a wistfulness he could only call childlike. "Like leaving here for somewhere safe. Civilized. Peaceful."

Deprived of, or rather spared, the polish of city and schoolroom, she retained an honest vulnerability rarely seen. He started to naysay her, talk about chamber pots emptied into city streets, unruly animals running amok, pickpockets and thugs, poverty and disease. But her winsomeness wouldn't let him.

They were drawing notice standing here. Despite the itch to tarry, he touched the brim of his hat. "Best see to business. Yours at the fort store and mine beyond the gates."

Ruth rounded the west wall of the smithy just then, calling Tessa by name. He walked away, his mind returning to the recent post he'd received from John Heckewelder about Keturah. The Moravian missionary was on his way to Fort Tygart, his arrival imminent. A beat of good news among the bad.

18

Ruth seemed a shade green. "Queen for a day, you are. A cake. A kiss. And now a sashay into Cutright's store."

"A passing fancy," Tessa said despite her pleasure. "Tomorrow I'll be back on the river and 'twill seem a dream."

"Cutright has some new merchandise, looks like, beyond the usual flints and furs."

Truly, the shelves had never been so full. Cocoa. Cloth. Pins, buttons, thimbles. Licorice. Snuff boxes. Blank books. Ink powder. Summer softened the British-milled soaps and sharpened the fragrance of the superfine teas. Even the dried figs smelled overripe.

Ruth chattered as Tessa looked, while Cutright stood in the rough-hewn doorway facing the common, pungent pipe smoke wreathing his bald head. Tessa lingered by a shelf of fripperies, drawn to a folding fan made of carved sticks and parchment. Carefully she unfurled its painted folds. The winsome scene was of a harbor with a tall-masted ship, a lovely palette of blues and greens.

"You don't mean it," Ruth exclaimed, examining a straw hat. "You'd take a bit of paper and wood over this?"

" 'Tis the sea," Tessa said, further extending the fan's leaves.

"Never saw the sea and likely never will." Ruth moved on, holding up a length of sheer gauze with the barest edge of lace trim. "How about this modesty cloth?"

But the lovely fan held an allure Tessa couldn't possibly put to words or make Ruth understand. Even Cutright, facing them now as if expecting a decision, seemed surprised, even a tad disappointed, in her choice. "Am I to tell the colonel you are content with a mere fan, Miss Swan?"

"Aye, with my thanks."

"Very well then."

She passed outside into a brilliant three o'clock afternoon, fan in hand, Ruth following. Wrestling matches were in full tilt beyond the fort's gates, the accompanying laughter and grunts of exertion jarring. Suddenly she was tired, the events of the day catching up to her — mostly that small emotional storm. Her very first kiss but not,

231

from the feel and heat of it, his.

"I'd best go spell Ma," Ruth said, wiping the sweat from her brow with a raised sleeve. "The babe's fractious, as he's cutting teeth."

Glad to be alone with her tangled thoughts, Tessa walked beneath the partial shade of the east wall. She spied Maddie outside the cabin she shared with Jude, well away from Hester's and the west blockhouse.

"Care for company?" Tessa called as she neared.

Smiling, Maddie gestured to the empty bench beside her. "What is that you're carrying?"

Tessa opened the fan and fluttered it in her hand, courting a breeze and scattering insects, before passing it to Maddie.

"Such a prettily painted scene." Maddie eyed it appreciatively. "Reminds me of Philly, namely the Delaware River. All those schooners and brigantines bound for England."

"Do you miss it?"

"Some things I miss." She handed back the fan. "Some things I don't."

"How are you feeling?"

"For an old woman about to have a baby, pretty fine."

"You're hardly old, Maddie. Nary a wrinkle do I see."

Maddie smiled, creating a few creases. "I disremember what year I was born, just somewhere in Philly. My mother was a washerwoman at the Blue Anchor Tavern. When she was felled by fever I got bound out to a Quaker lady uptown."

"I'm sorry. I hope she was kind to you. I've never known a town-bred lady."

"Mercy, Miss Tessa, with that bit o' finery you can just *be* one."

They laughed at this flight of fancy, and Tessa gave an exaggerated flutter of her fan. "What makes one a fine lady, Maddie?"

"Fine ladies follow fine rules." Tilting her head, Maddie took her time answering. "For one, a lady is never barefooted or bareheaded."

Sweet relief bloomed that she'd donned both her cap and shoes. "Go on."

"A lady ought to have a modest gait, not be in a hurry."

"Be graceful?"

A nod. "If a lady is about town on a busy street, she should be offered the wall next to the houses to pass by. And no looking about with immodest eyes."

"What if you trip over the cobblestones or soil your skirts with mud?"

233

"A lady raises her dress to the ankle and no higher. Just gather the folds of your gown with your right hand, like this." Standing, Maddie demonstrated. "Raising your skirts with both hands is vulgar."

"Says who?"

"Fancy folk. City rules, remember."

"There are neither here."

"Dodging wild animals and Indians leaves little time to fuss with your skirts."

"Tell me more, Maddie."

"More? Well, a gentleman'll call you Missus even if he married you, least in public. And a lady takes care to stand to a gentleman's right, never his left."

"I suppose a muster-day kiss is not to be borne."

Laughter shook Maddie's spare frame. "Red ears of corn and muster-day cakes and kisses are frontier doings."

The one question that most needed asking and answering gnawed at her. If Maddie but said the word, Tessa would set down her hopes and never look back. Though Clay had told her over breakfast that one morning he had no sweetheart, her heart craved confirmation.

"Does Colonel Tygart" — Tessa looked toward the gates, catching sight of him and weathering the woozy melt he made of her middle — "have a lady?"

Maddie sighed, leaving Tessa on tenter-hooks. "Nay, though a few have set their caps for him."

With effort, Tessa narrowed her sights to the delight of her new fan. If he had no sweetheart, why the distance? The sudden backtracking?

"And you?" Maddie asked. "Set your bonnet for some settlement gent?"

"Nary a one."

"Well then," Maddie said with a satisfied humph. "A right fine match in the making, if you ask me."

Tessa allowed herself another glance at the gates framing Clay. Earlier, when he'd slipped one hard-muscled arm around her waist, she'd been struck by the sheer physical strength of him, the fact that he'd nearly lifted her off her feet. But his kiss . . . such a mesmerizing mix of restraint and gentleness, and given none too hastily, as if he wanted to savor it despite the hundred or so onlookers.

Light-headed more from the memory than the heat, she thanked Maddie and turned toward Hester's, her thoughts circling back to the commander. How she wanted to call him Clay as Maddie did. There was something about it she liked, an earthy immediacy far removed from the formality of his full name or even his rank of colonel.

Mayhap she'd best content herself and call him Clay in her own private thoughts.

"Well, if you aren't the talk of the fort I don't know who is," Hester said with no small satisfaction when Tessa entered her cabin near suppertime.

"How fare your brothers?" Ma asked with a lingering look out the open door.

"At the rum," Tessa answered. "With all the rest."

"I hope they hold their liquor." Hester began making flip regardless, in case there was a shortage of spirits. "I'd hate to tangle with Tygart. He doesn't abide such."

Ma's knitting needles flew. "The evils of drink cannot be made light of."

"*Kiwsuwakàn,*" Keturah said with a frown. "Drunkenness."

All three women looked at her. Had the Lenape been plied with it in treaties like they'd heard? Liquor for land?

"A shameful business," Hester said with a wag of her head. "As for us, more than a few men need to stay sharp-witted and stand watch. Though I hate to say it, I sense this strange lull with the Indians bodes a deeper ill."

"By now, nearly midsummer, we've usually had a good run of trouble." Although Ma didn't miss a stitch in the gloom of the cabin and the heat of the day was still severe, her words sent a chill through Tessa. "I well recollect how it was before dear Lazarus was killed. That same unearthly calm. And then death."

"That black day was nearly the death of me." Hester began pouring the finished flip between pitchers. "There's been talk of Indians amassing for a strike all along the border here and deep into the heart of Kentucke territory."

"Where'd you learn such?" Ma said, her usual calm bestirred.

"You hear a heap of blether with spies coming and going night and day, post riders, stray settlers, and such."

"Meaning you're doing more than cooking for the colonel."

"I'd be glad to be relieved of the burden of that!" Hester spat out with vigor. "Now that he's come to his senses about my greatniece, surely some sort of declaration will follow."

Tessa turned from the doorway. "That kiss meant no more than a red ear at a cornhusking, Auntie." She withdrew the fan from her pocket and extended the painted leaves for them to admire, anxious to put an end to any nonsense. "But I am partial to this bit of hard-won frippery."

They made over the fan, though Hester still had that triumphant gleam in her eye, which set Tessa on edge. With eighty years stiffening her slightly bent spine, Hester was a caution she'd best be chary of. What would her great-aunt think of next?

Clay ate the cornmeal mush Hester served him the next morn, sunk in thought. A weathered copy of the *Pennsylvania Gazette* rested on the table, the notice about Keturah clearly visible. Beside it was the more recent letter from John Heckewelder, Moravian missionary to the Lenape.

"Tell Miss Braam I need to speak with her," he said to Hester as she banked the coals at the hearth and readied to return to her cabin.

"Keturah?" Hester looked hard at him, as if he'd misspoken and meant Tessa instead.

"Aye, Keturah," he answered, though her great-niece was firmly in mind.

Hester nodded and went out, leaving him to the uninterrupted reverie of her great-niece. He'd not spoken to Tessa since the cake cutting, but he'd observed her later outside Maddie's cabin, fan in hand. It impressed him that she'd chosen something pretty and practical, not the costliest item in the store. A mere trinket, Cutright told him with a touch of scorn. But if he read Tessa right, her telling choice reflected her heart and her desire for better things, to be anywhere but here.

"Kèku hàch?" Keturah stood in the doorway, giving a customary Lenape greeting.

"Kèku mësi," he replied, gesturing to a chair. Letter in hand, he left the table and moved to his desk. "There's been no word yet from your kin, though these things often take time." He proceeded slowly, speaking English. "What I do have is a reply to the letter I sent to the man in charge of the praying Indians."

"The Blackcoats?" Keturah asked, understanding kindling in her eyes.

"Aye, namely John Heckewelder on Beaver Creek."

Keturah's guardedness thawed, but she lapsed into Lenape again as she often did when English taxed her. "Heckewelder is a good man, a faithful friend to the True People."

"He's proven to be, aye," Clay continued in English. "He and his fellow Blackcoats want to start a new community called Fine Spring along the Tuscarawas River in the

Ohio country."

A prolonged pause. "The praying Indians are many. Some of Netawatwees's — my Indian father's — people are among them."

Netawatwees.

The name was an echo from another world. Clay staunched his surprise. Had Keturah been adopted by the great chief? Leader of the Turtle Clan, Newcomer, as the whites called him, was a loyal friend to Moravian missionaries if not yet a convert.

Her eyes bore a hole in him. "Why do you tell me this?"

Though he didn't want to alarm her, he said, "I have reason to believe you would be safer among the praying Indians and Black-coats than here."

Something filled her face he could only name as sadness, not fear.

"Brother Heckewelder is on his way west en route to the Ohio country. He wants to talk to you."

A flicker of uncertainty sharpened her gaze. "You will be here too when we meet?"

He nodded. "And if you decide not to go with him, I understand. We'll continue to wait for word from your family, though it would be wise to move you to the fort till then. There's soon to be an empty cabin by Maddie and Jude."

"The Swans . . ." Tears made her eyes a wash of blue. "Not welcome now?"

He was nothing if not forthright. "There's no protest from the Swans save Jasper, who despite his prejudices seems harmless. It's your coming and going in the woods that concerns me. I don't want you encountering any who might do you ill."

She was in double danger in a settlement so torn by war and strife. He wouldn't belabor the fact that the most grievous obstacle she was up against was the many settlers' murderous attitude against Indians.

"In the meantime, I'll send word to Swan Station when Heckewelder arrives."

Quietly, Keturah left the blockhouse, her beaded headband reminding him of the beaded tie of Tessa's braid. Would every rabbit trail circle back to her?

He leaned back till the creak of his chair told him to go no further and gathered his thoughts, trying to shut the door Keturah had just cracked open with the Lenape. Yet once again something as simple as the flash of wampum beads struck like a schoolmaster's lash. Even learning Keturah's Indian father was the ancient chief sparked a keen ache. Wise, peace-loving Netawatwees had treated him kindly. What other Lenape ties did Keturah have?

The little he knew now haunted. Keturah had been brought to Pitt in a prisoner exchange following another meaningless treaty. Her Lenape name was Wisawtayas. Yellow Bird. He should have dug deeper, asked for details.

Picking up a ledger, he uncovered the latest communication from McKee, a warning embedded within the usual politics and military maneuvering. Something was brewing among the Ohio Indians, the Iroquois farther north, and mayhap the smaller tribes around Detroit. Though his own report to McKee was bland, he couldn't shake the premonition of danger even in the face of scant sign.

"Colonel Tygart, sir."

He'd already turned toward the door before the voice sounded, a habit of the backwoods. His head spy, Captain Arbuckle, removed his battered hat, giving his matted hair a shake.

"More tracks along the Buckhannon by the ferry and near Swan Station." The report came out in winded spurts. "Two horses stolen from Westfall north of Swans'. Signs of passage at the salt licks further upriver."

"How many in the party?"

"A dozen or so by my reckoning, mayhap

a mix of Wyandot and Shawnee. We lost their trail at Clover Bottom." He reached into the folds of his linen shirt and withdrew a foot-long strip of birch bark. "Found this between the old Braam homestead and the Swans'. Some sort of picture writing."

Clay took the rough bark from his out-stretched hand and studied the etching of coal and pigmented clay on wood. *Wikhegan.* Indian symbols telling a story or relaying a message.

"I recollect you saying these bark maps are used amongst the tribes, detailing rivers and trails for those Indians unfamiliar with a region."

"Aye." Though he tried to look at it dispassionately, coldly, Clay could not. "Odd finding them in more settled territory."

The maker had drawn the sign of the moon followed by seven straight strokes in black. Below this were two red arrows in flight, both aimed at a woman fleeing, her dark hair spread out and flowing behind her.

"What do you make of it, sir?"

Clay set the wikhegan on his desk. "The red arrows and the woman fleeing are warnings. The moon and the lines beside it indicate the passage of time and the growing strength of their numbers, likely, be it

Shawnee or Wyandot or else. Mayhap a declaration of war, though not as telling as a black wampum belt. But something to heed, aye."

Arbuckle gave a low whistle. "Grim picture writing."

"Think no more of it." Clay turned away from the ominous sign with a ghost of a smile. "A hot meal and a gill of muster-day rum is owed you."

"Obliged, sir." Arbuckle passed outside, leaving Clay to ponder this latest development.

Other spies and other reports would soon follow. For the moment, he was most concerned about the Swans leaving out once the frolic was done. He was of a mind to escort them all the way to Swan Station. And now, melded with his conflicted attraction for a woman he couldn't court, this telling piece of wikhegan only fueled his angst.

Woodenly, without thinking, he abandoned his desk and climbed to the loft, the weight of his defenselessness amid the coming tempest pressing down like a hammer on an anvil. When the Swans left the relative safety of the fort, what could he do? Though the brothers' five guns were formidable as far as number, they were old and unreliable, a poor defense amid a volley of red arrows. What — or who — was the fleeing woman with hair flying etched so carefully in coal? Might it be Tessa? Settlement women in general? If so, why leave out children from the picture?

His backside connected with his bed and he sank his head in his hands, Maddie's words weaving through his inner turmoil.

You've got to get out from under that burden of believing a lie. Folks you care about get cut down, so you stop caring, stop letting folks in.

Might his prayerlessness, his occasional nod to God, leave him or a situation more defenseless, even powerless? Was it akin to facing an enemy without a weapon? He stood in the crossfire of fort life, the empty blockhouse calling for something he'd abandoned years before. His faith, watered down and mixed with Indian mysticism and superstition, had turned to rust.

If this gnawing attraction for Tessa drove him to his knees, all the better then. He hit the rough wood floor, the slight twinge warning of the rheumatism that followed so many backwoodsmen into old age. The odd posture felt awkward, even foolish, but he bent his head, fisting his hands together.

At once came the lick of another memory. Pale candlelight. The whistle of wind through cabin chinking. All the night sounds beloved to a boy, his mother's bent head and heartbeat most memorable of all as she'd gathered him close to pray. How he craved the words she'd once said, lost to time. No doubt they'd been aimed at his oft-absent father, away on a long hunt. Prayers for protection. Peace.

Peace, aye, peace. For Tessa. For all in this war-torn land.

Father, forgive me. It's been too long.

19

Tessa navigated the humid, briar-ridden woods, hardly batting at the insects bedeviling her. 'Twas not yet noon, and though Ma had wanted to leave the fort at peep of day, her brothers had business at the store and then with the colonel, delaying them further. But she was barely mindful of the time or the fretful arch of Ma's brow.

Despite repeated, secret talking-tos, she could not find her way past her romantic musings. Ever since that muster-day cake, Clay had kissed her not once but a hundred times in memory. It hadn't helped that he'd stood at the gate when they rode out. She'd allowed herself a last look at him, enough to see him give a tug to the brim of his hat as they filed past.

Oh, how his respectful distance vexed her. He seemed mildly interested at best. Was it wrong for a woman to woo a man? Did she dare? If he had no sweetheart, had he no hankering for one? Her brothers certainly did, though they took care to hide their feelings. Likewise, Clay was another question mark in britches she might never figure out.

Though Jasper usually forbade any woods talk lest they draw notice, Ross leaned near enough to say, "Ever since the colonel kissed you, you've looked pleased as a fox in a henhouse. But today, nay."

"Shush," she replied, still pondering her plan. To woo or not to woo?

Near their own clearing, their caution ebbed and talk turned to the coming harvest.

"Colonel Tygart's set a guard for each farm to bring the crops in," Jasper told them as he dismounted. "Won't have to work and watch our backs."

Lemuel nodded approvingly. "I reckon we'll get fifty bushels of corn to the acre in half the time then."

"I say eighty bushels," Zadock countered, igniting a full-blown discussion of the matter.

Ross went to round up the cows and horses, the faint tinkle of their bells heard in the direction of the river, while Tessa fetched a wood sled from the barn. She pulled it with a hemp rope, the slither of the runners reminding her of a snake. She and Keturah started toward the fields to gather melons grown so large they'd likely need help hauling them.

Chary of her steps in the tall grass, she noticed Keturah wore that distant, faraway look. Since meeting with Clay in the block-house, she'd seemed uncommonly quiet.

Her high spirits were so at odds with Keturah's own that she asked, "Are you downcast, *winkalit*?"

"The Blackcoat, he comes." At Tessa's questioning look, Keturah added, "A holy man among the True People."

Bewilderment took hold. Moravian missionaries? Hester had spoken of these faithful men and women in years past. "To Fort Tygart?"

"*Pìshi*. To talk. Këshkinko told me so."

Këshkinko. Tessa committed the odd word to memory. Was this Clay's Lenape name? Keturah was called Yellow Bird. Wisawtayas. It suited her somehow, sounded almost poetic, and surely spoke to her Dutch pale-ness. Once again Tessa felt on the outside looking in. So many questions, so few answers. And a wide chasm of misunder-standing between their Indian world and her white.

Had Clay returned from captivity near the time Keturah had been taken? How oft she'd wondered but never asked. "Did you know Këshkinko when you were Yellow Bird?"

"Mata." No. The firm word removed all doubt. "Much talk — of him. He made many afraid." She gestured to her eyes. *"Nataèpia."*

"His eyes?"

Keturah nodded. "They gave him power among the People."

A glimmer of understanding dawned. Clay's eyes, so striking to her, might be especially fearsome to the Indians. "How so?" Tessa asked gently, afraid Keturah would turn silent as she sometimes did.

"Ghost Eyes — Këshkinko — he is called. His blue eye, it sees heaven. His brown eye, earth."

The small storm of words ended, leaving Tessa wide-eyed in the aftermath. Never had Keturah spoken so, with vehemence and a sort of reverence. Indians oft attached extraordinary significance, a heightened mysticism, to the simplest things. Had Clay been protected somehow by his unusual eyes? Hedged from harm? And did this explain Keturah's noticeable regard of him, that respectful awe, if not affection?

"So you only heard of him during your time with the Lenape." Tessa's quiet question brought a nod of affirmation. "But never met him."

"Kёshkinko took a separate path," Keturah said at last.

In silence they walked on to the heart of the cornfield, unmindful of the cry of a buzzard and shrill chorus of cicadas, their reward an abundance of round, shiny melons beneath tall, tasseling stalks.

Keturah marveled. Had she no memory of melons? The three sisters were known and beloved to her — the Indian maize, squash, and beans. When Tessa thumped a watermelon, Keturah laughed.

"Tasty. Sweet," Tessa told her as they stepped around twisting vines and loaded the ripest onto the sled. Once cooled in the springhouse, the fruit would be savored till the juice ran down their chins. "When we were small, we'd have a contest and roll them to a finish line. The boys usually bested us. Remember?"

They grew still, the raucous call of a crow the only sound other than the rustle of the stalks. Keturah shut her eyes, then opened them. "Jasper . . . he won."

"Aye, being the oldest and the fastest." The burst of joy she felt at the sweet memory was short-lived, given her brother's hard-heartedness.

Keturah lost her faraway look. "Talk more of, then."

As they started back to the cabin, taking turns pulling the heavy sled, Tessa spoke of cranberry tarts at Christmas, the forest furniture they'd gathered for their rag dolls, the bear cub once shut up in the barn, the scourge of measles that spanned months before it was done, and her and Keturah's baptisms in the cold water of the Buckhannon by an itinerant preacher.

"I was made a" — Keturah hesitated as she often did, the white words eluding her — "angel?"

"A saint," Tessa replied softly, moved by the recollection. "But aye, I do remember Brother Merritt saying you looked like an angel when you came up out of all that water."

Clay had expected someone older but now faced a man his own age, an apprenticed cooper turned missionary. John Heckewelder was a remarkably unassuming man. "I'm serving as the messenger of David Zeisberger," he said almost apologetically upon arrival at Fort Tygart, his handshake firm, his manner warm. "But Brother Zeisberger sends his sincerest regards."

Zeisberger was the Moravian leader, a true

friend to all the tribes, with none of the prejudices afflicting so many. He'd established a successful mission named Bethlehem in eastern Pennsylvania, and his converts, mostly Lenape, were growing. Keturah's plight was of special interest to them.

In Heckewelder's party was a Mingo scout and his wife, three fellow converts, and his own assistant, all committed to establishing a new mission farther west. Greetings went round, and then Heckewelder was left alone with Clay after being shown the east blockhouse where they'd lodge.

Hester soon came with food and drink, then left the men to their talk. Keturah would join them in the morning, escorted by one of the Swan brothers and Tessa. He'd asked Tessa by letter to accompany them, his desire to have her safely behind fort walls as much in mind as Keturah's comfort.

He'd expected to answer Heckewelder's questions about Keturah, help smooth the way to their meeting, but once again the truth emerged that he knew precious little about her due to his own history with the Lenape and not wanting to delve further.

Now as they walked about the garrison at dusk, Heckewelder remarked on the fort's prime location, particularly taken with the bountiful spring. "Bethlehem, being a peaceful community, is without pickets." He stood beneath the elm's arching shade as a few children regarded them shyly. "We Moravians would deny you a job if we could."

"By converting every tribe and nation?" Clay mused, knowing their lofty aims. The peaceful prospect seemed especially ludicrous in light of their present surroundings. "Admirable but hard-won."

"We understand the tribes' plight, given so many of us Moravians have been driven out of our own homelands in Europe. We see their warring ways as a desperate effort to hold on to their territory, their way of life, mayhap their very existence. Admittedly, our stance on the frontier is conciliatory rather than defensive." Heckewelder studied the sentinels guarding the half-open front gates. "What is your greatest challenge here as commander?"

"Murderous attitudes."

Heckewelder nodded in understanding. "Both settlers and Indians, you mean."

"Most here have known violence and death at Indian hands, or they will. Many seek an opportunity to repay in kind. The rule of law, even military law, is nearly unknown."

" 'Tis understandable in light of their losses, but certainly not biblical."

"Most prefer 'an eye for an eye' and overlook 'blessed are the peacemakers.' "

"And you, Colonel, are you not a riddle, raised by both Friends and Indians and now defending the westernmost border?"

"My position here is primarily defensive. I have no plans to mount an offensive unless provoked."

"Has an attack been made on the fort or settlers?"

Clay gave a nod. "Before my coming, aye. I assumed command in early May but have yet to fire a single shot at the enemy. Fort spies regularly report sign, mostly on well-traveled Indian trails, but other than a few stolen horses the country is remarkably quiet."

"A most peculiar circumstance." Heckewelder's calm demeanor continued. "Who are the foremost raiders?"

"Prior attacks were at the hands of the Wyandot, Delaware, and Shawnee living on the upper Sandusky and Scioto."

"The very places we hope to sow peace."

They bypassed the powder magazine, hardly a point of interest since the Moravians, like Quakers, were pacifists. Clay pointed out the common garden with corn, beans, and squash in abundance.

"I'm partial to Indian fare." Heckewelder's lean frame was in sharp contrast to Cutright, who stood watching them from his storefront. "Succotash in particular."

"I well remember," Clay said, never having lost his taste for the Indian dish.

"How long were you with the Lenape?"

"Ten eventful years."

"And your family? Captive or killed?"

"Killed," Clay replied without the usual mental flinch.

To his credit, Heckewelder spoke of such things without emotion. The bane of the frontier was that death and captivity were commonplace.

"And what of Miss Braam?"

"Best let her tell you her story, in her own words," Clay answered as they returned to the west blockhouse.

A week they'd been away from the fort, long enough for the muster-day cake to fade from memory, if not the unexpected kiss. *That* Tessa kept alive like the broken-winged sparrow she'd once saved in a rude cage of Cyrus's making, feeding it seeds and refusing to let it perish.

'Twas the same with a pleasurable recollection, was it not, keeping it alive by continual rumination? Or maybe she was simply a weak-willed woman grown too fond of the fluttery feeling the fort's hero wrought. No matter. 'Twas a marvel that no other man had made her feel so in all her years.

Her fan rested on the little shelf above her bed, another pleasant keepsake from a day gone by. She used it, as did Ma, who seemed right fond of such finery, though Keturah's turkey feather fan was just as handy.

When a spy delivered the missive summoning Keturah to the fort, Tessa took it from his hand in wonder. She alone could read it, perusing it privately, then pocketing it to share at supper's end in the soft glow of candlelight.

Dear Swans, read the flowingly bold, masculine hand. *Brother John Heckewelder has arrived at the garrison and seeks a meeting with Miss Braam on Saturday morn. Would be wise to have a male escort, Miss Swan included. Yours entire, Colonel Clay Tygart.*

'Twas an honor being singled out, yet maybe it was mere courtesy, an afterthought from a man she was unsure of. Still, the summons created a hullabaloo as her brothers debated who would set their work aside and accompany them.

"You'd think you were escorting royalty," Tessa teased as their arguing grew more impassioned. "Not two homespun women on an old mare."

"I'd like to meet this Heckewelder, friend to the Indians," Zadock said, lighting his pipe.

"So would we all," Lemuel said to their surprise. He was never one to want to trade a day in the fields for even a frolic. "Wish Heckewelder and Colonel Tygart would venture out here instead."

"Seems like you older rascals always go and I'm the runt who gets left behind." Ross glared at them good-naturedly, taking another slice of the dripping watermelon.

"I've not seen you smile so broadly since that muster-day kiss, Sister." Cyrus gave a sly wink. "What might the colonel mean, asking for *your* company?"

"He means to make Keturah comfortable and not leave her at the mercy of you men," she fired back. "Think no more of it." She waved her fan about, further amusing them as talk turned to other matters.

On Saturday morn they rode to the fort in response to Clay's summons. Surrounded, she was, riding between not one but two of her brothers, Zadock leading, Cyrus behind. Today Keturah had her own mount, preferring to ride bareback. A sense of expectancy spurred them through the woods. Everything held that peculiar over-ripe scent, that final, intense green before giving way to autumn's rust.

Any comeliness she'd aimed for when pinning her hair beneath her cap or donning her flounced petticoat melted away by the time they spied the fort's far pickets. Sweat trickled down her neck and bodice and turned her itchy. Dust left a browner cast to her skin. If not for her gladness to go, she'd have let the simmering day turn her sour.

Clay was at the gates when they rode up, as if wary they'd be fired upon or ambushed. The tension of being a moving target drained from her as she slid off Blossom. Theirs always seemed a small victory to be safely within.

"Morning, Colonel Tygart," Zadock said as he dismounted.

Behind the colonel stood Hester, dwarf-like in his shadow. Would Tessa spend the morning with her great-aunt or be expected to accompany Keturah when she met with Heckewelder?

Hester embraced her like always as Clay tipped his hat to them both. She returned the nod with a small smile, mindful of Hester's sharp eye.

"We'll be making the noon meal for Brother Heckewelder and company," her aunt told her. "From the best of the fort's garden to boot."

Was that the reason Clay had asked her here? To help cook? "What of meat?" Tessa asked as they all began walking toward the blockhouse.

"Colonel Tygart has brought down a buffalo. Don't you smell the marrow bones roasting?"

"Aye, Auntie." Tessa breathed in a dozen different scents that a blessed breeze mingled, not all of them savory. "Fine feasting, then."

"You'll grind the meal and make the bread. I've beans to snap and corn to shuck."

Into Hester's cabin they went, while her brothers were left to their own business and Keturah disappeared inside the blockhouse.

20

Heckewelder greeted Keturah with the same easy affability that had already won over many of the fort's inhabitants. If he was surprised by her beauty, her thoroughly Indian ways, even the beads she wore, he gave no sign. She stayed stoic, almost guarded, despite Heckewelder's humble manner and his fluency in Lenape.

He began, "Would you prefer to converse in English or the language of the True People?"

Clay was unsurprised when she chose Lenape. It allowed her an ease of expression not yet mastered with English. He well knew the struggle of exchanging familiar words for the unfamiliar, a loss not unlike a small death as words and whole phrases in the Indian tongue were abandoned and then forgotten.

"Word reached us at our mission in Bethlehem that you were given up by the People.

In fact, some of our brothers and sisters there were overjoyed when they learned you were here. I have come to see if you would consider joining us, at least until word of your family reaches you."

Keturah eyed him with renewed interest. "Who are these sisters and brothers you speak of?"

"These Lenni Lenape have taken Christian names, though you know them as Neolin, Shingas, Pesquitomen, and Chulili."

"They are now" — her pale brows arched in surprise and something akin to alarm — "praying Indians?"

"Aye, Christian Indians. They have heard the Good News of our risen Lord and embrace Him." Heckewelder smiled as if to lessen her sudden anxiety. "Why don't we go back to the beginning. Tell me how you came to be with the Lenape."

They sat before Clay's desk, their backs to the closed door. Even in the shadows, the sole light streaming through the cabin's chinking and the loft window, Keturah's shifting expressions were plain.

"Much I have forgotten." Her soft voice was tinged with sorrow. "It was corn-planting time. The season of strawberries. I was with my white sisters." She looked toward Clay. "Tessa Swan . . . another girl named Ruth. I went ahead of them to pick berries. The woods were thick with sounds, and I did not hear the warriors approach."

She spoke so clearly and precisely that the scene played out in Clay's head. Heckewelder seemed just as riveted, though he'd no doubt heard such accounts before.

"I was much afraid. These men made motions they might kill me. They took me northwest, toward the Scioto, so very far I knew I could not find my way back again."

"Many days of travel," Heckewelder said.

"Yes. When I came to the one village, my white clothes were taken away. I was led to a river and told I was their new daughter, all my whiteness washed away."

Clay's own story was much the same, though it had begun more violently with the firing of his family cabin. When he'd reached that last Lenape village, he'd run a gauntlet, dodging sticks and clubs. He'd stayed standing, earning him the respect of watching warriors before his own river cleansing.

"My Lenape mother was good to me. She taught me many things. My Indian father, the sachem Netawatwees, was kind. Still, my heart was on the ground. No one came for me from the white world. I had to learn Indian ways. Indian words. My thinking became more red than white."

"How long were you among them?" Heckewelder asked.

Again she looked to Clay. Time was not counted in minutes and months but by moons and seasons.

"Ten or twelve years, by my reckoning," he answered.

Heckewelder nodded thoughtfully. "Long enough to make you forget much of your family and life along the Buckhannon."

Keturah toyed with her braid. "I have little memory of Keturah but became Yellow Bird. There was much to see and do. We camped many places but mostly along the big waterfalls for a night's lodge."

Brow furrowing, Heckewelder looked at Clay for confirmation. "The same as a night's watch?"

"Aye, a stay of one year in Indian time. Along the Cuyahoga River." It had been his favored camp, heavily timbered with wide, cascading falls. Plentiful game and fertile places to plant the three sisters.

"Cuyahoga Town?" Heckewelder asked. " 'Tis what we Moravians call it."

"The True People live on the north side of the river," Keturah told them. "The Iroquois live to the south."

"And Netawatwees is — was — your

adoptive father. I heard the same from your friends at Bethlehem," Heckewelder said. "Is it also true that you had a husband?"

The question, gently stated, startled her nonetheless. Expecting a nay, Clay reached for his pipe and started to take out the tobacco pouch a Shawnee had given him. Keturah's attention swiveled to Clay as he filled the bowl with Indian tobacco, the *këlëkënikàn* made fragrant with sumac leaves. He did it if only to ease her, as the questions turned more personal and mayhap more painful.

"My husband . . ." She swallowed and looked to her lap. "He is a warrior. A chief."

"So, he still lives," Heckewelder asked quietly, "or was alive when you were returned to Fort Pitt?"

Her prolonged pause had Clay on tenterhooks, pipe forgotten in his hand.

"Alive, yes." She nodded. "He is Tamanen of the Wolf Clan."

Her revelation flew by quickly, but Clay nearly choked on his pipe smoke as her words came clear.

Tamanen.

Another echo from another world. Tamanen. Warrior. His Lenape brother, born to his Lenape mother. Raised alongside him. And now a chief.

265

Clay turned toward Keturah so suddenly her eyes met his. The fragrant smoke circled in lazy rings between them but did not cloud his sharp surprise or the telling awareness in her gaze.

"He was against my going to Pitt. Nothing would move him to part with me until the redcoats said they would kill him lest he give me up. Even then he vowed to reclaim me." Her voice held a tenderness Clay hadn't yet heard. "He was a good husband. A good provider. I was never in want. He is far more than the warrior the redcoats say he is."

Clay said nothing, letting Heckewelder talk on while he grappled with the dire ramifications of this new truth. Keturah had been taken from one of the leading men among the Lenape, a chief well known among Indians and whites for his intense resistance to white encroachment. It did not bode well for them.

"May I ask if you had children while in captivity?" Heckewelder said next.

Another pause. "A son." Again Keturah was visibly moved. "Taken by the white man's disease. The running sores sickness."

Smallpox. Another strike against them. A wife lost. And a son. Clay drew on his pipe, the stem clamped between his back teeth, remembering Tamanen's strength of will and depth of feeling. If he had wept when Clay was returned to the whites by force years before, what would be the toll of a missing wife and lost son?

"I wish I could restore him to you," Heckewelder told her. "I fully believe your child is now healed and in heaven."

Keturah's chest rose and fell with a suppressed sigh. The anguish of her loss seemed to gather round them like a coming storm.

Clay was relieved when Heckewelder changed course. "It is said you are a healer of some renown . . ."

Clay was no longer listening, still mired in the truth he'd just learned. Did Tamanen know of Keturah's whereabouts? If so, why had he not struck Swan Station and taken Keturah back? The heavy presence along the Buckhannon, the Indian sign about Swan Station, seemed to speak to the Lenape being aware of where Tamanen's wife had been taken. Or mayhap his own fears were drawing false conclusions.

Would Keturah return to her Indian family in time? Countless captives, once redeemed, escaped and returned to their Indian lives at the first opportunity. He'd taken her passivity for being here as willingness. Cooperation. Not once had he asked her how she felt about matters. He had no inkling. He likely never would.

One thing was certain. She would be safer among the Moravian brethren than here. The praying Indians, with their neutral stance and their widespread reputation for peace, would help protect her. She would be among Lenape she knew. A Moravian settlement was the ideal place for her white kin to reclaim her. And it would remove the threat she might be to the Swans and any of the settlers against whom a raid might be aimed.

But would Keturah go with Heckewelder willingly? Or would Clay as fort commander have to order her to go?

Tessa endured Hester's bossing, helping prepare the noon meal. Her high feeling turned slightly skittish as the morning wore on and the blockhouse door remained shut. Something would come of this meeting with Keturah. 'Twas not a simple matter. Heckewelder had journeyed a long way for a reason.

As much as she wanted to return to the time before Keturah was taken, there was no going back. The Braams were gone. They would likely never resettle along the Buckhannon, so beautiful yet treacherous. They'd moved on. And their eldest daughter had moved on too, becoming a far different woman than the child they'd raised. Keturah's years as an Indian had forever altered her and everyone around her.

Any rosy notions about a love match between Keturah and one of her brothers had turned to ashes. To think she'd once considered Jasper, whose animosity still festered. It had Tessa examining her own attitudes and prejudices. She continued to wear the beaded tie on her braid, but was that not aggravating his mind-set? Making him more hard-hearted? The feeling betwixt her and Jasper, once easy and affectionate, was now roiling and rebellious, and it grieved her to the heart.

"You're woolgathering something awful." Hester stood beside Tessa as she worked the hand mill. "What's this business between Keturah and the Moravian and the colonel, I'm wondering?"

Tessa ground the corn more vigorously. "If we were meant to know, we'd be in that blockhouse."

"Well, that doesn't stop my ears from burning."

"Patience, Auntie." Tessa kept her own temper. "How much bread do you reckon we'll need?"

"Plenty." Hester eyed the mound of meal. "A peck should do it. I'll go tend the meat while you finish."

Now at almost midday, the buffalo roasting outside Hester's door would be done and falling off the bone. Tessa began making corncakes, praying the meeting with Heckewelder would bear fruit. For all she knew he'd brought news of Keturah's Lenape family.

As she thought it, the blockhouse door groaned open at last. Keturah emerged into stark sunlight, blinking at the glare before ducking into Hester's cabin. Tessa greeted her, gesturing toward a pitcher of spring water. As Keturah poured herself a drink, she kept her eyes down, cloaked in silence. She looked distressingly spent, even wan. To fill the stilted silence, Tessa hummed a hymn.

In time they assembled around Hester's table, Clay at the head, Brother Heckewelder and his party filling the other places. Naturally, Hester contrived to plant Tessa as close to the colonel as she could, directly to his right. Amusement overrode her irritation at Hester's continued scheming. Did Clay mind?

Forking a few bites of the succulent meat, she watched the butter melt atop her corn-cake, wishing someone would talk once Heckewelder said grace. No one did. Flies darted through the open door and window, a welcome breeze lifting the edge of the linen cloth with which Hester had dressed up the rough table.

"Bountiful dinner," Heckewelder said at last with an appreciative nod aimed at Hester and Tessa.

"Always is, this time of year," Hester told him, passing him another helping of green beans and potatoes. "Soon we'll have plenty of roasting ears."

"Thankfully, crops are plentiful at Bethlehem. We have common gardens of several acres, a church, and a schoolhouse."

Tessa voiced a secret hope. "We've need of such here. A preacher and a teacher both."

"In time, mayhap," he replied with a reassuring smile. "Once the western border settles down."

"Peace might be had sooner if such things were in place." Hester rose to replenish pewter tankards. "I'd sure like to witness both before I go to glory."

Clay seemed lost in thought, saying little, his steady presence adding to the swelling pleasure Tessa felt to be gathered around this bountiful table. At meal's end, as she anticipated coffee and pie, he scrambled her composure when he set down his fork and said, "A word with you, Miss Swan."

A word? Hester all but crowed when Clay rose from the table and escorted Tessa to the blockhouse. She went in ahead of him, sure every settlement wag in the fort had their eye on the blockhouse door, if not privy to the conversation within.

Standing by the fireless hearth, he rested an arm along the mantel while she sat in the Windsor chair facing the andirons. The air was still cloudy with smoke, the seats arranged as they'd been for their meeting with Keturah.

"You need to be made aware of some things." His voice lowered to that measured tone he used when he didn't want to be overheard. "And since you're one of the few women here who has the gift of discretion, I'll say it plain."

She folded her hands atop her aproned lap. "Speak plainly then."

"Miss Braam is wed. To a leading Lenape war chief."

Her mouth went slack. Keturah wed? To a . . . war chief? If he'd struck her with the fire tongs she'd have been less upended.

"She had a métis child, a son, who died of what sounds like smallpox."

Wonderment engulfed her. For a moment she sat mute, trying to make this stunning piece of Keturah's past fit into the puzzle of her Indianness.

"Her safety is in question, given her Lenape tie to a war chief. I have reason to believe he and the Lenape may know or will learn of her whereabouts, which puts your family at risk in the event he tries to retake her."

Her thoughts spun back through the time Keturah had been with them, sifting through the days, hours. "She's often alone in the woods gathering her medicines. Seems like there's been ample opportunity to reclaim her. Or for her to run if she had a mind to."

"She's made no effort to do so? Given you any reason to believe she wants to be elsewhere?"

That faraway part of Keturah she sensed so strongly at times — was this because a large part of her was with her husband, who was still living, or with her child, forever gone? "Betimes she seems distant. Like she's just bodily present. But never has she given us reason to believe she wants to be somewhere else."

"Heckewelder has offered her asylum at Bethlehem in eastern Pennsylvania or the mission the Moravians hope to establish in the Tuscarawas Valley further west."

"Sounds sensible. If you heard from her Braam kin, you'd send word to her there, aye?"

"Aye, but the hard truth is, some don't want redeemed captives back. They're considered befouled, especially once they learn they had an Indian family. Reunions can be agonizing for both sides."

Did he speak from experience? Her gaze held his. "You know it by heart. I can tell you do."

"Aye."

How would Keturah's family react once they learned of her return, if they ever did? Did an Indian husband carry more clout than her own white kin? "Would it not be wise to ask Keturah where she wants to be? With her Lenape husband or here?"

"So, you would recognize a marriage between a savage and a settler."

"Why wouldn't I?"

He looked more pleased than surprised by her vehemence, as if she'd passed some test most failed. Did he think her like Jasper, blinded by mean-spiritedness?

Lord, nay.

"Is that any different than marriages made hereabouts without benefit of a preacher?" she asked. "Those settlers who come together and wait to make it legal?"

"Your logic is flawed, but I admire your spirit."

"Indian ways can't be compared to white ways, true. But surely if Keturah cares for this man, she should be allowed to return to him if she chooses."

"An unholy union, by white standards. And almost certain death."

She squared her shoulders. "Are all military men so grim, Colonel?"

His sorrow tempered his harshness. "When you've seen as much bloodshed as I have, there's little room for any mawkishness."

Something kindled in her, a desire to soften that side of him. To take the terrible things he'd known and turn them into something else entirely, to give him reason to rejoice. Or maybe that was the Lord's doing entirely, bringing beauty from ashes.

"I'll miss her if she goes. I never stopped missing her after she was taken." *Though she's not the same, nor am I.* "Keturah was the sister I never had."

"There's Ruth." His voice had gentled. He seemed moved enough by her words to try to console her. "You're oft in her company."

"Ruth, aye." Caught in a rare moment of

vulnerability, she weighed sharing her heart. Would such a man understand? "There are friends, and then there are bosom friends. I believe as Scripture says, that there are those rare times your spirit is knit together with another's and you love them like your own soul. That's how I've always felt about Keturah."

He pushed away from the hearth, and before she realized what was happening, he'd dropped to one knee and enfolded one of her hands in both of his. Her heart turned over. His eyes — oh, his beautiful, marbled eyes — seemed soft as candle wax. They told her what words and the touch of his hands did not, that he did indeed understand her, or wanted to. And that he knew she would miss Keturah if she went away again, but in a way altogether different than before.

"You truly have Keturah's well-being at heart. I sought your counsel because of it." His thumb caressed the back of her work-roughened hand. "Will you stay here while I ask her whether she wants to go with Heckewelder or return to the Lenape?"

"All right," she answered.

He let go of her hand and stood, as if pondering just what he would say to Keturah, or maybe giving Tessa time to collect herself. Her gaze roamed this masculine den of his, the log walls bearing maps and furs and weapons, and finally snagged on an odd strip of bark rife with Indian symbols. Flying arrows, a fleeing woman. Despite its simple, maybe hasty rendering, her soul went still.

Before she could ask about it, Clay strode to the door and called Keturah to come over from Hester's cabin. Looking more at ease than when she'd first left the blockhouse, Keturah smiled at Tessa and took the chair nearest her. Slowly Clay stated her choices. Join the Moravians at one of their settlements while awaiting word from her kin, or return to the Lenape.

Keturah showed no surprise. Maybe Heckewelder's coming had prepared her for such a choice. "This Blackcoat — Heckewelder — will bring light to the True People along the Tuscarawas?"

"A new mission, aye, deeper into Indian country than any white man has gone before."

"The Blackcoat has a warrior's spirit then."

"God goes with him," Tessa said, silencing the voice that said these Moravians were more foolhardy than brave.

"Then I would like to go too," Keturah

said without hesitation. "If it is true what the Blackcoat says, and my child is with God, then I want to stay close to Him. To the light. When I die, I want to see my son."

Again Tessa bent her mind to the Tuscarawas, when what she wanted for her friend was the far safer, established Bethlehem.

Clay set his pipe aside. "What does Tamanen think about the Blackcoats? Their talk of light and peace?"

Keturah's lovely features darkened. "Every praying Indian is one less warrior, my husband says. But if he knew our son lives with the Father, he might listen more to the Blackcoats."

Knotting her hands in her aproned lap, Tessa fixed her gaze on Clay's boots, letting go of Keturah bit by bit. Her prayers would include Tamanen now, not only Keturah. Though she was still unsteady from the shock of learning about a Lenape husband, she sensed Tamanen cared for Keturah and she for him.

"Very well then." Pushing away from the mantel, Clay gave Tessa a last look. "Cutright has more goods that might serve Miss Braam well on the trail. I'll talk with Heckewelder while you help provision her."

The simple task seemed an honor. Together she and Keturah left the blockhouse and crossed the common beneath heavy clouds amassing like cannonballs, the air heavy with the scent of coming rain. A squealing piglet ran past, several gleeful children in pursuit. Bestirred by Heckewelder's talk of peaceful times to come, Tessa tried to picture a schoolhouse, a church. Would the Buckhannon ever know such noble things?

"Welcome, ladies," Cutright greeted them. "What do you buy?"

"Keturah needs provisioning for a long journey," Tessa told him, "at Colonel Tygart's request."

"Very well."

Keturah began examining the shelves more intently. True to Clay's word, here were ivory combs and printed fabrics, candied lime peel, and wool blankets not to be had on muster day. Though Tessa had never made a journey of any kind, she had helped Jasper prepare and so gathered those essentials, with a few extra items sure to please a woman. Keturah stayed near the stroud, that coarse woolen cloth known to the Indian trade, till Tessa took it from her hands.

" 'Tis yours."

Their task done, they watched as Cutright entered the items into his thick ledger.

'Twould be a long, risky journey, but at least provisions were in place. Tessa took some comfort in that.

New purchases in arm, they went out, nearly bumping into Maddie as they cleared the doorway.

"Never a dull day at Fort Tygart," Maddie said. "Clay said you'd be in directly. Spending the night too?"

"Likely," Tessa said. 'Twas her next hope in a long line of them. Another private moonlit talk by the fort's garden wouldn't be amiss even in the rain. "You look well, Maddie."

"No longer sick to my shoes, aye," Maddie returned with considerably more sass than when they'd last seen her. "Eating like a farmhand too. Just ask Jude."

"How long now?" Tessa asked, finding it impossible to tell with Maddie so slim.

"About Christmastime to my reckoning. Granny Sykes will be on hand. We're prayin' for a mild winter."

Tessa refrained from saying their border winters were wicked, the fort's mud ankle deep before freezing in an onslaught of heavy snows. But surely Maddie knew, trail worn as she was.

"Keep your baby abed with you," Keturah was saying. "Drink stinging-nettle tea."

The sorrow in Keturah's words lanced Tessa's heart. Her advice was born of a mother's love, no doubt.

"I'm glad for these high walls after all the forays I've spent outside them." Maddie's gaze lifted to the pickets. "Jude's crafting a cradle and Hester's making a proper feather tick."

"I've started some garments to give you," Tessa told her. "So small I can hardly see my stitches."

"Obliged," Maddie said, her gaze trailing after the children still in pursuit of the piglet. "Soon our babe will be underfoot and raising dust with the likes o' them." She rested a hand on her slowly rounding middle. "Now look smart, here comes Clay."

Her back to him, Tessa made peace with her bittersweet feelings, preparing to bid goodbye to Keturah if that's what the moment called for.

Lord, whatever happens, let it be right and good for Keturah.

Clay came to a stop just outside their circle, his words for Keturah. "You'll leave out in the morning for the Ohio country, ferrying across at Swan Station, where you'll collect your belongings."

One final eve at the fort, then. Keturah nodded as a warm rain began falling, giving a smile of genuine joy in the gloom of the waning afternoon. Maddie showed no surprise, aware Heckewelder's arrival spelled some change.

"You'll be a welcome addition to their party, understanding the Lenape like you do," Clay continued. "And if word comes from your kin, I'll see that it reaches the Tuscarawas."

They scattered, each to their respective cabins. Tessa and Keturah headed for Hester's.

Suppertime came, and Tessa helped Hester serve the colonel and Heckewelder's party, now including Keturah, in the blockhouse. As they refilled tankards and dishes, Tessa listened to them discuss the coming journey, Clay giving insight about rivers and ranges to cross and trails to be chary of.

Mindful of their early rising, Keturah sought her loft bed while Tessa began reading from her book of poetry and Hester turned to her handwork. The rain began an outright drumbeat, the deserted common soon the color and consistency of molasses, dousing Tessa's hopes along with it. She and Clay wouldn't take a turn outside on such a night.

Her voice was hardly heard above the downpour.

"My days have been so wondrous free,
The little birds that fly
With careless ease from tree to tree,
Were but as bless'd as I."

"What foolishness," Hester barked from her corner. "My ears cannot abide such sentiment."

Which is probably why you remain unwed.

Tessa bit her tongue against the hasty retort and paged to another bit of verse. Surely this was more to Hester's liking.

"Hence loathed melancholy,
Of Cerberus and blackest midnight born,
In stygian cave forlorn,
'Mongst horrid shapes, and shrieks, and
    sights unholy."

"Easier on the ears," Hester said, jabbing her needle through the cloth. "And fits the sorry weather."

Tessa paused. Lantern light cut through the blockhouse's chinking and gilded the open door. Voices carried, robust, even merry, Clay's among them. Would he soon step outside that door and make his nightly rounds as he usually did? The fort cat, a tabby no one claimed but all petted, yowled and swished its plumy tail in the doorway

283

as if seeking shelter.

Hester yawned. Seconds spun forward. Clay emerged from the blockhouse, hat pulled low against the damp, tin lantern in hand to light his way.

Without so much as a glance toward Hester's.

Watching him, Tessa held tightly to the memory of the man on bended knee in the blockhouse. That was the Clay she loved. The Clay who had been buried beneath layers of upheaval and hurt, who seemed at times so distant, as if he didn't quite know what to do with her. Who raised her hopes one minute, then dashed them to the floor the next.

Her hungry heart skipped after him.

21

By the time they'd reached Big Sand Run a few leagues beyond Fort Tygart, the night's rain had pushed farther west, and an odd south wind rustled the thick July leaves. Jude rode silently behind Clay as the sun cracked open bright as an egg yolk on the eastern horizon. Already they'd come across plentiful sign since leaving the fort, confirming the latest scouting report. The territory seemed to be swarming yet the Indians stayed hidden, tomahawks sheathed.

Half a dozen spies had ridden out at daybreak, scattering in different directions. Jude was assigned to the gaps and low places in the mountains for thirty miles or so, to a point where he'd meet with spies from the next fort. But the well-placed plan didn't give Clay any ease.

"Don't get near enough to danger that you can punch it with your ramrod," Clay told him as they forded yet another stream. "I just need fresh word of any movement or action."

"Aye." Jude's bay horse snorted, nearly masking his assent. "Glad I am of the rain. Otherwise we'd sound like buffalo coming through a canebrake with the woods so dry."

Clay gave a nod, recalling Maddie's long look at Jude as they'd left the fort. "I've a mind to keep you forted up. Or assign you to the settlement harvest."

"Naw, Clay. Lord knows I'm always itching to roam. Soon enough I'll be tied to home with winter and a baby comin'. And me still feeling like Methuselah. For now, I need to be free of fort walls."

"Take heed then. There's no replacing you."

"A babe needs a father, amen. See you at week's end." With that, Jude was off, eclipsed by the deep woods.

Clay pressed on, skirting the Buckhannon as it flowed north, thinking once again how well suited it was for a gristmill, not only a ferry. He'd seen Tessa laboriously grinding a great quantity of corn with a hand mill outside Hester's, no small feat. With so many brothers to manage the labor of building and so much riverfront acreage, a gristmill seemed a worthy pursuit. Mayhap on his own land along the Monongahela someday . . .

His thoughts canted backwards, not forward. He'd not bade Tessa good night once Heckewelder and his party returned to their blockhouse quarters. He'd simply made his rounds despite the downpour, passing by Hester's at the last, half hoping a candle would still be burning. If so, he might have stopped by that unshuttered window. The temptation had been just about more than he could stand, hastening his step as he checked the horses and magazine, the watch and both gates. As he finished, his disappointment at finding that light out was keen enough that he'd fallen asleep far later than he wanted. Tessa Swan even stormed his dreams.

His double-mindedness gnawed at him. With her continually in reach, he'd lost his edge. He'd come here without any ties or motivations besides manning a garrison in the midst of an ongoing border war. A besotted commander was unfit for the job.

Back off, Tygart.

Despite that, he'd wanted to escort Tessa home this morning, a fool's errand when she already had her brothers and Heckewelder's party as escort. So he'd left out ahead of daybreak when she was just stirring. In the cabin next to him to boot, hair streaming down behind closed doors, in her smallclothes. *That* contemplation was enough to drive a man mad.

He bent his mind to the trail once again, coming to a deep gorge rimmed with hemlock, the water snow-white as it twisted and foamed over boulders on its journey to the west fork of the Monongahela River. How he wished he could cleanse his own thoughts, wash his mind free of Tessa in kind, and return to the untethered man he'd been. Yet when he was near her, his resolve crumbled like a sandy wall.

He tried to take a step back, look at her dispassionately. Raised with so many brothers, she bore that unflinchingly honest edge considered unbecoming in most women, yet it only turned her more fetching. No powder. No pomp. Just unadorned decency. And a bone-deep beauty beginning with her startling violet-blue eyes.

Was he wrong to pray that the Lord would remove this ill-timed attraction and his growing need for her?

He'd been moved to his boots when she'd joined hands with him across the breakfast table that May morn. Praying seemed as natural as breathing to her. Only she'd asked him to say grace, making him resurrect the long-forgotten blessing of his child-

288

hood that may well have fallen from his father's lips. It only added to his yearning for a family to call his own.

And then yesterday, alone with her in the blockhouse, he'd been so taken by what she'd said about one's soul being knit to another's that he'd opened the Bible Heckewelder left him and tried to find the passage she spoke of. At midnight he'd put it down with the hope he'd return to it tonight.

Even now, sunk in reflection, he wasn't fully present. The faint tinkle of a bell carried on the rising wind, a warning he might have missed. Before it faded, he'd slid off Bolt. Up this high, with cabins far below, the sound didn't ring true. 'Twas a favorite trick of Indians to steal from belled livestock and lure settlers near enough to ambush.

Had he and Tamanen not done it?

He gripped his rifle harder, the memory carrying a lick of regret. Keturah had married well within the tribe. Tamanen of the Wolf Clan was well chosen. Mayhap her desire to go with Heckewelder was founded on a desire to reunite with Tamanen. Clay's own marriage had been thwarted by the treaty that took him away from the Lenape, yet his thoughts stretched back to a misty memory of the woman his Indian mother hoped he would choose. Ganoshowanna. Falling Water. What had become of her?

The bell ceased tinkling. The sigh of the wind was the only sound other than a hawk's cry. He got back into the saddle and pressed higher, harder, rocks scattering beneath Bolt's clambering hooves into the streambed far below.

No matter how hard he rode, how far he roamed, Tessa followed.

Without Keturah the cabin seemed less like home. The time she'd been with them had added a new depth and dimension keenly felt in her absence. Pondering it, Tessa gathered the rest of the melons by herself, sitting down beside the burgeoning wooden sled when done and allowing herself a moment's melancholy.

This morning when she'd awakened to that empty trundle bed, she'd lain very still, listening to Ma's usual noises at the hearth. The thunk of wood added to the cook fire. The dry scent of toasted bread. And finally, coffee, its fragrance filling the cabin's far corners, teasing her brothers awake in the adjoining blockhouse.

This morn there was no sleepy *wëli kishku,* which surely meant good morning or good day. What she most remembered were

Keturah's last Lenape words, which Heckewelder had translated when he'd seen her chin trembling as she and Keturah embraced.

Làpich knewël. Goodbye. I will see you again.

Would she? Keturah was going so far. There were countless dangers, even though she was dressed again as a Lenape woman in the clothes she'd abandoned upon coming here.

"Take care, Keturah. Our door is always open to you." Tessa's words were shaky as a surge of emotion threatened her stoicism. "There's been no friend to me like you. I expect there never will be."

Keturah gave a tremulous smile suffused with joy and heartache as she stepped away from Tessa's embrace. The hide pouch about her neck bulged. The old doll?

Tessa took a long look at her, praying the memory held. As she watched Heckewelder's party vanish into the dense woods, all her hopes seemed to vanish with them.

Keturah did not look back. *That* tore Tessa's heart in two. 'Twas all she could do not to run after her. Gone was her beloved childhood friend. Again. While her family looked on, all but Jasper, she'd fisted her hands at her sides and set her jaw till it ached. Ma cried openly, dabbing at her eyes with her apron, while Zadock seemed the most bewildered, finding the woman he'd hoped would look his way instead wed to a warrior who could lift his scalp.

Keturah's going left more than an empty place at table, one less hand to lighten the work. It seemed a small death, reminding Tessa of Pa's and the bottomless well of emptiness he'd left behind. Even Snuff seemed mournful, ears drooping. How she wished she was more like Ross, face turned toward the sun.

"Don't tie yourself in knots," he said quietly as they lost sight of Heckewelder's party and resumed their chores. "Look how the Lord provided a companion in that Mingo woman. And how Heckewelder talks Indian like he was born to it. Could be a sight worse. But I'll miss Keturah, I'll give you that."

Ross always dwelt on the light side, his faith practical, almost childlike, forever mining the good out of the darkest depths. Even when Pa passed he'd received a thrashing from Jasper when he'd said with raw honesty, "Just think on it, Pa's gout don't vex him now that he's in his eternity box."

Tessa had chuckled through her tears at the time, earning a stern look from the rest of them, but what Ross said was true then and now. Keturah could not have better company than the Moravians, no matter where she roamed. And surely heaven was the best remedy for what ailed Pa, or anyone else, for that matter.

"I pray we see her again," was all Ma said before seeking the solace of the garden.

Recalling it now, Tessa shut her eyes and tried to make peace with it all, only to ponder matters more sore than satisfying.

Like Clay.

Someday, maybe, she'd work up the nerve to speak his name. She'd thought to say it when they left the fort yesterday morning. But the west blockhouse yawned empty and Bolt was missing from the corral. Maddie told her he'd gone out on a scout. Though Clay never left the fort for long, he did take a turn like the rest of his spies. Somehow it comforted her knowing he was out there somewhere. Even now he might be near at hand.

Her eyes roved the tasseling cornstalks, her whole being wishing he'd materialize before her. Their occasional encounters always left her craving more. They'd begun an uncertain dance, she and Clay, and she was unsure of the next step. How did a couple arrive at courtship? When did a man and a woman move beyond a very public muster-day kiss? Maybe she was making too much of matters. His hot-cold regard of her left her in a continual muddle.

Slowly she stood, a bit stiff from sitting so long. Woolgathering, as Hester called it, left her forgetting the time. Taking the hemp rope, she began pulling the sled with its load of melons toward home, the sun at her back.

Lord, let Keturah find happiness. And let Clay find his way to me in Your time.

Clay sat down at Maddie's table, the fare rivaling Hester's. Betimes his blockhouse quarters yawned too empty. Hester needed a rest, so he sometimes came here, just as hungry for good company. Maddie and Jude's tiny cabin was spare but as tidy and clean as Maddie could make it. The finished cradle rested in a corner, crafted from walnut, awaiting winter's use. Jude had always been a hand with wood.

"Have another helping, Clay." Like it or not, Maddie replenished his plate, mounding it high with the first of the corn she'd taken from the cob and fried with butter and sweet milk.

"Thought you said your mother was a laundress," Clay said between mouthfuls. "How'd you become so good a cook?"

"Helps to have a big fort garden," she returned with a smile as she finished frying the last of the catfish. "And a husband handy with a hook."

"Sure beats being on the trail." Jude pulled a fish bone from between his teeth. "Though I did partake of a fine slab of blackberry pie at Cox's Station near the tail end of my last scout."

"Berry, you say? The berries are drying up on the vine, Hester tells me." Maddie gestured to the rafters, where a berry basket Keturah had made hung empty.

The sight put him in mind of Heckewelder, how far their party had traveled. Though Keturah was no longer at Swan Station, Indian sign abounded up and down the border, confirmed by the string of forts and stations. Should he heed the growing cry for reinforcements, more soldiers? If Fort Tygart was undermanned and fell . . .

Maddie's voice drew him back to the present. "Wonder what's happening a bit south of here?"

He chuckled. "Just say it plain, Maddie."

"All right, I will. How is the lovely Miss Swan? I see you're wearing a pair of the stockings she made you."

"You don't miss much."

"I was trained to keep a sharp eye, being

a camp follower with the army. Same as you, remember."

"Fair enough." Clay set down his fork. "I haven't seen Miss Swan in a fortnight or better, not since Heckewelder's leaving."

"Shame on you, Clayton Tygart." Her aggravation always warranted the use of his full name. "Here it is late July and the belle of the Buckhannon is languishing."

Jude gave a low whistle. "You sure use some hoity-toity words."

Maddie shot Clay another beseeching look.

"Once the harvest is in, things might be different." Clay knew his noncommittal remarks earned him no favor with Maddie no matter the reason or season.

"Well, Colonel Tygart," she said in her gruffest tone, "I urge you to be a part of the guard you assigned at Swan Station once the harvest commences."

He winked. "Is that an order, Maddie?"

"As close as I can get to ordering you, aye." With that, she whisked his empty plate away. "Strike while the iron's hot, as they say?"

"Winter's a mite better for courting."

"Hmm." She began stacking plates. "Winter, my eye, when the snow's so high you can't even get the gates open, much less shuffle south."

He chuckled despite himself. Maddie meant well, but he didn't need her meddling any more than he needed Hester's matchmaking. "All in good time."

"*Good* time?" She arched her brow at him. "You —"

"If I could get a word in . . ." Jude winked at her, his voice taking on the gravity of a preacher's. "Such talk puts me in mind of what ol' Daniel said. All you need for happiness is a good gun, a good horse, and a good wife."

Maddie paused. "Boone said that?"

"To my hearin', aye, right before we buried Braddock in '55." Jude sat back, eyeing Clay with intent. "You just lack a good wife, is all. Now hear me out. You been stewing about all that Indian sign hereabouts. Stands to reason you'd have one less worry if you just married Miss Swan and brought her to live here at the fort."

Maddie tossed Clay an I-told-you-so look and poured coffee from a kettle. "Too hot for coffee, but here it is."

Clay took the dark brew, adding a piece of hammered sugar from Cutright's store. Despite his resistance, the teasing and talk, their concern for his happiness was genuine and appreciated. "I'll keep in mind your advice. But since it's my *wife* . . ." Even the word sat oddly on his tongue. "And because I'm here to hold the frontier from ene—" he couldn't use the word *enemies* though he heard it oft enough — "from Indian outrages, matters of the heart seem frivolous."

That was as simple as he could state it. Though he wouldn't speak ill of the dead, he had been one of the officers who'd rolled the heavy wagons over Braddock's grave beneath the road they'd traveled in retreat. And the few terse, whispered words among the officers about General Braddock were seared to memory.

A man of weak understanding and very indolent . . . Slave to his passions, women and wine.

Let no one say that Clay Tygart, though a humble, near half-breed commander of a rude fort in no-man's-land, was a man of weak understanding and enslaved to his passions.

22

Standing on the edge of the Swan cornfield ringed with armed men, Tessa paused to watch the work. So many laborers made short shrift of the midsummer harvest. Her small part was helping Ma bring the gleaners the noon meal and enough switchel to drink. Hatted and sweating heavily, these settlement men banded together to cut and bundle the sheaves.

Later, she would work alongside her brothers to pull the blades from the nearly naked stalks, bundling them once again for those lean winter months when the livestock needed fodder. White dent corn was her favorite, sweet and full of milk. The delectable ears were left to harden and dry till first frost. For now, her brothers kept up a robust debate about storing the crop in the corn house they'd built of notched logs near the springhouse.

"I say we pick by day and husk by night,"

Lemuel told them during the noon rest.

"I beg to differ," Zadock replied. "Pa always said it's best left in the husk. So long as you store it dry, it won't go to ruin."

"I'm most worried about the winter wheat. Should have been sown between corn rows like Pa told of overmountain." Jasper kicked at a field stone. "Mayhap we should consider the flour trade, grind our neighbors' corn by gristmill. The river's calling for it right where it forks into Cane Creek."

"Become a millwright?" Cyrus's brow lifted. "Seems sensible. Plenty of stones to be had for the foundation just upriver. Highly profitable enterprise, Tygart says."

Hiding a smile, Tessa gathered up the empty baskets from the nooning. Tygart this, Tygart that. You'd think he was part of the Trinity the way her brothers revered him. Squinting, she raised a hand to the sun to shield her eyes as she turned toward its golden gaze.

She kept to the edge of the field, hemmed in by the armed guard and the reapers, her arms ringed with empty baskets so cleverly crafted by Keturah. How she missed her old friend, the work of her hands an ongoing reminder.

Nearer the cabin, a crow's raucous squawk greeted her. With a practiced eye she probed the outbuildings and cabin for anything amiss. With so many working the corn, the place stood unguarded. Oddly empty. Even Snuff had gone to the fields.

She stopped at the well. The cold limestone water made a fine drink. Lowering the pail, she ignored the slight chill that skittered through her like a touch of winter on a summer's day. Halfway to the bottom, the rope stilled in her hand. Gooseflesh rose on her arms. Fear was never far away. She'd felt its cold clutch since childhood. Till now that fear had to do with other people. Keturah. Pa. But this . . .

This felt near. Personal.

Lord, help Thou me.

Her hands shook. The breath she was holding burned her chest. All at once she let go of the rope, hearing the splash and plop of the pail as it smacked the water below. Whirling, she faced whatever was at her back. But no arrow whistled through the air, no upraised tomahawk. Just deep-green woods all a-rustle in the wind.

Relief jellied her legs, yet the chary feeling remained. How had it been for Pa that fatal day? Had he known the same terror, that deep-rooted sense something was amiss, before he was cut down?

"Miss Swan?"

She swirled round again, so fast her skirts ballooned. Still in the grip of something she couldn't name, she faced the man she couldn't quite push from her conscience.

Clay slid to the ground from Bolt's back. His own expression, ever watchful, turned more so in response to hers. He wasn't looking at her but in back of her now, at the westernmost woods. Slowly he walked to the well, rifle in hand. For the first time she saw a tomahawk dangling from his belt. And a long knife. Her own gun, carelessly left inside on so busy a day, was pointedly amiss.

"You all right?" he asked her.

"I am now." Odd how a body found relief in company. The skittery feeling began to retreat, Clay's presence solid and reassuring.

They stood without moving, the well between them. "Go ahead and draw your water." His voice was so hushed she sensed he felt what she felt, that same nameless caution.

She returned to drawing her water. The bucket resurfaced, and at last she had her drink.

He winked, dispelling the remaining tension. "Adam's ale."

The old name for well water made her smile as she handed him the gourd dipper. Behind him, Bolt began to rip and tear at a particularly rich patch of weeds. Horses, of all creatures, were especially nervy when danger neared. This stallion seemed to have nary a care.

Clay hung the gourd dipper from a rusted nail. "How goes the harvest?"

"Well enough." She began picking up the baskets she'd discarded in the grass. "I'm surprised to see you . . ." Her voice trailed away. Surely a man who paid her any mind wouldn't let so much time pass.

"I regret that." He removed his hat, the wind smoothing out the dark strands, like she longed to do with her fingers. "A harried season."

He spoke the truth. She'd seen the ledgers and posts on his desk, the endless interruptions, his never-ending turn at watch, the steady stream of folks in and out of the fort. Far more.

"Ever think of making a better life beyond those pickets?" she asked, straightening.

"Aye, Tessa."

Something melted inside her. She'd not had to say his name first. He'd said hers. And the way he said it . . . soft and gentle, almost like a caress. Like he'd reached out and placed his hand at the small of her back. But he hadn't touched her, least not with his hands, just his eyes. They held hers with an intensity that forever banished any doubt as to his feelings.

Still, she was cautious. "I suppose you're here for the harvest, Colonel."

"In time. But first I —" He was still looking at her, the warmth in his voice another caress. "I want to hear you say my name."

"Well, fancy that. I've always wanted to call you *Clay,* Clay."

He smiled then, the broadest she'd yet seen, his teeth strikingly white in his deeply tanned face. He even looked a bit bashful, as if this was all new and untried, like a first dance or a new suit of clothes.

The sun ducked behind a cloud, and she gestured to a bench beneath the shade of a chestnut. "Care to sit?"

She stored her baskets in the nearby shed, then returned to find he'd sat down, when she'd expected he'd head straight to the fields. Now every thought in her head emptied. She took a seat beside him, so close her skirts brushed his leg.

"You missing Keturah?" he asked, resting his rifle across his knees.

"Nary a minute goes by that I don't think of her." *Though I think of you more.*

"They should have reached the Tuscara-was by now."

Should have. No promises.

"How will we ever know?" she wondered aloud.

"Pay them a call at some peaceful juncture in future."

"So far," she lamented. "A hundred miles or better?" *With you, I'd brave it. Especially if we went east.*

"A day's walk, aye," he said.

Her smile was wry. "You've got sturdier moccasins than I."

"Beautiful country. Takes the tired right out of you."

She looked to her lap, smoothing a crease in her apron. "Still no word from her kin?"

"Nay. There might be none. I believe she'll be more content with the Moravians."

She swallowed. Dared. "How was it for you when you were taken and returned?"

A pause. "Harsh."

She waited for more, his one-word answers wearing a discontented hole in her. "You never speak of it . . ."

"I favor the Lenape custom of not discussing the dead." Even though they sat talking quietly, his gaze made a repeated sweep of the clearing and edges of the forest. "Let the past stay in the past."

His simple explanation only stoked her curiosity, the yearning to know more, to tread the untraveled, untrammeled parts of him.

"I felt the same after Pa died. But I find it helps not to skirt around him, not tread too carefully. I want to remember, if only the good."

"I'd like to have met him." He traced the scrolled engraving on his rifle's brass mountings with a callused forefinger. "Which of your brothers is most like him?"

"Ross," she said without thought. "Pa rarely spoke a surly word. He stayed on the sunny side. Ross is the same."

"And you? Or are you a bit waspish like Hester?"

"You tell me," she replied, raising her chin to look at him.

"I could put you to the test, as Daniel Boone did with Rebecca."

"What means you?"

"He mislaid his hunting knife and made a tear in her cambric apron."

"On purpose?"

"Aye, to try her temper."

"The rascal!"

"Nary a complaint did she make."

"I'd likely have stayed a spinster."

His low chuckle lent to her warm skin. "You might have mimicked Hester, aye. But as it stands, there's hope."

"Hope?"

His decisive nod ensnared her further. She couldn't look away, captured by his face in profile with all its handsome lines and angles, the heavily fringed lashes, darker even than his charcoal hair.

"I know a man who's right fond of you."

Surprise pinched her. "And who might that be?"

He hesitated as if trying to collect the details. "New to the settlement. Stands over six feet tall. Not much to look at —"

"Says who?"

"Hester," he returned with another chuckle. "But he's a quick study. From parts east. Outshoots any gun along the Buckhannon, if not the border."

"I'd be pleased to meet him."

"All right then." He pulled himself to his feet, rifle dangling from a large hand, leaving her hanging just like he'd done after that muster-day kiss.

Reaching out, she took his other hand in her own and gave it a little squeeze before releasing it reluctantly. "Give him my regards then."

He smiled down at her before retrieving his hat in the grass. It looked in need of a good washing, though the rest of him was tidy, his once-bewhiskered jaw smooth as

307

newly tanned buckskin. "Better hie to the fields."

Jasper was approaching in the distance, the ball of a two o'clock sun behind him. Clay turned his back on her. Called his horse. She had no clue as to when she'd see him again. Here was ample opportunity to stake his claim, yet . . .

"What are you afraid of, Clay?" she called after him.

He swung round, pinning her with that startling gaze. "You been talking to Maddie?"

"Nay," she said. What did Maddie have to do with it?

Touching his hat brim as if signaling an end to the conversation, he kept on, pausing briefly to speak to Jasper on his way.

"Is there a wedding in the offing, little sister?" Jasper said once Clay was out of earshot.

She stared at Clay's back. "Hardly."

"Well, Ma may have a suitor, if you don't."

She followed him to the barn, bemused. "Where is Ma?"

"At the edge of the cornfield, courting." He sunk his axe into a chopping block. "Old Eb."

"The widower Westfall? I wondered why she was tarrying in the fields."

Jasper seemed pleased. "A worthy match."

Worthy in the sense that Westfall owned more acreage than any in the valley, maybe, and served as county magistrate. Jasper was all pounds and pence and position.

She left the barn and returned to the cornfield to find Ma indeed in Westfall's company beneath a spreading sycamore tree. And Clay with them to boot. Such sent her scurrying back to the cabin and Jasper, wondering if Westfall would join them for supper.

Though it was hours away, the venison needed tendering on the spit outside, the corn with the husks left on to roast in the ashes. She chopped potatoes with a vengeance, her brisk movements making short shrift of the work.

Sure enough, near five o'clock, Westfall stood at their door. "Miss Tessa." He removed his hat, revealing a full head of white hair despite his sixty years. "Your ma asked me to supper."

Tessa wiped her hands on her apron and welcomed him in. Would Clay follow? Hope barely crested before disappointment swept in. Ma appeared, toting a piggin of milk, Ross following. He winked at her, clearly enjoying the turn of events. She'd paid it little mind when Ma had paired with the widower for a reel or two at the frolic, but truly, the matter begged pondering.

Westfall quietly took Pa's place. Tessa felt a twinge. The head of the table usually sat empty, though after Pa passed she'd had a hard time breaking her habit of setting his place, then whisking away the fork and spoon and tankard amid her tears.

Six men now ringed the long table once again, she and Ma serving. Talk centered upon the harvest, the usual tittle-tattle of the settlement when folks got together. This was no doubt a novel supper for the childless Westfall, surrounded by the Swan brood. Tessa said little, content to listen and try to make sense of the events of her own unforeseen afternoon as well as Ma's new-found courtship.

With a telling glance at his sister, Zadock picked up his fork and commenced eating. "I thought Colonel Tygart would join us."

Jasper shook his head, sparing Tessa an explanation. "Tygart had matters to see to upriver."

Wed to the fort, he was, and rightfully so for the betterment of the settlement. She tucked her disappointment away and smiled as Ma served bowls of apple tansy brimming with cream. To their amusement, at Westfall's leave-taking Ma disappeared with him into the moonlit night.

Once the door shut, Ross's whisper rocked them all. "Reckon he'll try to kiss her?"

Lemuel shook with silent laughter. "He'd be a fool not to."

"Likely Pa's turning in his grave," Zadock sputtered around his pipe.

"Pa, my eye." Cyrus snorted. "What about Mistress Westfall? In her eternity box but six months!"

With a wink, Jasper brought an end to their merriment as Ma came back into the cabin, cheeks rosy as pippin apples. If ever a woman looked like she'd been kissed . . .

Tessa began clearing the table amid the aroma of pipe smoke as plans were made for the morrow's work. At last the cabin settled and she climbed atop her thin mattress, lying on her back and staring at the high rafters. Try as she might, she couldn't nod off, couldn't even keep her mind on Clay. Summer thunder growled, threatening the ongoing harvest. She preferred the gentle spring peepers and warm rain. The brittle rustle of wind in the autumn leaves. Even the perfect stillness of a winter snowfall.

Tonight all creation seemed to groan, as Scripture said. The wolves especially made a terrible night music. She listened to their howls, haunting and otherworldly. That shadowy feeling that had overtaken her earlier at the well returned. Something felt different, some strange, cold force pressing in on all sides of them.

God, help us. Spare us. Please.

23

Clay struck the soil with a shovel, driving the pointed end hard past rock and weeds to overturn one too many graves. Eight — nay, nine. He miscounted then recounted, gorge rising in his throat. Seven children, one of them but a fortnight old. Smoke from the ashes of the cabin and outbuildings writhed and purled in the night, turning everything a dull charcoal gray. That overwhelming burnt smell was one he'd never gotten used to since the firing of the Tygart homestead when he was a boy. It smelled of heartache and despair then and now.

He tried not to look at the still, lifeless faces or the stricken men who'd helped with the Swans' harvest and come here. Other neighbors gathered, Jasper and Cyrus included, each overcome with varying emotions, namely outrage. It hung as thick as the smoke in the air. Silent to a man, they wrapped the bodies in quilts and sheets, burying the baby with his mother.

By the fifth grave, someone brought Clay a drink from a flask. He tasted blackberry juice. Vinegar. Sugar. It steadied him, eased his protesting arms and shoulders. At last he threw down the shovel and removed his hat, angling it over his sore heart, his mind empty. Around him stood a knot of somber men, rightly fretful about their own unguarded homeplaces, their heads bowed while others stood open-eyed, rifles ready.

He had no idea what he prayed, only that he said the words with urgency, aware these men needed to be on their way to bring their own families to the fort. He'd sent fort spies on a dangerous chase to relay the woeful news to other outlying settlers and stations.

Leaving Swan Station near dusk, he had ridden here with Jude. Tomorrow was the day assigned the guard to help the Clendennins harvest their corn. Clay had wanted to make sure they were ready, to plan for the morrow. They'd arrived to this.

Never had Clay been so glad for Jude's presence. They went from charred cabin to smokehouse to springhouse, making sure the flames did not leap to the woods and set them afire. The Indians had done a thorough work. Nothing remained alive or of use. Even the dog had been dispatched. Jude gathered the cur in his arms, buried it beneath an apple sapling, and rolled logs meant for firewood atop the grave to keep out the wolves.

"God rest their souls," Jude said with a swipe of a grimy sleeve across his brow. "Best hie on back. That runner you sent to the fort should have them on full alert."

Weary beyond words, Clay took a step toward Bolt, the agreeable afternoon he'd spent at Swan Station besmeared by fire and blood.

"You think we'd get used to such," Jude told him.

Was he thinking of Braddock's defeat? The field strewn with the bodies of red-coated soldiers and frontiersmen, female camp followers and children? Even now, years later, heaps of bleached bones were still scattered about, lying as they'd fallen, too many to bury.

One recent fact loomed large. "I received an unconfirmed report a fortnight ago that Chief Bull and five Shawnee families, all friendly to the whites, were cut down near Wheeling by settlers. This may well be retaliation, if true."

Jude gave a low whistle as they traded the

smoky clearing for the night woods. Moving cautiously, saying no more, they both gave a sigh of relief when the lights of Fort Tygart came into view. A volley of shots welcomed them in, carrying a ring of defiance to any enemy who might be watching from the woods.

In no mood to eat, Clay let Jude see to the horses while he crossed the common to the blockhouse. After being halted numerous times en route to answer questions and concerns, he finally pulled free. Hester stood at her cabin door, arms akimbo. For once she was silent.

He went into the blockhouse and closed the door, stripping off his bloodied shirt that was stained beyond repair and throwing it into a corner. His leggings were no better, but his boots would scrub clean. If he could only launder his ravaged thoughts.

Once he was dressed, a knock at his door led to more questions and then a hasty meeting on the common by the flagpole. This was followed by a breathless post rider who'd nearly been waylaid by what was thought to be the same war party.

Anxious, harried settlers began streaming through the heavily guarded gates. Time and time again his hopes to see the Swans rose and then fell as people gathered in tight bunches on the common and doubled up in cabins.

Clay climbed the rifle platform, the tension fairly crackling despite triple the guard. Even on so dark an eve, with nine fresh graves but a few miles away, the moon broke free of thunderclouds and a south wind awoke, as picturesque an evening as he'd ever seen within these wilderness walls.

Time ticked toward midnight but still no Swans. Had they stayed on in the barred blockhouse and cabin? Even with seven guns, it could not hold forever. Jasper was as hardheaded a man as Clay had ever seen. Formidable as a militia captain yet blinded by stubbornness and pride. If anything should befall Tessa . . .

Just when he could sweat no more, grow no more harried in waiting, a ruckus was raised at the gates. A stray shot had been heard in the woods a minute before, enough to raise every hackle. Then came the Swans at full gallop, riding hard across the stump-littered clearing, Tessa leading. Her hair was down, flying out behind her like the image of the woman fleeing in the wikhegan. One brother — Lemuel? — was on foot, bringing up the rear and running full tilt for safety. Had his horse been shot or stolen?

Relief drenched Clay as he descended the

ladder. The gates swung open to admit them, one rider slumped across a mount, reins dragging. The moon ducked behind a cloud, hiding the man's identity.

"They're out there, sure as doomsday," Zadock panted, swinging to the ground in the dust storm raised by skittish horses. "Cyrus is hit."

Tessa had dismounted, already at her brother's side. Hair streaming down in a torrent of waves and tangles, her cap missing, she made such an arresting sight Clay felt his breath hitch. He came up beside her, catching Cyrus as he fell from the saddle.

"Take him to Hester's," Tessa said, voice and hands trembling.

Lemuel threw down his hat in disgust, so out of breath he spoke in winded snatches. "Those redskins got my prize roan!"

"Better that than your scalp," Zadock returned hotly.

Clay hefted Cyrus across the common with his brothers' help, Tessa keeping up with their lengthy strides. Hester had seen them coming, was busy gesticulating toward a bed in a cabin corner. Clay laid Cyrus down, the blood coming from his wound in short bursts. Not gut shot, praise God.

They cut his crimson shirt off with a knife to lessen moving him. For a few breathless moments Clay stared, staggered. A tomahawk had sheared Cyrus's right side, so deep he was in mortal danger. Clay had seen many injuries, and this one sent him back to Braddock's field.

"Get Maddie," he said to no one in particular. He did what he could in the meantime, staunching the damage with linen rags Hester brought, glad Cyrus hadn't yet come to his senses. Such an injury would cause a powerful hurt. Whiskey would be needed in time.

"For now, cayenne tea." Hester moved briskly to the hearth, where a kettle steamed. "Pour some down him."

Beside Clay, sitting on the thin mattress by her brother's side, Tessa finally spoke. "Keturah swore to flaxseed for poultices."

"Maddie is a hand at both." Clay sought to cheer her as her hovering brothers fed him bits and pieces about the ambush.

"Came as close to an Indian as I ever was before . . . Cyrus was in front . . . One buck tried to grab my reins, but I brained him with the butt of my rifle . . . Tessa broke free . . . Fell off my horse when it got spooked and bolted . . ."

It came to him that Rosemary Swan was missing. They had a ready explanation for that too.

"She wanted to warn Westfall. Said she couldn't live with herself if he didn't come in." Zadock shook his head. "I was going to warn him instead, but she wanted to go herself. Saw her to his fence line and then came here."

"I'll go see if they've come in." Jasper turned on his heel and left the cabin.

'Twould be an all-night vigil with Cyrus. Tessa's pained expression said she'd not leave his side, her pallor nearly the same as her ailing brother's.

Maddie finally came, managing her shock well enough when the dim lantern light shone on the gaping wound.

"Colonel Tygart." In the doorway behind them stood a member of the militia. "A roan horse with no rider just came up to the gates, and we let it in."

"That would be Lemuel's," Clay returned, taking a step away from the bed and looking at Tessa's brother for confirmation. Lemuel nodded.

"Better take a look at it, sir," the man persisted.

Injured, mayhap? In need of putting down? The Swans were known for their fine horses.

Clay passed out of the cabin with Lemuel following, the rumble of thunder at their backs. They threaded through unsettled people and roaming animals, stopping just shy of the corral where a great many nervy horses were penned. The roan reared at their approach, its bridle held by none other than Jude, the set of his mouth bespeaking trouble.

"Look there on the right flank, Colonel."

Clay circled the skittish mount, speaking to it in low, soothing tones, while Lemuel stood back. No visible signs of harm other than he'd bolted, thrown his rider, and . . .

Clay stopped. Squinted. Behind him someone held up a pine-knot torch to illumine the painted flank. Though hastily made on an animal that wanted none of it, two black arrows were clearly drawn, each tip facing opposite directions. Hanging from the pommel on a leather strap was a wolf's paw. Clay grabbed the torch and looked closer.

Tamanen. His symbol. His unmistakable mark.

A small storm burst inside Clay. He ran hot, then cold. His turmoil wasn't easily hidden. Jude knew. Their eyes met in weighted understanding.

"Wash it clean," Clay said with a calm he didn't feel as Jude did away with the dangling paw.

With a nod, Jude turned the horse over to Lemuel. Clay took to his heels and returned to Hester's, wanting to make sure Tessa was all right.

When Clay did finally tumble into bed at dawn, Tessa kept him awake. Lying on his back, arm behind his head, he let the sweet memory of her on harvest day return to him, overriding the horror that had followed. Their easy if heartfelt banter. The way she'd taken his hand at the last. And then her parting words, so softly spoken yet arrow-sharp. They'd gone straight to his soul, rattling his carefully constructed defenses that Maddie had first begun to tear down.

What are you afraid of, Clay?

He wasn't afraid of the wilderness or Indians or tomorrow or any matter that might be brought to him that begged resolution. He wasn't even afraid of Tamanen and his outright, personal declaration of war.

He was only afraid of loving a woman with soulful eyes and hair as black as moonless midnight.

24

Even an expected siege didn't keep the fort's inhabitants from table. The next morn, Hester served up a formidable mound of biscuits made from newly ground wheaten flour. Slathered with butter and molasses, they satisfied the fussiest appetites. With Cyrus asleep in the corner and Lemuel at the wall, the rest of them sat down together. Ma was now among them, another reason to give thanks, as she and Westfall had made it in by midnight.

The tragic details about the Clendennins were revisited, and Tessa listened with deep-seated horror. She couldn't abide a renewal of war. She desperately wanted to cover her ears.

"So, the savages have finally struck," Hester lamented. "And struck hard."

"All killed," Jasper told them. He reached for the bread, but the news turned Tessa's stomach so she could not eat. "The colonel helped bury the dead."

"So many young ones . . ." Ma looked like she might cry. "And a new babe too."

"Wonder why they didn't take 'em captive?" Ross said. "The colonel says they oft adopt whites into the tribe to replace their dead."

Jasper shot him a warning look. "None of that heathen talk at table."

"If they're traveling fast and captives can't keep up, they're killed," Zadock continued despite Jasper's irritation. "Only the hardiest survive."

"I've lost count of all the raids, the burned-out homesteads, since settling in this valley. Seems like we could just abide together in peace." Ma's worn hands cradled her steaming teacup. "Reckon the colonel's going to send out a party to track them?"

"Nay. Such would weaken defenses here." Jasper swallowed another mouthful. "He's doubled the spies and now all the border is on alert, nearly everyone forted up."

"Which gives the Indians freedom to plunder whichever farm they please," Ma said.

"Nothing short of the king's army can halt that," Hester told them. "And those redcoats have their hands full in the East, trying to maintain order with rebel colonists."

"King's men don't know how to fight." Ross shook his head in disgust. "Standing all in a line waiting to get mowed down by Indians smart enough to take cover behind brush."

Jasper stared at him. "Like they did us in last night's ambush."

"The colonel thinks that was a different party than raided the Clendennins."

"All the worse then," Jasper returned, reaching for another biscuit. "Too many redmen overrunning the country."

"It was theirs to begin with, remember." Zadock echoed Keturah's line of thinking. "If Pa had property where he'd staked his claim and put in crops, how would you feel if somebody rode in and pushed him over and proclaimed it his own?"

Jasper flung down his fork. "You'll do well to keep your red-tongued —"

Ma stood, chair scraping hard across the floor, bringing an end to the matter. "There'll be no arguing amongst ourselves with the enemy at our gates. You're worn to nubs, all of you, which is why I'll excuse your fits of temper. Now go on and be about the business of this fort."

"I'm needed at the wall," Jasper said with another ugly glance at Zadock.

Hester began spooning the last of the fried

325

potatoes onto Jasper's plate. "If you're going to die, at least go to glory with your belly full."

"I'm not sure glory's where he's headed," Zadock said, to muted laughter.

A shiver convulsed Tessa, her mind circling to yesterday afternoon. Had the war party passed close by Swan Station, then decided with the presence of so many men at their harvest to keep heading north toward the Clendennins'? Might their misfortune have been her own?

A narrow escape, truly. 'Twas just after she'd fallen into a restless sleep last night, the wolves a-howl, that the warning had come to hurry to the fort. Bleary-eyed, stumbling on the hem of her nightgown as she pitched forward from her bed in haste, she gathered up her garments to dress in the darkness, leaving her hair unbraided and completely forgetting her cap.

The ride through the woods had been a living nightmare, the fracas that caused Cyrus harm so near the fort's gates a frantic blur. And Clay risked his own life most of all to bury the dead, scouting territory no man wanted, staying up all night, or nearly so, to spell those who couldn't manage another minute.

Once again the everlasting pull to go east

rose like the sun deep within. To be in a place where the man you cared for was busy working a trade and not burying the dead. To say farewell of a morning with no worry he might be scalped by sunset. When the only things that stalked cobbled streets were disease and pickpockets. Not savages, be them red or white, who marauded and burned and betook folks to lonesome, forsaken places.

"You all right?" Ross whispered next to her.

She looked up from staring at her untouched plate. "Nay."

Her brother's kindly eyes, so like Pa's, tore at her too. He was as big-hearted as Jasper was harsh. Seemed like the Almighty might have given them both a more balanced temper.

Westfall appeared in the open doorway, attention on Ma while giving the rest of them a hearty greeting. Had he heard her brothers arguing? They welcomed him in, though the mood stayed somber.

"Best take stock of the good," Ross told her quietly as more peaceable conversation resumed around them. "I'm all bent up about the Clendennins same as you, but at least they've all gone to glory together. Cyrus is still breathing. And not one shot has been fired at the fort."

She nodded, glad to the heart not to be running hot bullet lead in her apron or spelling a man at the wall. She eyed Jasper as he quit the table. All the ill will in the cabin seemed to vanish with him. "I'm just sore over it all."

"So am I," he murmured, before leaving to see how he could lend a hand.

She helped Hester tidy up, her great-aunt all too interested in Ma's fondness for Westfall as she peppered Tessa with questions. Their sudden courtship seemed to be progressing smoothly despite the dangers. As for Clay, Tessa set thoughts of him aside to tend Cyrus. He was feverish, the poultice they'd applied at daybreak making a mess of the bed linens as he thrashed about.

Lord, heal him, please. No more losses. No more empty places.

She bathed her brother's damp face with cool spring water, wishing he'd come to himself and take a drink of Hester's tea. She hadn't seen his attacker or seen him fall. She'd only been aware of Jasper's shout to flee and someone slapping the rump of her mare with his reins to send her bolting forward ahead of the fracas.

'Twas a miracle they'd not fared worse, in light of the Clendennins. What horrors Clay had seen. The gray cast to his face last night had to do with all those buryings, surely, though he'd looked unabashedly glad to see her when she rode in.

"How's Mister Cyrus this morn?" Maddie leaned over Tessa's shoulder, smiling. Her new bloom couldn't be denied. For a moment Tessa was more taken by Maddie's glow than her brother's plight.

"He's feverish." The lament in Tessa's voice caused a crease in Maddie's brow. "In need of Keturah's medicine."

With a nod, Maddie held up boneset to break a fever, raising Tessa's hopes. She canted her gaze toward the sunrise beyond the open door. "What's happening out there?"

"Calm as the Sabbath," Maddie returned. "Spies that came in at dawn brought no ill news, no more sightings. Tracks lead north toward the Ohio country, is all."

"How long are we to fort up then?"

"Best ask Clay." Maddie gave her a knowing smile. "But he's in no mood to say goodbye to you just yet."

Ever mindful of Hester, Tessa lowered her voice. "What do you mean?"

"Your brothers — Lemuel, mainly — is already wanting to return home. He's not alone. But Clay's urging caution. He's yet to recover from seeing you fly to the fort with Indians at your back."

"We've got to leave sooner than later. It goes hard on the men to be away at summer's peak."

With Tessa's help, Maddie tied a strip of cloth around Cyrus's middle, binding the wound with boneset as tight as she could.

The hum of background voices ceased, and Tessa looked up to find Hester, Ma, and Westfall gone. "I have a feeling the Swan household is about to go arsy-varsy."

Maddie's chuckle was low in her throat. "I heard some tittle-tattle about your ma and a certain widower, aye."

"I have this feeling Ma is going to be wed before long." Letting loose a sigh, Tessa spoke what weighted her. "And since Westfall isn't about to leave his land, that means I'm the only woman to look after five men."

"Let your brothers look after themselves. Might inspire them to find wives to do for them."

"You know we're far and few, Maddie."

"There does seem to be a drought of women and a flood of men. But that's neither here nor there. I'd rather talk about Clay."

"Is something the matter with Clay?"

"Aye, he's lovestruck." Maddie's low voice

spared Tessa another worried glance at the open door. "And you are the cause of such."

"Lovestruck? That hardly describes Colonel Tygart."

"It does indeed. If you were to somehow fort up longer than a few minutes, it might amount to something."

"You're woolgathering, Maddie."

A rustle came from the bed. "You two done discussing Tygart? I'm parched and in need of water for my thirst and some whiskey for my misery."

Both women looked to Cyrus, then burst out laughing. "Well, I'll be switched," Maddie exclaimed, going to fetch both. "Our patient has risen from the dead!"

Looking at her brother, seeing the pain etched in his sunburnt face, turned Tessa somber again. "How're you feeling?"

"Never mind me." Gently, Cyrus reached out and encircled her wrist with a workworn hand. "Listen, Sister. Don't forsake a chance to be with the colonel. He's a good man. You won't find better. I don't want you to end up like Hester."

"You know Ma looks to be leaving."

"All the better. Pa's passing has gone hard on her for too long. Westfall is a decent man, besides."

"What about you?"

"We're young yet. More women are coming into the country every day. In time, mayhap."

His words bolstered and unsettled her all at once. Couldn't she summon a thimbleful of gladness for her mother, who'd found love again? And take to heart Cyrus's earnest words? Even Maddie encouraged her to be at the fort more often. Could it be done?

Her mouth twisted wryly. Rather, could she survive Hester?

25

The day unwound slowly, the watch changed, and fresh spies were sent out while saddle-sore ones came in on lathered horses. The country looked calm, all said. No other fort they knew of had taken so much as one musket ball, one arrow. All indications pointed north to the Warrior's Path. The marauding Indians seemed to be moving toward the Ohio and beyond. Had they truly forsaken the settlements?

At nightfall, they all gathered in the west blockhouse for a wedding. Truly, Westfall was wasting no time. He wanted to return to farming and take Ma with him. Considering their fragile, ever-shifting circumstances, no one raised an eyebrow.

"We covet your blessing as the matron of the Swan clan," Rosemary told Hester, who stood with arms akimbo, gaze trailing to Tessa. "Colonel Tygart has the authority to join people in holy matrimony."

"Everybody but himself," Hester muttered moodily.

While it was all moving along at a faster clip than Tessa found comfortable, she donned her best smile and stood up with Ma as the vows were said. Truly, few observed mourning on the frontier and often remarried at a pace deemed scandalous overmountain.

Touched by Ma's look of girlish delight, amused by Westfall's trimmed hair and new if wrinkled weskit hastily sewn of printed fabric from Cutright's store, Tessa was hard-pressed to keep her eyes off Clay. He stole her attention as he read from a Bible in hand. His own? She liked him in the role of preacher, if that was what it was. His voice, thoughtful and resonant, carried to the far corners of the blockhouse as he pronounced the new couple man and wife.

Tessa looked to her feet as they kissed, the resounding cheers and huzzahs nearly as enthusiastic as those for her and Clay's muster-day kiss. Her brothers were smiling, back slapping and hand shaking all around, before making their way outside. Hester had slipped out before the ceremony ended to mix her celebrated flip for the toasts to follow.

"Tessa."

She turned, a step away from the door. Clay stood behind her, Bible closed but still in hand.

"Aye, Clay?"

"You at peace with all this?" The question surprised and touched her. Lately she was a bundle of emotions, her own feelings for him foremost, growing stronger the nearer she was to him. Did he sense that?

"I'm glad for Ma. Just trying to prepare myself for her being gone."

He nodded and set the Bible on his desk. Her eye was drawn to his Indian pipe, the beaded pouch of tobacco beside it. How she craved to know its story.

"Your brothers plan to leave out in the morning, but Cyrus is in no condition to move. Are you willing to stay on and tend him till he's on his feet?"

"Gladly." She nearly smiled. Maddie's doing? "But there's always Hester, remember."

"You're better medicine." He winked at her, his slow smile making her wish she could sit her woozy self down.

Wanting to prolong his company, she pointed to the map on his desk, laid open from corner to corner, the ends anchored by sadirons. The black markings denoting mountain ranges and rivers, the finely wrought script and compass points, drew her. The map was their world in miniature, the Ohio country plainly laid out beyond a long stretch of rivers that seemed to have no end.

Coming to stand beside her, he moved his pipe and tobacco pouch out of the way. "We're here. This small scrolling line is the Buckhannon. Your homeplace is marked by an *X.*"

She leaned nearer, following his pointed finger. "And this path lined in red?"

"That's the main Indian trail, the Warrior's Path, connecting north and south and cutting through the hardest terrain east to west — the endless mountains, to borrow an Indian phrase. Passage is easiest in the valley here."

"And the Tuscarawas River?"

"Marked in blue. Keturah and the Moravians are near the forks, establishing their mission."

She dared a more personal question. "Where did you camp with the Lenape?"

"Along the Cuyahoga here, near the falls." His finger moved northwest. "We made other camps in different seasons but always returned there."

She couldn't imagine it, having been born and raised on the Buckhannon and nowhere else. Indians were rovers, yet how could they be otherwise, forever pushed west, as Keturah said? She'd spoken of terrible cold, near starvation, though there were times of plenty too. Surely the Moravians would keep her friend warm and well fed.

"When the smallpox struck, I was one of the few who survived. Our band was reduced by half. Not long after, a treaty was made and I returned to my Quaker kin. I might have starved otherwise."

Her eyes roamed the map west to east. The distance from the Ohio country to Philadelphia seemed impossibly vast. "So far you must have traveled."

"Hundreds of miles, aye."

"I've always been taught to fear Indians, but in truth I know little about them. Mostly hearsay."

"Mayhap one day I'll tell you more."

She pointed to the painted bark near a pegged buffalo skin. "For now, you can help me understand this."

"You don't miss much." His expression held respect — and something else that looked like reluctance. "Wikhegan."

"Indian picture writing?" She looked away. "Whatever 'tis called it gives me chills."

"Supposed to. 'Tis a warning."

He said no more. Well and good, then, as

she'd lost the heart to hear it.

She stepped back from the map with a bittersweet smile. "Care for some of Hester's flip?"

"Gladly." He put a hand on her elbow and they went outside, where everyone had gathered to celebrate the nuptials. 'Twas an odd celebration, muted by their watchful circumstances. Men looked down at them from the rifle platform with cheerless faces, the rising moon reflecting off myriad gun barrels.

Clay soon drained his cup and asked for seconds, leaving the throng to disappear inside Hester's cabin. Tessa followed, heartened by the sight of him bearing two drinks and handing Cyrus some flip of his own.

"Mighty kind, Colonel." Cyrus raised up with a wince, his back against the log wall. His color was a shade better, but still Tessa fretted. "Suppose I'll tarry here a while longer, aye?"

"Would be wise. Sometimes we even have a physic pass through. But between your great-aunt and your sister and Maddie, you should recover in time."

"Still can't stand without getting woozy-headed."

"You lost a great deal of blood." Clay took a drink of his own flip as laughter erupted outside. "Keep to bed for the time being."

"Ma is now Mistress Westfall, sounds like." Cyrus looked to Tessa for confirmation, or maybe to gauge her feelings about the matter.

Tessa sat down on the side of the bed with a smile while Clay stood in the open doorway with his back to them. "I'm glad Westfall's isn't far."

Cyrus motioned her closer. "Wish it was your wedding instead."

Putting a finger to her lips, Tessa shushed him unnecessarily, the building laughter masking her brother's whispered words.

In time Ruth appeared, slipping past Clay to stand at the end of the bed. Cyrus flushed to the roots of his tawny hair.

"Need some company?" she asked, sporting a basket. "Checkers? Or cards?"

He nodded, still looking a bit sheepish, while Tessa fetched a small table to set between the bed and Ruth's chair. She then left them to their game, drawn outside again, but Clay was back in the blockhouse meeting with two spies who'd just ridden in.

Ma and Westfall were clearly enjoying their new circumstances, the details falling into place. They hoped to leave come morning, after spending their first night in the cabin Westfall always occupied when forting up.

With a glance at the rifle platform, Tessa moved away from the merriment into the summer twilight. The flip she'd drunk made her a bit loose limbed, lessening the tension she'd felt since coming in at a gallop the night before. She gave thanks as she walked along the fort's perimeter. The horses jostled and nickered softly as she passed, no longer milling about moodily or restlessly like they did in times of danger.

No one was near the spring. Bending low, she ran her fingers through an eddy of cold water and cupped her hand for a drink. Unlike those fearful moments at the well, her being here was free of that shadowy feeling, the silhouette now walking toward her reassuring.

Clay.

"You're a worthy watchdog," she teased. "Just needed to take a turn."

"Already feeling the pinch of these walls, no doubt."

"Betimes, aye, but 'tis safer here than home," she admitted, drying her hand on her apron. "I can't imagine how it must be for you."

"Like caging a panther," he confessed. "Come morning, when most of the settlement gets beyond these gates, I'll want to go with them."

"You have your scouting."

"That keeps me sane, aye."

They fell into step together. "I never figured you for a farmer, Clay. Staying put in one place."

" 'Tis tempting. I've been awarded a tract along the western Monongahela for my stint in the Seven Years' War. Prime bottom land for farming."

"Have you walked it?"

"Twice, aye." He paused at the rear gate and looked out a loophole. "A square-mile piece, well timbered along the river with two springs. Worthy of a stone house like my kin's in outer Philadelphia."

"A solid stone house then, like our springhouse," she said as he pulled back from the wall. "More to my liking than logs."

"More enduring." They walked on, bypassing the black hulk of the smithy with its taint of iron and ash. "This garrison was built with green wood that won't last more than a few years at most."

"My hope is we have an even bigger frolic taking these pickets down than we did putting them up."

"Wish I'd witnessed it. You helped feed the builders, no doubt. You're a fine hand at the hearth."

"You're remembering that muster-day cake."

"Nay. I'm remembering that muster-day kiss."

She couldn't resist a little ribbing. "That called-for kiss?"

"Your first, I'd be willing to wager." He turned toward her, bringing a sudden standstill to their walking.

"My very first," she said, looking up at him. "But not yours, I'd wager."

He removed his hat and let it dangle in one hand. "Called for or nay, such a kiss is not easily forgotten."

He reached for her, his hands framing the curve of her shoulders where the ruffled edge of her fichu ended. Her breathing, shallow till now, all but stopped as his hands moved down the length of her arms before entwining her fingers in his own. In the near darkness she couldn't see his features plainly but sensed his purpose.

With a seamless step not unlike that of a dance, he moved her beneath the smithy eave, out of sight of any on the rifle platform who might turn around and look down on them. He was close, so close she smelled the leathery-tobacco scent of him. He let go of her hands and encircled her with his arms. Gently yet boldly, as if sure of her willingness.

His mouth met hers as if he'd been kissing her for a long time. *This* was no called-for kiss. It felt true and sweet and good. Not obligatory but passionate. Not hasty but lasting. When it ended she wanted to begin all over again.

"To be honest, this has been on my mind since that first day we met," he whispered against her hair.

"Truly? When I followed you outside and asked you to bring Keturah's belongings?"

"It's a smitten man who wants to kiss a woman at first meeting."

"What took you so long?" she chided, wanting to reclaim all that time lost to them.

"Pure Tygart stubbornness." The smile in his voice made her nestle closer. "If I'd known you felt the same . . ."

"I felt lightning struck at first meeting. I went into the barn when you rode off and fell back into a pile of hay. I've not recovered yet."

His low laugh so near her ear was the richest sound she'd ever heard. "So, what are we to make of all this?"

"We're not going to let any more time get away from us. Or settlement business come between us." She sighed, mostly in pleasure, her desire for his company and to be outside fort walls equally strong. "I'll not hide the fact I'd like to be away from so many prying eyes."

"Didn't I hear Cyrus say something about a pie? There's a mess of berries a half mile from here in that deadfall near Slade Creek. Might make a good jaunt." He seemed to reconsider. "But chancy."

"I'll risk it for nobody but you." She slipped her arms about his shoulders, unwilling for their closeness to end even as his hands tightened about her waist. "A pie might help bring Cyrus round."

"We'll see what morning brings," he told her.

Another lingering kiss. More whispered words. Then he took her hand and they started to inch their way toward the merriment. She'd nearly forgotten about her mother's nuptials. How she wished they were her own, hers and Clay's.

When they came into the circle of light made by the flickering of a pine-knot torch, heads turned. Pride and pleasure turned her bashful. She didn't miss Maddie's knowing smile or Hester's unmistakable glee, or even Ma's own pleased surprise as she stood by her groom.

Only when spies came in to give a report

did Clay release her hand. There was a warmth and security in his touch that left her missing him even though he was only a few feet away in the blockhouse.

Time ticked on and Hester brought another round of flip. The watch changed. Ruth was still inside the cabin entertaining Cyrus, intent on their game. Stifling a yawn, Tessa went to sit near the doorway of Hester's cabin, wondering what, if any, news the spies brought.

Open-eyed, she prayed for peace. For Cyrus's healing. For Keturah and the Moravians far beyond the Buckhannon. For Maddie's baby to be born well and safe. For Ma and Westfall to make a good beginning. In a sea of needs, her and Clay's romantic leanings seemed small and swallowed up. How was she supposed to pray about that?

Giddy as a girl, she was. Over a few kisses. Whispered words. The clasp of a callused hand.

26

The morn was blessedly cool. Clay rued being away from the fort, from Tessa, but he couldn't rest till he saw for himself there was nothing of concern to prevent settlers from returning to the harvest. Yet no matter how vigilant the fort spies and settlers, the Indians might strike again anytime, anywhere.

"Never saw better country," Jude said, removing his hat to fan his face. "Except your land along the Monongahela."

"Pity it's a hundred miles north or we could lay out a house site."

Jude gave him a knowing grin. "I always wondered what woman would make you want to end your roving ways. The Spinster Swan it is."

"If she'll have me."

"Have you? That wedding last night should have been a double. No sense waiting. But who's going to marry you? You can't marry yourself."

"That's the trouble. As it stands, there's no one to officiate unless an itinerant preacher happens by. I'll not do as some and pledge troth without benefit of clergy."

"Take her to Pitt. I recall a sober preacher there."

Clay said nothing, committing Jude's words to heart. They reined in beneath an ancient chestnut tree near the idle Swan ferry, resting their horses after a ten-mile circuit. The day held a touch of fall, the leaves of late July showing a summer's weariness, their vibrancy fading. In the distance came the reassuring ring of an axe. The Swan brothers, all but Cyrus, were home, the sound blessed confirmation. Ross, usually at the ferry, was likely in the fields. Folks would have to swim or float their belongings across, but lately there'd been few travelers, given word of the Clendennin massacre had spread.

"Why do you think that war party took no prisoners?" Jude asked, eyes on the river.

"They were traveling fast, not wanting captives but vengeance after what happened to Chief Bull and his party."

"What do you make of them that nearly ambushed the Swans that night? Think it was the same who attacked the Clenden-nins?"

"Nay. The Clendennins seemed to be the work of Shawnee or mayhap Wyandot. That wikhegan on Zadock's roan was pure Lenape."

Jude gave a low whistle of consternation. "You ain't said much, but I know you well enough to see the hackles it raised. Care to tell me more?"

"It's personal." Clay reached for his canteen and took a swig of water. "Hearkens back to my time as a captive."

"Living with the Wolf clan along the Cuyahoga?"

Clay gave a nod. "You recall that Lenape brother whose brother I replaced when he died of disease?"

"Ghost eyes, they called you. Këshkinko. I recollect his was Tamanen. 'Twas him who marked Cyrus's horse."

"We were raised together, shared a father and mother. Sisters. Everything we did was to best the other. Close as blood brothers, we were." Clay took another drink, still stung by the uncanny circumstance. "Keturah was his wife in the Lenape tradi-tion. Nothing binding under white law, but still his wife as far as the tribe is concerned."

Jude grimaced. "And you knew nothing of

the bond between them?"

"None. Keturah was made captive of another band of Lenape before marrying Tamanen and becoming part of his clan. I'd since left them and had no knowledge of their tie till she spoke of it that day with Heckewelder."

"And somehow, for some reason, Tamanen came here and spooked the Swans, then marked their horse to send a message to you."

"That's part of it, aye. Bad blood, mayhap."

"Bad blood? Because of you living like brothers and then you forsaking your Lenape ways?"

"Stands to reason, aye? He's a war chief. He's lost not only his Indian kin to disease but also a white brother and a wife. I had something to do with Keturah. Who knows the depth of his reasoning or his wanting revenge, if that's what it is."

"I'd be mighty nervy then." Jude looked over his shoulder with a grimace. "When a grudge becomes personal, it ain't likely to end easy."

"Tamanen's clever — and ruthless." Clay turned his horse east, recalling the many times Tamanen had bested and outwitted him. "It's his nature to settle a score, no matter how small or how much time has passed."

They rode back to the fort in silence, daylight giving way to the flash of fireflies and a pale sunset. 'Twas hard to keep his mind on the task at hand, as Tessa met him at the beginning and end of every thought. But he felt an odd peace undergirding it all, knowing she was behind those picketed walls, hopefully anticipating his return.

He half expected to see her serve him supper, but 'twas Hester who was at his hearth, concocting venison stew and wheaten bread.

"How's Cyrus?" he asked.

She poked at the hearth, scattering the embers beneath a kettle to end its singing. "Taken a turn for the worse."

Dismay overrode his weariness. He hung his shot pouch and powder horn from a peg and stored his rifle, then went straight to her cabin.

Tessa was by her brother's side, head bent. Was she praying? Her small hand was clasped in Cyrus's much larger one. His eyes were closed, his pallor disturbingly washed-out. His wound was grievous, but with time and attention Clay figured he'd get well.

He rested a hand on Tessa's shoulder. She looked up at him, her gaze holding a well of hurt. Cyrus's breathing was alarmingly shallow. It shook Clay that a man could go from playing checkers to lying motionless in a matter of hours.

"Your ma leave with Westfall?" he asked her softly.

"Aye." She reached up and laid her hand on his. "When they went, Cyrus was on his feet, and then afterward he began to bleed again."

He bit back a rebuke about Cyrus being up and around so soon. The Swan men were many things, including willful. Dropping to his haunches, he pondered what to do. Indecision often spelled disaster, a life lost. Keturah's remedies were never so needed as now. Maddie did what she could but was no physic or Lenape healer.

His own mostly minor injuries, gotten in wartime or with the tribe, trickled through his memory before becoming a deluge. He rubbed his scarred jaw. "Slippery elm bark."

Tessa searched his face as if seeking all he could possibly remember, as if knowing her brother's life depended on it.

"Mayhap the wound needs suturing with linen thread. I'd hoped to avoid such, but if needs be we ready a needle." Here there'd be no stitching skin with the inner bark of basswood or the fiber from the long tendon of a deer's leg. Or the purifying properties of steam. But in truth he put more stock in them than white man's medicine.

"I can ride out to fetch slippery elm," Tessa said. "Shouldn't have far to go. But first, mightn't you pray with me?"

His mind became blank as inkless paper, but the plea in her lovely face couldn't be denied. Removing his hat, he bent his head, feeling the warmth of her fingers lacing through his own. Her lips were moving but he couldn't make out the words. Still, it was a rare, hallowed moment that seemed to fight back the darkness of the unknown future as they said *amen.*

He pulled himself to his feet. "As for that remedy, I'll ask Jude. You try to get some water down Cyrus in the meantime."

Ruth and Maddie helped Tessa and Hester keep watch of Cyrus, the slippery elm remedy and careful stitches soon in place. Meanwhile, Clay kept the door open to his blockhouse quarters, able to watch the comings and goings of all who entered and exited the fort.

It was almost a relief to return to the mundane the next morn. He sat at his desk and managed various interruptions by settlers wanting to address some matter, returning to his paperwork between times. His latest report was half written, penned with no small sorrow.

> There has been no mischief done in this county since the 17th instance when a family of nine persons was killed and scalped about eight miles above this, on the North Branch opposite . . .

Having no heart to finish, he set down his quill and tried to read. He perused the latest laws from the colonial government tongue in cheek. Some he overlooked as petty, and others, if enforced, would fine half the settlement.

In the interest of good morals and the suppression of vice, a penalty of fifty cents was to be exacted for swearing. For drunkenness, ten lashes across a bare back. For laboring on the Sabbath, one dollar was owed. Stealing land warrants resulted in death.

His attention wandered to the open doorway. Toward Hester's.

What about kissing a spinster in the nighttime shadows?

He leaned back, the creak of the wood slats against his weight a testament to their age. That somebody had hauled a Windsor chair clear to the back settlements was more than a tad befuddling. That it ended up in this blockhouse, more befuddling still. Most frontier furniture was a far cry from eastern colonial parlors. A stump for a seat and a couple of planks nailed down for a table sufficed.

If he returned to the Monongahela country and laid the foundation for a stone house, what would he furnish it with in time? What belongings would Tessa want? He could send east for what was needed. York and Lancaster had fine furniture makers. The orders could be delivered in wagons to Fort Pitt, not too far from his acreage, or floated downriver.

Tessa had a hankering for finer things. Things not even a stone house along the Monongahela might offer. She craved poetry. Hand fans. English tea. Yet she made do with what her rusticated life offered.

He stared without focus at the list of colonial laws, allowing himself a look into the future. Why did he see it so clearly? A house of solid stone. Fencing around a colorful garden with Tessa at its heart. Around her, running and playing, were sons and daughters that bore both their features. Held captive by the scene, he shut his eyes, trying to picture himself there, somewhere.

"Clay?"

Tessa's voice snatched him back to the present. He opened his eyes. She walked toward him, her smile encouraging. Cyrus hadn't worsened then.

"He's awake and taking some of Hester's tea. And he's asking for blackberry pie." She held up a basket. "Don't want to take you away from your work, but if you could spare some time . . ."

He reached for his powder horn and shot pouch in answer, unable to keep a smile from his own face. With the country calm, there'd be no reason to deny her even a half hour. The morning's fair scouting report that had let the settlers loose surely extended to them.

Bolt was glad to be free if only on a short jaunt, snorting softly and pawing the ground as they readied to ride out. Tessa sat behind Clay with her pail, their closeness an outright declaration. As they left, Maddie waved from her cabin doorway while a dozen other fort dwellers stared in brazen curiosity.

For once the heat wasn't oppressive, the noonday sun tucked behind cloud cover that stretched for miles. He felt no sense of danger, not only because fort spies spread out like spokes on a wheel in every direction. His own soul bespoke peace. For the first time in a long time, all the tension drained from his frame, the enjoyment of the moment foremost.

The thicket they sought was still abundant, the berries spared the summer's sun by a dense surround of white oak. Tessa stood within reach of a rich harvest, gleeful as a girl. He chuckled as she flew through her task, her lips soon stained a telling purple. Ever generous, she fed him the plumpest, juiciest berries. Bolt ignored them both, tearing rapturously at a patch of bluestem.

"I prefer whortleberries to blackberries," he told her as her basket filled, overcome by a vivid memory. "Baked into cornbread, they were a prize."

"Whortleberries, aye. I was fond of Keturah's strawberry cakes."

Keturah and Heckewelder were never far from his thoughts. Had they safely reached the Tuscarawas? Already laid out their newest mission in pursuit of peace? He leaned back against an oak's rough bark, mindful of all that was at stake. He was here to help bring about safety and peace in his own small way. Yet he was growing increasingly disheartened defending a cause he didn't wholeheartedly believe in, pushing back the

Indians till they lost not only their lands but a way of life. Unrelentingly, his part in their demise cut across his conscience whenever he gave orders in the blockhouse or scouted land that surveyors and settlers had grabbed and gouged with their implements, refusing to stop till they'd claimed every acre. The Indian in him hated such. The settler and officer in him saw it as a grim necessity. The spoils of war.

But for now, a moment's peace. Tessa. She glanced up as a sudden breeze teased the leaves overhead. Her throat was bare, and he kissed the hollow of her shoulder where her fichu had slipped slightly. She sighed, the sound content. His own heart was so overfull he couldn't speak.

"I wish I owned time and could slow it down, especially when you're near me," she said.

"How about forsaking the Buckhannon for the Monongahela?"

"I hear the Mon is a mighty big river." She studied him, their noses almost touching. "Makes the Buckhannon look like a creek. Most fertile land west of the Alleghenies, Pa always said."

"A garden as big as your heart is set on, aye. As near paradise as I've ever seen in my rambles. Unless you'd rather live overmountain."

Her expression clouded. "I don't know that in town is where you belong."

He didn't know either. Emptying his mind of the notion, he breathed in the scent of a coming rain and called for Bolt. "We'd best hasten back. Mayhap one day soon we won't have to."

Helping her into the saddle, he kissed her again. Already he was dreading her leaving and returning home. She was becoming as necessary to him as his daily bread.

They returned to a fort no different than when they'd left, with just as many eyes on them. But his mind remained on the expansive Monongahela and what needed to be done to begin a life there. Or mayhap, in a wild flight of fancy, he would trade it all for town.

Tessa showed her brimming berry bucket to a heavily bewhiskered Cyrus, who was awake now and being fed bone broth by Ruth. Hester was busy gossiping beneath her neighbor's eave, the women's spare frames clothed in dark homespun, their cackling reminiscent of crows. Setting out the ingredients she would need, Tessa began making the requested pie, her mind not at all on her task.

All she recalled was Clay's talk of the Monongahela. Were his thoughts sprinting hard ahead just as hers were, no longer content with a happenstance courtship, a chance meeting, but something more enduring? His wistful words cracked open the door to an altogether different life. A life lived without looking over one's shoulder, Lord willing.

"What are you smiling about, Sister?" Cyrus had finished eating, and Ruth took the empty bowl away. "More the colonel than your peck of berries, I'm thinking."

At Ruth's chuckle, Tessa glanced up from the cookbook Clay had given her, a copy of *The Complete Housewife Suitable for the Virginia Kitchen,* printed in Williamsburg. She devoured it as much for the reading as the recipes.

"And I'm thinking that pie's more the colonel's too," Cyrus said with a wink at her continued silence.

"Big enough for the both of you," Tessa returned with a smile, pouring the berry filling into the rolled crust.

Cyrus lay back and plowed a hand through lank hair, his boredom at being in bed apparent. Ruth went to fetch cards, giving Tessa an opportunity to whisper, "Seems like Ruth is sweet on you."

"She's set her sights on me today." His features grew ruddy. "I can't speak for the morrow."

"I'd be pleased to have a brother married and gain a sister."

"So you'd feel better about running off with the colonel, I suppose."

"Amen," she said, not caring who heard. But Clay was again in the blockhouse, hearing someone's complaint over a stolen pig. The man's voice rose in agitation as he recited a list of grievances against another settler.

On the Monongahela their future shone brighter yet still held the mists of a winter's morn. All she knew was that she'd gladly trade town for Clayton Tygart.

27

Cyrus found his feet within a fortnight, the sutures were removed, and then in a blink both he and Tessa returned to the Buckhannon, her fort tryst with Clay seeming a hazy dream. Ma was at the cabin to meet them, making Tessa believe for just a moment nothing had changed. But after a brief visit, Ma headed to Westfall's again with a favorite kettle and other necessities, leaving Tessa the sole woman in charge of Swan Station.

Her August days were unendingly busy now as she did the work of two women. At week's end Ma helped share the burden of soap and candle making, half going to her new larder. A calm Sabbath unspooled, and they went to Westfall's. Mention was made of Clay's coming, but as the day wore on, no horse and rider materialized.

Her spirits sank to her Sabbath-shined shoes with their tarnished brass buckles. Might he have had a change of heart about her? Though he'd left little doubt of late about his feelings, his cool regard of her in the past still made her skittish.

By and by a low growl from Westfall's hounds foretold someone's coming. Tessa all but jumped up, having lost count of how many days it had been since she'd seen Clay. And now here he was, standing tall in Westfall's doorway, welcomed by all. He smiled and said little, but the haggard lines of his face bespoke much. The latest dispatches from Fort Pitt foretold trouble, of raids on farms and on smaller stations to the north and south of them. The men discussed matters in low, solemn tones while she and Ma prepared supper.

"Seems like the raiders give Fort Tygart wide berth," Ma said as she turned corncakes onto a platter. "Except for that one night you and your brothers were ambushed, or nearly so, coming into the fort following the Clendennins' burial."

A shiver rode Tessa's spine, more from the fate of the Clendennins than their own narrow escape. "Cyrus took the brunt of it but seems to be mending."

"What's this I hear about him and Ruth?"

Tessa set a bowl of applesauce on the linen-clad table. "He's said nary a word to me about Ruth since we left the fort."

"Some grandchildren would be a fine thing." Ma expelled a rare sigh. "This cabin's a mite big for just us two."

Was Ma missing them? Tessa couldn't imagine so light a load with just she and Westfall to do for. But despite Ma's wish for grandchildren, she seemed content. The place held a dozen womanly touches, including the coverlets and trunk she'd brought from home.

"And you and the colonel?" Ma's green gaze speared Tessa. "You're nigh as bad as Cyrus for keeping secrets."

"There's little to tell, Ma." She glanced toward the porch at the men. "But Clay's right here. Surely that bodes well."

The men came in and sat about the unfamiliar table. Talk turned to mundane matters like the new irons Jasper was considering for a future gristmill and Westfall's need for oxen. Beside her, Clay set his fork down again and again to answer questions of the latest news from Boston, of British troops firing into a crowd of people calling themselves Patriots who were protesting at the customs house.

At meal's end, Clay's hand felt for hers beneath the table. 'Twas bliss to have the warm pressure of his fingers on hers, the reassuring heft of him on the bench beside her. Even the guns lined up along the log wall failed to hold the foreboding they usually did.

Sabbath's end brought a walk in the twilight through Westfall's orchard, the fledgling apple trees reminding her of children in varying stages of growth, some thriving, some struggling. Though young, a few of the trees bore fruit. The bee skeps near the orchard hummed, promising honey in time. One bee danced around her, alighting on her shoulder.

"English flies are what the Indians call them." Clay flicked it away lest it sting. "You can tell white people are coming by the advance of the bees."

She pondered it, squeezing his hand. "I do prefer molasses over honey, and maple sugar over both."

"Sugar, aye." Something came over his face she could only describe as wistful. He'd removed his hat as he always did in her company, a courtesy she found endearing, allowing her a better look at his tanned features. Though the Indians had left their mark, so had his genteel Quaker kin. "Used to be the spring hunt began after the sugar making. My last season with the Lenape was my most memorable. Many horse loads of skins."

"Were you more hunter or warrior?" She'd always wondered.

"I preferred the hunt. Four bears in one day on that last hunt, three the next. That final stretch I brought in fifty-six deer."

"The Lenape relied on you for meat, then."

"We were always one step away from starvation."

"Your leaving would have gone hard on them."

"I recollect the lean winters all too well. How glad we were at the return of spring."

They were in the middle of the orchard now, hidden from view. Sunlight speared the turning leaves, yellow arrows all around them.

She touched an apple, a Virginia crab, its pale, pebbly skin stained red. "These blossoms are showy in spring. Might make a good cider apple to have in your orchard someday."

"*Our* orchard, Tessa? Apples, peaches, cherries, pears. Mayhap a quince or two."

"You've given it some thought."

"And you?" He looked down at her, rifle in hand, and she tried to imagine him in their orchard with gun stored, buckskins traded for a simple linen shirt and stock and breeches, even buckled shoes. But he was so handsome as he was, she shuttered the thought.

" 'Tis time, at least in my heart," she answered. "Time to do different. Time to look forward instead of over my shoulder. But I'll leave the rest to you."

He nodded. "The more I think on it, the more I sense you need to bid the wilderness farewell. Live somewhere civilized."

"In town?" Her smile faded. "I'd likely shame you."

His face flashed surprise and an almost palpable hurt. "You think you're something to hide, to keep in the back settlements?"

"Town-bred women are different, Clay. Your Quaker kin might expect something more than what I am."

"You're not marrying my Quaker kin. I'll have you be no different than you are."

They'd not spoken the word *marrying* till now, though they'd danced around it. His reassurance she need not be some fan-waving, silken-clad belle sent a little tremor of relief through her. But she did aim to be better than she was, to master the finer graces, to make him proud. She swallowed the question begging to be said as he kissed her, scattering every other thought like garden seed.

When?

She sensed it wasn't time yet for him, not the way it was for her. If he asked her to marry him tonight, she would. She'd give up the Swan homestead for good, let her brothers fend for themselves. Even as her heart raced on, her head reminded her there was no preacher or magistrate to be had.

"Sister?" Jasper's voice carried through the dense foliage of the orchard. "Needs be we head home."

Clay released her, and a decidedly bereft feeling overtook her. Forcing a smile, wishing for more tender words, more time, she moved toward the waiting horses. No telling when she'd see him again. There'd been talk of his returning to Fort Pitt for some sort of military gathering. But he vowed he'd not leave till reinforcements arrived first.

Once mounted on Blossom, she turned back and saw Clay atop Bolt, eyes on her as she turned south, her brothers ringing her, rifles in arm. With a wrench of her head and her heart, she met his gaze a final time in silent farewell.

For where thou art, there is the world itself . . . and where thou art not, desolation.
Though learned in Quaker school years ago, he'd never felt the truth of Shake-

speare's line till now. Fort Tygart seemed hollow, lifeless, even weary. The pickets profoundly ugly. Lacking. Tessa seemed to be needed everywhere he looked, not on the Buckhannon where he couldn't ensure her safety.

He tripled the spies, sent them out in continuous batches, heard their reports, which included one skirmish at the smallest station upriver, and perused numerous dispatches from Fort Pitt. Privately he'd warned Jasper not to have Tessa at the ferry where there'd been repeated sign. Neither was he comfortable leaving her at the cabin with the men in the fields, but without reason to voice this other than he was in love with her and wanted her safe, he'd stayed silent. His unending prayer was for direction. Protection.

"What's this I hear about you spending the Sabbath with my great-niece?" Hester never failed to serve his supper with an inquisitive question or two.

"Not only your great-niece but your five great-nephews and the new Mister and Mistress Westfall," he said, sitting down to eat.

"Humph." Hester poked at the coals in the hearth. "I suppose courting in all that company slows one considerably. But I reckon you can't marry her yet. Sometimes I'm sorry you're not the sort to promise a preacher and just pretend you're wed till then."

"Nay." He forked a bite of catfish fried to perfection. "She deserves better."

"That she does, and don't you forget it!" Hester straightened, a hand pressed to the small of her back as if it was ailing her. With her other hand she aimed the poker at him. "But I'd like to see her nuptials before I go to glory."

"I'll see what I can do," Clay answered, hoping he could indeed fulfill that final wish.

She went out, shutting the door to the blockhouse firmly as if to allow him to ponder the matter more thoroughly without interruption. He'd considered sending to Fort Pitt for some official capable of marrying them according to colonial law. But with the frontier so hunkered down, he couldn't put anyone at risk. Nor would he take her to Pitt, an unholy place to begin wedded life.

He reached for the salt cellar and sprinkled his potatoes. All he wanted now was Tessa. Tessa opposite him at table, doing her handwork by the fire, reading to him in the firelight. Tessa right here, in whichever way he could have her. To talk to and laugh with. To welcome winter in together.

All the little details about her drove him to distraction. The dark fall of her hair with its threads of red. The startling hue of her eyes with their forthright gaze. Her smile, a bit crooked, her mouth soft and dimpled. The way his hands spanned her waist . . .

Lord, let it be.

28

The cloudless August day dawned with a sky so blue, the air so crisp, it bespoke the change of seasons. Tessa rose before first light, swinging the kettle on its crane over the ashes she'd banked carefully the night before. Breakfast was a blur of bowls and mugs and terse words as her brothers hurried to their tasks at field and ferry. Ma was never so missed as at peep of day. But she'd made peace with Ma's going just as her brothers would make peace with her going in time.

Six days had passed since she'd seen Clay. Would he ride in on the Sabbath like last week? Or would some fort matter keep him rooted? She filled a wash bucket with lye, scrubbed her brothers' shirts clean, and set out her own Sabbath best. Draping the laundry across a near fence, she pondered what needed doing next.

Taking the whetstone she'd gotten from

the creek bed, she began sharpening knives, the sound rasping her nerves. Next she gathered the last of the greens from the garden, braiding the onions to hang from the rafters. For supper she'd make fried mush with maple sugar that Zadock had expressed a hankering for. Such required a rasher of bacon.

Bent on the smokehouse, she took a step toward the open cabin door when the hard, shuddering thwack of an axe stopped her. The thud had an odd sound unlike her brothers' wood chopping. The jarring thwack came again, right outside the door. It sent her back a step. A dark form filled the doorway that had been so flooded with light but a second before. It reminded her of an eagle's shadow in passing. Her bare skin turned to gooseflesh.

A lone Indian looked at her, tomahawk in hand, one moccasined foot clearing the threshold. His eyes were like flints in his lean face. Half his features were swathed red, the other half painted black. A bold paw print — a wolf's? — marked his left cheek. The garish display nearly tore a scream from her throat.

He circled behind her, the hard thwack against the cabin's outer logs continuing. He'd not come alone then.

Lord, spare us.

Her legs twitched. She fought the impulse to run like a rabbit before a red-tailed hawk. Slowly, the intruder prowled through the cabin, poking at this or that with his tomahawk. A string of dried beans rustled like a rattler. A basket of cleaned wool was emptied. With one menacing sweep of a tawny arm, their prized salt-glaze pitcher tumbled from its mantel perch and shattered with a fearsome clatter.

Her back pressed against the cold hearthstones, Tessa watched him, riveted to his tomahawk. If she turned her back to him, mightn't she find that terrible weapon sunk into her scalp? She had no means to fight with but an iron poker. Her rifle rested nearer the Indian than she.

The warrior passed outside the cabin, taking her rifle with him. Woozy, she leaned into the trestle table, Pa's fate taking hold of her afresh. God was here. God was near. Yet terror held the firmest grip.

Clenching her shaking hands, she looked at the steaming pot ready for the mush she'd been about to make. Outside, the tomahawk throwing continued, accompanied by loud, wrathful voices. Would they hack the cabin to pieces?

The wolf-marked Indian was at the doorway again, a hand on the hilt of his scalping knife. Tessa turned her back to him against her will, dumped the cornmeal she'd ground into the waiting pot, and stirred it, as she would have done had she been making supper for her brothers.

Would she meet a bitter end before this hot hearth?

Excruciating moments ticked by, the mush finally made. Raising a hand, she pushed back a strand of damp hair before heaving the pot off the crane and moving toward the door. Bypassing the Indian, she now faced nearly a dozen outside. They regarded her with steely silence, their painted features and ready weapons nearly buckling her knees.

An empty sugar trough rested at the edge of the garden. She set the pot down and turned into the springhouse, a squat Indian following. When she emerged with a crock of milk, he poked a finger into the creamy top and tasted it, shadowing her as she poured the mush into the waiting trough. Thick and hot, it spread down the length of the wooden vessel in a pale stream, then mixed with the milk she poured next. Setting her jaw against her rising panic, she went back into the cabin to fetch molasses and spoons.

She knew her brothers. Surely these red-men were the same. A full stomach was far better than an empty one. Her very life depended on it. Hardly aware of what she did, she handed each Indian a spoon before adding molasses to the trough of mush. Were these men Shawnee? Wyandot? Lenape? Stepping back, she dredged up one of the few words Keturah had taught her.

"Mitsi." Eat.

The warriors' watchful intensity switched to momentary surprise. Again every eye was upon her.

"A-i," one brave uttered. What that meant she did not know.

She gestured to the steaming trough. They soon ringed it, dipping their spoons with relish. All seemed hungry, even famished. When one grew especially greedy, he received a rap on the head with a tall Indian's spoon and a terse warning, as if he'd violated some rule of Indian decorum. Unbidden, Tessa felt a beat of amusement.

At a whippoorwill's trill on the path to the fields, a fresh fear overtook her. If her brothers came into the clearing . . . Though she'd delayed the danger, she couldn't shake the certainty something dire was coming. Some soul-crushing moment where both the past and the future would be forever altered.

The trough emptied. The spoons were dropped onto the ground. The warriors were all looking at her again as if silently deciding her fate. One gave a shrill war whoop, turning away the instant Ross came around the barn.

Dear Lord, not Ross!

"Run!" She took a step toward him only to collide with the tall Indian, who blocked her way. With a practiced ease, he slipped a cord around her wrists, bound her hands behind her back, and pulled the rawhide so tight she winced.

Ross came on, straight toward her. As if he could help her. Save her. His rifle was in one hand, the barrel pointed at the ground. What could he do against so many Indians? She well knew what they might do to him.

Something more than these warriors had bleached his face the hue of new linen. Her gaze fell from his stricken expression to his shirt. A scarlet stain covered one sleeve, another splash of scarlet across the shirt's front. Was he hurt? Nay.

Another brother.

Had the Indians come upon Jasper and Zadock in the fields before coming here? She saw no dangling scalps. Two Indians strode toward Ross, one wresting the gun from his grasp. Ross let it go without protest, his odd gaze still on her. He was trying to keep peace, protect her, not provoke them into a fury.

Her voice broke. "What about the others?"

He shook his head as if unwilling to say. Or so eaten up with grief he could not. His scarlet shirt bespoke much. He stood still as he was put in a neck noose, his hands bound like hers.

Two braves entered the smokehouse and emerged with a ham and other provisions. At that instant she was shoved from behind, past the garden and around the back of the springhouse and into the woods. One look back at Ross earned her another shove, this time so hard she nearly fell. In the melee of the moment came the distressed whinny of horses. They were her brothers' prize mounts, now being rounded up by the Indians.

Their party waded through the shallow water, her stockings and shoes sodden, the hem of her skirt making walking a chore. If her hands were free she'd leave a trail, bits of fabric from her threadbare apron, along the way. As it was she could only press her heels deep into the ground once they left the water to try to mark her hasty passage. A broken branch here, a trampled flower there.

The Indians were having trouble with the horses, high-strung mounts, all but Blossom. Tessa could see the concern in their dark faces as they attempted to curb the stomping, rearing animals. One brave mounted and was thrown. With no bridles or saddles or even a whip, the most that could be done was drive them forward till they tired. The stony creek bed soon bore the harsh clatter of hooves.

The tall Indian seemed to have charge of her. He led the party, his stride strong and purposeful. His muscled, swarthy skin bore a sheen of something rank, some grease. Bear fat. Coupled with the hot air, the strong smell spiked her wooziness. She tried to match his pace. Her life depended on it.

Clay, Clay.

Never far from her thoughts, he'd been all but forgotten in the nightmare of the last half hour.

Lord, help him get to us. We might have a chance if Clay came . . .

For now, Ross consumed her, his stricken face betokening some unspeakable grief. Deep in her spirit she sensed at least one of her brothers was with Pa. Not knowing who plunged her into the blackest pit, her mind and heart racked with angst.

Their party vanished over the brow of the

hill that marked the boundary of Swan land, pressing farther west than she had ever been before. Up creeks and streambeds that left no trail, past waterfalls spilling from clifftops like a giant pitcher poured from on high, through laurel thickets she could not admire and ripe whortleberries she could not pick. Once, her foot caught on a grapevine and she stumbled, nearly pitching headlong into the tall Indian. He turned midstride, never slowing, his look forbidding. She'd oft heard the tragic penalty for falling behind, for slowing them in their dash to distance themselves from any settlers in pursuit.

In time they mounted the horses, which were now trail worn. Bareback, she missed her familiar saddle. Strength ebbing, she clung to Blossom's mane to help anchor her atop the unforgiving ground.

These red warriors were untiring, taking to the heights like goats. One of their party scouted ahead to inform them of danger, one behind to watch any approach from the rear. The bony ridge was dry, the sun pulling to the west and throwing a veil of gossamer light over the unbroken forest below. She tasted dust, her throat so dry she could hardly swallow. That beloved spicy-sweet scent of autumn had taken hold, but now it held a bitter taint. She rode toward the setting sun, dazed, winded, and disbelieving.

'Twas milking time, that sweet, earthy half hour atop her small stool, head pressed against the cow's warm side, the noisy stream of white steady inside the dark pail. But here and now they were making a sort of rest stop beside a miserly trickle of creek due to some fuss about a gun.

Ready to drop from exhaustion, Tessa leaned against her mount, eyes burning from too much sun and dust, finding no solace in the spectacle before her. Ross stepped up to the Indian with the broken musket, taking the weapon in hand like it was his own, his rapt expression an aggravation to Tessa.

Tears of fury blurred her view. Long minutes ticked by, followed by some tinkering, and then a pleased grunt and unintelligible word signaled the stolen weapon was fixed. The surrounding Indians eyed Ross with unmistakable respect. New interest. Her beleaguered spirits simmered. 'Twas the first time in memory she'd been vexed by her brother's resourceful bent as he helped the very Indians who might have killed Pa, who no doubt had dispatched another Swan this very day, who might well strike them down next. Turning, she spat into the dirt, earning a wicked glance from the wolfish warrior.

29

The field of winter wheat was sun-drenched and silent, the heated August air already blackened by buzzards. Wolves would be next, yet Clay had no time to think about a burial. His aim was to get to the Swan cabin even as horror slowed him at the spectacle of death right here. Two of the Swans' horses had been killed in the harness, their unwieldy bodies collapsed atop untilled ground. A severe struggle had played out, a brave fight. The upturned earth and shattered gunstock led him to Jasper's broken body, a wad of black hair still clenched in one callused fist.

While armed men took care of the burial, Clay raced to Swan Station with a small company of settlement men, Westfall included. As Bolt jumped a split-rail fence and came down hard, Clay tried to brace himself for the wrench of what was yet to come. Cyrus had escaped when the Indians struck in the field, running to alert the fort while Ross backtracked to the Swan cabin. No telling what had transpired with Tessa and her other brothers.

A breathless dread spiked as Clay drew nearer the homestead. No smoke curled above the tree line where the cabin and outbuildings lay. The place was as silent as the field. His restless gaze swept the clearing for any carnage. The open smokehouse door foretold raiding. Jude cautiously looked inside, the shake of his head negating a closer look.

The ground at the cabin and corral bore a great many moccasin and hoof prints, leaving off toward the westernmost woods. But the trail was quickly washed away in the creek. A few deeply placed heel marks leading to the water's edge confirmed his suspicions that Tessa and at least one other had been taken captive, the horses stolen.

Zadock roamed about with a loaded rifle, calling for Tessa in that wrenching way a bereaved brother would, as if expecting to come upon her body as he had his fallen brother.

Clay studied the disturbed ground that led into the woods. "Let's waste no more time."

No telling when he'd return to Fort

Tygart. Though the fort was weakened in the absence of even a few men, more prey to attack, they had a formidable supply of powder and bullet lead.

Clay pressed upward, leaving the valley, knowing the raiders would eventually take to the heights, where travel was easiest and ambush unlikely. The search party followed with a frightful noise. He half wished he was alone and could overtake the Indians, pick them off one by one from the rear in a silent, deadly pursuit. Yet this might well spell death for Tessa. 'Twas a treacherous chase. Even the best plan might fail, the outcome tragic and irreversible.

His gut churned, that odd breathlessness causing a sharp twinge to his ribs. Fear cut into him, never so personal as now. Not since the attack on his own homestead so long ago, the tattered memories jumbled into a tight knot he couldn't unravel, had he been so jolted. He felt naked. Exposed. Nearly helpless. Everyone here knew how he felt about her. Their hand holding and walks within fort walls, the heaven-sent day they'd spent berry picking outside them, bespoke much. And even now they were watching to see his reaction if the worst happened.

Though these men didn't know his underlying fight with what Maddie called the lie, they knew he loved Tessa. And she had been wrenched from his life as surely as if his loving her had propelled her there, proving once again that whatever he set his heart upon was shattered.

Almighty God, please.

The brokenness that had begun inside him long ago, only half mended, now fractured anew. As he rode at a furious pace, all manner of things flew through his head till he seemed naught but a barrel rolled downhill, every bump and crash jarring loose a tormenting possibility. Scalping. Burning. Worse.

A man can only take so much.

Spent, he finally paused at a spring to let Bolt drink. Precious moments ticked by, each widening the distance between himself and Tessa. He could only imagine her fear, her shock. Her captors were traveling fast, leaving little trail, and intent on putting the wide Ohio River between them. Only then would the chase slow on the Indians' part.

Still they pressed on, the ridge showcasing a spectacular crimson sunset that was lost on him. Soon darkness would overtake them, and they must eat. Rest the horses. Mayhap split ranks if warranted.

When the time came, Jude dropped to his

haunches beside Clay as the horses were watered and the men ate from pouches of jerky and meal.

"Been ridin' hard now for hours." Jude wiped his brow with one of Maddie's neatly sewn handkerchiefs. "You've had plenty of time to think things through. What's the gist of it?"

"A war party of ten or twelve. Lenape, likely. Tessa among them. Thank God we've come upon no corpses." Clay swallowed, too bestirred to take the jerky from Jude's outstretched hand. "They're traveling fast, mayhap all night. They might divide at some point, try to fool us, or lie in wait and ambush us."

Jude expelled a heavy breath. "I hate to ask, but do you think . . ."

Clay nodded. Tamanen. He wouldn't speak his name. Not without it leaving a bitter taste.

Lord, let me be wrong.

But in his spirit he believed the Swans were marked by their association with him, that somehow Keturah was a part of that. No doubt Tamanen wanted to cut short any chance of happiness Clay had in future, that his rage at the whites was at its most personal in seeking revenge for Clay's turning against the people who had raised him.

Whom he'd betrayed by not returning to them when he had the chance.

"Don't think overmuch," Jude said. "Just pray and keep followin' hard after them."

The misery of the moment was so acute that Tessa swung between fury and fear. When she could not take another step without a drink of water, a bubbling rage made her nearly shout at her captor's tawny back, *"Mënihi."* Give me a drink.

'Twas what Keturah had said to them early on, before she recalled the white words. Tessa's strangled demand brought a halt to their frenzied pace, the wolf-marked warrior turning to regard her with a menacing gaze that faded to cold irritation. Her own ire darkened to sorrow when he removed a strap from about his neck and thrust at her a flask she knew all too well.

Jasper's. Had it been just this morning she'd made him switchel? Though the drink was quenching, it still hurt to swallow. Her oldest brother was no more. Deep in her spirit she knew. If she'd grasped this day was to be his last, she would have embraced him when she'd handed him the flask, taken a long look at him in the golden haze of daybreak, made sure there were no lingering hard feelings between the two of them.

With effort, she swallowed a second mouthful, then hung the flask around her own neck before the steady gaze of the wolfish warrior. Would he jerk it free? With a small smirk, he faced forward, studying the sky and giving her a moment to glance back, seeking Ross. He was at the rear of the column, looking as haggard as she felt. Her heart twisted anew, her earlier aggravation long gone. She yearned to go to him, comfort him. Free him. The neck noose cut into his skin, making a circlet of blood about his throat. If he fell he was in danger of being dragged by the horse in front and trampled by the one behind, both the most excitable of the Swan mounts.

Near full dark they came down from the ridge to the forest floor. Here the Indians spoke in low, quick exclamations as if agreeing on a camp for the night. She dropped to the ground, her petticoats cushioning her near fall. Across from her, Ross sat beneath a bent willow, brambles and briars raising red welts on his exposed skin. He was missing a shoe, his bare foot raw. Her own shoes had rubbed blisters, but in her dazed state she was only now aware of the throbbing ache.

The tall Indian bent to untie her hands, another doing the same with Ross. She passed the flask to Ross, stumbling over a root in her weariness. Though the desire to run was strong, they hadn't the strength to get away. As if sensing this, their captors treated them almost carelessly, tossing them a pouch of parched corn while they feasted on the smokehouse stealings, turning their backs to examine the guns they'd taken.

She had no appetite, yet without food she could not endure another day's journey. Her mouth worked slowly, finding the maize strange and dry. Before the third swallow she fell into an uneasy sleep, head pillowed on her arm.

She awakened to Ross holding a bayoneted musket, head bent as he examined what looked like a broken hammer. The wayward cub! Would he continue to help those who might well fire the musket at him when fixed? Or stab him with the bayonet? The urge to cry out for him to stop was once again stifled by sheer, jaw-clenching will. On he worked as daylight eroded, the Indians observing closely as he repaired the old gun.

She lay still, eyes closed, trying to grasp for the good amid the bad. How thankful she was not to lie on cold winter ground. Though the snow might leave a plainer trail, bitter weather might be as dangerous as the tomahawks and scalping knives glinting in the last of daylight. In winter food was scarce, blankets hard to come by . . .

When the wolves began to howl, she awoke again. Around her Indians slept, dark, still lumps in the moonlit night. Two stood watch. If her feet weren't bound, she'd try to flee. Jump atop one of their horses hobbled nearby. As it was, she could only slap at insects bedeviling her as she lay. Ross was just across from her, tied to a tree, head lolled onto his chest in slumber.

In and out of sleep threaded one unceasing thought. *Clay, come to me.*

Was he even now on their trail? Had he been the one to bury Jasper? Her heart could hardly hold the weight of it. Pa had been too much. Just when they'd begun to make a sort of peace with his empty chair, the pipe and tools and clothes remaining, now this. Yet her life, their lives, were made up of a thousand little losses. Even Keturah's leaving and Ma's remarrying were losses too, holding more sadness than joy, leaving a lonesome place. Some said 'twas the way of the frontier, to take and take again. She'd never make peace with that. Wouldn't life on the Monongahela be the same? Wasn't the city safer? If Clay was beside her . . .

Life with Clay would be different, aye, because he was different, so far apart from the ragged-edged frontiersmen she'd known. Somehow his Indianness and his whiteness melded to form an experienced, honed survivor of both worlds. Much like Keturah, he was a breed apart, the best of both worlds.

Holding that close, she slept, only to be awakened before daybreak as they took to the trail again, this time at a breakneck pace as if the Indians sensed someone was overtaking them. There was no denying the spiked tension, the heightened wariness. She was equally aware of the Indians' capacity for sudden violence. Short-tempered, almost childlike in their impatience, they had little tolerance for any show of weakness.

The woods spun by, the autumn smells and sounds of the forest a brittle blur. They were on horseback again, sparing her blistered feet, but her old homespun dress and stockings were being torn to pieces by briars and brambles as they raced on headlong. Morning became afternoon, and their arduous pace began to tell on the horses. Lathered, stumbling, they kept on, but her mare threw her once. Her body was jarred anew by the tumble, which earned her another menacing look.

In time they descended onto a flat plain where buffalo wallowed. A river spread before them, bluer and wider than she'd ever seen. 'Twas more than a river, more a great divide between the world she'd known and the world yet to be. They paused on the bank of a rock-strewn stream that fed into that tremendous river. The Indians were excited now, as if they'd accomplished something by coming here.

She slumped across Blossom's neck, fingers digging into the coarse mane. Ross was on his feet just ahead of her, several warriors talking and gesturing as they ringed him. He looked toward her, one bare foot in the water. His linen shirt was little more than a dirty gray rag, his britches no better. Dark hair lay lank about his shoulders, a startling contrast to the Indians' scalp locks and dangling feathers. Her brother looked small. Bewildered. Beyond weary.

The leader gave a thrust of his hand northward. The horses were divided, her brother tied on the mount Jasper had favored. Ross did not look back. Slowly he crossed the stream, and her heart cleaved in two.

With a little cry, she slid off her horse and began a clumsy run toward him.

If he left, if they were parted —

A hard hand spun her around. The tall Indian loomed over her, his painted face so near she smelled his fetid breath. *"Ikih!"* The commanding word held a warning. He jerked her toward her horse, lifting her onto its broad back, and they were on their way west, not northward like Ross and the warriors with him.

Down the bank she went, plunging into the river's cold, the current soaking her skirts. There were but six of them now, she at the center. 'Twas getting harder to stay atop her mount. At the end of her endurance, she began to lose hope.

They climbed the opposite bank, the hoofprints seeming of no consequence now that they'd come such a great distance. Her impressions blurred as they climbed another ridge and then descended into yet another forested valley. Fainting or sleeping, she fell off her horse once . . . twice. They tied her back on with wild grapevine.

No grief had been so great as this separation from Ross. Greater than Pa. Than Jasper. Had she not tended him more than Ma? Watched over him, rocked him, soothed him day in and day out when he was little, then delighted in his company when grown?

Stars marked their passage, and a great

harvest moon. They pressed on to unknown parts, her hopes unraveling before eroding completely, her prayers unanswered.

30

Though passable riflemen and hardy farmers, the rescue party was slowing him. Harassed by worries of their own homeplaces, their mounts plodding rather than pursuing, they looked to Clay for guidance, for success, and thus far they'd met with one obstacle after another. Two horses were lamed, provisions had been lost in a river crossing, a gun had misfired and injured a hand, and one man was fevered.

At this tempo the Indians would soon outdistance them. Reining in at a salt lick, Clay faced the wearied party. If he was to recover Tessa and Ross, even own a chance at such, he'd have to go ahead of them.

"I'm going to press on with you at my back as fast as you can travel. Jude is a master tracker and won't lead you astray. If there's any question as to your whereabouts or mine, fire a single shot, but only one lest the Indians come down on you. I may be close enough to hear it. One way or another, Lord willing, we'll reunite."

"How far ahead do you think the war party is?" one man asked.

"A few miles, by my reckoning. We're close to losing their trail, but I aim to pick it up again." With that he wheeled round and set off as if breaking a restraint, only Jude realizing his desperation to be free of them.

His pursuit, the coming confrontation, was about far more than recovering Tessa and Ross. It bore a personal grudge, a festering, that would likely end in the death of himself or Tamanen. He felt to his bones his Lenape brother had been the one to wreak havoc at Swan Station, his killing Jasper and capturing Tessa as close to injuring Clay as he could come. Indian grudges went deep, but so did white. He'd borne Tamanen no ill will till now. And he understood the depth of Tamanen's success in this. Bringing back a white captive — not just any white woman, but one who was affianced to Clay — bore highest honors. And Tessa might burn because of it.

The noon sun was hottest atop the rocky ridge, and a copper snake coiled in his path, then slithered away at the beat of Bolt's hooves. Fear clawed a new hole in him as he lost the trail and then picked it up again in a shadowed draw, pausing to examine a piece of linen no bigger than a flint. A scrap of apron?

Tessa.

Unbound and on horseback, no doubt, and clever enough to leave sign of her own. He clutched the fabric in one fist and kept on, eyes stinging beneath the brim of his sweat-stained hat. Blessedly iron shod, the Swan horses left undeniable traces yet were remarkably swift. He'd have to press Bolt beyond anything he'd required of him yet if he was to overtake the war party. And if Bolt wore out, threw a shoe, or was lamed . . .

Clay left a buffalo trace and traveled a burned section of forest before reaching a tributary of the mighty Ohio. Here a scuffle seemed to have occurred, the hoof prints deep, the party dividing. Dismounting and allowing Bolt a drink, Clay scanned the opposite shore, knowing he was an easy target in the open. Indecision warred inside him. Which way?

God in heaven, help Thou me.

The wrong path could prove fatal to them all. He dropped to one knee on the stony bank, bent his head in a plea for direction. The hot wind shook the trees overhead, the cicadas raucous.

He mounted Bolt and started into the water, holding his gun high overhead in case of another mishap. His gaze narrowed to the opposite shore, hope rising in his chest.

There, on a sticker bush at the wood's edge, was another tendril of cloth. His heart lurched. Tessa. Still alive. Still able to leave a remnant of their swift journey, providing clear direction as to which way she had gone. The sign was nothing short of miraculous, somehow escaping her captors' unwavering scrutiny and confirming the trail he must take. He broke through the brush with renewed haste, his confidence seeming to spur Bolt on as well.

Was their reunion almost at hand? Any wrong move on his part might prove disastrous. He was one man against what looked to be five or better. He could get a couple of strategic shots off that might let her get out of harm's way before he reloaded and took aim at the rest. It helped that she had that frontier quick-wittedness, one of many reasons he admired her. Her life depended on his response — and hers.

He ducked to escape a low-hanging branch, his thoughts crammed full of her even as his gaze swept the forest floor. Time had never been so precious. He needed to find her, hold her tight. Take her to Fort

Pitt out of ruination's way and marry her. Resign his post. He ached with the weight of his love for her and the uncertainty of the moment.

The sunset was a crimson smear, the murmur of thunder distant. Coming to the bottom of a gorge crisscrossed with fallen timber, he inched past a noisy waterfall, leaving Bolt hobbled out of sight. A high, sharp whinny of another horse sent him to his knees. It had come from just over the rise as it led out of the gorge. Crouching low, he moved upward, higher, his breath coming in repressed bursts, the hungry hours honing his senses.

His aim must be true.

The bay horse's high whinny overrode the murmur of thunder. Tessa's worn senses sharpened even as her guard shoved her down behind a laurel bush, her face to the earth. Around her the other Indians quickly took cover, weapons pointed toward the rise looming over them. Her pulse quickened as her painted captor stood over her, moccasined feet firmly planted on her loosened hair to keep her pinned.

The forest seemed to be holding its breath, waiting. Even the birdsong ceased. Tessa lay motionless, scalp taut as her hair was yanked, the laurel's blooms pressing against her with bony stems.

Lord, I want to live. Let this come to a quick end.

Two Indians circled back, climbing up the hill through dense brush so stealthily they made no sound. As they stepped closer to the top, treeing in their ascent, nary a twig snapped or a leaf rustled. Her skewed view took in what she could.

Her captor shifted, the ache to her scalp heightened. Thunder threatened louder but the rain withheld. The horses behind them grew more unsettled, at risk of bolting. At the bedrock of her awareness came a sense of dread. Not her own but the Indians'. Keturah had told her of the Lenape's fear of Clay. She had not understood, yet she felt the Indians' wariness. Clay had come for her. Was crouched somewhere behind that rocky, leafy rise. Knowing it, sensing all that was at stake, she felt at once a thrill and terror.

The Indians raised their guns as they took positions behind brush and trees. All but the man who stood over her, firmly fastening her to the ground, his own rifle raised. She had no doubt he'd use the tomahawk and scalping knife at his belt if it came to that.

So exhausted was she bodily that even her thoughts were sluggish but for one ongoing, hope-filled plea.

Almighty God, help Thou me.

His Quaker roots wouldn't give him any peace, their "Thou shalt not bear arms" a constant reproach. But how many men, even Friends, caught in the crux of saving a loved one or not violating a tenet, would choose the latter? Clay peered through a spicewood thicket, able to see down into the bowl-shaped hollow from his position, though the Indians could not see him. But they were ready, guns raised. If fear had a smell, it was here, both his own and theirs. His for Tessa. Theirs because they feared more than his rifle, steeped in superstition as they were.

Summoning all the life within him, he let out a hair-raising war whoop. It had been his rallying cry, his call, when he was with the Lenape in battle. Never had he used it against them till now. One Indian broke and ran at the sound, the rustle of brush eliminating one target, at least. But Tamanen stood his ground, as did the other warriors, muting Clay's fleeting burst of pleasure. Their horses scattered, nervy about the thunder of both guns and skies. Slowly, Clay raised his rifle, intent on the man who held Tessa to the forest floor.

Keturah's Indian husband. His own Lenape brother.

Emotion rose up and clouded his eyes, and he silently cursed the weakness. He stayed stone still when a shot rang out. The ball nicked the tree nearest him, widely errant of its mark and spraying bark. They meant to call him out of hiding, end his advantageous position.

Shifting a bit to the left, he trained his sights on Tamanen, who was well hidden behind a thick maple. He could make out Tessa's dress, her slim silhouette on the ground below him. The humbling sight steeled his resolve. Tamanen was a good two hundred yards distant, but Clay's charge of black powder could reach farther. A hot wind smacked him, unseating his hat and threatening his aim. He closed the frizzen and cocked the hammer. The slight click seemed to echo, a forewarning of the trigger pull.

When Tamanen's dark head appeared for a spare second, Clay fired. The charge tore through the narrow hollow like cannon fire.

"Run!" he yelled at Tessa.

Amid the bellow of white smoke, he got off another shot, this time at the warrior climbing up the rise nearest him. The warrior toppled backwards, crashing through brush, his bare body rolling till a stand of laurel caught him. Out of the corner of Clay's eye came a flash of indigo. He raised up ever so slightly to better see down the narrow defile. In that instant a shattering pain rent his skull, sparks exploding in his brain like a hammer on a red-hot anvil. Before Tessa could get to him, his world went black.

Bile shot up Tessa's throat as she watched Clay drop. Frantic, she rolled from beneath the tall warrior, his body partially covering hers when he slumped to the ground, her fingers catching the sharp edge of his tomahawk. Blood ran from her clenched fist, staining her filthy skirt scarlet. The shock of it set her heels on fire. With a last look over her shoulder at the warrior's still body, she clawed her way up the draw, clear of the Indians still firing.

Head a-spin, she made it to the top of the rise where she'd seen Clay fall, blood and dirt beneath her fingernails, a sticker bush tearing one side of her petticoat away, the rise and fall of her chest excruciatingly tight. She had no weapon, yet never was one so needed. Before her, at the very top of the

403

hill, a now roused Clay grappled with a warrior in a deadly struggle.

A cry rose in her throat, so winded it was more a feeble screech. Blood pulsed from Clay's skull, making a scarlet mask of his eyes. Lying on his back, he held the warrior's upraised hand with its long knife in a slippery grip, seconds away from the knife's fatal plunge.

Desperate, Tessa looked about for a stick or a rock to hurl at his enemy. Fingers curling around a sharp piece of limestone, she pulled it free of dirt and fallen leaves. Careful to come at the warrior's back side, she crept toward him, nearly dropping the heavy rock. The deathly struggle played out before her gaze, Clay's hand slipping down the bare arm of the Indian as if losing its grip.

A musket ball whirled past, so close she heard its whistle. Stumbling then righting herself, she kept on. In one frantic heave she brought the rock down on the Indian's exposed scalp with all her might. He stiffened, arms outflung before he toppled backwards. In one swift motion Clay grabbed for his rifle on the ground before reaching for her and pulling her behind a rocky outcropping.

Raising a shirtsleeve, he swiped at his eyes before reloading and firing a final time. Unable to look, Tessa kept her head down, his hard-muscled body like a wall in front of her.

Once the smoke cleared, the forest was still as a grave.

Her heart, so bruised over Ross and what she was sure was Jasper's fate, fractured anew in the eerie lull. But Clay, God be praised, was alive, every fiber of his being so tense he had the look of a skulking panther. *Lord, have mercy.* His head wound fretted her. He needed it bound and cleaned. She tore at her ripped petticoat, freeing a long piece that would serve.

"Stay still and let me see to your wound." Her voice was a whisper. She didn't want to touch him without warning in the heightened state he was in. Shifting to her knees, she tried to wipe his face clean before winding the makeshift bandage around his hatless head.

They hunkered down for a good quarter of an hour. She could see the fallen Indians, including the one she'd brained with the rock. Guilt licked at the edges of her conscience. Utterly spent, she wanted nothing more than to lay down atop the rough ground and sleep. Her throbbing hand beat along with her heart, giving her little rest.

As the sun flickered behind a bank of

thunderclouds, new noises turned them on edge. Brush being trampled. Horses nickering and snorting.

When she saw Jude's worried face appear, she nearly wept with joy. The search party soon framed him. Two of the men began rounding up the stolen horses while others stripped the fallen Indians of their weapons.

Famished, thirsty, she took the jerked meat and canteen Jude thrust at her without a word of thanks. Her only thought was for Clay. She in turn passed him the offerings, but he simply shook his head. She ate, taking tiny bites, as Clay descended the draw to where the wolfish warrior had fallen. Several Lenape had been killed. One had run.

But the one who'd pinned her to the ground . . . gone.

31

Jude gave a chuckle as they reached another nameless riverbank in the twilight. "So, you served the savages mush?"

"I thought it would go harder on us if I didn't act hospitable," Tessa confessed, cast back to that terrifying moment when she'd first heard tomahawks cleave the cabin logs.

"No doubt your scalp would be hanging from a belt if you'd done otherwise," Westfall said. "After what we saw of Jasper . . ."

Clay shot him a look that bespoke much. A grievous silence ensued, the rush of the river not at all soothing. So, Jasper had indeed fallen, been buried by now near Pa, surely, facing east in readiness for resurrection morn like most settlement graves. How Ma was holding up beneath the loss of a husband and son — not one but two, counting Ross — was lost to Tessa too.

She fixed her gaze on Clay as she rode behind him and crossed the river, the cold water wetting what was left of her skirt and numbing the scratches on her skin. They were all a sorry, dirty lot, in need of a hot meal and a bath and a long night's sleep.

She groped for gratefulness. She had but a few scrapes and sore fingers. Clay had survived that deadly tussle. Though her heart was torn to pieces about Jasper, she was more torn up about Ross, out there somewhere and unaccounted for. Now her fervent prayer was that the other party would return with him, intersect with them as they made their way back to the Buckhannon. But as night closed in, the men growing silent and forming a protective ring around her, she fell asleep to tormented dreams.

She was unaware she cried out till Clay loomed over her, the glint of his rifle in the pale moonlight a fearsome sight. He dropped to his knees at her shaking, the thin blanket around her no mask for her trembling. Letting go of his rifle, he reached out and drew her near, unmindful of the sleeping, snoring men surrounding them or the alert ones on watch.

"Tessa . . ."

She burrowed into him at the tender utterance, seeking strength. Solace. They'd not spoken privately since he'd found her.

"How's your head?"

"Still attached." His wry words ended with a chuckle. "I'm more worried about my hat lost back in that draw."

"Blast that hat. You saved my life, Clay. And I've no doubt you would have bested that Indian in the end. As it was, you took on all of them single-handedly."

"I was most concerned about the tall one."

"The buck who nearly scalped me by stepping on my hair as I lay there, then took your bullet and disappeared?"

He nodded, his sudden silence raising new qualms.

She rested her head against his shoulder. "Did you know him?"

Again that prolonged pause. It boded ill. She knew before he answered.

"Aye," he said.

She waited, overcome by some unspoken regret, some grief weighting him that surely had to do with the wolf-marked warrior.

He drew her nearer. Lowering his head, he kissed her brow. "I never thought to see your hair unbound till we wed."

She pushed back a wayward strand with her good hand, a twig tangled in its length. Pulling it free, she looked up at the moon. It resembled a scythe, bringing to mind Jasper at work in the fields, drinking the

409

switchel she'd made him. And then her mind circled round to Ross when Clay said, "Tell me what happened at the cabin when the Indians came."

She retold the terror of the day, focusing on Ross. "Later, on the trail, he fixed an Indian's gun. I couldn't believe my eyes but daren't speak, lest it bring down their wrath on the both of us —"

"He's no fool. Once they know he can mend their guns they'll likely keep him alive. And he's young yet. If he stays with the tribe, he'll fare better than most. Mayhap grow fond of their ways —"

"Fond?" She couldn't bear the thought. This chancy separation, this waiting and not knowing, was inconsolable. "You've got to bring him back, Clay. I thought —"

"You thought we were on the trail to find him? Nay, Tessa." The firmness in his voice was like the closing of a door. "The other party we broke with at the river is charged with returning him if they can. My aim was to find you and bring you back."

"But not without Ross." Her fingers curled round his hard forearm. "I won't rest without him."

"Ross went north on the warrior's trail. Once that happens it becomes harder to track him. There are countless paths to countless tribes. He might end up with the Iroquois, a far greater foe than the Lenape. But no matter where he lands, he'll be considered a prize with his gunsmithing. At least he won't burn."

"Burn?" She'd feared it when taken, yet it spelled a blessed end once done. "Betimes that's the better way."

"Not if you've seen it done, nay." He shut her down with his quiet vehemence. "If he's not found he'll make his way among them, be adopted. Mayhap he'll run in time. But not all captives want to return to the white world. Some choose to stay red."

His words kindled fresh fear in her heart. To lose a father and then two brothers, one of them to a people who would deprive them of his beloved presence, made her soul sick. Then to face the possibility Ross would betray them by remaining with the very people who'd torn them apart? The memory of him bent over the Indian gun, striving to repair a weapon of the enemy to be used against them, stole the last scrap of her composure.

Tears fell onto her torn bodice as an anguish she'd never known crowded in black as the night, seeping through every worn and weary part of her. Of all her brothers, Ross had hold of her heart. Would the Indians rob his sunny spirit? Change him into a dark-hearted warrior?

"You've got to go after him." Her voice turned pleading. "Those other men in the rescue party — they aren't you, Clay. You can find Ross. I know you can. Every delay spells disaster. I feel it."

He shifted, the arm holding her more iron-like. "I'll not veer from returning you home. I can't risk the fort any longer besides."

Dander high, she pulled away from him and lay down again. Though she was exhausted, ire kept her awake.

When they roused well before sunrise, she didn't look Clay's way but mounted her mare, spine stiff. Let him be stubborn and hard-hearted then. She'd not forgive him if Ross was lost. She'd rather her brother join Jasper in the ground. This infernal waiting and wondering would drive her mad.

Clay had sensed a stubbornness in Tessa from the first but had never felt the brunt of it till now. He admired her, loved her, but she was unbending as Hester in matters best left to him. All he could do now was pray for Ross's swift return and contact Fort Pitt and other stations to alert them to his capture and hoped-for ransom. But it was a chancy matter with the utmost complexities.

As they rode east into the sunrise, the rift between him and Tessa took root. He felt it as keenly as the wound to his skull, but here, amid so many men in such haste to return to the garrison, there was no time to address it. He stayed at the head of the column, Jude as rear guard, their party with so many horses making a clamor no matter how hard they tried to pass unnoticed. The undergrowth had turned brittle in the heat, sun-dried with shades of autumn, the slight rain a distant memory.

His ongoing prayer was that Fort Tygart, though undermanned and worn down by the slightest skirmish, stood stalwart. How could he explain to Tessa that the good of many trumped the loss of one, even a beloved brother? Few withstood the horror of a fort's fall, the once-proud pickets a heap of smoking ashes, mangled and mutilated settlers strewn like seed across acres of red ground. The day of the Swan raid, he'd read a report of the Indians and their allies bringing cannon against the westernmost outposts. Nothing could withstand cannon. All must surrender or die.

They rode on, through canebrakes and salt licks, along buffalo traces and deer paths, up and down till their horses grew lathered and clumsy, before coming to the north fork of the Buckhannon. Morning fog curled like smoke along the riverbank, blurring the lines of cornfields and fences as they neared Fort Tygart.

The fog was lifting in the face of the rising sun. His distant scrutiny of the garrison gave way to profound gratitude. *God be thanked.* No taint of charred timbers. No corpses. There the fort sat on the rocky bluff, bristling with guns, a lone shot and loud huzzah welcoming them in.

He gave a look over his shoulder, heartened to see a sort of pained relief on Tessa's face as she rode behind him. He wanted her behind walls. He'd still not settled down at finding her gone, that frantic, gutted feeling not yet dissipated. And with this new chasm betwixt them, what next?

Through the fort gates they hustled. For once Clay was glad to see Hester rush forward and take Tessa to her cabin. Maddie and Jude accompanied him to his blockhouse quarters, where a good hour was spent hearing reports of spies and answering questions of their own mission, only partly successful with Ross and half the rescue party still missing.

As if expecting a crowd, Hester spread a

414

great many dishes before them in her cabin at suppertime. The presence of Cyrus, Lemuel, and Zadock only reminded them of who was missing. Rosemary seemed more grateful than grief-stricken, having both a daughter and a new husband returned. They all sat at the burgeoning table at sunset, wrestling with Ross's loss, Jasper's death, and what to do with Tessa.

"You'll stay here, of course, till you heal," Hester announced with a pointed look at her great-niece and her bandaged hand as she heaped more fried corn on Clay's plate. "Nothing short of the Lord's second coming would send me back to the Buckhannon at such a time."

Tessa sat mute, eating little. Rosemary tried to draw her out in conversation, but Tessa was having none of it. Westfall did most of the talking, asking pertinent questions about the rescue and what other Indian activity had been reported along the border. Clay answered as best he could, tiredness overtaking him and almost slurring his answers.

He hardly tasted Hester's coffin pie, though he dutifully washed it down with coffee. At supper's end, he said quietly, "Obliged for the fine meal."

"Obliged to you, Colonel, for rescuing my

daughter." Rosemary looked to Tessa, whose bandaged hand was in her lap. "You're in need of rest. A bath." She shot Clay an understanding smile. "As are you, Colonel Tygart."

His own rankness was not lost on him, a further deterrent to any romantic thoughts. Tomorrow, bathed and clear-headed, he'd make time alone with Tessa, if she'd talk with him. The set of her features said she might not. Mayhap by morning she'd come around.

He left to attend to fort business, a deep-seated restlessness taking hold.

The next morning he was back in Hester's cabin again. How could he tell Tessa the latest news? He took the seat nearest her as she sat by the open window with her sewing.

"You likely saw the search party come in without Ross a half hour ago," he began. They'd raised such a commotion no one could miss it.

She simply nodded, tears in her eyes.

"I can't tell you how it grieves me to say that." He knew, too, she blamed him in some way. She never said it outright, but he sensed it. What else would explain her sudden and prolonged coldness?

"I wish you'd gone after Ross instead of me," she said softly. "I know you could have saved him."

Was it not enough that he'd saved her? Aye, a captive brother was a grievous matter, but if she only knew what it had taken to reclaim her, not to mention Keturah's possible loss and his own complicated tie with Tamanen. Knowing he'd lash out angrily if he spoke, he left without another word.

At day's end he sat down to pen a letter to Heckewelder to be read to Keturah in the event it ever reached them. He inked the quill, his hand poised over the paper, the dull ache in his head keeping words at bay. He wanted to turn back time to when Tessa was making him stockings and he was simply giving her a pretty book of verse. Not this. Not a debacle in the field and the woods, where good if misguided men had died on both sides and a brother had vanished. Two brothers. Had Tamanen not once been that to him?

To expunge some of the ill feeling, he pressed the ink to the page and scrawled, *Brother Heckewelder . . .*

Guilt ambushed his next thought. Gripping the quill, he forced the next line.

I trust you and your party are well and have met with success establishing your mission along the Muskingum.

He nearly rolled his eyes. Such foolish greetings when he was driven by one irrefutable fact.

I regret —

At that he almost slashed the word out. He did regret the killing he'd done that day. No peace was to be had violating "Thou shalt not kill." But it was either Tessa or the Lenape, and the choice was never clearer. Bending his head, he grasped for gut-wrenching words to ask forgiveness.

Still, he could not say, *I regret to tell you of the death of Tamanen, Keturah's Lenape husband.*

When he'd fired the shot to save Tessa, his one consoling thought was that it would be quick. A merciful end when it might have been unmercifully drawn out. But nay, he could not say in truth, *He fell in an ambush near the west fork of the Little White River.* Instead, he wrote only what he was sure of.

I regret to tell you of the capture of Ross Swan, last seen on the banks of the Little White River.

The quill shook. He set it down.
What had become of Tamanen?

32

A fortnight passed. August waned with a thwarted attack on a small station downriver. One man perished, and then the raiding Indians melted away. Clay kept a quarter of Fort Tygart's men constantly reconnoitering. He resumed his scouting rounds, more at peace outside the garrison than in it. He and Tessa had barely spoken since he'd gone to Hester's to tell them the sorrowful news that the search party had returned without Ross. Tessa's hand was healing, and he saw her about the fort — drawing water at the spring, talking to Maddie, doing one-handed chores — but mostly she kept to herself and the cabin, turning her great-aunt uneasy and raising fresh concerns of his own.

She seemed a shadow of herself. Gone was the quicksilver smile that rose to light her lovely eyes. That lilting laugh. Her clothing began to hang on her slender frame. When he came in and out of the blockhouse he often saw her sitting by the cabin window less than a stone's throw away. She looked at him without emotion, meeting his eyes only briefly. It cut him in ways he couldn't fathom.

There was no help for a moment in time that couldn't be undone. "There are other ways to try and recover him, understand," he'd told her once. "I've written to Fort Pitt, sent word to various outposts. Trappers and traders often bring word of captives they've seen or heard about. The chase is far from done."

She regarded him dully. The lackluster look she'd taken on since his recovering her hadn't altered. A sense of hopelessness lodged like a millstone in his own soul. He vowed not to seek her out again. Let her come to him if she would. *If.* The crushing uncertainty of it hung over him like a hatchet.

Hester darkened his door, all but wringing her hands. "Can you do nothing?"

"About Ross?" he said, a hair away from exasperation.

"Nay. Tessa." She shut the heavy door with surprising strength despite her small frame. "She'll soon join Jasper if we don't take action, pining away night and day like she is."

"What do you advise?" The words came out harsher than he wanted, his own sense of helplessness skirting fury. Passing a hand over his jaw, he fumbled for answers.

"Her spirit's troubled and there's no help for it. 'A merry heart doeth good like a medicine: but a broken spirit drieth the bones.' "

The proverb was not one he liked to dwell on.

Hester came nearer his desk, all but pacing between it and the hearth. "Was it just my silly, gray-haired hopes, or did I sense some spark betwixt you two?"

"It's since ebbed," he said stoically.

"On her part or yours?"

"Not on mine." There was no letting up with Hester. Once begun, she'd not rest till she had a remedy. "But Tessa is in no temper for courting, as you yourself just said. And I have far more on my mind than frolicking."

Hester snorted. "A little frolicking might do you both a world of good."

The kisses they'd shared in the all-too-distant past cobwebbed in his memory.

"This fort is crawling with soldiers, given reinforcements from Fort Pitt just arrived." She faced him, arms akimbo on her narrow hips. "Seems like you could take Tessa beyond those pickets anytime you please."

He withheld a sigh. His self-made vow to not approach Tessa till she first approached him wavered before Hester's persistence. While he didn't believe Tessa would lie beside Jasper anytime soon, he was concerned enough that she kept him awake nights.

"I'll speak with her, aye." But not take her beyond fort walls, nor try to revive the spark that had once nearly turned him on end and now seemed like it never was.

Hester looked hard at him as if awaiting details. He gave none. With a harrumph she went away, leaving him to ponder this new predicament.

He was at the end of his tether regarding Tessa, soldiering on despite her, hoping something would turn in matters of Ross. Since the recent raiding and murders, he himself felt like a target, not knowing if Tamanen was dead or alive. If alive, he'd best watch his back. If dead, Tamanen's fellow warriors would surely retaliate, might even now be watching the fort, awaiting his riding out alone.

Within these walls, his head and heart were engaged in full-blown battle. Even if Tessa stayed stone cold toward him, he must make a move. Either regain what was lost between them or make peace with the fact she'd never forgive him, their tie irretrievably severed.

His heart, so guarded, was now almost broken by circumstances beyond his control — a brother he couldn't bring back, the woman he adored eroding before his eyes. He needed answers.

The night was starlit. Clear. A coolness had crept in, carrying a promise the first frost wasn't far off. Clay came down from the rifle platform at the change of the watch, the brilliant sunset long since faded. The clarity he'd prayed for had finally come, but would Tessa agree to it?

He approached Hester's cabin, which was brimming with kin. Had he overlooked something?

Standing outside the open door, Zadock answered his perplexity. " 'Tis the date Pa died. And now Jasper lies beside him."

Clay removed his hat in respect, second-guessing himself. Hester had told him a while back the Swans marked the day by gathering but hadn't said which day it was. They didn't make a loud show of it, just assembled for a family meal.

Should he stay his plan till a better time?

Nay. There was rarely a better time. No guarantee of the next minute, nor tomorrow.

The cabin quieted as his frame filled the open doorway. He wore his Sabbath-best linen shirt and breeches, buckled shoes, and the clocked stockings Tessa had made for him. In his pocket was the heirloom usually secreted in his trunk. The heart-shaped locket bore a slight crack in its tarnished face, but the entire necklace was still intact, the frail chain a filigree of gold. Once it had hung upon the bodice of the woman he loved best, the queen of his own boyish world. Somehow, miraculously, it survived the firing of the Tygart cabin before finding its way back to him, mayhap meant for Tessa herself.

"Colonel Tygart, do come in." Rosemary stood, turning toward the hearth as if to fetch him a plate or some coffee, but he shook his head while others murmured greetings.

"I've come to speak with Tessa. Walk out with her if she will." There, he'd said it. Issued the invitation. Would she deny him in front of all? Send him away to return the heirloom to the trunk, and all his hopes with it?

Though alarmingly pale when he'd first

come in, she was now a becoming pink as she stood. Clad in her Sabbath best — a dress he hadn't seen before of pale green cloth, the fichu and apron an unspotted cream, her lace-edged cap with its dangling strings covering her bounty of carefully pinned, upswept hair — she made him unashamedly weak-kneed.

He all but held his breath as she came his way, skirting the full table, every eye on them both. He'd missed her. Her voice. Her unique mannerisms. Her warm presence. Would Ross stand between them now? Or had she come to the place where she'd forgiven him for what he couldn't rectify, couldn't control?

They walked out into the night, candles from a few cabins casting yellow squares of light hither and yon. In his skittishness, he'd forgotten a meeting was playing out in the blockhouse with the new command, a great many soldiers rambling about the common. He sought the place between a cabin and the far blockhouse nearest the spring that afforded them a bit of privacy. It smelled of mint, the herb growing wild in this shel-tered, shady spot.

The moonlight allowed him just a glimpse of her, but already he felt the droop of her once-steadfast spirit. He'd thought she was beyond a lasting melancholy as she'd been so full of life, but mayhap a father's loss followed by two brothers was too much to cast off. It emboldened him in his purpose, though he was still unsure of her response. Gently, his hand reached for hers in a first, tentative bid. She didn't pull away as he thought she might. His thoughts became the simplest sort of prayer.

Lord, please help me get this right. His nerve wavered for a second as emotion knotted his throat. *I know what needs saying but don't know how to say it.*

At that instant came a slight squeeze to his hand, the pressure of her fingers heartfelt. Coming on the heels of her indifference, it choked him further. For another long minute filled with the wink of fireflies and the rhythmic croak of frogs, he battled for composure.

"You look awfully handsome, Clay." Her voice was warm if weary. "I've never seen you out of buckskins and plain linen."

"I feel like a skinned bear," he admitted, which gained a little laugh from her. But appearance was not on his mind. "Do you forgive me, Tessa, for failing to find Ross?"

"There's nothing to forgive, Clay. You did what you could. I see that now, though 'tis a hard loss to take." She touched his cheek.

427

"Forgive me for being cold. My feelings for you never changed, they just got buried beneath the hurt of it."

He nodded, the feel of her hand so small in his. He wanted the world for her, wanted to recover Ross and see her smile again. But at least he still had her heart. "You need to be away from here. I see it plain, though you've told me so from the start."

"You mean go overmountain?"

"Aye." Even as he said it he knew what it would cost the Swans. Her brothers had need of her. Her mother too, even Hester. Hester had talked of an outing beyond fort walls, not clear to Philadelphia. But he forged ahead. "Would you be willing to venture to Fort Pitt? Marry me there if we can find a preacher, before making our way east to Philadelphia?"

His gaze never left her face, gauging any shred of resistance. This was not how he'd intended their courtship to play out. But nothing in his life had been framed by sameness, including this deciding moment.

"With all my being." He brought her hurt hand to his lips, kissing the bandaged fingers, when what he wanted was to take her fully in his arms. Again that knot in his throat nearly forbade speech. "If you'll have me."

She nodded, discarding the *nay* he'd expected. "When do we leave?"

Leaving, not marrying, was most on her mind then. "As soon as you like. With reinforcements here, we're free to go." He'd considered resigning his post more than a time or two, though this was not how he'd considered doing it. Now the hour had come to take her away, restore her fractured spirits. He'd nearly lost her. He'd not chance that again.

"Let's tell them then," she said softly.

They made their way back to Hester's cabin to find the group ringing the table as they'd left them. Clay took the lead when Tessa didn't speak. He still had hold of her hand, their fingers intertwined. "We've decided to marry, and we'd covet your blessing."

A short gasp from Hester and then Rosemary's face broke into a joyous smile. Rising, Westfall clapped him on the back while Tessa's brothers hooted their glee.

Hester spoke for him, laying out the dilemma of why they couldn't be present for the occasion. "You'll not wed here, with no one to officiate."

"We'll likely wed at Fort Pitt on our way

to Philadelphia. Our hope is to leave out tomorrow if there's no further trouble reported."

Affirming nods went around, though they all seemed surprised by the suddenness of the plan. Tessa said not a word, just continued holding tight to his hand as if her life depended on his laying things out. She was hardly the blushing bride-to-be. No smile graced her face. No hint of expectation.

"With Major Jennings in charge, the valley should be in good hands," Westfall said.

"Plenty of men to hold," Clay agreed. "And if I resign my command there's always another posthaste." A great many wanted to make a name for themselves, rise in the ranks. What better way to do it than tread west where the danger was the thickest?

"We'll begin packing then," Rosemary said with a glance at Hester. "I've set some fancy things aside over the years. Needs be they go east with you."

Hester nodded, turning toward a trunk. "We'll try not to weigh you down, just give you a fine send-off."

"How many days' ride to Philadelphia from Pitt?" Westfall asked, taking out his pipe.

"If we go hard, four sleeps — days." Clay righted himself after lapsing into the Lenape mind-set as he was prone to do when worn down. "But we'll take our time through the backcountry. Shouldn't be much trouble that way, given the heavy military presence."

"You know the best routes, the trails to be chary of."

"We'll see Philadelphia before the first frost." He looked to Tessa, who gave him a small smile. God help him, he'd be a good husband from the outset. Get her safely to Pitt and then Philly.

He'd not yet given her the locket. The time wasn't right. Best wait till she was more wholehearted about things, mayhap their wedding day.

33

Morning dawned. Tessa lay on Hester's loft bed, the old ropes sagging beneath her weight. The key was lost to tighten them, so she slept sway-backed atop the feather tick, which was flattened with age and repeated washings. She rolled onto her side, and thoughts of Ross rushed in — and Jasper — hollowing out her middle till she felt empty as a gourd.

It was nearly her wedding day. Her wedding journey. That alone should spark some joy. Yet it did not. That deep hopelessness she'd felt along the riverbank when Ross had gone the other way with the Indians still weighted her here in the dark rafters smelling of herbs and smoke. Below, Ma and Hester made the usual noises of redding up and preparing breakfast. Her stomach, always a rumble of anticipation, turned.

Closing her eyes, she drifted. Snatches of time flashed through her mind. The hair-raising instant she'd heard the tomahawks cleave the logs. Ross's stunned features as he came into the cabin clearing. The moment she realized Jasper was gone. The breathless second when the Indian took the ball and fell, coming down on top of her. Clay grappling for his life in the leaf mold with another Indian. Jude's jest about her serving mush to the savages.

She slept again. The smell of turnips and apples roused her, then more voices. Westfall's . . . Clay's. Someone began climbing the loft ladder. Hester. Her great-aunt lay a hand across her forehead as if checking for fever before going below again. Someone had left a piggin of water by her bed. Slowly, she swung her bare feet to the floor, leaned forward, and drank till her stomach felt overfull.

As she dressed, tying her stays and raising her arms to settle her petticoats into place, her brothers came into the cabin. Three brothers when there'd been five. They were discussing raising the toll of the ferry crossing next spring.

She came down the ladder like an old woman, one rung at a time, sore hand still tender. Zadock, Cyrus, and Lemuel stared at her. Though they were not given to emotion, their eyes were nonetheless damp. She sat woodenly at the table as Ma poured her a cup of dittany tea.

"Brought some of your belongings from home early this morn," Zadock told her quietly. "Suspect you'll want to pack your hand fan and such."

Tessa smiled her thanks, feeling their sore-heartedness. Any happiness they felt about her coming marriage was overshadowed by their new grief and impending goodbyes.

In time Maddie poked her head in the doorway, her steady presence bringing a sense of normalcy to the hushed cabin. She sat down by Tessa, eyes alight. "Guess you get to go to town and see those fancy folk yourself."

"Guess I do." Tessa swallowed a bite of toasted bread smeared with butter and Hester's quince preserves. "Can't go back to the cabin."

"I understand." Maddie sipped her own tea. "You been through an ordeal. Might be good to get away. Just have time alone, you and Clay." A slight chuckle. "Suppose I'll have to start calling you Mistress Tygart."

Tessa Swan Tygart.

Why did this, something she'd dreamed about, only leave her benumbed?

"Clay has some fine city kin. You'll feel like a queen among those wealthy Quakers.

Friends come by their name on purpose. They're hospitable folk, mostly. Clay's kin especially."

"I don't have the slightest notion how to act, what to say." Would these fine Quakers be shocked if she came unadorned? "If I had some proper clothes . . . manners."

"Come town, Clay will see you dressed proper. As for your manners, they're in no need of altering. If he'd wanted a town-bred girl he'd have married one. Just stay true to yourself."

The reassurance bolstered her for what felt more hurdle than honeymoon. Trying to overcome her lethargy, Tessa poured herself another cup of tea, as the beverage braced her. "Pray we get there safe and sound."

Thus far Maddie had steered clear of any talk about Ross or Jasper. Heartsick as she was over them, Tessa feared she'd burst into tears at the mention. She fixed her gaze on her chest of pretty things. Where was her joy? Her anticipation? It had gone north with Ross, been buried with Jasper. Ross had always teased her about marrying, said he'd dance the night through. Jasper had promised to take Pa's place and give her away.

She unwound the bandage from her hand.

Almost mended. Clay's head wound was still cause for concern. A fine pair they were, beat to pieces by what they'd been through, drained to the dregs with hardly a word of comfort to share between them. They were free to leave the valley, but Tessa sensed she wasn't the sole reason they were going. Something had shaken Clay so that it seemed he was as ready to leave as she.

Having breakfasted and dressed, she helped Ma and Hester gather her belongings into saddlebags. Clay had already readied Bolt and a packhorse near the gates. She longed to go to him. Touch him. Comfort him as only she could. But his hands remained at his sides, as did hers. She couldn't recall the last time he'd embraced her. Kissed her.

The distance chafed. Yet she had no heart for any sweetness, for kisses or sentimental words. Sharp-witted as he was, that didn't escape him. He kept his own counsel, simply talking, not touching. Somehow it seemed wrong to make merry when so much had gone wrong.

He approached her, a new hat in hand. "Tessa . . . You're sure about this?"

Was she?

"Never surer, Clay," she finally heard herself say, setting her jaw for the farewells at hand.

Her family ringed her, their faces a study of emotions. Save Ma, never had she seen them cry, not even at Pa's passing. Tears stood in Zadock's eyes while Lemuel hung his head. Tessa embraced Cyrus first as he stood closest, his thickset arms holding her for several long moments, his face pressed against her shoulder. Hester, long schooled in life's miseries, simply thrust a handkerchief into Tessa's hand, her cherished dream finally realized. Ma was nearly undone by the sight of her tender sons.

'Twas not just their sister's leave-taking they cried for, but Jasper's and Ross's as well, Tessa knew. Ruth and other fort dwellers soon joined them, wishing them well and offering a prayer for safe travels.

Drying her eyes, Tessa finally mounted Blossom and held the reins with her good hand while Clay bade goodbye to the officer now in charge.

"Be sure and write when you get to Pitt," Hester admonished. "And then Philly. We won't rest till we know you're there unscathed."

With a wave of his hand, Clay led them out Fort Tygart's gates, a new burden settling on Tessa's shoulders. Would they ever see the garrison again?

■ ■ ■ ■

By the time they'd cleared the Buckhannon Valley, their party of two had swelled to twelve. A wounded soldier and a chance meeting with a family of six fleeing their homestead both slowed and changed the tenor of their party. There was safety in numbers and added guns, and now Tessa had feminine company, given the wife and daughters among them. She seemed glad of their presence, and Clay made his own peace with it, realizing the Almighty might well be hedging them in, though not one Indian did they see.

In a hundred miles the trees thinned, and evidence abounded that the white tide of settlement was subduing the wilderness league by league in a relentless advance. Endless acres of winter wheat and fences now crisscrossed the landscape, the forts they saw looking out of place, rustic oddities in a land becoming so firmly settled.

His own land along the Monongahela was not far but didn't warrant a closer look with such a large party. Still, he made note of the ridge and stream that led to it in his own private thoughts, glad to the heart to have something to show for his stint in so long a war.

On the outskirts of Fort Pitt, he drew an easier breath as they parted with the group and entered town as a couple, intent on finding a pastor to unite them in holy matrimony with little ado.

Riding alongside him, Tessa seemed a bit wide-eyed, reminding him of his first time at the unruly outpost. "If it's any solace, Pitt bears no resemblance to Philly. Word is the fort is about to be decommissioned."

"So, we'll not lodge inside its walls?"

"Nay, farther north along the Mononga-hela River. Semple's is the best lodging hereabouts. They have a few amenities you might like." He'd say no more. Best let Semple's speak for itself.

A finer day couldn't be had, the river as blue and placid as he'd ever seen it, the town's more sordid corners brightened by sunlight.

"This is where you met up with Keturah," she said.

It wasn't a question. He simply nodded, hoping the mention didn't usher in dark thoughts. "As you can see, there are many Indians here from various tribes. They come to trade, treat, and make merry, among other things."

She took in the color and confusion on all sides of her. Pitt always seemed like an unending fair, muddy and sprawling and uncivilized with a great many sounds and smells, oft obnoxious and unwelcome but never boring.

They dismounted near Semple's stable, the tavern's door and windows open wide on such a clear day. As Clay led Tessa through a side entry, Mistress Semple herself met them.

She dismissed Clay in a glance, her shrewd gaze on Tessa. "Well, Colonel Tygart, I see you are in fine company today!"

Her hearty welcome made Tessa smile, while he himself managed to say with a beat of pride, "This is Miss Tessa Swan, my intended from the Buckhannon River country."

"A border belle, I see." She ushered them into a parlor, ringing for a servant to bring refreshments. Mistress Semple had many talents, her uncanny ability to sense a need one of them. "What can I do to help ensure your stay here is a memorable one?"

Clay cleared his throat. "A preacher is in order."

"Of course. None more respectable than Pastor Guthrie. I shall send for him as soon as you say the word."

Clay looked to Tessa.

"Aye, once I've cleaned off the dust of the trail, thank you," she answered.

"Glad I am to be of help." Mistress Semple's pleasure was genuine. In a border town full of disorderly girls and unruly men, marriage was a rare, elevated state. "Your timing is quite felicitous. Colonel Washington was here in early August, but his rooms are now vacant and suitable for such an occasion. None but the best for an officer and his bride, aye?"

"Obliged," Clay replied as refreshments were served, a dram of whiskey for him and cider for Tessa. He'd heard of Washington's private rooms but had never seen them.

"A generous supper awaits you too. Even lovebirds need feeding." As they finished drinking, their hostess produced a chatelaine, intent on a skeleton key. "Follow me, Miss Swan, and prepare to meet your handsome groom."

34

Taking Tessa up a back stair, Mistress Semple led the way to the end of a narrow hall. Where Clay would ready himself was a mystery. Since Mistress Semple seemed to have all in hand, Tessa wouldn't ask. The faint clink of a key in the lock opened a door without a single creak to its brass hinges.

"I'll have the maids bring up hot water." Mistress Semple crossed the room and began drawing the drapes closed. "Every bride deserves a fragrant bath."

Murmuring her thanks, Tessa took in the bower before her. The room might have been in Philadelphia, so lovely were its refined lines. Papered walls. A mahogany bedstead with brocade hangings. Bed steps. An uncracked looking glass. Sterling candlesticks. Framed floral artwork. The scent of beeswax was everywhere.

In such a sumptuous room she felt smaller and more homespun, dirtier and more disheveled than she'd ever been. But surely this was not Mistress Semple's intent. Her appreciative gaze strayed beyond the immediate. In the adjoining room was a parlor. Two bookcases lined the walls, holding more volumes than she'd anticipated seeing in a lifetime. 'Twas all she could do not to run across the carpeted floor and ransack the shelves in delight.

Instead she took a step toward a striped brocade loveseat — but mightn't she soil it if she sat on it? A knock sounded, sparing her the dilemma. Two servant girls delivered the promised hot water and hip bath. As they readied everything behind a painted screen in a corner, the memory of her own humble quilted curtain in the cabin turned her pensive.

Clay, one maid said, had gone to clean up in the men's common area below. Pastor Guthrie had been sent for. The facts were coming hard and fast, cushioned by their genteel surroundings. A table was reserved for them in Semple's dining room following the nuptials. Cook, having gotten wind of it, was fashioning a small cake. The maids chattered like a mob of sparrows, clearly enjoying waiting on a bride-to-be.

Towels and something called a sultana were laid out for her near the bath. Its steam was scented with lavender, the only familiar anchor in this strange new world. She tried to shed her unease along with the filth of travel, her soiled garments a tawdry heap on the carpeted floor. Soon they were whisked away by one of the maids to be washed — or maybe thrown out.

Stepping into the shiny tub, Tessa set her teeth, the bathwater was so blessedly hot. She was used to the startling chill of river water, cold in any season. On a small table within arm's reach were toiletries laid out for the taking. No gourd of soft soap but carefully cut hard ivory bars and a wonderment of pretty-smelling creams in small pots, even a hair wash redolent of roses and mint.

Half an hour later, she stepped out of the bath and studied her water-wrinkled fingers and toes. A maid returned and helped her dress, combing out her hair before hauling the hip bath away. Powdered, pinned, and wrapped in the soft sultana, Tessa sat on the love seat by the window, parting the drapes and half expecting to see a lamplighter on the street like Clay had told her about. But this was still a rough border town, not the civilized likes of Philadelphia.

Laughter resounded below, followed by Clay's reassuring voice. Had the preacher come? Were they waiting on her? She began rummaging through her belongings, searching for her best dress. About to embark on another journey, this one so new, so untried, left her near tears one minute and overcome with a strange joy the next. Hester's presence seemed to hover, and regret stung her that she must deny her great-aunt the joyous moment to come.

Shift. Stockings and garters. Stays. Petticoats. A flurry of preparation, even a hastily plucked flower from Semple's garden for her hair. The purple blossom was a bit limp, but it stayed put with a carefully placed pin. Drawing a breath, Tessa turned away from the ornate looking glass and readied to meet her groom.

Tessa came to him freshly washed, still damp and smelling of mint, in her best linen dressed up with a bit of lace at the sleeves and neck. She'd fastened a flower in her hair, the inky mass sun-lightened in places and glinting Scots-red, her skin tawny too. Frontier born and bred to the bone, she was. Clay wouldn't have her looking like a city miss.

As for himself, out of buckskins he always felt a tad odd, though today he was as well groomed as she. For a few seconds they just stood a handbreadth apart, regarding each other with exhausted pleasure.

"Are you both ready to begin?" the pastor asked with a bearded smile.

"Aye," they replied in unison like obedient pupils before a schoolmaster. The heavily Scots words of the marriage rites were somewhat lost to him as they stood in this frontier parlor, the best Pitt had to offer.

Clay's roiling emotions settled as his bride-to-be looked so calm. More like the Tessa of old. And then a sudden qualm intruded on his ease. Was she missing her kin? Dogged by regrets?

They faced each other, holding each other's hands, and he remembered the locket. At ceremony's end, he kissed her lightly on the lips before he brought the heirloom out of his pocket. Her eyes lit with surprise, then darkened with emotion. His hands were a bit unsteady as he opened the clasp, moved behind her to encircle her throat, and draped the locket across her bodice once he'd fastened it securely.

"My mother's," he murmured.

Her fingers touched the gift, expression softening. It wasn't as glittery as city baubles went, but it was all he had, and the sentiment behind it was priceless. She seemed to think so too, for she reached up and kissed him on his smoothly shaven cheek, eyes awash.

"How did she come by it?" she asked, holding his gaze.

Again that keen wistfulness took hold in his chest. "I wish I knew."

Pastor Guthrie congratulated them, his hearty effusiveness raising their own quiet joy a notch. Before they could adjust to their newfound state, a servant led them into the overflowing dining room to a private table. Supper smells swirled around them, a tantalizing hint of the fare to come.

Tessa placed a callused hand on the linen tablecloth, eyes on the sterling candlesticks, her wondrous expression caught in the yellow glow. His mind leapt from supper to the night ahead. He'd not seen their upstairs rooms, but Tessa had whispered they held the biggest bed she'd ever seen, and books.

Their plates were heaped with veal chops, celery, and thyme. She sipped her Madeira wine as he did, saying little but caught up in the currents of conversation on all sides of them. Dessert was just as impressive, almond creams served in fluted glasses with tiny spoons. *And* cake.

She looked at him, fingering the locket. "I feel I'm in Philadelphia already."

"Semple's is a good imitation." He set his

napkin aside. "In all honesty, I recall none of this finery from when I was here last. But I was with Maddie and Jude and we stayed near the stables."

From the connecting chamber came an oddly melodious sound. Clay smiled. "I think you'll find the parlor worth visiting."

They left the table and threaded their way past diners to the front parlor, which was, for the time being, empty. Anticipating her delight, Clay led her to a far wall where an elegant mahogany case clock stood, engraved with floral scrolls. Opening the glass window, he pointed a gilded arrow to some lettering and stepped back as the selected tune began playing. Above the clock's face, several automaton figures tapped their feet in time to the music, a little dog jumping up and down.

"This is one of the wonders I told you about. Crafted by a Philadelphia clockmaker."

Lips parting, Tessa studied the separate dials showing the phases of the moon and the alignment of the planets, until Clay took her in his arms and began dancing her slowly about the room. They had once danced in the blazing firelight of a fort frolic, the humid air and exertion leaving them all undone. Here all was closeted and cool and elegant.

"Superb!" Behind them came Mistress Semple's gentle applause. "I know a good pairing when I see it. Our case clock boasts twelve lovely tunes."

Their hostess selected another, "Shady Bowers," and left them to their dancing with a smile. Pulling his gaze from the open parlor door, Clay mastered his self-consciousness and lost himself in Tessa's pleasure. Let her have this one night away from the dust of the trail, the dark memories, and any cares of the unknown future. She seemed at her best, cheeks pink, smiling up at him without that taint of sorrow.

As the notes faded, he perused the other offerings. "Hob or Nob." "The Maid of the Mill." He bypassed "Indian Chief." No need to remind her of that. Or himself either. He chose "Marquis of Granby," a familiar, merry tune.

A half hour passed. Tessa yawned behind her hand. When a few sated diners joined them and the parlor became crowded, they slipped away up the back stairs. Clay drew a relieved breath to be free of trail companions and Semple's staff and their fellow lodgers.

She led him to their rooms, pushed open the door, and stood on the threshold to await his reaction. The bedchamber still held the rose fragrance from her bath, her discarded robe draped over the dressing table.

"A big bed, aye," he agreed, gaze straying from that to the small parlor beyond, which did indeed seem to hold a great many books. "Enough to keep you up all night reading."

" 'Tis early yet." She turned to him, palms flat against his linen-covered chest. Her heart was in her eyes. Standing on tiptoe, she kissed him softly and said entreatingly, "Mind if I read to you a bit?"

Was she jesting? Or a mite bashful? Reading was not on his mind. Denied time alone till now and they would . . . bury their heads in a book?

In what seemed the first test of their married life, he gave a long-suffering nod and released her.

The room was growing dark, though one taper had been lit within a glass globe atop a small table. Into the parlor they went, taking the light with them. She stood before the bookcase as he held the light high enough for her to read the titles.

Though the events of the day were catching up to him, he'd rarely seen her so enthralled. She chose a thick, leather-bound volume, then curled up like a cat atop a sofa, not beginning till he'd settled down beside her.

Leaning back against the stiff brocade frame, he closed his eyes as she opened the book. Her dulcet voice wooed him.

"How Candide was brought up in a magnificent castle, and how he was expelled thence . . ."

By chapter two the weight behind his eyelids grew heavier, the sofa more comfortable. Her nearness excruciating.

Reaching out a long arm, he plucked the book from her hands. "How a borderman wed the belle of the Buckhannon and nearly missed their wedding night . . ."

Her soft chuckle followed the book's fall to the floor. "Fooled you," she whispered. "I was merely trying your patience like Daniel did Rebecca."

"The Boones . . ." Understanding dawned. "When he cut her apron, aye." Bemused, he reached for her, rewarded with her warm, rose-scented, linen-wrapped softness.

Enfolded in his arms, she reached up and unbuckled the small clasp that held his neck cloth. The linen strip fell to the floor like the discarded book. Heart a-gallop, Clay threaded his fingers through her hair in search of the carefully placed pins that

451

bound it into a loose knot. The rush of anticipation that washed through him nearly jellied his knees.

Between kisses, she said, "Clay, why not keep to these rooms till week's end? Push back Philadelphia a bit." Her soft words suffused all the affection-starved, sin-darkened places inside him with healing light. "Let's stay right here, just the two of us, till we know the beginning and end of each other. Every nook and cranny, heart, body, and soul."

Leaning away from her, he snuffed the candlelight with a snap of his fingers.

35

Tessa awoke with a start, heart thudding as if she'd run a mile or more, to find Clay beside her, pulling her back to the present. He didn't know she dreaded sleep, her dreams uneasy, at times terrifying. In them she seemed to be trudging toward something, trying to make peace with something, to no avail.

Morning bloomed, forcing yellow light past the drawn shutters as the river town came to life. A rooster crowed. Someone was hawking hot cross buns on the thoroughfare below. But Tessa was mostly aware of the warm bulk of the man beside her, his rhythmic breathing telling her he was still asleep. Since arriving at Semple's he'd seemed more comfortable, less haunted, the faint lines in his sun-darkened features less visible.

As for herself, she tried to leave the past behind, at least for their honeymoon, all that was new and distracting aiding her. But when she'd fallen asleep long after midnight, she simply traded her fretful memories for troubled dreams. Ross and Jasper were there in her mind's haze, even Keturah with the Moravians in the far west.

She touched the locket's face, feeling its unfamiliar weight against her skin, reliving the feel of Clay's rough fingers against her throat, the gentle yet bumbling way he'd worked the clasp so that the necklace held fast and was hers. How she craved its story, longed to know the woman who'd been Clay's mother.

Turning her head on the goose-feather pillow, she spied the book they'd abandoned last night. Soon they'd leave the comforts of Semple's behind and press east, onward toward Philadelphia. But first a meeting with the commandant at Fort Pitt. Clay would confirm his leave of Fort Tygart and they would inquire about Ross. But now that she'd seen Fort Pitt and the throngs who came and went on land and three rivers, what hope had they of learning anything of her brother or putting in another plea for his return?

Best ponder more immediate things, like the sleeping giant beside her who had a look of wakefulness though his eyes were still closed. Leaning in, she kissed him full on the mouth, which curved into a lazy smile.

His voice was raspy from sleep. "I dreamed I married a belle of the border . . ."

"Who kept you up reading *Candide*."

He traced the curve of her cheek with a gentle finger. "There's always tonight."

"Aye, we need to know the rest of the story."

A wry smile. "That's not what I meant."

He pulled her closer and she kissed him again, long and lingering. He returned it with fervor. Still, a trace of bashfulness crept in, his and hers. She could feel a tender befuddlement rising at this new intimacy, of things fresh and untried.

"About that book . . ." He rolled over. "Better borrow it for the journey to Philly. But ask Mistress Semple first."

"I will. Mind if I read in the saddle?"

"I've seen it done by an army chaplain with his Bible." He threw the covers off. "What's the hour? We're wasting daylight."

"Six o'clock, by my reckoning." But in an unfamiliar room facing west she could not tell. She couldn't slow Clay now, intent as he was on leaving Pitt. She sensed he had no great liking for the rowdy town, though Semple's was civilized enough. "Don't you want to delay leaving a bit?"

Standing at a washstand, he splashed water on his face. Drying off, he said over his shoulder, "Do you?"

She raised up on one elbow. "I reckon we can't lie abed all week."

"If we leave out by noon we'll be near Parsons Creek by dusk." He talked as he dressed, his belly rumbling from halfway across the room. "Hungry? There's no better mush to be had than Semple's, but don't tell that to Hester."

She cracked a smile, trading her town garb for the trail.

Delayed by a few kisses, they finally made their way to breakfast and ate heartily before walking to the commandant's house, the only genteel dwelling Tessa saw. How odd it looked among its rough surroundings, though its river view was scenic enough. They were ushered inside by a servant who took them to a paneled office with a desk that rivaled Clay's at Fort Tygart.

"Colonel Tygart, welcome back." Edmonstone shook Clay's hand and kissed Tessa's in a gallant gesture. "An officer should be able to take leave for his honeymoon, no doubt. Glad reinforcements arrived just in time. But I sense you're also here to follow up on the latest raid along the Buckhannon, the one involving your wife's brother."

Tessa liked Edmonstone all the more for coming to the point. She took the offered chair, hands folded in her lap, breathing in a distillation of stale tobacco smoke and spirits. As they talked, a long line of men began arriving, snaking beyond the front door as they awaited their turn.

"There are so many raids up and down the frontier at any given time, 'tis impossible to track who has struck where and those who have been taken captive."

Listening to the man who kept the pulse of Fort Pitt and beyond, Tessa felt her high spirits sink.

"Unless a future treaty is arranged, necessitating a prisoner exchange, I doubt the Lenape will give him up. He's young and in good health, of value because of his gunsmithing skills, and has likely replaced someone deceased within the tribe by now. He could also be used for trading purposes given the Lenape have something to gain, thus ending up as far north as the Huron or as far west as the Shawnee."

Every knowledgeable, authoritative word chipped away at the remaining hope in her heart. Ross had not been gone long, but so much had happened since. Already she was dealing with a shadowy haze at the recollection of his features, the tone of his voice, the last conversations they'd had. A tumult of heartache and false hopes now weakened their bond, stealing her precious memories of him.

"I'm sorry to tell you there is seldom a satisfactory ending to recovering these captives. As it is, Fort Pitt may be decommissioned and no longer serve as a meeting place for the tribes and colonial government, a place to treat and enforce peace or to make war."

Her fingers went to her locket as Clay and the commandant talked on, her gaze straying beyond the men. The maps on the office walls only underscored how vast was Indian territory, a confusion of mountains and valleys, a wash of lakes and rivers without end. Where in this web was her beloved brother? Was Ross even alive?

"I bid you a safe journey then." Edmonstone was on his feet as Clay ended the matter, his attention pulled to the door where the line waited. "Mistress Tygart, I hope to see you again. And I will do everything in my power to enlist your brother's safe return."

The words, though kindly said, seemed rote. How many times had the commandant had to deliver this same message?

On their way out, Clay was delayed by

McKee, the Indian agent. A half blood, he was a curious mix of two worlds, both red and white, his respect for Clay obvious. Unlike his commander, he didn't indulge in pleasantries and protocol and spoke Lenape with Clay as if wanting to maintain some sort of privacy. A third man joined them, his attire and manner as Indian as McKee's. His stony eyes took her in so intently she nearly flinched.

He spoke in Lenape too, gesturing to her in a manner that returned her gaze to him, if only briefly. Standing aside as the trio talked, she watched an Indian woman with a baby on her back walk past, her step light, her doeskin garments colored with beads. Tessa's thoughts, always so full of Ross, left room for Keturah too. How did her old friend fare? Was she happy with the Moravians, glad to return to the territory she'd lived in for so long with the Lenape?

Clay was speaking as emphatically as she'd ever heard him, McKee and the third man listening closely, occasionally asking an unintelligible question. Occasionally even McKee's gaze would stray to her, then back to Clay again. Though their words were lost to her, she sensed the matter being discussed was more personal than passing. After several intense minutes, the other two men walked in the direction of the fort.

"Who was that with McKee?" she asked, looking back over her shoulder at them.

"Simon Girty."

Her brows peaked. Hester seemed to hover and hiss. *Dirty Girty.* All her life she'd heard of him, but never had she thought to encounter him. Taken by Indians as a child, he'd never forsaken his feral ways, even turning on his own white kin. "He's not soon forgotten."

"You never know from which corner help will come," was all Clay said. Did he mean the matter with Ross?

She mastered the shudder in her spirit, the sense that Girty and even McKee were not lightly dealt with, nor men you could turn your back on. But Clay had shown no unease in their presence and had from all appearances known them for a very long time.

"Needs be we head east straightaway. Once we have our fill of Philadelphia we'll return here to see what's transpired in our absence." Clay took her by the arm, turning in the direction of the inn.

His decisive words kindled new courage. "If you think that best, aye."

36

Clay settled accounts with their hostess and bade the officials farewell, and then they started east. Soon Fort Pitt was a speck of brick on the far horizon. Three hundred miles spread out before them, the distance daunting. Though Tessa set her sights forward, she couldn't quiet the notion that by leaving Pitt she was somehow leaving Ross. Turning her back on the border, the far-flung west, was somehow akin to turning her back on her brother, or so the knife's edge of pain said. But waiting along the Buckhannon seemed unendurable too.

When they came upon a boundary marker along a particularly alluring stretch of the Monongahela River, Clay said, "Here marks Tygart land."

"Whatever would we call it?" she wondered, spying a treed rise that begged for a fine house. "Surely not Tygart Station. These woods seem peaceable in a way the

Buckhannon's never been."

"Plenty of oaks. Oak Run. Oak Grove. Oak Hill." With a shrug, he turned in the direction of Fort Pitt. "A home of solid stone, not logs. Furnishings from over-mountain. Enough fancies to make you feel you've one foot in town."

She smiled, envisioning it. "But first, Philadelphia."

They set a brisk pace, their hard riding through the foothills of the mountains eclipsing conversation, though in time a companionable silence ensued. Since leaving town, Clay had become quieter, as if his conversations with McKee and Girty weighted him in ways he couldn't share. To counter it, she forced a gladness she didn't own, if only to lighten his load. No need to burden him with cares he couldn't control. As for herself, she tried to outrun her sorrow with every league they traveled. Yet no matter where she went, flashes of Ross followed. And Jasper.

Daylight trickled to dark, turning their thoughts to bedding down. They slowed, searching for a suitable spot to overnight, their horses spent. Together they removed saddles and bedrolls and what was needed to keep them till first light. The weariness of the trail had taken hold again, that sun-lined, sunburnt look born of the heat and dust and miles.

"You look deep in thought," he said, settling beside her on a saddle blanket.

She smiled, fingers seeking her locket again, afraid she might lose it in the rigors of travel. "I'm remembering that blessed bath and bed. What followed . . ."

"We're making good time," he told her with a wink. "Should see the spires of Philadelphia by week's end."

Lately at close of day they'd been joining hands and murmuring cumbersome if heartfelt prayers. For those at home on the Buckhannon and at Fort Tygart. For those far away like Keturah and Ross. For themselves as they pushed into the unknown. They partook of Semple's beaten biscuits and some jerked meat as the wind awoke, a touch of autumn in its grip.

Clay draped an arm about her, pulling her closer, the both of them a knot of warmth in the chill, blackening woods. He kissed her softly, an invitation. She returned the kiss, burrowing nearer, forgetting the insects and sideways slash of the wind. But 'twas impossible to ignore the howling wolves or the distant thunder of approaching hooves. At once, Clay pulled away from her and got to his feet, rifle in hand.

A man's voice grated in the near dark. "Tygart, that you?"

A split second's surprise.

"Aye, Girty," Clay answered as the buckskin-clad man appeared in their make-shift camp. "What brings you?"

Long minutes passed. The men were speaking Indian again. Did it give them greater expression than the white tongue? She sat completely still and waited for the intrusion to come to an end. The moon rose, white and full as a melon from the field.

In time Clay turned toward her, his expression unreadable, the shadow of Girty in back of him. "Prepare to return to Fort Pitt at first light."

She got little sleep. How could she rest with the snoring, volatile Girty but a few feet away? There was little time for questions. She would trust Clay that returning west was what was called for. Secretly, she rejoiced. Maybe the Lord was answering their persistent prayers. She just hadn't expected help to come in the form of the renegade Girty. Or a return to Fort Pitt.

At first light she rode in back of them, glad the miles they'd traveled from Pitt hadn't been many. The weather, so sunny at the outset, was now clad in mists and spiderwebs. Maples brightened the landscape, the first trees to color their leaves, and she dwelt on the beauty around her instead of the unpredictable present.

When at last they headed downhill toward town and the fort, Girty bade them farewell. Breathing easier, she looked at Clay, withholding the dozen or so questions begging to be asked.

"I don't want to raise your hopes, but I told Girty and McKee I'd give half my land along the Monongahela to return Ross." He lowered the brim of his hat against the setting sun. "Seems there's been a move made by the Lenape in that direction, though I don't yet know the gist of it."

She stared at him, reins slack in her hands. Blossom moseyed along toward Semple's as if she was as anxious to return there. "You'd give up half your land? Clay . . ." She swallowed, so moved she couldn't finish.

"Like I said, I don't know details, but I need to talk to McKee and Girty again once we're settled at Semple's."

"Can I go with you? See what this is about?"

"I'd rather you wait till I find out more." He swiped a hand across his unshaven jaw, eyes narrowing to take in the busy waterfront. "All I know at present is that it involves Netawatwees, a *sachem* — chief — of the Lenape."

Tessa said no more as the tavern came into view. Did the news have to do with Ross? Keturah? The warriors Clay had taken down in the woods that eventful day? Pondering it, she dismounted at Semple's, giving Clay a last look as he reined Bolt toward Fort Pitt.

37

Clay awaited McKee and Girty on the arrowhead tip of land where the three rivers mingled, surely one of most spectacular sights in British North America. Small wonder both Virginia and Pennsylvania waged an ongoing territorial war over which colony claimed it. Few white men ventured past Pitt. Until the border settled and peace was achieved, the West would remain no-man's-land.

Girty and McKee appeared along Fort Pitt's westernmost wall, walking past Edmonstone's dwelling. Clay prayed silently as the men walked toward him, trusting McKee but never sure of Girty. They greeted him in Lenape and told him what they knew and had learned since his leaving Fort Pitt with Tessa the day before.

He listened, saying little, as Girty did most of the talking, McKee adding what he knew. In a mere quarter of an hour the matter was laid out. Would he agree to it? If so, the plan would be enacted in the morning when the sun was two fingers high. No mention was made of his land along the Monongahela, but surely it had sweetened this chancy endeavor.

Out of the corner of his eye Clay caught sight of Tessa. She was walking toward them, her indigo skirts unsettled by the wind, one hand on her new straw hat to keep it in place. The locket about her throat glinted in the late afternoon sun, a reminder of their new, everlasting tie. His wish that she remain at Semple's was short-lived.

Her face was pinched in concern. "I'm sorry, Clay. I couldn't stay away. Your dealings with Girty don't set well with me. I'm not even sure about McKee."

He wouldn't argue. Both men had critics aplenty. Warmed by her concern, he took her hand and led her to the shade of an ancient elm where one leafy arm extended over the water. They sat atop an overturned canoe, boats of every kind tied to moorings along the river's edge.

"Please, Clay, tell me everything. Two heads are better than one, aye?"

He pondered his reply, carefully navigating the proposition before him. "The Lenape chief, Netawatwees, is said to have called for a meeting at Keturah's request."

"Keturah? Is she well?"

"It would seem so, considering her summons."

Tessa's expression eased. "Would the meeting be here?"

"Nay. Downriver a bit, well into Indian territory. The chief won't come to Pitt — a den of poisonous snakes, he says."

She nodded in understanding. "So he wants to meet with you? No one else?"

She had him there. He wouldn't lie. "He asked that you come too. Keturah is his adopted daughter among the Lenape, remember. When she first came to be with the People years ago, Netawatwees took her into his family."

"We must go, then."

"I told McKee and Girty I would, aye. But not you."

"Nay? Why not? Keturah — and the chief — asked for me."

"I'm not yet sure of the truth of that. Such might be an outright lie, a ruse. I won't know till I get there." The words were tight, the tension ratcheting inside him word by word. "In the morning I'll leave with McKee and Girty by canoe. Keturah might well be the key to Ross, but I could be mistaken."

Tessa paused, obviously trying to make

sense of matters. "I've never pressed you, but I sense the Indians you killed that day you came after me, including the one who fell then disappeared, were known to you."

"The one marked like a wolf, he was my Lenape brother. He was also Keturah's husband. And kin to Netawatwees. He was —" He had an inkling Tamanen still lived — "rather, *is* a chief in his own right."

"Oh, Clay." Tears stood in her eyes. "If you go downriver you might be —"

"I might be ambushed, aye." Her blatant alarm fed his own. He was taking a frightful risk. "Taken captive again. Made to pay for what I did in the woods that day. Girty obviously wants my land along the Mononga- hela. McKee has some stake in this I'm not sure about."

"Will you let Captain Edmonstone know?"

"I will if only to make him aware some- thing is afoot. If I don't return in a timely manner, then Edmonstone will investigate."

"I'm going with you." She stared at him as if wanting to commit every last detail of him to heart. "I can't lose you. You —"

"Tessa . . ." He took her hands in his, enfolding them and holding them firmly. "Tomorrow you'll stay safely at Semple's and pray against any trickery, any deceit. For now, it's nearing supper." He silenced the voice that taunted it would be their last. "We'd best turn in early if I'm to be up before first light."

She dressed for travel. Did Clay notice? She was clad in her sturdiest shoes, her most enduring dress and stockings, even her plainest fichu, but her hopes were dashed when he said, "Pitt is no place for a lady even at dawn."

"I'm no lady, remember," she replied, but he was so preoccupied getting ready to depart he seemed to pay no notice.

At the bedchamber door, he drew her into his arms but kissed her with only a spark of the passion of before, as if his mind was already on the river and what awaited. She listened to his footfall on the stair and then the closing of a door.

Careful to stay well behind him and out of sight, she left Semple's and walked the back alleys till she came to the waterfront just as the sun touched the rooftops. This early, the town was like a sleeping, cantankerous giant struggling to awaken. Few were out at such an hour, especially the revelers who stayed up all night, as the taverns never seemed to shut their doors.

McKee and Girty were waiting. How it grieved her to stand at a distance while they climbed into the waiting canoe, the stoutest she'd ever seen. Clay took the middle position while Girty sat in the bow and McKee the stern. Their rifles, shot pouches, and other accoutrements were near at hand. Little time was wasted. The sun was indeed two fingers high when they launched, their oars slicing through the water with a quiet trill.

At the last, Clay gave a look over his shoulder. Did he know she'd followed? If ever a heart was in a look, it was in his. Her stomach somersaulted and she felt breathless, even light-headed. Memories rushed forward, her last of Pa, Jasper, Ross. Only then, she hadn't realized how final those moments were. If she had she would have looked harder. Longer. As it was, she watched till Clay turned into a speck on that vast river now swathed pure gold as the sun rose.

The Ohio was the mightiest river she'd ever seen, so large and so long it seemed to have no end. Indian territory. Few ventured there. Many never returned. She'd heard the stories. They were even more frightful than those along the border.

Steeling her resolve, she ran toward the waterfront as if her life — and his — depended on it. Her heels sank into the sandy bank as her hands fumbled with the rope tying a canoe to shore. She'd not been raised on the river for naught. In seconds the boat floated atop the water, and she settled in the stern on her knees, the oar in her hands smooth if unfamiliar. No one watched or ran after her or called her thief.

The shore became smaller and smaller as she paddled in Clay's wake. Though she could no longer see him, as he'd gone around a bend, she was thankful this river road went west and there was no tangle of waterways to choose from, no rocks or rapids as it curved lazily. Here the water wasn't deep. She could see the pebbly bottom. Thankful, too, the rising sun was at her back and not in her eyes, her straw hat forgotten at Semple's.

The day was warm. Clear. The river was mercifully calm, no wind to ruffle its smooth surface. Soon she settled into a steady rhythm, the dull ache in her arms measuring the distance. A lone flatboat or keelboat was all she saw, though great herons and a black bear dotted the waterfront as she glided past.

No longer did she see Clay's canoe. With three men paddling, they easily outdistanced her. Undaunted, she kept on, unable to shake off the foreboding that losing sight of him meant losing him forever. Unsure of their meeting place, she kept a close watch on the banks, which were nearly a half mile apart in places, looking for any movement, any landed canoe.

As the sun climbed, Indians appeared along the waterfront. Women and near-naked children. A few men. Their lingering stares raised the hair on the back of her neck, and she paddled harder, gaining momentum, heart thrumming in her ears more from disquiet than exertion.

Lord, please, peace. And some sign.

Another sharp river bend that blocked her view of the watery road ahead, and then . . .

There sat Clay, his canoe turned like a wall to block her way. Girty and McKee were regarding her with amused scorn, their oars idle. But Clay — fury roared through his features at the sight of her. 'Twas in the tightening of his tanned features, the lightning-quick sternness of his eyes. His mouth was not merely a grim line but so pronounced it slanted downward into a fierce frown.

To Girty he said tersely, "Fashion a tow rope and tie her on."

Doused with cold humiliation, Tessa rued ever setting foot on the riverbank. Only a fool would follow a man into the wilderness when he'd told her to stay behind. Not only had she defied Clay, now she would slow them unnecessarily. Eyes down, she lay aside her oar, the wind hardly cooling her fiery face while Girty tethered her canoe.

Lord, forgive me.

It took all the self-control Clay had to keep from overturning Tessa's canoe in anger. Her flushed, repentant features didn't assuage him one whit. He'd married a strong-willed woman and here was proof. He paddled harder, ire stiffening his strokes. The semblance of peace he'd had thinking her safely at Semple's took wing. Now their present predicament called out every protective instinct he had. Not only was he in grave danger, but so was she. And if this all went wrong and propelled them headlong into an ambush . . .

In another mile or more they left the middle of the river where they'd been out of firing range. A hard sweep on the right with their oars turned them toward the bank. They beached the canoe, making little noise.

Clay lifted Tessa out like a wayward child and planted her firmly on the bank. Being experienced woodsmen, they left little trail once they cut into the woods. Soundlessly,

Girty and McKee led the way, Clay behind Tessa at the rear. That bone-deep certainty of being watched overcame him, though he saw no one.

Tessa cast him an entreating look as they traversed what was little more than a game trail. He paid her no mind, still a-simmer at her rebelliousness. The forest was different here than along the Buckhannon, autumn's entrance more telling, sassafras and sweet gum leading the colorful charge of leaves. Half a league in, the swift tumbling of a stream had them pause for a drink. When Clay stood, he smelled smoke. Indian tobacco. Girty and McKee wiped dripping water from their faces and communicated with hand gestures.

As Clay watched them, Tessa faced him. He put a finger to his lips. The apology he guessed she'd been about to make remained unspoken. Wretchedness marred her lovely face. Was she fretting over the ill feeling between them? Wanting to make amends if the worst happened?

They continued on. The longer they walked, the less wary Clay felt. Surely, if there was any trickery, they'd by now have been overtaken and dispatched. Though their combined rifles were formidable, they couldn't withstand a surprise attack.

At last they came to the edge of a small meadow, an awning of skins at its heart providing shade from the sun. Beneath it sat an aged Indian in eagle headdress.

Netawatwees.

Taking cover behind a sprawling laurel bush to better assess the clearing, Tessa stood in back of the men as they peered through the waxy leaves. The awning shaded an Indian who was seated and appeared to be waiting. Keturah's Lenape father? Winded and sore over defying Clay, she vowed to cause him no more trouble. She simply stood, absently fingering the locket, and prayed for peace as McKee stepped into the open, then Clay.

Girty hung back with her, saying, "Any sign of your brother?"

Her gaze sharpened and probed the shadows behind the chief. A flicker of movement was their answer. Her brother was on his feet now, though he made no move toward her. She closed her eyes to dispel any woolgathering. Ross was alive. Well.

Not a ruse then. Not a ploy to draw them here and harm them. Or was it too soon to be sure?

As Clay and McKee seated themselves facing the chief, Girty led her into the clearing. Netawatwees studied her as a heavily beaded, buckskin-skirted woman drew her beneath the awning toward the waiting Ross.

There, in the shade, his beloved grin erased every fear she'd ever had about recovering him. He embraced her tightly, looking as if his entire ordeal was more adventure. Save for a welt on his cheek, he seemed robust as ever, his good humor intact. "Welcome, Sister. I never thought to see you so far west."

"I never thought to see you again," she whispered through her tears as all the events of summer's end caught up with her. "What a time we've had since the raid on the cabin that day."

They sat down atop reed mats, facing forward to better see the smoking ceremony now taking place between the chief, Clay, Girty, and McKee. Unspeakably weary, arms still aching from her furious paddle downriver, Tessa fell quiet, savoring the sweet fellowship of her brother's presence. And then . . .

"Don't be fooled." Eyes on the woods, Ross lost his joyous spark. "There's an army of Lenape surrounding us."

The unwelcome words tore Tessa's attention from him to the dense foliage ringing the meadow. "They mean us harm?"

"I pray not. Plenty of bad blood between

Clay and Tamanen, Keturah's husband, though."

"Is Tamanen here?"

"He's recovering with the Moravians along the Tuscarawas. His fellow warriors brought him to Keturah after the fight with Clay."

Relief flooded her. Since Keturah was a noted healer, this made sense. Though there was ill feeling between Clay and his Indian brother, Tessa knew Clay had not wanted to harm him.

"How did they know Keturah was there?"

"Indian spies. Messengers. Not much that goes on in Indian territory is missed."

"No doubt."

"Tamanen told Keturah that I'd been taken north," Ross continued quietly, eyes on the smoking men. "Keturah knew your heart would be on the ground, so she sent word to her Indian father, Netawatwees, to help bring me back. It took time, but here I am." Ross looked at her, eyes soft. "What's more, Keturah traded herself for me, told Tamanen she'd return to the Lenape if they would give me up. Seems like a healer is worth more to the Indians than somebody who tinkers with guns."

Throat tight, Tessa looked toward Clay, stone pipe in hand, features stoic. But did

Keturah want to return to her Indian life?

Reaching into his shoulder pouch, Ross withdrew something familiar. Beloved. The worn doll she'd found in the Braam cabin prior to Keturah's return. Tessa's fingers closed around the small cloth figure. 'Twas no worse for wear, unaltered but for one thing. On its bodice something had been stitched in vermilion thread.

A red heart.

Tenderness smote her, the warmth in her chest and haze in her eyes intensifying as she studied the new adornment and what it meant.

A true friend, Keturah was. One who "loveth at all times," one born for adversity. She was no swallow friend who flew to you in summer but was gone in winter, as the preacher Matthew Henry said. Her affections did not turn with the wind or change with the weather. No matter where life took the two of them, the bond between them would be unbroken.

"You all right, Sister?"

"In time, maybe." Swiping at her eyes with a quick hand, she tucked the doll inside her bodice, where it nested with Clay's locket.

The smoking had come to an end, and the talking commenced. Nothing was done hurriedly but in a manner of quiet courtesy.

Since their conversation was in Lenape, the words were lost to Tessa. But watching Clay in this unusual setting, she saw him in a new light. His direct, measured speech. His gracious, controlled mannerisms. All bespoke the Indian influence.

Though her nerves had settled, she was still anxious to see Ross and Clay on the banks of Fort Pitt, if not the Buckhannon. Ma needed telling, Ross returned. Keturah must know her noble mission was complete.

Sitting was nearly unendurable when she felt like flying. Her heart, so full where it had been fractured, resumed an easier rhythm.

At last Clay came to her without a trace of anger. Extending his hand, he clasped hers and led her to Netawatwees. She bowed her head respectfully, unsure of what was required of her. The chief's lined face registered pleasure as she spoke a final word Keturah had taught her.

"Wanìshi." I thank you.

Where the mood had been unhurried before, now a sense of urgency overcame them. With sure-footed haste they took their leave of camp — she, Clay, Ross, and McKee — while Girty remained behind with their second canoe.

With a last look at the woods, Tessa sat at

the canoe's middle, hands in her lap, as the men paddled. The swift ride upriver was taken with the noon sun high above them, the water a restive blue.

When the bastions of Fort Pitt came into view, Tessa wanted to weep as joy gained the upper hand. She had only to look at Ross and Clay to feel whole again. Thankful.

"Where to next, my wayward wife?" Clay winked at her, pausing in his paddling for just an instant. "East toward Philadelphia?"

"Nay," she replied with a growing certainty. "South toward our land along the Monongahela. Maybe once we send word to Ma, Ross can help us get settled before he returns to the Buckhannon. Philadelphia can wait."

Clay smiled as Ross hooted his glee. McKee laughed and paddled harder, finally returning them safely to shore in the shadow of Fort Pitt. Together they stood on solid ground and looked farther down the Monongahela as it stretched to distant foothills, blue and beckoning, theirs for the taking. Tessa felt a stirring of something she'd not felt in a long time. Renewed hope.

A fresh start awaited. A new land. A new life.

ACKNOWLEDGMENTS

So many hands, heads, and hearts go into the making of a book. The Revell team has now published eleven of my novels and are among the very best at bringing edifying books to readers everywhere, as is my agent, Janet Grant. Special thanks to Revell's art director, Gayle Raymer, who put a face on this novel, giving me the frontier cover that is so true to the story.

A special shout-out to my first reader and faithful Kentucky friend, Patti Jones, who bypassed the novelty of the final published story to peruse the first draft. Her savvy eye for superfluous wording is second to none and so appreciated. Here's hoping the finished, polished book surprises and delights Patti's succinct, historical-loving heart.

To dear friend and author Joan Hochstetler — I'm beyond honored she read the manuscript despite her own brimming schedule and offered valuable insight and direction about this story. Given her rich family heritage and knowledge of both the American frontier and the American Revolution, this book is better for it. Her own work has inspired me in countless ways, especially her Northkill Amish and The American Patriot series.

Last, but never least, a huge, heartfelt thanks to reading friends who find frontier America as fascinating and novel worthy as I do. You are one of God's best gifts (Phil. 1:3).

AUTHOR'S NOTE

Since childhood I've been fascinated by the remarkable captivity narratives of Jemima Boone, Mary Ingles, Jenny Wiley, Mary Jemison, Susanna Hutchinson, Frances Slocum, Elizabeth Archer Renick, Mary Rowlandson, Regina Leininger, Simon Girty, the Ruddell brothers of Kentucky (one Ruddell descendant is a reader of my novels), and others. The women's stories most intrigue me and led to the creation of Keturah Braam.

Researching these captivity stories led to a treasure trove of accounts involving those first settlers in western Virginia, now present-day West Virginia. Several scenes in this novel were inspired by the historical record, such as Jasper's final fight in the field and Tessa's serving a meal to the Indians. Much of this rich, even astonishing, frontier history has been buried and nearly lost to time. *An Uncommon Woman* is

485

a tribute to those unflinching souls who risked so much in so dangerous a region. Their courage, fortitude, and faith are not forgotten.

Many sources were of help to me when writing this novel, particularly the *Diary of David Zeisberger: A Moravian Missionary Among the Indians of Ohio.* Zeisberger and fellow missionaries, including John Heckewelder and other missions-minded men and women, had an extraordinary ministry among the tribes in their reach. Of special note is *White into Red: A Study of the Assimilation of White Persons Captured by Indians* by J. Norman Heard.

Writing a book is always an education for the author. I quickly became immersed in the colorful world of the Lenape, also known as the Delaware tribe of Indians. While researching, I came across an account by the Florentine navigator Verrazano, who encountered the Lenape in 1524 along the East Coast before white contact and disease took a toll: "These people are the most beautiful and have the most civil customs that we have found on this voyage. They are taller than we are, they are a bronze color, some tending more towards whiteness, others to a tawny color; the face is clean-cut, the hair is long, and their manner is sweet and gentle, very like that of the ancients. They have all the proportions belonging to any well built men. Their women are just as shapely and beautiful; very gracious, of attractive manner and pleasant appearance."[1]

Several dialects were originally spoken among the Lenape in addition to Munsee and Unami. The Lenape Talking Dictionary (http://www.talk-lenape.org) includes audio that allows one to hear their language firsthand. Native languages are especially complex, and any errors within this novel are mine and unintentional.

Often it is not till the end of a book that I grasp what the book is truly about. While writing, the theme of friendship stayed steadfast. Though Keturah Braam is not the heroine in the novel, she could be. Keturah is an uncommon woman and an uncommon friend. Her character is based on this beautiful passage from the commentaries of Matthew Henry, an English minister who lived in the seventeenth and eighteenth centuries: "Friends must be constant to each other at all times. That is not true friendship which is not constant; it will be

1. Fred N. Brown, *Rediscovering Vinland: Evidence of Ancient Viking Presence in America* (iUniverse, Inc., 2007), 126.

so if it be sincere and actuated by a good principle. Those that are fanciful or selfish in their friendship will love no longer than their humour is pleased and their interest served, and therefore their affections turn with the wind and change with the weather. Swallow-friends, that fly to you in summer, but are gone in winter; such friends there is no loss of. But if the friendship be prudent, generous, and cordial, if I love my friend because he is wise, and virtuous, and good, as long as he continues so, though he fall into poverty and disgrace, still I shall love him. Christ is a friend that loves at all times and we must so love him. Relations must in a special manner be careful and tender of one another in affliction . . . A friend that loves at all times is born (that is, becomes) a brother in adversity, and is so to be valued."[2]

2. Matthew Henry, *An Exposition of the Old and New Testament: Wherein Each Chapter Is Summed Up in Its Contents: Job–Solomon's Song* (Chicago: University of Chicago, 1839).

ABOUT THE AUTHOR

Laura Frantz is a Christy Award winner and the ECPA best-selling author of eleven historical novels, including *The Frontiersman's Daughter, Courting Morrow Little, The Colonel's Lady,* and *The Lacemaker.* When not reading and writing, she loves to garden, take long walks, listen to music, and travel. She is the proud mom of an American soldier and a career firefighter. When not at home in Kentucky, she and her husband live in Washington state. Learn more at www.laurafrantz.net.

The employees of Thorndike Press hope you have enjoyed this Large Print book. All our Thorndike, Wheeler, and Kennebec Large Print titles are designed for easy reading, and all our books are made to last. Other Thorndike Press Large Print books are available at your library, through selected bookstores, or directly from us.

For information about titles, please call:
(800) 223-1244

or visit our website at:
gale.com/thorndike

To share your comments, please write:

Publisher
Thorndike Press
10 Water St., Suite 310
Waterville, ME 04901